DRAGON'S BREATH

Crimes Against the Crown

By Wendy Bayne

Other Books in the Series

Crimes Against the Crown

Disclaimer

This book is a work of fiction. Unless otherwise indicated, all the names, characters, businesses, places, events, and incidents in this book are either the product of the author's imagination or are used in a fictitious manner.

Any resemblance to actual persons, living or dead, or actual events is purely coincidental.

Any dialogue, actions, or events that I attribute to actual historical figures are only from my imagination and are not necessarily based on any historical fact.

Some of the wording and words used are archaic by today's standards and reflect a dialect of the time, including reduced forms that are not written in English but are frequently used by native speakers.

Also, you will find that many words are spelt the British way. Again, these are NOT spelling errors.

Copyright Information © Wendy Bayne

Published October 2021

ISBN: 987-1-7780492-2-4

Dedication

To my loving family and supportive readers, Thank you.

Acknowledgements

Inspiration for many of my characters comes from family, people I have met, read about, worked with or observed and an overactive imagination.

Thank you to my beta readers and proofreaders, who have been invaluable and unforgiving of my errors or omissions. They have been my harshest critics, most incredible supporters, and fans.

Cover designed by using Canva.
Photograph by Ivan Vujicic from Getty Images

Table of Contents

Chapter 1

August 1836

The Past Revisited

Gwen and Derek spent the month of July with us, their children Artur and Kathleen, the twins, and the youngest Angus revelled in the wide-open spaces and the nearby sea, but they eventually missed their beloved highland home. They left after extracting promises that we would visit them in the spring. Our time in Dorset was glorious. Even the dark and rainy days at the Rambles were full of laughter and love.

Eventually, we had to return to London. The day we left, Granger was already deep into planning the kitchen expansion and refurbishment with Bita.

Miles was chewing on his lip as we pulled away from our home, and I chuckled. "We can go back and put off our departure if you'd like to be there to supervise the work."

He waved a hand. "No, it would be unfair to ask Bita to cook for all of us on an open fire. She would never forgive me."

I smiled. "You gave Granger a budget, didn't you?"

He glanced down at Alex, sitting on his lap, looking up at him and smiling at our son, then whispered, "I forgot to." Alex laughed aloud at the sour face Miles made. He glared at Alex and said,

"Come on, old man, you are supposed to be on my side." Alex giggled and shook his head.

I was surprised and tried to puzzle out what could have distracted him. He was usually so focused on such details. Bita and Granger could get carried away, so I asked, "What's wrong, Miles? It's not like you to forget something like that. Is this to do with me feeling ill recently?"

He pursed his lips and shifted Alex leaning down to smell his hair. "No love. I received a letter from Lord Burley."

My breath hitched, and then I swallowed. "Justin Browne contacted you; whatever for?"

He refused to make eye contact with me and seemed to debate if he should tell me. So, I wondered if the Burley heir had stepped into his deceased Father's shoes after all and resumed his smuggling activities. He finally conceded and told me, "It's to do with his sister."

Now I was puzzled. "Arabella?"

He glanced at me, saying, "No, Marianne."

"Oh, God."

He nodded. "Precisely."

I inched forward, "What's happened?"

"She's disappeared."

I sat back, shocked. "Disappeared—how?"

Miles sighed. "He says he doesn't know, and according to him, no one at the asylum is giving him a coherent answer."

"Why write to you?"

Miles cleared his throat. "He wants us to find her."

Now I was taken aback. "Us! What can we possibly do that he can't?"

"It seems that Marianne has been fairly lucid for some time and has been compiling a record of their Father's business dealings and associates. He warns that it's extensive and could cause an unimaginable furore in the country. It could even topple the government or worse."

"He's seen it?"

"No, but she wrote to him about it, and he understands the repercussions of such a document falling into the wrong hands."

I narrowed my eyes. "Then Burley should collect it and take it to the King or Sir Thomas."

Miles nodded. "I agree, except the document is missing as well."

I felt the blood drain from my cheeks. "Is that really why he's contacted you?"

"Yes, he wants me to intervene on his behalf with the Agency. He says that he took her disappearance to Sir Thomas and your Father, but they wouldn't commit to doing anything. He wants his sister back, saying he doesn't care about the record she's compiled. I think he's baiting us with the promise of turning over

11

this record to get us involved in finding her."

"Did he tell my Father and Sir Thomas about this document?"

"I don't know."

I clasped my hands in my lap, taking in his troubled expression. "Are you sure that he's telling you the whole truth? Do you think that such a document even exists?"

He bit his lower lip and started bouncing a restless Alex on his knee. "I am not sure of any of it, including that he doesn't know what happened to Marianne. But I don't believe that we can ignore it. I need to speak to your Father and Sir Thomas. But I am more concerned about what Edward might do when he finds out she's missing."

"Miles, your brother is in love with Fiona and ecstatically happy with his family."

"Yes, but you know Edward and how guilty he felt about Marianne. He will do whatever he can to help Justin find her, which makes me worry about what trouble they might find themselves in. I am also concerned that I might not be the only person that Burley has contacted."

I stared out the window before saying, "I suppose you are right. Burley might do anything to protect Marianne, including seeking help from some of his Father's former associates."

"More likely to protect the family name he's trying to rebuild. He doesn't need Marianne popping up in the visitor's gallery at Westminster or some other event yelling out their secrets."

I reached over and took a fussy Alex from him, pulling him into a close snuggle. Hopefully, he would fall asleep like his older sister, who was leaning against me, dozing. "You said that Burley wrote that she was getting better?"

He nodded. "I remember what the doctors told Edward. They held out little hope that she would improve. While she might be better now, I suspect she's still mad. I am more concerned about what damage she could do by spewing out what she knows to the wrong people. Her life could be in jeopardy."

"You know you can't keep this from Edward. He will find out somehow if he doesn't already know."

Miles pulled on his ear. "I know. Either way, this is going to be unpleasant."

We spent a night with the Wilsons surrounded by their magical garden, then left early in the morning, arriving at our London townhouse with Mr Malcom to greet us with the rest of the staff. Once Miles wrangled the children bouncing around greeting all our staff, he turned them over to our young nanny Anne who marched them up to the nursery with a promise of a story. Scurrying up the stairs behind them was Bard, our dog, and the cat Patches. Miles watched them with an amused smile, then turned to Mr Malcom. "I take it both of those animals have had the run of the house?"

Mr Malcom smirked. "I swear that cat can open doors, milord. They have been inseparable since you have been gone." Miles shook his head as Mr Malcom added, "May I suggest tea in the library after you change and refresh yourselves?"

I sighed. "Thank you, Mr Malcom, that would be lovely."

He grinned, then turned to Miles. "I placed your post on the desk in your study milord."

"Thank you, Mr Malcom."

He left us then, and I took my husband's hand, trying to pull him towards the stairs. He smiled but said. "I should check the post first. Then I will be up."

I arrived in my room to find Meg waddling about, holding her back as she unpacked. "Meg, I told you to have Rennie or Jane take care of that. You need to be off your feet."

She shook her head. "I am fine, milady. I prefer to keep busy, but I swear this baby is making me pay for wanting him so much."

I giggled since I could appreciate the feeling. Mine liked to somersault at night, waking both his Father and me.

She helped me change and left, taking my travelling clothes with her. I sat at my dressing table, expecting Miles to join me, but after a while, it was plain that he wasn't. I finally left our room, and as I came to the head of the stairs, I heard yelling from the library. It was Edward. I bit my lip, wondering if I should join them or stay out of this brotherly altercation.

I hesitated long enough to see Edward walk out of Miles' study, turning and yelling. "I expect you to get results, Miles. You owe me!" He grabbed his hat and gloves from Tyson and then stormed out. Tyson grabbed the door and closed it just before Edward could slam it shut. He glanced up at me with eyes wide and full of surprise.

I made my way slowly to the study, hoping that some of the rage that was bound to permeate the room would have dissipated. Miles was pouring himself a brandy when I entered. I arched a brow as he turned towards me with glass in hand. I looked down at the glass, saying, "Rather early for that, isn't it?"

Miles gulped back the contents of the glass and set it aside. "No."

I pursed my lips, took a seat, and watched him pace in front of the window. Tyson came in pushing the tea trolley. He glanced at me before he left, indicating he would be nearby if needed. "Well, at least the staff will have something to talk about now that we are home."

Miles spun on his heel. "What are you prattling on about?"

I bit my tongue and poured him a cup of tea to keep from spitting out an angry retort. Then I waited for him to take it and decide if he would talk to me about Edward's visit. He finally moved to take the cup, then set it down on a table by his favourite chair and threw himself into it, so I ventured to ask, "Do you want to talk about it? I heard Edward leave."

He laid his head back, looking up at the ceiling. "Everyone in the neighbourhood heard Edward leave. I am sure you have already deduced the crux of our discussion."

"Perhaps, but a few details would be nice. Such as, will I be refused entry if I take the children to see Fiona, Vincent and baby Elspeth?"

He sat forward, biting his finger, then ran a hand through his hair. "I don't know, possibly, unless I can get your Father and Sir Thomas to agree to take on this investigation."

"Why didn't he go to them himself?"

Miles took a deep breath and exhaled, "He did. But you know Edward when he's emotional. He must have made a hash of it this time."

"Then what are we going to do about your Father's birthday next month?"

He reached over to a pile of invitations and pulled one out, handing it to me, grimacing. "It looks like it will be the event of the season. Jane has turned this into a picnic taking over the grounds at the Tower of London. Unfortunately, I don't think there will be enough room for all her guests unless we put some of them in the cells."

I shook my head, smiling at the thought of my Mother-in-law haranguing the Constable of the Tower, the Duke of Wellington. "How did she get His Grace's permission?"

"She's the daughter of a hereditary Duke with a pedigree that goes back nine hundred years or more. No one says no to her, not even Wellington."

"Then you had best solve this issue with Edward before then."

He chuckled. "I can always lock Edward in a Tower cell." I glared at him to show that I didn't find it amusing, "Fine, I will speak to your Father tomorrow."

A voice from the doorway said, "Speak to me about what?"

Miles groaned, then stood to shake hands with my Father and wave him to a seat while I poured a tea.

"Where's Mother?"

He shuddered, "Interviewing a dance instructor for your brothers."

I smiled, remembering my dance instructor, who had been my parent's former butler, Mr Allan. He had also taught me history and etiquette; he was a kind man but a demanding teacher. "Have you checked to see if Mr Michael can dance?"

He chuckled, "Yes, but Ballroom dancing is not among his many talents, my dear."

He accepted a cup of tea and settled in, looking Miles over, noting his dusty boots and the empty glass by the decanters. "I see you have just arrived." nodding toward the glass. "And I believe it is safe to say that Edward has been here before me." His eyes twinkled as he said, "He certainly has a short fuse and doesn't listen very well."

Miles guffawed. "You noticed that?"

My Father took a sip of his tea and sighed, "Yes, and that's why I decided to come here. From the frown on your face, I assume that Lord Burley has also been in touch with you."

Miles nodded, selecting a cake from the tea trolley. "He has. I received a lengthy dissertation from him a week ago. It's quite the story."

Father crossed his legs and watched Miles. "You don't believe him?"

"That Marianne has disappeared? I suppose it's possible. But I am not sure that she has dire information that could—what was his word—topple us, the government and worse. How can we credit the ramblings of a woman whose wits have been shattered by the brutality of her husband and cousin?"

My Father considered what he had said, "I agree, but can we afford not to?"

"You know about the documents?"

"Burley was very loud and clear about that and the risk it might pose to the Agency if we ignored him. Therefore I suppose we should try and find her and see what she has to say."

Miles speared my Father with a look of shock. "You are joking."

"No, I am not." Father glanced at me. "Montgomery is in France conferring with Richelieu about what we can do to discover who is behind Brocklehurst. McMaster is preparing for his wedding, which we are all supposed to attend next month. I want to deal with this little issue and have it out of the way before then."

Father nodded. "I will have to put you and Lissa on this. He glanced at me. Are you going to be able to help?"

I smiled at him. "I am nowhere near my time. So yes, I will be fine." Miles glowered at me, and I hissed, "Stop it, Miles. I promised to subject myself to an examination by Dr Jefferson and heed his advice, but you will not override what he says I can and cannot do."

My Father stared into his cup, avoiding eye contact or the need to comment. He used to be highly protective of me even after I married, but he had finally realised that it was Miles' job to protect me unless I asked for his help.

Miles scowled at me. "Fine." Then he turned to my Father, "So we are off to Scotland?"

"Actually, no. Burley informed me that while he was away on the continent, his other sister Arabella and her husband moved Marianne closer to their home, a decision based on a doctor's recommendation. As a result, she was transferred to a small private hospital from which she has now escaped. He is furious about the whole thing and blames Lady Arabella and her husband."

Miles nodded, pursing his lips and tapping his leg. "You think someone helped her escape or kidnapped her?"

Father licked his lips before answering, "Sir Thomas and I agree that Marianne had no reason to leave on her own based on what Burley told us."

Miles glanced at me, then my Father. "Have you considered that he might have lied about this record she compiled just to get us involved?"

"It was one of the reasons we didn't immediately agree to help him, and I suppose that's why he appealed to you, then Edward."

I was perplexed and inquired, "Why would Burley create such a stir by writing to so many people? If someone has Marianne or is looking for her, they must be watching him to see what he would do. Are we just playing into their hands?"

Miles smirked. "That is a circular argument."

My Father seemed to agree as he turned to me, "Sir Thomas and I have considered your question, Lissa. The Burley family hasn't exactly dealt fairly with us in the past, and Justin has kept his distance from us, understandably, when you consider we were integral to their ruin. Yet there's no evidence that he has been in touch with his Father's former business associates."

Miles grumbled, "Yet he expects us to find Lady Marianne in London?" Miles sighed. He sounded prepared to capitulate as he added, "Very well, where is this private hospital supposed to be?"

"In St. John's Woods, it's a massive Georgian mansion." My Father took a sip of his tea and smiled as he crossed his legs, adding, "Apparently."

Miles rubbed one eye. "Sir Thomas agrees we should investigate." He shook his head, mumbling, "This is an impossible task. It's been more than a week since she disappeared."

My Father pursed his lips, then said, "I doubt Lady Marianne would go anywhere with someone she didn't know, and if she escaped on her own, she would seek out someone she trusts."

Miles' voice dripped with sarcasm. "That's helpful. At least it might be easier than searching all of London. Now we only have to search the length and breadth of Britain for somewhere she felt safe with and someone she trusts."

My Father raised a hand to staunch his whining, "Only if she went willingly."

Miles stared into his cup when he asked, "Is this really about us finding Marianne or the document she has compiled."

I wasn't surprised by the question and looked to my Father, who was not forthcoming with a response, so I said, "I would think it's one and the same."

Miles shook his head. "It is not, though, is it, Colin."

My Father sighed. "The document is of paramount importance. If we are lucky, Marianne will be found with it in her possession."

I ventured to ask, "What about her sister Lady Arabella? Does she know anything about this?" Miles shrugged as my Father's face suddenly became pensive. "What is it, papa?"

"Lady Arabella's husband, Lord Harris, is under investigation by the Home Secretary's office. There is some question about his personal finances. He lost a considerable amount a few years ago and has miraculously recouped it all and then some just recently."

Miles steepled his fingers. "Why would the Home Secretary find that interesting."

"That's not all. The Foreign Secretary Lord Palmerston is also suspicious that his newfound wealth is coming from Russia in exchange for state secrets."

"So, it is safe to say that you don't think we can approach Lady Arabella."

My Father sighed. "Sir Thomas is concerned that if Palmerston is correct and Russia gets its hands on this document, it could prove significantly harmful to Britain, depending on its contents."

Miles was genuinely shocked. "Could it be that far-reaching?"

"He can't afford to dismiss the idea, and neither can we."

Miles nodded. "How do you want to proceed?"

"First, we have to rein in Burley from running around telling half the Beau Monde about his sister without telling him about Harris. Then we need to put some men on investigating what happened at this private hospital."

I mulled over what had been said. "I think we need to ask Derek to find out why the Scottish doctors reversed their initial decision about her chance of improvement and then recommended that she be transferred to London."

My Father narrowed his eyes, staring at me with a furrowed brow. "I imagine her sister just wanted her closer to the family?"

"But why? Lord Burley and Lady Arabella don't impress me as the types to visit regularly. After all, someone would note it, and it would become a source of gossip. Marianne would be an embarrassment to the family. If you are trying to reclaim your family's place in society, openly acknowledging a madwoman as family wouldn't help. They couldn't be seen coming and going from a mental institution. I know that sounds harsh, but Lord Burley and Lady Arabella have been concentrating on forgetting what their Father and brothers had been involved in, including Marianne. They left her in Scotland, for God's sake! I would never do that to one of my family."

Father quirked a brow and nodded. "You have a point, Lissa."

Miles was watching my reaction. "What has you so bothered

about this, my love?"

"What bothers me is that the welfare of a woman brutalised to the point of madness is secondary to your discussion!"

Miles frowned as my Father snapped, "That's not fair, Lissa."

Miles put up a hand. "No, she's right. No matter how insignificant, any stigma can jeopardise a person's place in society. I have lived it. We were even aware of it when Peter died. We couldn't publicly express our full remorse and pain at his passing. The Beau Monde would have rejected us for such a display regarding an orphan from the lower class." His words jolted me, but he was right. We had both lived with the humiliation of being considered bastards for a time. It is not something you forgot.

My Father could see where my thoughts had drifted. "You are right, but that doesn't negate that our focus must be on the document."

I was irked now. "You will find it faster if you find Marianne first. She is the source; even without the written document, it can be recreated if you have her."

My Father frowned at me. "I understand your altruistic motives, but we must keep the document out of other people's hands."

I leaned forward and almost pleaded, "We can do both, papa."

He sighed, but all he would say was, "Perhaps."

Miles pursed his lips. "So, what's next?"

Father slapped his thigh. "That's the reason that I am here. You

23

are expected at dinner tonight. We have invited Burley, his sister Arabella and her husband, Lord Harris."

"Is it wise to have all three in the same room?" I asked.

"Time is of the essence. Marianne has been missing for over a week now. I will send a courier to Scotland to ask Maurice to check at the hospital as to what affected their decision to have her moved."

Miles' brow furrowed. "Is it wise to involve Maurice?"

"Edward said I could trust him, and I believe we can." Miles didn't look pleased he was very protective of the Bruce family since they had embraced him from birth and never treated him as anything but family.

My Father took note of his reaction, "He will be making an innocent inquiry as a friend of the family, nothing that will put him in jeopardy."

Miles snorted, "You can't be sure of that, Colin, but I agree he is capable of doing the job—no matter how much I wish he weren't. Derek, Gwen and the children should be in Edinburgh by now or close to it. Their Uncle Douglas was picking them up in Portsmouth."

I felt my concerns were slipping away, and I decided to force them to commit. "About Marianne, will we concentrate our search on finding her?"

My Father considered it, then nodded. "It does make sense that she will at least be able to tell us where she has put the document or who has it."

I sighed. "I suppose that is the best I can expect. But you should know I will concentrate on what is best for Marianne."

My Father appeared perplexed. "I think we have the same objective, Lissa."

"I hope so."

Then Miles, out of nowhere, asked about Jibben, "What about Locke? His connections and insights would be invaluable. Don't you think he's been punished for his lapse in judgement?"

"Trying to infiltrate Brocklehurst could have had far-reaching implications. In any case, he is still working with Jean Campeau, reconstructing his brother's records that the French did not send us. But I believe they have gone as far as they can, and Campeau is anxious to leave London."

Miles asked, "When will he be leaving?"

"Montgomery should be back next week. Then he will take him to his home in Sussex and around the coast and onto one of our packets to Pembroke."

"I take the circuitous route is to put off anyone following him?" My Father only nodded. He was watching me instead.

So, I decided to push him to answer Miles' original question, "What about Jibben? Will he be allowed to work with us, papa?"

He sighed. "I have no problem with him. I think he has learned his lesson, but Sir Thomas must agree." He put his hand up before I could say anything else. "Sir Thomas and he should be meeting with Locke about that very thing right now. If they both come to dinner tonight, I assume you will have your answer." Then he rose. "Now, I would like to see my grandchildren if that is possible."

I smiled. "Of course, papa, let me take you up."

He waved me back to my seat. "Sit, daughter, I know my way."

When he left, I turned to Miles. "Well?"

He came and sat beside me, pulling my legs onto his lap, removing my slippers and massaging my feet. "We don't have to go to dinner if you don't want to."

I smirked, "Why, Lord Tinley, are you afraid I will create a scene tonight?"

"Hardly, my love. But we will have to be careful about what we say and how we say it."

I nodded slowly. "So rein in my outraged passion and be the perfect gentlewoman."

He smiled. "It would help."

I giggled. "Are you saying that I am not normally a gentlewoman?"

He sat back, staring at me. "You are a minx. But I am asking you to be your usual compassionate self without prejudging anyone at the table."

I smiled at him and sighed over the continued massage. "As long as you make the same promise."

"Agreed."

Chapter 2

Dinner and Indecision

After my Father left for the Agency, Miles returned to his correspondence while I went to the kitchen to review the week's menus with Mrs Jonas, our cook and her assistant Kit Wright. Then I met with Mr Malcom and Dolly Wright, our housekeeper, to discuss the needs of the staff and the house.

Dolly suggested that Rennie be trained to substitute for Meg when she reaches her confinement time. I agreed with the idea but asked that she leave it to me to convince Meg.

When we were done, Miles and I took a light luncheon, after which Miles told me he was going to hunt down Edward before he did anything foolish, promising he would return in time to dress for dinner. I went to play with the children in the garden until they were tired, and Anne took them up for their nap. Then I took advantage of the peace and quiet to lie down and rest.

I woke to a light tapping on the door. After blinking and thinking I was hearing things, the light tap was repeated. I stood, smoothed my skirt, and said, "Come in."

It was Dolly. She smiled shyly. "I am sorry to disturb you, Lady Tinley, but Lady Arabella is downstairs. She insists that she needs to speak to you. Mr Malcolm is in the middle of polishing the silver, so I offered to deal with it."

I smiled at her timidity. I had seen her interacting with the staff, and she wasn't this shy, but she was still new to her position and feeling her way around me. "Thank you, Mrs Wright." I watched her reaction to the honorarium. Her brow wrinkled. So I asked, "Is there something else?"

She stood up straight and looked me directly in the eye. "Yes, milady, I would prefer you call me Dolly or Miss Wright in company. The Mrs doesn't feel right even though I know it's proper in such households."

"If you wish. What if I call you Miss Wright in company and Dolly in private?"

She grinned and curtsied, "Thank you, milady." She turned to go, then spun around. "Oh my gosh, I almost forgot. Lady Arabella is in the small sitting room, and I have sent for tea."

"Thank you, Dolly." She blushed and rushed out.

I checked my appearance in the mirror, but before I could reach the door, Meg came in, tutting, "You can't go down there with your hair looking like a bird's nest." It took her no time to have it looking perfect as she glanced at my gown and pronounced, "You will do." Then she gave me a cheeky grin and walked into my dressing room, where I saw Rennie hanging on Meg's every word. It appeared she was already training Rennie, which convinced me that the walls here seemed to have ears since I had not discussed the possibility with Meg yet.

I smiled, went downstairs to the small sitting room, and found Lady Arabella settled on the window seat, her reticule clasped firmly in her lap. I noticed her grip was tight-fisted as if she was unsure or afraid. She had a heavy veil on her hat and a cloak folded on the chair beside her. Both were out of place for August. So, when she didn't appear to hear me enter, I coughed to draw her attention. She didn't turn but continued to look out the window and, in a soft raspy voice, said, "You have a magical garden Lady Tinley, and so large, it must be an immense joy to you. You really should consider having a garden party. You would be the talk of the Beau Monde for months."

Then she pulled back her veil and turned to look at me. I was taken aback and gasped. Her right eye was almost swollen shut, and that side of her face was a livid bruise. She looked down at her lap as I knelt by her "Lady Arabella!"

She moved to look away as I reached out to her, "No, don't."

I rang the bell, and Tyson came to the door, "Ask Mrs Jonas to make me a tea poultice and send for Dr Jefferson." He nodded without staring at my guest and closed the door gently.

Then I turned to her as she barely whispered, "You needn't have sent for your physician."

I stared at her. "Let me be the judge of that." She swallowed, and the very action appeared to cause her pain. I moved to turn back her dress's high collar, where there were unmistakable purple fingerprints around her throat. She didn't shy away from my examination, but a single tear rolled down her cheek while I looked at the apparent marks of a man's fingers. "You are coming with me, and I won't take no for an answer."

She didn't resist me as I led her out the door and towards the stairs, but her legs buckled after climbing just three steps. Tyson was returning with the poultice and tossed it aside to catch her and swing her up in his arms, saying, "Lead on milady." He followed me up the stairs to one of the guest rooms. I opened the door and called out to Jane, coming down the hallway, "Jane! Send Meg and Miss Wright to me and fetch my medicine chest." She nodded and ran off.

Tyson placed her on the bed and asked if I needed anything else. "Will you retrieve the poultice for me?" He blushed, nodded, and left.

Meg and Dolly arrived, and both gasped as they neared the bedside. Meg was the first to say anything, "My Lord, what happened to her?"

"I don't know, but I would guess her husband beat her."

Dolly nodded her head. "That's why she wore the veil. I didn't see any of those marks when I showed her in. I am so sorry."

I patted her hand. "It is all right, Dolly. You did nothing wrong. Would you ensure that Dr Jefferson has his usual basins, alcohol, and boiled water. You best fetch some linens for bandages as well. I don't know what else we will find after undressing her."

She hurried off as Meg, and I began removing Arabella's clothes. As we peeled back each layer, I wondered how she could have even tolerated being dressed. Then it occurred to me to question where her maid was. Dolly returned and passed me the linens while Jane and Rennie brought the other things I had requested. "Dolly is Lady Arabella's maid downstairs?"

"No, milady." then her brow furrowed. "Come to think of it.

The lady came in a hackney."

Meg glanced at me. "My God, what happened that she left without her maid." Meg blanched. "You don't think she was hurt, too?"

A croaking voice filled with emotion came to us from the bed where the naked Lady Arabella lay under bed linens. "She's probably dead by now—he would have killed me, so I doubt he would have hesitated to kill her. I can't remember, but I believe Brewster intervened to stop it, or I would never have escaped." She lay there with her eyes closed, then with raw emotion, she pled, "Please, you can't tell my husband I am here!"

"Don't worry. We will protect you." She made a gurgling sound in her throat that I took for a chuckle. "Would you like us to send for your brother?"

She opened one eye. "No, he has enough to worry about right now. It is best that he doesn't know where I am. It is safer for him that way."

I sighed. "Do you think your husband will come looking for you?"

She coughed. "Harris will never admit that I left him. Instead, he will make up some story to convince your husband that all this was self-inflicted or footpads accosted me."

"What of your maid, Brewster?"

She coughed again. "Anderson, his valet, is a slippery devil—he will find a way of disposing of her." She grimaced and moaned in pain, but I had to press her while she was still conscious.

"Marianne, do you know where she is?"

"She's afraid—" That was all she said, then she lost consciousness.

I sent Meg and the others off to their regular duties while I waited at Arabelle's side for Dr Jefferson. Miles arrived first and came upstairs immediately. He gave a perfunctory knock and walked in, halting in astonishment, "My God, what happened to her."

I walked over to him, pulling him back out into the hallway. "Lord Harris did that—she believes her maid is dead because she intervened, allowing her to escape."

"Why come here and not go to Lord Burley?"

I arched a brow. "Who knows how he might have reacted? After all, husbands have the freedom to treat their wives however they please. He might have sent her back to him, or he could have called him out. Neither choice would help Lady Arabella."

Exhaling loudly, he puckered his lips together. I was sure he was disturbed by the thought of one of those two men landing on his doorstep. "What are we supposed to do with her?"

I laid a hand on his arm. "Hide her, care for her. She came by Hackney with a heavy veil. Only our staff know she's here."

We heard someone racing up the stairs and turned to face Dr Jefferson. He stopped abruptly. "What the—I mean, I thought you were hurt, Lissa."

"Not me, Matthew. It is Lady Arabella. She's in there." I

pointed to the room where the door stood open. "She's been badly beaten."

He looked stunned. "Why is she here, is her husband with her?"

"Her husband did it."

He rocked back on his heels and made a silent *'oh.'* Then he squared his shoulders and entered the room, medical bag in hand. I followed, and Miles started to walk in, but I turned and placed my hand on his chest. "I think you should wait downstairs in case she awakens again."

He nodded. "Yes, of course. Should I contact Burley?"

I shook my head. "I don't think we should, at least not now. Let's wait until she's awake, and we can ask her again."

Matthew called out, "Lissa, could you lend me a hand?" Miles made to step forward. I placed a hand on his chest. "If we need help, I will call for you, Miles." He nodded and turned to walk towards the stairs.

Matthew's examination was thorough. Thankfully, Lady Arabella was only semi-conscious during it, mainly expressing pain and not much else.

Matthew was almost finished when he said, "Lady Tinley, perhaps you should join your husband. I will finish this examination alone, and then I will be down."

I nodded at first but was confused, and then I realised he would look for signs of her having been violated. There was blood

34

and bruises over a great deal of her body, but I hadn't considered the significance.

I found Miles in the library staring into a glass of whisky, but he didn't look up as I entered, asking me, "Who would do something like that?"

I didn't know, so I offered, "Someone extremely angry and out of control—a monster."

He shook his head, staring upwards. "I remember Marianne telling us that Arabella had married for love. How does someone who is supposed to love and care for you do that."

"Perhaps he changed—perhaps he never was a loving husband. Arabella may have loved him, but that doesn't mean it was reciprocated, especially considering the scandal that the Browne family would have embroiled Lord Harris in publicly."

Miles didn't respond, so I went to him and sat down, taking his hand in mine as we waited until Matthew could join us. He came in and walked to the decanters without a word. He poured himself a drink, gulped it back, poured another and came to sit across from us. Then, holding the glass in both hands, he leaned forward. He glanced at me and frowned. "Perhaps you shouldn't hear this, Lissa."

I arched a brow. "Tacitly, she has asked me for protection, Matthew. I have a right to know the extent of her injuries."

He inhaled deeply, then exhaled, "You saw much of the damage. Fortunately, Lady Arabella wasn't violated. But there is evidence of internal bleeding, and if she lives, I am afraid for the eye—I don't know if I can save it and even if I can, I am not sure it will ever function normally again."

I felt like my heart was in my throat. "Oh no, the poor woman."

Matthew nodded. "You said her husband did that to her?"

I felt ill thinking of what her life might be like if she lived and said in a hush, "Yes."

Matthew finished his drink without saying anything more and rose, "I can have a nurse sent over to care for her."

I shook my head. "No, I think it best that we involve as few people as possible. I will ask Meg and Dolly to care for her. Both have nursing experience."

"Alright. I will find them and leave instructions for her care. Then, I will check on her before your parent's dinner party tonight."

He left, and I turned to Miles. "What should we do?

He huffed. "Well, we can't tell her husband or brother you are right about that. But she can't stay here either."

"Miles, she can't be moved, not yet."

He sighed. "I know. We will need to speak to your Father."

I reared back, "Not Sir Thomas?"

"I think it is better to approach your Father first. He is liable to be more understanding."

"I agree. I think I will sit with her before we have to get ready."

I started to get up. "Did you find Edward?"

He chuckled. "Yes, I did. He was ready to draw my cork until I told him we were committed to finding Marianne."

"Thank goodness that's been taken care of."

I moved off, and before I reached the door, Miles said, "Lissa, be careful what you say to Lady Arabella. We don't know what happened yet."

I nodded, "I will."

I entered the room to find Dolly straightening the bed sheets and pulling the curtains so that the light didn't fall directly on Lady Arabella. "Dolly, you can go have your tea. I will sit with Lady Arabella until I have to get ready for the evening."

"Yes, milady, she's been sleeping."

I sat beside her after Dolly left and found her breathing was even but shallow, and her countenance appeared relaxed, most likely due to the laudanum that Matthew would have administered. As I watched her breathing, I was lost about what to think. She didn't say that her husband had beat her, just that his valet would dispose of Brewster. Was Lord Harris a pawn, or was he responsible for what happened to her?

I didn't know much about him other than what my Father told us about Lord Palmerston's belief that Harris was selling state secrets to Russia. Did Lady Arabella know something about that, or was this about Marianne? Would Marianne have left a safe place if she had not been threatened? What was her state of mind that made her leave? Had Burley even asked that question? Once again, we had too many questions and not enough answers.

Meg came in and tapped my shoulder, which startled me. I must have been wool-gathering or dozing. "It's time for you to start getting ready, milady. I have your bath drawn." I smiled at her and patted her hand. As I stood, Dolly crept in and took my seat.

I undressed and slipped into the warm water while Meg added some jasmine oil and washed my hair. Once I was done, I went to my room to sit by the fire and brush my hair dry. At one point, Miles took the brush from my hand and continued. "I have been thinking, love, there are still many things we don't know."

I sighed. "I know. I am unsure if she meant it was her husband who beat her. On the other hand, she did say he would deny her having left him and that his valet would dispose of her maid's body if needed. So I inferred from that it was her husband."

He put the brush down and turned me around to look at him. "That's a reasonable assumption, love. But you are right. We must consider that someone else might have been involved. I don't know Harris well, but I would never have thought he had such violence in him."

"Could it have been the Russians that Lord Palmerston is worried about that attacked her? They might have meant her beating as a message to a reluctant Lord Harris."

He sighed. "It's a tempting idea, but we can't start making unsubstantiated assumptions without evidence."

"We have enough questions about Marianne alone, such as

why the doctors in Scotland recommend she be moved closer to London. It just doesn't make sense to send away a wealthy client."

"Enough, we need to dress, or we will be late." He rang for Meg and Robert. My hair was the issue trying to tame it into the braids that would form a cornet. I wore a beautiful seafoam green gown with a deep décolletage decorated with delicate blonde lace and the hem of the wide skirt embroidered with tiny butterflies and vines.

Miles came in and smiled approvingly. "Are you wearing your amethysts?"

"I thought I would wear my pearls. After all, it's only a family dinner, more or less." He nodded as he came to my mirror to finish tying his cravat, and Meg helped me fasten my pearls. He leaned over and kissed my shoulder, whispering, "You look beautiful darling, but we had better leave."

On the short carriage ride, I had the uncomfortable feeling that we were being watched, and I feared for Lady Arabella's safety. Fortunately, Miles insisted that the house be locked up when we left and that the footmen and grooms were armed as a precaution. We arrived and found many of our family and friends already gathered in the drawing room, including Lord Hamilton.

Since our adventure in Scotland, we had limited contact with him, much to Nell's chagrin. She came to us, embracing us both. Hamilton followed, looking somewhat contrite as he leaned in and kissed my cheek, which was more familiar than usual. He cleared his throat. "I have been told I behaved badly and should work to ingratiate myself into your good graces once again."

I glanced at Nell to see if she had influenced this decision, but she giggled before saying, "It wasn't me that finally convinced him; it was Lord Russell. Both his Lordship and I gave him the same message."

Hamilton wiped a hand across his brow and looked at Nell in surprise. "I believe you called me a horse's ass and not worth well—I won't repeat what you said in mixed company. Nevertheless, she was right, and I have missed all of you a great deal."

Miles chuckled. "Has Palmerston been speaking to the Home Secretary?"

He sighed. "You mean about the Russians?"

Miles snorted, "Yes."

A sudden noise in the entry hall could only mean that Jibben had arrived. He walked in with Judith on his arm, followed by Jean Campeau. "Ah, my friends, it is so good to be back." Everyone stared at him, expressionless. Jibben's shoulders slumped, and then he rolled his eyes. "I have been reinstated to the Agency! Jean helped to prove my innocence." Campeau looked at him askance and shook his head.

The Frenchman bowed to all of us and came to Miles' side. "I understand that when Sir Colum returns, I will start on my journey to Wales. I find I am intrigued. Sir Derwyn and I have been in correspondence, and I think we will provide Lord Blackburn with a more efficient and modern accounting system. With Sir Stephen's assistance, the Brotherhood's investments should improve considerably."

My husband shook Jean's hand smiling. He and Jean had bonded over a love of fencing. Something Miles had given up while we refurbished the Rambles. However, he had picked it up again and, to his immense pleasure, had found a partner equally devoted to the sport in Jean Campeau. "I shall miss our matches, Jean. You have challenged me to improve my form."

Jean grinned. "Ah, but you will visit, no?"

I smiled at Jean. "Yes, Christmas is to be held in Wales this year."

Jean grinned and patted Miles on the back. "I shall look forward to it. Now, if you will excuse me, I must speak to Lord Blackburn."

Miles leaned into me. "I shall miss him. Perhaps I should teach you to fence?"

I smiled. "I would love to learn."

Then he looked at my belly. "Well, perhaps later."

My face fell. "Next year?"

He hugged me and whispered, "By this Christmas." I hugged him back.

The only people who hadn't arrived were Lord Burley and his brother-in-law Lord Harris. Mr Michael had come in to announce dinner, but my Mother had asked him to hold it.

Finally, Burley arrived without his brother-in-law. He seemed preoccupied and gave the ladies only a perfunctory bow while apologising for being late. He also offered an excuse for Lord

Harris that he had been called away on business, and Lady Arabella had taken it into her head to go to the country at the last minute. Minutes later, we were called to dinner.

The first course came and went with only casual conversation. Then Burley suddenly put down his fork and addressed my Father. "Have you decided anything regarding my request?"

My Father nodded to Sir Thomas, who answered, "Yes, we have, and we agree your concerns have merit, and we will begin an investigation."

Burley glared at him. "Which investigation?" I felt my heart sink, waiting for what he would say.

"To find your sister Lord Burley. I won't lie to you, our first choice was to find this document you say she compiled, but I have been convinced that finding her first is our best chance of finding it."

Burley glowered at my Father, then Sir Thomas, "Do I have your word that you will keep her safe?"

Sir Thomas stared down his nose. "It is not our habit of sacrificing innocent people, Lord Burley. On the contrary, I will guarantee that when we find her, she shall have our full protection." That seemed to satisfy him.

I leaned forward. "Lord Burley, I am curious; why did you agree to move Marianne from the hospital in Edinburgh?"

He took a sip of his wine and then glared at me. "May I ask what your interest is in this, Lady Tinley?"

I arched a brow. "I thought you were aware, Lord Burley, that everyone at this table contributes to the work of the Agency."

He seemed puzzled and stared at my Father. "Your women are Agents?"

My Father took umbrage with his tone, "When they desire, or the need arises. The ladies who work for us are highly skilled, and I take exception to your insolent tone. But if you have a problem with that, Burley, perhaps you need to hire a private enquiry agent to find your sister. While we concentrate on finding the document."

Lord Burley bristled, "I apologise. It is just that I have a great deal on my plate on top of Marianne missing."

Miles pursed his lips and stared at him thoughtfully. Then he said, "Then perhaps you will answer my wife's question."

Burley cleared his throat and looked at me, seated across the table. "Arabella and Rupert visited her and met with her new doctor. This new man suggested that she was well enough to be transferred."

"A new doctor. Had you been made aware of this change?"

He glanced down and fiddled with his napkin. "I have been extremely busy, so I have let Arabella deal with any issues regarding Marianne. But to answer your question, no, I wasn't aware of the change."

I frowned and wanted to chastise him for delegating his responsibilities to his older sister. But instead, I asked, "We will need to follow up on that with our Agents in Scotland. Do you know the doctor's name?"

He sighed as if annoyed. "Yes, it was Cooper, Dr Graham Cooper. But that won't help you. The hospital denies that they ever had a doctor by that name. Sir Charles Bell is the director there and has never heard of the man. They insist that Marianne was removed against their best advice, but Harris says he has the documentation to prove it otherwise, yet he seems to have misplaced it."

You could have heard a pin drop in the room. I collected my thoughts and asked, "When did Lady Arabella and Lord Harris meet with this Dr Cooper?"

He sighed. "Late last year. October, I believe—yes, it was October. But, regrettably, I was on the continent at the time. I was not made aware of the changes until my return."

Edward was incensed. "Harris has misplaced the documentation! Have you ever considered he's been lying to you? After all, he has been selling state secrets to the Russians and probably would love to get his hands on the names of your Father's compromised connections in the government! Graham Cooper is not a doctor. He's a killer and is now dead!"

My Father and Sir Thomas groaned while Burley sat utterly stunned, his mouth hung open and his face drained of colour. Miles glared at Edward and yelled, "Edward, I told you that in the strictest confidence to make you understand our dilemma. It was not for sharing!"

Fiona looked at me, then put a hand over her eyes and yelled, "Stop it, both of you. What's done is done." Miles scowled and

Edward looked sick.

Burley drank down his glass of wine, held it up for Mr Michael to refill, and then drank half of it back in one gulp. He sat back and bit on his thumb. "Oh god, Arabella sent me a note asking me to meet with her today that it was urgent." He looked around at us. "I didn't go to see her. Urgent to her in the past has been the choice of colour for drawing room curtains. You have to realise she wouldn't know anything about what Harris might be involved in."

Judith and my Mother were staring at him in disbelief. Mother was the one to broach the subject. "So you ignored her request? How often has she ever summoned you for urgent curtain matters?"

He opened his mouth to answer, and she put up her hand. "No, don't say anything. I don't know Lady Arabella well. But I have talked to her on several occasions. She is a highly intelligent woman, and I would say she is not given to requesting assistance with emergency drapery decisions. Being male does not make you the sole possessor of intelligence."

My Father sat forward, sucking on his lower lip before saying, "We will need to speak to Lady Arabella. She should at least have some information about your sister Marianne. Since you didn't seem involved, she must have been aware of the move to the private hospital in St. John's Wood." Burley stared at him as my Father continued, "Tell me, Lord Burley, why are you so concerned about Marianne now?"

Edward's fists were white, and he was vibrating with anger. "You bastard Justin this is about what she knows about your

Father and his business dealings. You want us to find her so you can put her away forever, so she never sees the light of day again. You bloody liar—here I thought you cared about her! I swear to god I will do all I can to ensure that you do not retain guardianship of her."

Burley threw down his napkin. "You people have no idea what it has been like to live with the name Browne. I don't want her talking to the wrong people. Or, for that matter, that bloody document getting into anyone's hands that will seek to use it against me."

Edward grit his teeth. "Does Arabella know this?"

"Of course not! She doesn't know anything. Marrying Harris has kept her immune from any hate our family has collected."

I glanced at Miles, who barely shook his head at me, I knew I couldn't tell anyone at the table about Arabella, but I wanted to. Jibben, Campeau and the Hamilton's sat askance. Just then, Dr Jefferson came in. Isabel told us he would be late because he had an important patient to check on first. He scanned the table and seemed to read the tension. "I beg your pardon, but a new patient had need of me. It took some time to resolve the issue."

I stared at him intently. He blinked as he sat, then tapped on the table using the hand code that Murphy and my Father had contrived to convey messages. It was just three words *'All is well.'*

I felt I could take a deep breath now and nodded my thanks. Miles grabbed my hand to draw my attention to Edward. He had noted our exchange and looked on the verge of asking about the message when Matthew engaged him in a conversation about an ill friend. But Edward had a sharp mind, and I knew he thought Matthew's new patient was Marianne. Nothing could be done about it now, but I was sure Matthew or Miles would pull him aside later and explain since they had both noted his interest.

With a lull in the conversations, Mr Michael snapped his fingers at John and Richard, the footmen, to start serving the next course. He pulled out a clean napkin and handed it to Dr Jefferson, who accepted it and thanked him as a plate was placed before him.

Sir Thomas then offered Lord Burley an olive branch "Despite our objective, we will still look for your sister, and when she is found, I will ask the King to make her a ward of the Crown. Then we will actively discredit any information she may share publicly." Burley frowned but nodded in agreement. I wouldn't trust him until he thoroughly explained his reason for wanting to find Marianne.

The meal progressed as our conversation changed to strategy, but my stomach felt full of ground glass thinking of Arabella's plight. When we left the men at the table, Aunt Mary took me aside, noting my discomfort and asking, "Clarissa, have you been feeling well? You look a tad pale."

I saw Isabel Jefferson watching me closely, and I wondered if Matthew had told her anything. "I am fine, Aunt Mary." We moved to sit with the others, and as I looked about the room, I felt terrible at keeping Arabella's presence in my home a secret. I made up my mind then that I had to tell them. Our daughter Charlotte noticed everything and was likely to blurt out that we had a guest if any of these women visited.

"Miles may be furious with me, but I need to tell someone, and

I trust all of you implicitly. Lady Arabella arrived at our home earlier today—she had been savagely beaten." I paused to see their horrified faces. Isabel nodded for me to continue. "We aren't sure who beat her, but she believes that her maid, who facilitated her escape, was possibly murdered."

Mother was infuriated. "Lord Harris must be devastated?"

I swallowed and glanced about the room before saying, "Her husband may have been her attacker." There was a collective gasp, and I watched each face crumple into abject horror and disbelief.

Aunt Mary shook her head. "No—no, that can't be. I have known Rupert since he was a child. He's been a bore most of his life but was never violent. I can't see it in him."

Mother pursed her lips. "We thought the same thing about Sir Lawrence Vane, and he beat his wife to death over an undercooked filet of beef." my Mother glanced at My Aunt. "We can never know what a person is like in private." Aunt Mary glared at my Mother, but her face fell, and she nodded in agreement.

Judith was deep in thought, "Why would he attack her?"

"I don't know, Judith. She is extremely ill right now and hasn't said much. She doesn't even want Lord Burley to know her whereabouts. Besides, I am uncomfortable with his stance on Marianne and his seeming lack of genuine concern for her. He may feel the same towards Arabella."

Nell and Fiona had been whispering, and it irritated me so

much that I snapped, "Do you disagree, Fiona, Nell?"

Nell frowned. "No, of course not, but we need to find Marianne. We agree that Arabella's whereabouts must be kept secret as long as possible. At least until the King can be applied to."

Aunt Mary stared at her. "Apply to the King to what end?"

Nell looked to Fiona, who swallowed and said, "Divorce."

Aunt Mary gasped, it just wasn't done in the Beau Monde, and it was almost impossible for a peer. "He would never intervene, Fiona, never. He didn't even support his brother when he wanted a divorce."

Fiona looked perplexed. "That was different. George was Regent then and a wastrel. Besides, he had no cause to divorce Caroline. The people would have revolted."

Aunt Mary shook her head. "It is not different, Fiona. The King will use it as an example to test such a request."

Fiona was incensed. "But Lissa said he's beaten her to the point of death and perhaps has been complicit in murder!"

My Mother's expression was one of resignation, "That is a husband's right. The law is on his side."

"Then, the law is wrong!"

Aunt Mary nodded, "I think we can all agree on that, Fiona."

Mother glanced at me. "Do you feel up to visiting this hospital where Marianne was staying?"

I sighed. "It is as good a place as any to start."

We made plans for the morning to visit the hospital. Then we would call on Aunt Mary's friends, who were inclined to gossip. "They notice everything that happens in the Beau Monde. So we can find out what they know about Lord Harris." She seemed to relish the idea of using her social connections once again for what she called *'the greater good.'*

When the men joined us, their tempers seemed stoked once again. There were pointed, grumbling remarks exchanged as they entered the room. I glanced at Miles, conversing with Edward and Hamilton, their eyes occasionally stealing a glance at Lord Burley, who was in a heated discussion with my Father and Sir Thomas.

Jibben, Jean Campeau and Dr Jefferson seemed content to stand by and observe, not a posture I was used to seeing Jibben assume. He was generally in the thick of things and one of the loudest. He caught me watching them and came to sit beside Judith, and across from me, the other two ventured to set up the chessboard and settled into a game.

Jibben arched a brow at me. "If you want to know why everyone is at sixes and sevens as we came in, Lord Burley is determined to be included in our investigation. Regrettably, he's too emotional and conflicted to be of much use, but Montgomery is due to return in the next day or so, and he can babysit him."

"I thought Montgomery was charged with taking Mr Campeau to Sussex, then to Wales?"

He sighed. "Since Dr Graham Cooper's introduction into the conversation, it seems he has some information regarding Lady

Marianne Braithwaite. Therefore, he will be staying with us for a bit longer."

Judith tipped her head to the side. "Does that disturb you?"

"Only so long as he represents a threat to us."

I was surprised at his comment, "You think he will turn on us?"

He shook his head. "No, but I feel we are being watched because of him. I haven't caught them yet, but I will."

I felt a shiver roll down my spine. "I have had the same feeling coming here; do you think it is Brocklehurst?"

He shook his head. "No, this feels more lethal, not duplicitous like that bunch. Despite being blackguards, they were once Templars, and they still have a code. This feels different—it's not Brocklehurst, of that, I am almost certain." Then he grinned. "So what are you ladies plotting, and do you need my help?"

Judith giggled. "We have plans, and you would just muck them up."

He placed a hand on his chest. "Come now. I have an innate charm and charisma that could be helpful."

I smiled. "If we need your charm, we will call on you." Then, I endeavoured to change the subject by asking, "Where is Magda tonight?"

He shrugged and glanced at Judith, who answered, "She's off with Kezia somewhere."

That was strange. Magda rarely missed an opportunity to visit with all of us. She seemed to view us as if we were part of her clan. That we were strategising and she wasn't here felt very odd. "What could be so important that she would miss this."

He waved a hand. "Kezia arrived in a flap, but I couldn't make any sense of it other than Grandmama must go with her immediately." I stared at him, not believing a word he had said. Then, finally, he threw up his hands. "All she said to Grandmama was that it was more important than a meal."

It still puzzled me, but I accepted what he said as the truth. Miles then came to me, "You have been plotting something. I can see it in the lines of your brow—what's wrong?"

I was disconcerted and told him so. "Magda and Kezia ran off, and Jibben has no idea why. Kezia felt it was more important than meeting with us about this latest dilemma. It's not like her."

Miles shrugged as if to discount my concern. "Kezia is her daughter."

"And Jibben is her Grandson."

Miles sighed. "Kezia is more of her blood than Jibben."

Jibben nodded. "That's true Little One. Grandmama loves us all, but blood will always tell."

Chapter 3

Come Find Me

The next day I took our carriage to collect my Mother to meet at Judith's home. Sadly, Fiona was unable to come with us. She was meeting with a client of Edward's about furnishings for their new home. She had a good eye and didn't have Edward's expensive taste.

When we arrived, we were taken to the drawing room, where Judith was in a temper, pacing back and forth and huffing. Magda sat on a settee, watching her while trying to look innocent. Judith glanced at us. "Can you talk some sense into her?"

"What happened?"

She threw up her hands. "Kezia! She is insane. She has applied to the hospital to work as a nurse and was accepted."

"She's given up her school?"

Judith shook her head. "No, Father Kelly will take care of it for the time being."

"Then why does she want to work at a hospital?"

Judith stopped. "I am not explaining this very well. Magda, tell them. It is your crazy idea!"

Magda arched a brow and waved to the chairs. "Please sit.

When the others come, I will tell you our idea."

It wasn't long before Nell, Isabel, and My Aunt Mary arrived. I supposed the look on our faces told them everything they needed to know when Aunt Mary said, "What's wrong?"

Our eyes turned to Magda, and theirs followed. Judith grimaced in discomfort. "Well, tell them, Grandmama."

Magda folded her hands in her lap and smiled. "Kezia has taken a position at Blane House, where Lady Marianne was a patient."

Everyone was astounded. I was the first to recover. "How—I mean, why?"

"Benedictine Nuns manage this private place. The same Clan of Nuns that Kezia belongs to."

Aunt Mary sniffed, "I believe the correct term is Order, not clan, Magda."

Magda ignored her and continued, "No man will be allowed across the entryway of that hospital. Only women are cared for there, and only women care for them. None of us is Catholic, and we would be suspect."

I leaned forward. "But Lady Arabella and Lord Harris aren't Catholic either. So how did they gain admittance for her."

"Lord Harris is related to the Duke of Norfolk. They are a powerful Catholic family."

Aunt Mary sniffed, "Rupert is a very distant relation. I doubt the Duke is even aware of the connection."

I sat back, shocked. "If Lord Harris is selling information to the Russians. I agree with Aunt Mary the Howards would never be involved."

Magda stood. "Or he used their name without their knowledge. Now we will go to the hospital." She glanced around. "Come, everyone, we go now."

We all obeyed her command and moved to leave just as Jibben came down the stairs blocking our way. "I am going with you."

Magda slapped his arm. "Out of the way, Jibben."

"No! People are following us—I will not have you go anywhere unprotected."

I stepped forward. "We all have weapons, and the grooms do as well."

He nodded. "I am still going with you. If not with your carriage, I will go out as a Tinker again."

He stared at Judith, who rolled her eyes. "He means it, ladies."

Aunt Mary shifted her position. "This is ridiculous." She took Jibben's arm. "Come along. Tell me, how good are you at pretending to be a Catholic?"

He chuckled. "I have met the Pope, Mrs Spencer, but he is a despot."

She nodded. "So you are not good at pretending."

Jibben smiled and helped us into the carriage before moving towards his horse. Then turning back, he asked in a puzzled voice,

"What is the plan?"

Aunt Mary leaned out, calling to him, "We are looking to support a deserving charitable institution."

He jumped onto his horse. "I thought it was a private hospital."

She snorted, "I have been given to understand that their client's care is paid for by generous donations from their families and others."

He frowned, "You know this for a fact?"

Aunt Mary sighed. "No. Sir Stephen, but it is a place run by a religious order. They are always looking for money and look the other way regarding who makes the donation when supporting a deserving loved one."

"Then who is going to be the patient?"

Magda's hand popped out the window waving at him as she laughed and Jibben came to the window. "No! You are not going to enter that place as a patient. I forbid it!"

Magda motioned him closer. She reached up and patted him on the cheek. "I need the rest." Then she cackled with delightful laughter. Jibben mumbled something in Romani and called out to the coachman to move on.

No one seemed to want to broach what Magda had in mind, but Nell felt adventurous enough to ask, "Magda, do you expect Jibben and Judith to commit you to this hospital?"

She grinned. "For a few days perhaps, then I will leave."

I stared at her in disbelief and said, "Magda, you can't just leave."

"Lady Marianne did, and I have more skill in leaving places where I do not want to be."

Judith was mortified and anxious "They could have killed her, Grandmama!"

"They are Nuns. I don't think they kill people, even for money." I almost burst out laughing, but Judith glared at me as soon as I started to giggle.

"This is not funny, Lissa. Grandmama's life is at risk."

Nell leaned forward and took her hand. "They may not even accept Magda as a patient Judith."

Magda picked up the satchel at her feet. "They will when I show them this." She opened the satchel, and it was stuffed full of banknotes."

We were shocked, and Judith hissed, "Where did you get that?"

I picked out a five-pound note and noticed as I looked in the bag they all appeared to be five-pound notes. I arched a brow at her. "Magda, are these counterfeit?"

She smiled at me and said as if it was a matter of course, "Yes."

"Magda, you can't use these, and besides, where did you get them?"

She sat back, giving us an appraising look, then pursed her lips.

"Sir Thomas said I was not to tell."

I was astonished. "Sir Thomas gave you these?"

She grinned. "Yes, he approves of my endeavour. Kezia and I spoke to him yesterday."

I frowned. "Sir Thomas didn't say a thing last night."

"He couldn't. He does not know if Burley or Campeau would betray me."

Now I was concerned that Sir Thomas was back to his old tricks. There were other ways to communicate with us about his plan. "He doesn't trust either of them?"

She shook her head. "He doesn't know them well enough to trust them, Little One. Your Father trusts Campeau, but he understands Jean's brain. The man is Templar and Roma. Jean would not betray me, but Sir Thomas does not know this in here—" She pointed to her head and heart "as I do."

"What of Burley?"

Magda screwed up her face. "Him, I do not know, is he his Father's son, or is he his own man? He may be too young to know yet."

The journey of a relatively short distance turned out to be a chore. The traffic was heavy, and we seemed to be confronted by obstacles at every intersection. Eventually, we entered the area known as St. John's Wood. It was rather titillating as it was known as a place where gentlemen kept their mistresses and where artists and the less salubrious members of society lived.

Aunt Mary was practically vibrating. "This is where the Prince Regent's Mrs Fitzherbet lived after her last break with Prinny. William Pole-Wellesley lived here too. You know he's Wellington's nephew. He never was accepted back into the best circles after his affair with Mrs Bligh. I have even heard that there are houses of ill repute scattered about the area."

Nell peered out the windows. "Seems like a fairly normal neighbourhood Mrs Spencer, not quite as grand as Mayfair but not down on its heels either." Growing up in London's Seven Dials, Nell was always rather nonchalant about such things. Then she asked with a child-like curiosity, "Do you know which house was Mrs Fitzherbet's?"

Aunt Mary gave her an imperious look. "One does not enquire about such things, Lady Hamilton." Nell cocked a brow, knowing that My Aunt Mary would know precisely where the infamous Catholic mistress of the Prince Regent had lived. She finally capitulated, saying, "I believe it was Stockleigh House on Prince Albert Road, but we will not be going past there."

She continued to chat about the infamous people who lived here and those who had fallen from society's grace and lived on the edge of fashionable society. I glanced at Magda, who always relished such stories in the past. But she seemed absorbed in her own thoughts. I glanced at Judith to catch her attention. Then I tipped my head towards Magda. She took note of her preoccupation and leaned against her shoulder. "Grandmama, you don't have to go through with this scheme."

Magda didn't answer her immediately. Instead, she turned to stare out the window as we were delayed once again. I looked out the opposite window to see an older, heavy-set man with bushy side-whiskers and a long flowing moustache staring at our carriage as if he could see the interior and who sat there.

His eyes were dark, intense, and unsettling. I glanced at Nell, who was also staring at him and seemed just as perturbed. I glanced out to see if Jibben had noted him, but he was busy haranguing a young buck who had entangled his cabriolet with a hackney. The young man, while yelling back at Jibben, was also staring at our carriage.

I decided then it was best to alert the other ladies, but as I glanced at where the older man had been standing, he was gone. Soon after, the young man was up and into his equipage, then off down the road. I didn't mention the older man watching us to the others since it had happened so quickly. I wasn't sure I hadn't imagined it after all, except that I knew Nell had taken note of him. But I couldn't dismiss Jibben's talk of being followed after feeling the same last night.

I was determined to be more vigilant in the future and kept a wary eye as we moved along to our destination, which was made nearly impossible by the countless villas with high walls or shrubs. There were far too many ideal hiding places.

We finally reached our destination and pulled onto a short circular drive stopping under an impressive portico. No one appeared to be about, so one of our grooms jumped down from the back of the carriage to knock on the door. We waited, and some time passed before Jibben directed the man to knock again. The door was finally opened by a plump, smiling woman in the full regalia of a Benedictine sister.

She took in our conveyance with the Hamilton crest. Then she looked up at Jibben mounted on an impressive roan gelding, and her smile disappeared as she asked in polished English what she could do for us. Jibben, by this time, had dismounted, and Nell had ordered the groom to open the carriage door and let down the steps to assist us to alight. As we came to the door ourselves, it was to hear the Sister insist that this was a convent and not a hospital for the mentally ill, that we had been misinformed.

We were all taken aback until Magda stepped forward, shoved her satchel into the woman's arms, and quirked a brow. "Is this place still just a convent?"

The Sister eyed the bag's contents and then examined all of us. Her brow furrowed before saying, "Please wait a moment." Then she closed the door in our faces leaving us standing on the doorstep.

Aunt Mary was outraged, and Jibben was ready to bundle us back into the carriage when a taller, older sister precipitously opened the door. She had a hawkish nose, brilliant blue eyes, and a wrinkled porcelain white face. She studied each one of us with a look of distaste.
As she said in a lilting Irish accent, "Good morning to you, and what can we be doing for such grand people such as yourselves?"

Jibben moved to take charge, but Nell stepped in front of him and made the introductions, then said, "We heard about your establishment and how discreet you were about your clients." The Nun frowned, taking in our dress and carriage again, and then moved to close the door.

Jibben put his foot in the way and a hand against the door to prevent such action. "Excuse me, sister, I understand that what Lady Hamilton said could be construed more than one way. However, I hope you understand that the Lady only meant that we are aware of your reputation as a compassionate, caring facility for the mentally afflicted."

The sister glared at him as if mulling over his words. Peering over her shoulder, I could barely hear someone speaking behind her. Finally, she opened the door wide "Please come in, and Reverend Mother will see you shortly."

We all filed into a beautifully proportioned and scrupulously clean but austere entryway. It was devoid of pictures or art of any kind. The only exception was an exquisite cross on the wall positioned, so the light from the front windows illuminated it.

In contrast, the room we were shown into was stunningly appointed and would not have looked out of place in any Mayfair home. There was an Aubusson carpet, a fragile teak escritoire that must be at least a hundred years old and French in design, as were the other furnishings, all distinctly from the old regime.

Jibben was admiring a fine pastoral scene with all the earmarks of a Gainsborough, and over my shoulder, I could see a portrait of a regal-looking couple and their three children done by his great rival, Joshua Reynolds. This was indeed a rich house. Jibben continued to walk about the room, examining its furnishings and artwork. Until a large tea service was wheeled in by a maid, who couldn't be more than fifteen at most and not a sister, and she left without a word. Aunt Mary eyed it, but it would be bad form for anyone to help themselves.

Another few minutes ticked by, and then the door was opened

and in walked a sister of indeterminate age with a flawless alabaster complexion and twinkling vibrant green eyes. She seemed to float across the floor to take a seat. Then she looked at the tea service and sighed, "You will have to excuse Milly. She's new here and not quite up to her duties yet. She's still learning."

The sister had a slight accent, but I couldn't quite place it. But it sounded French, though something harsher reverberated underneath. "I am Sister Mary, in charge of this—convent." Jibben came to sit beside Judith. He didn't look convinced of her assertion as Aunt Mary introduced us. The sister nodded at each one of us in turn. Then she leaned over to pour the tea. Once it was passed around, she smiled. "Now, what is it we can do for you?"

Magda, I noticed, was watching her closely, and the Sister was aware of her scrutiny. She abruptly turned to Magda and said something in a language I had never heard before. Magda was shocked, but she sneered at the woman who was scowling at her. Magda responded in something that was not Romani. I looked to Jibben to see if he understood this bilingual diatribe happening before us.

Both women rose and started yelling at each other until the door opened again, and in came the wizened old Irish Nun who had greeted us at the door. "Enough, both of you!" She shooed the other woman to another seat. "You will have to excuse me for our deception, but we have had several people coming here asking questions that were not appropriate in our view. Sister Mary knows several languages and has had various experiences that are not commiserate with the bulk of our Sisters."

Jibben scrutinised Sister Mary while Magda was still sending mental daggers her way. Then, finally, he glanced at the older woman and said, "And you are?"

She blushed and pursed her lips, having been caught out in missing a social nicety. "Quite right, Sir Stephen. My name is Reverand Mother Clare." She seemed flustered, and her Irish accent had all but disappeared.

Aunt Mary had been watching Sister Mary intently. Then she smiled slyly. "I know you. You are Irina Bagration. Last year, I met your uncle, Prince Andre Gregor, at the Embassy dinner. You were there with him and dressed very differently at the time. You look like your Mother, with the same eyes and flawless skin. The Sister did not smile. She merely nodded.

The Reverand Mother patiently watched this exchange, then said, "Now perhaps you can tell us why you have come here." She quickly glanced at Magda, then added, "With, I believe, Sister Bride's Mother."

Magda grinned. "Kezia told you I was coming?"

Mother Clare nodded. "We do not lie here, Madam Magda. As she told you before coming, that she would not lie."

Magda waved a hand back and forth. "True."

Mother Clare turned to the nun and said, "Sister Mary, will you please retrieve their satchel?"

Sister Mary nodded, rose and left with her chin tilted at a haughty angle. Mother Clare sighed. "Some struggles are eternal. Sister Mary's greatest struggle is humility." She scanned the room.

Jibben then leaned forward. "Sister Mary is Russian?"

Mother Clare nodded. "She is."

He bit a lip. "Can I ask you how long she has been with you?"

Mother Clare smiled. "Is this about Lady Marianne?"

Mother nodded. "Yes, it is Mother Clare; there seems to be a Russian connection to her disappearance."

She nodded. "Hence your question about Sister Mary, I see." She rose as Sister Mary returned with Magda's satchel of counterfeit money. "Thank you, Sister, now if you would be so good as to locate Sister Bride for me and send her here. Then you may go about your morning duties."

Sister Mary left with a scowl on her face. Mother Clare waited for a moment, then opened the door again to find Sister Mary had only just started to turn away from the door. She glanced over her shoulder and asked, "Did you need something, Mother Clare?"

Without thinking about it, Mother Clare said, "Yes, if you don't mind, would you please ask Milly to bring up the almond biscuits? She seems to have forgotten them." She closed the door, picked up a plate of biscuits on the tray, opened the window, and then tossed them out, placing the plate back on the trolley. She brushed her hands down the front of her habit and then sat down with an impish grin. "I hope all of you will forgive my little deception."

We all sat waiting for Milly to bring the other biscuits, which didn't take long. Finally, she apologised, "I am sorry, Mother Clare, I was sure they were on the trolley."

Mother Clare smiled at the shy girl. "They were, sweet girl, but they were so good we ate them all. A gentleman's breadbasket can hold more than you and me, child." Milly gawked at Jibben, nodded, and then hurried out the door, closing it behind her.

"Now, drink your tea before it gets cold. We can hold off our talk until Sister Bride can join us."

Not to be put off, Aunt Mary started the conversation, "How long have you been in London, Mother Clare?"

She chuckled. "Many years now, I worked with Father Kelly when he first arrived in London. He is our pastor and was instrumental in obtaining the funds to buy this place. On his word alone, we would have welcomed you. There was no need for deception."

Nell blushed at the chastisement. "Oh my—I helped with that fundraising. He didn't tell me it was for a hospital of this nature."

She shook her head. "No, he wouldn't. It is hard enough to get funds for a children's school, let alone a facility for the mentally disabled."

"That's why you are open to only those that could afford to pay for quality?"

Mother Clare looked confused. "No, of course not. We run on donations from the families based on what they can pay."

"So it's not only aristocrats that are admitted?"

She shook her head. "We recently started taking charity cases at the direction of our new medical director Dr Graham Cooper."

Jibben rolled his eyes. "How long since Dr Cooper visited?"

She sighed. "It has been some months, and truthfully, he hasn't answered any of my correspondence."

Nell's face drained of colour immediately, and she groaned. "It can't be?"

Judith was pensive when she asked, "This Dr Cooper. Can you tell us how long he's been associated with your endeavour here?"

She didn't hesitate though she seemed concerned about Nell's reaction. "Less than a year, our previous Doctor died suddenly in a terrible carriage accident. Dr Cooper came forward as a colleague and offered his services as our director."

Jibben perked up. "So he didn't care for your patients?"

She shook her head. "Oh no, his speciality wasn't diseases of the mind. He was merely interested in using his influence in the medical community to help us achieve credibility with his colleagues. We base our care on kindness, fresh air, wholesome food, and prayer. We have a medical doctor who will see our patients for physical maladies and prescribes sedatives when necessary."

There was a tap at the door, and it opened to show Sister Bride or Kezia as we knew her. She looked rather sheepish as Mother Clare invited her in. Then, glancing at Magda, she said, "I told you I wouldn't lie to the Reverend Mother. It was an insane idea anyway, Mama." Kezia bit her lip, realising the double meaning and mouthed, *'sorry.'*

The Reverend Mother pursed her lips, then said, "I should

probably throw all of you out, but I have to admit that I am curious to know what this is about."

For some reason, her eyes locked on me. "You have been very quiet, my dear. Perhaps you would care to explain."

I couldn't see any way around it, so I explained our connection to Marianne Braithwaite, how we had found her some years ago, that her family had taken her away to Scotland to be cared for, and now her brother's urgency to find her. She listened attentively, nodding, "I see."

She steepled her fingers and took a deep breath before speaking. "We did take in Lady Marianne as a resident on Dr Cooper's recommendation. When she arrived here, she was not in a lucid state. I believe that the woman who brought her here was overmedicating her. Once she had arrived, I sent for Lord Harris. He came immediately and was very explicit that no one was to know that she was here. He visited regularly and spent as much as five hours at a time with Lady Marianne. He often left her so distressed and exhausted that she became ill. I wrote to him a few weeks ago, suggesting he shorten his visits or curtail them until she was better. But he didn't take my advice."

I interrupted her, "Did her sister or Lord Burley try to visit her?"

She appeared disturbed by the question, "Not until recently, and I was surprised by their visits. Lord Harris had stated that they would only agitate their sister, and they had agreed to stay away."

I was interested in hearing about these visits. "How often did they visit?"

Both only came once and separately. "Lord Burley seemed upset when he left, saying he would make arrangements for her removal. But, sadly, I didn't have a chance to show him the court order Lord Harris had given me that made him Lady Marianne's sole guardian. He must have forgotten in his anxious state that he had signed that paper in agreement."

So, he omitted telling us that he had been to visit her, but I think I understood why he was upset, so I asked about Lady Arabella instead, "What about her sister?"

"That was very distressing. She tried to leave with Lady Marianne. She was highly perturbed and, strangely enough, outraged that her husband had written authority over her sister's care, and she didn't believe her brother had agreed. So it was like—well, never mind."

"No, please go on. It was like, what?"

She put her cup down and clasped her hands in front of her. "As if she didn't know her sister had been moved here. She had her sister halfway out the door before we could stop her."

I was starting to see a pattern. "When was this?"

Mother Clare was perplexed and sounded concerned. "About a fortnight ago."

"When did Lady Marianne go missing?"

She coughed, and the blood drained from her face. "That night."

"Did Lord Burley return?"

She seemed distressed now. "Yes, the very next day. You must understand that we were beside ourselves with her disappearance, and he was so angry. He left saying that he would have the highest authorities in the land involved."

"What did you do to find her?"

She wrung her hands. "I contacted Father Kelly. He said he would pray on it and speak to some people who might be able to help."

Then she glanced at Kezia. "That was when Sister Bride first came to us. She told us that the Crown had investigators that could help and that she knew them." She looked about the room and focused on Jibben. "I take it you are one of those people Sir Stephen?"

He smiled. "We all are."

She looked aghast. "Really! Even the ladies?" then she beamed. "How wonderful—times have changed since I was a girl." She seemed fascinated by all of us now.

I arched a brow and looked at Kezia. "You took this to Sir Thomas?"

She smiled serenely. "It was Father Kelly, and I approached him together, and he said he would consider it. Then I went with Mama, and she told him what she thought, and he came around to our way of thinking. He likes mama."

Jibben ran a hand over his face. "You could have talked to me first! What did you tell him to convince him to change his mind, Grandmama?"

70

"I had just returned from Cornwall. Kezia was waiting for me, and you were not home, so we left quickly and went straight to Sir Thomas, and well, I stretched the truth."

Jibben chuckled. "You lied?"

"I stretched the truth, Stephen. It is not the same."

Mother Clare stared wide-eyed at Magda, then at Jibben. "Does this happen often?"

My Mother smiled at her. "Yes, it does." Then she changed the subject and asked, "Mother Clare, may we see Marianne's room?"

She sighed. "I can't allow all of you up there, and Sir Stephen most certainly cannot leave this room. Therefore, I must extract a promise from you first that whoever you see here, you do not talk about them outside of these walls."

I agreed, "We promise, unless it affects our investigation, we will do everything we can to protect their identities."

"I suppose I can't ask for more." She suddenly looked incredibly sad and much older than when she entered this room.

It was decided that Nell and I would go with Mother Clare and Kezia. "As we climbed the stairs, she stopped. "I should mention that Lord Harris came here the day after she went missing and went through all her personal possessions."

"What was his mood like?"

"He was fine initially, even after he found out she was missing. Then we packed her things at his request and gave them to him. But he did the strangest thing with them. He dumped them out on

71

my desk. Then his mood abruptly changed. He was furious and stormed out, leaving them behind. Saying that he would kill her."

"That's when you contacted Father Kelly?"

"Yes."

Nell asked, "Do you still have her personal effects then?"

Mother Clare nodded, "Yes, Sister Bride can fetch them for you." She turned to Kezia and handed her a key. "You know which door?"

"Yes, Reverend Mother."

I saw Sister Mary watching us from the top of the stairs and reached out to stop Kezia. "Be careful."

She gave me a puzzled look, but she seemed to understand after Mother Clare called out to Sister Mary, saying, "Ah, there you are, Sister. Would you be so kind as to entertain our visitors in my sitting room?"

I was concerned that Kezia would be at a disadvantage with only one leg in a confrontation with the tall Nun, and for a moment, I considered following Kezia. But Mother Clare was waiting for us, so I trailed after her and Nell. As we passed Sister Mary, I felt her eyes on us as we continued down the hall.

The room we were shown shocked me. Lord Harris and Burley could have afforded a suite of rooms. Yet here was just one room of moderate size with a bed, armoire, and chest of drawers and near the hearth were two chairs and a small table on bare floors. "This is it?"

Mother Clare nodded. "It is one of our smallest." It didn't even have its own water closet, only a chamber pot and basin with a wide mouth ewer. "Lord Harris insisted that luxuries would only overstimulate her."

"And you believed him?"

She chuckled. "I may be old, but I am no fool. Lord Harris didn't care about her comfort. The only thing Lady Marianne ever asked for, and Lord Harris insisted she have, was paper and a pen. Yet, she never sent a letter to anyone. When we found her gone, all her papers were also gone."

Nell was walking about the room inspecting everything. "Do you recall anything that she was writing?"

"She didn't write anything; she only drew pictures. They were extraordinarily complex pictures. Lady Marianne told me she had learned the technique from a good friend in Scotland."

Nell's brow was furrowed as she searched the chest of drawers. I looked behind the paintings and in the armoire. There wasn't a scrap of paper anywhere. Nothing was written on the walls, and there was no discernible hiding place under a loose floorboard. Nell finally threw up her hands as I closed the door to the armoire "Nothing."

Mother Clare nodded. "Milly is very thorough when it comes to cleaning the rooms."

"Milly, the young maid that brought us the tea?"

Mother Clare smiled. "Yes, she's a hard worker and asked specifically to be able to clean Lady Marianne's room. They had bonded over their shared experiences."

I was shocked. "She can't be much older than fifteen."

Mother Clare's expression was so sad. "She had a frightful life before coming to us. Villainy is no respecter of age or class."

"May we speak to Milly?"

I could tell that the Reverend Mother was reluctant. "I must warn you that she's timid and easily frightened. But, if I allow it, I must insist that I am present."

That set off a warning bell in my head but so far, other than the initial introduction, Mother Clare had seemed to be open and honest with us. "Agreed."

"If you will wait here, I will fetch the child. Nell stepped forward and rang the bellpull by the door. "There's no need for you to climb up and down the stairs Mother Clare."

She stared at Nell, then smiled. "I don't blame you for not trusting me—but the bells don't work in any of the rooms." She showed us that the mechanism had been disabled.

I examined it and nodded. "How do your residents call for assistance?"

"Their doors are locked at night, and the night Sister makes hourly rounds to check on them. During the day, they come down to Sister Francis's office on the first floor and make their requests. If they are ill, we have an infirmary that our nursing sister watches over them during the day, but at night, it is just the night, sister."

Nell ventured to ask, "Just one sister?"

"We are a small group, Lady Hamilton."

Nell licked her lips. "May we speak with the night sister?"

"I will have to look to see who was on duty the night Lady Marianne left us, but I believe it was Sister Francis—I will check."

She left us alone to find Milly and look up who was assigned the night duty. The door to the hallway was open, and a beautiful, fey-looking woman walked or rather danced into the room and spun around.

She bowed before us, whispering, "Applause is usually appropriate after such a perfect pirouette." Nell and I obliged, which seemed to please her. Then, in conspiratorial tones, she bent forward to say, "Marianne is gone—she left with her golden angel. She floated down the stairs as quietly as a whisper and spirited her out the door. I wanted to go with her, but it was dark outside, and the night scares me."

She spun around the room, and despite our attempts to ask her questions, she continued to spin. Finally, Mother Clare returned with Milly and sighed, "Mrs Danvers come with me. You shouldn't be in here."

The woman looked at her and said, "Why, of course, Montrose, you are right." then she danced out the door and out of sight.

The Reverend Mother looked back at us. "If you will excuse me, I must see to her." Then she touched Milly's shoulder in a gesture of comfort. "Milly, this is Lady Hamilton and Lady Tinley. They would like to ask you a few questions. It is all right that you speak to them but speak truthfully." Then she rushed out of the room.

Milly stood in the doorway, looking for all the world, like a scared rabbit. I stepped forward and said, " Please sit with us, Milly." I looked at the two sad chairs, but Nell climbed onto the bed and invited Milly to sit with her. This caused Milly to giggle. Then she turned to look at me as I placed a hand on my belly. She rushed over to pull a chair to the bedside for me, then climbed up beside Nell.

Milly sat, pleating her apron and biting her lower lip and seemingly found it hard to make eye contact with either of us, so Nell reached out and took her hand, saying, "Milly, that's a beautiful name." She smiled shyly but didn't say anything.

Then glanced at me when I asked, "Milly, did you know Lady Marianne?"

She nodded. "She was nice to me and let me watch her draw sometimes. She drew every day using wee letters and numbers, not like a proper artist." She bit her finger and looked at the door. "That was supposed to be our secret."

"That was very nice of her, and I promise we won't tell anyone." She nodded as I tried to keep my voice calm and quiet. "Did you see her sister when she came to visit?"

Milly nodded. "Lady Marianne asked if she could have tea in her room, and I was the one who brought it up when Reverend Mother said she could."

"Did they speak about any secrets?"

Her breath hitched, and her eyes were like saucers. I was afraid she was going to cry. But, instead, she said the strangest thing "I can't tell yee unless yee knowed the secret."

Nell looked puzzled, and I tried to think of what she meant, thinking back to my only conversation with Marianne and repeating the only thing I could recall word for word. "Was it that she knew everything about her Father's secret books?

Milly was astounded and whispered, "Yes! She said the secret keepers would come. Is that who you are?"

I smiled at her, "In a way, we are."

I looked at Nell to see if her thoughts seemed on the same path as mine, so I had to be careful with my next question. "Do you know where Lady Marianne is?"

She shook her head. "No, her sister took her away."

"Did you help her?" She shook her head no, though I wasn't so sure, I let it go, and Nell smiled her approval.

"Thank you, Milly."

I slipped a hand into my reticule, pulled out a half-crown, and placed it in her hand. She stared down at it in awe. "What is it?"

Nell smiled. "A half-crown, Milly."

She glanced up at a loss for words. "I can keep it?"

I nodded. "It is yours to do with as you wish." She grinned from ear to ear, scooted off the bed, gave us a hurried curtsey, and left the room at a full run.

Nell climbed off the bed and straightened the counterpane.

Then we walked out of the room just in time to see the hem of a black habit disappear around the corner that led to the stairs. Nell pursed her lips and glanced at me. She had seen it, too and whispered, "I wonder how much Sister Mary heard."

"If that was her, I think it is safe to say she heard enough. Not that there was much to hear."

Nell frowned. "What are we going to do?"

I shrugged. "Warn Mother Clare, I suppose."

"Is that wise?"

I peered at Nell in surprise. "You think she might be involved?"

She shrugged. "I don't know."

Mother Clare came into sight at the head of the stairs. "I am sorry, ladies, that I had to leave you. Was Milly any help?"

I shook my head. "Not really. She only confirmed things that we already knew."

Mother Clare stared at me, saying with a sly smile, "Or that you surmised." She pursed her lips, then asked, "I need to know if Milly is in danger because of what she told you?"

Nell answered when I hesitated, "It is possible, Reverend Mother."

She nodded. "Then I think it's best if Sister Bride takes Milly and goes with you. Please keep them safe." I frowned, wondering what the men would say about bringing a skittish young girl under our protection. But in truth, I couldn't leave her behind and believe that she was safe. "We will gladly take her with us."

She smiled. "I will go fetch her and Sister Bride. Lady Marianne's personal effects are with your companions in my sitting room. You know your way?"

"Yes, thank you." She smiled and walked off with head high, and a firm footing towards what I supposed was the servant's stairway.

We started in the opposite direction when a cry of alarm came to us from behind. Nell and I turned about and rushed to where a doorway stood open. Mother Clare stood there with tears streaming down her face. Milly lay at her feet with her throat slit. Mrs Danvers stood below where Milly lay and said, "A crow did it—the nasty black crow that likes to pinch."

Nell took Mother Clare in hand and pulled her back through the door while Mrs Danvers leapt over Milly and bent to look at the half-crown in her open hand. "Crickey, she would only need a penny to cross the River Styx." Then she danced up the stairs and through the door.

I glanced at Mother Clare. "Reverend Mother, do you want us to send for the police, or would you prefer that we handle this?"

She was sobbing on Nell's shoulder but turned to look at me. "I will send for Father Kelly. He will tell us what we should do." Sister Francis came up the stairs with a pile of linen in her arms and stopped dead with her mouth open.

I took a sheet from the top of her pile and said, "Sister Francis, will you please bring Sir Stephen here and hurry before anyone else comes along." She dropped the linen, nodded and turned, flying down the way she had come.

It was just a minute or two before Jibben arrived. He quickly took in the scene, saying, "Why is it always stairwells?" Then, he gently picked up the child and carried her to Marianne's room, laying her on the bed. Mother Clare said a prayer over her with us standing by. Then she locked the door behind us as we left.

Sister Francis was lurking in the hallway with Mrs Danvers. When the Reverend Mother glanced at her, she said, "Please take Sara back to her room, Sister, then send for Father Kelly."

We returned to the sitting room and informed our companions about what had happened upstairs, but we didn't tell them everything Milly or Mrs Danvers had told us.

It was decided that we would wait for Father Kelly to arrive, and in the meantime, we asked to speak to the lay staff and the other sisters. Mother Clare was reluctant to agree, but Kezia convinced her, "Reverend Mother, any evidence could be disposed of, and stories could change the longer we wait."

"You trust these people?"

"With my life, and so does Father Kelly."

Jibben and Judith went to the kitchen to interview the laundress, cook and scullery maid. They had nothing to add to the narrative none of them had seen or heard anything unusual. Kezia and Mother Clare gathered the remaining eight nuns. Again, no one had anything of interest to add to what we already knew.

The only one we didn't interview was Sister Mary. She was

gone mysteriously missing. Mother Clare didn't seem surprised and explained that she had recently arrived from a convent in France but was from an aristocratic Russian family with some members attached to the Embassy, which she often visited.

Magda and Kezia searched Milly's room and returned with one drawing, obviously done by Marianne, using numbers and letters in the style Milly mentioned. They were so small that you would need a magnifier to read them. Everyone looked at it but couldn't make any sense of the jumble of characters.

Father Kelly arrived as we were interviewing the last nun, Sister Francis. She couldn't tell us anything about the murder, but she did part with an interesting tidbit regarding Lady Marianne's disappearance. Indeed, she was on duty that night and had seen someone in the garden through the infirmary window. She insisted it was a man, but she couldn't find him when she went to check. Then, right after making her next round, she found Lady Marianne missing. So did Arabella have assistance? Was it a coincidence, or had they been followed?

Judith looked out the window towards the front garden and asked, "Were the doors still locked that night?"

Sister Francis looked puzzled. "Of course they were."

"Did you check them all?"

"I had no reason to. Mother Clare locks up every evening and unlocks them every morning."

Jibben groaned after she left, then asked, "May we speak to your residents, Mother Clare?"

81

She shook her head. "I am sorry, I cannot allow that without their family's permission, and I can assure you none of them will be willing to risk the exposure."

"What of this Mrs Danvers that Lady Hamilton and Lady Tinley mentioned? She seems to elude your staff readily enough."

"Why would you say that?"

He gave her a sceptical look. "By your admission, your resident's families would not want exposure, so I assume your hesitance in admitting us was to make sure they were tucked away in their rooms, and I gather you locked them in. Yet Mrs Danvers managed to escape twice despite your best efforts." We all watched Mother Clare's reaction; it was as if the reality of his statement had jolted her.

Father Kelly had been quiet to this point, but he sat forward then and asked, "Reverend Mother, I doubt that Mrs Danvers brother would care. He never comes to see her."

The Reverend Mother nodded and sent Kezia to collect her. Aunt Mary gasped when they returned. "Lilly?"

Mrs Danvers looked at her and smiled. "Lady Alford—how nice of you to come." Aunt Mary made the requisite introductions. Once she had, Mrs Danvers took a seat next to the Reverend Mother and smoothed her skirts out. Then she cast her eyes around the room. When they landed on Jibben, she smiled graciously and said, "You look like a kind Tinker I once met." Jibben nodded but didn't respond, which didn't bother her as she moved on. "Now, to what do I owe the pleasure of such auspicious company?"

Father Kelly cleared his throat to garner her attention, then clasped his hands in front of him. "Mrs Danvers, there are two recent events I would like to clear up, and you may have some information for these people that is vital to that cause."

She nodded. "I assume that would be the disappearance of Lady Marianne and the murder of poor Milly?" If truth be told, we were all shocked by Mrs Danvers' lucidity.

He smiled at her and said, "Yes, that is correct."

She glanced at Nell and me. "I believe I already told these ladies about her Golden Angel. Poor Milly must have known something that someone didn't want her to repeat."

Father Kelly's brow was furrowed as he broached his next question, "How do you know that, Mrs Danvers?"

"Which one?"

"I beg your pardon?"

"Which event do you want me to attest to, or is it both?"

He smiled at her. "Both, if you may."

She glanced about the room again, and her eyes lit on my Mother, "Your General Hughes daughter aren't you, my dear?"

My Mother nodded. "Yes, I am." Then she turned to me. "Then you must be the bastard he recognised." Everyone in the room gasped, "I am sorry I shocked you, it was a bad choice of words, but Richard didn't make a secret about it. Even though everyone knew it for a lie, we didn't tell him Irene—but I think he knew just the same. "You look more like your Father, Colin Turner and his

Mother, Lady Violet."

Father Kelly was embarrassed, but it wasn't the first time I had come across someone who had known the General and made similar statements, if not in such blatant terms. Nevertheless, he endeavoured to regain her attention, "Mrs Danvers?"

She swung her head around to look at him again. "Yes, Father Kelly?"

"What can you tell us about the night Lady Marianne disappeared?"

"Oh, that's simple. We played cards after dinner, Marianne is very good, almost as good as I am, but then I cheat." She grinned as if seeing us all surprised at such an admission. "We aren't allowed to wager, the sisters forbid gambling and disapprove of cards, but they indulge us from time to time. But that night, Lady Marianne and I did wager it was rather one-sided, come to think of it. If she won, I would let her out of her room and unlock the front door. Those tasks weren't terribly challenging for me, but our game was fraught, and we kept going back and forth. Yet she somehow won the final hand, so I delivered on my promise."

"You said her Golden Angel came for her—do you know who that was?"

She grinned. "No, when I opened the front door, she entered wearing a golden mask and a dark cloak, then swept up the stairs and came back down with Lady Marianne, they left, and I closed the door."

"Did you lock it again?"

"Of course I did. That was part of the wager. Then I returned to my room."

He nodded, then clenched his hands. "And Milly, do you know anything about what happened to her?"

Mrs Danvers put her finger to her lips. "Secrets—there are so many secrets Father Kelly."

"Milly knew these secrets?"

She sat up straight and pursed her lips. "She must have. Sister Mary asked what Lady Marianne had told her whenever the child left her room. She asked about her books. She was always asking questions about books. I even helped the Sister search Lady Marianne's room once, but we found nothing."

I hadn't found any books in her room either, so I glanced at Mother Clare, who looked just as surprised. The Reverend Mother said, "Lady Marianne never had any books."

Mrs Danvers turned a haughty stare on the Nun. "Of course, she didn't." Then she tapped her head. "They were in here, in amazing detail and written in red. Marianne told me it was blood—so many people had died because of what was in those books."

Father Kelly took charge again. "So, back to Milly, did you see anything?"

She leaned forward, glancing at Jibben, frowning, then back to the Father. "Sister Mary listened to Milly tell her secrets to Lady Hamilton and Lady Tinley. She is a wicked person. Her robes should be red. There is blood on her hands."

Suddenly she rose, yawned and danced out of the room without acknowledging anyone. Sister Francis came from behind her desk in the hallway and took Mrs Danvers by her arm, moving her toward the stairs. I looked back at the group. Mother Clare was gobsmacked. "I have never seen her so coherent."

Father Kelly looked at Jibben. "She mentioned a Tinker; do you know her?"

Jibben's eyes glistened as he nodded to Magda, who answered. "He found her in the park rocking her dead baby. The pitiful thing was impossibly thin. It was born early and hadn't thrived; it broke her spirit. She was extremely ill following the child's birth and could not produce milk. When her husband wanted to bury the baby, she wouldn't let it go and ran out into the night. Jibben saw her and brought her to our camp for help, but her mind was broken. He went back out searching for her home the next morning. It took him most of the day, but he found her husband and brought him to the camp. He took the poor woman and her baby home. That was the last time we saw her until today."

Mother Clare frowned. "Her brother brought her to us and pays for her care. Her husband has a new wife. How he obtained a divorce, I don't know. But her brother doesn't come often. Still, she wants for nothing. He told us that his Father had their Mother committed to Bedlam, where she died, and he wanted better for his sister."

I felt tears sliding down my cheeks and looked at the rest of us. We were all emotional. Even Jibben looked tense and cold with fury.

Father Kelly looked to be undecided as to what the next course of action should be. He sucked in both lips as he thought. "We can't ignore what happened here. I know Inspector Gerald Fry of the Metropolitan Police, who will understand the need for discretion. I will send for him."

He stared at the rest of us. "I believe that you are familiar with him. He was once with the River Police under the command of Inspector Stewart." I was glad to know he would be familiar with us and our methods.

It was decided that Nell, Jibben and I would stay. The others would send for Inspector Fry, then return home, relate what we had discovered to the others, and send the carriage back for us. Kezia and Magda disappeared into the garden, perhaps looking for evidence of Sister Mary's flight. Father Kelly then went with Mother Clare to view Milly's body and pray for her.

Nell walked over to the table and picked up the drawing that had been found in Milly's room. "Do you think this drawing is a code of some sort?"

Jibben strolled over, took it from her hand, and then held it up to the light coming through the window. "That is a possibility, Lady Hamilton." He continued to peruse the drawing. "The numbers and letters appear to be scrambled randomly. I have no idea what they mean."

Magda returned with Kezia, who said, "Grandmama found signs of a vehicle that waited outside the garden gate, and it appears there was a scuffle. But we have no idea if Sister Mary went that way or not."

Inspector Fry arrived in short order, and after a cordial

greeting, he interviewed us all individually and then sent us on our way with a promise he would follow up with us. Sister Francis saw us out. She was agitated and seemed on the verge of saying something as we filed out, but she kept silent. I wasn't the only one who had noticed, and Kezia stopped beside her, whispering to her. Sister Francis smiled and nodded.

Chapter 4

Perception

Our companions who had left earlier sent the Hamilton carriage back for us, and it was a quiet ride home. When we arrived, it was to find Miles entertaining Judith and Lord Hamilton.

Miles glowered at all three of us and snapped as he ran a hand through his hair. "This was your great plan to investigate Lady Marianne's disappearance? Now it's resulted in the death of an innocent child!"

He turned his focus to Jibben. "You were supposed to control them and stop them if necessary."

Jibben glared back at him. "Have you ever tried to control five women when their minds are made up? I am only thankful that Edward's red-haired crusader couldn't attend. I kept them safe; what else could I do?"

Miles rolled his eyes. "My wife and Lady Hamilton were within an arm's reach of a possible murderer."

Jibben growled, "As a man, I was prevented from accompanying them further into the building. Other than carrying the child's body to a room, I was relegated to the front sitting room. Even after our friend Fry arrived, he was not allowed past the Reverend Mother's guard dog, Sister Francis. That's why he will be coming here before too much longer. He will want to talk to these ladies about all they saw and didn't tell him within the hearing of the Nuns."

Magda suddenly stormed in with Kezia rushing behind her. "Mama!"

Magda paid her no attention, "Jibben, we must go. There is much to be done. Wicker can yell at you later."

Miles looked bemused while Jibben looked sick as he said. "What is there to do, Grandmama?"

"We need to speak to Lady Marianne. So we must find her."

Jibben threw his head back and stared at the ceiling. "We don't know where she is?"

"I have an idea about that."

She had Miles' full attention now. "What idea, Magda?"

"We must find out where Lady Marianne would go when she was in London before she was married. I must speak to her brother."

Hamilton's brow furrowed. "How is that going to help?"

Magda waved at everyone. "Sit, and I will try to explain."

"Lady Marianne would not stay anywhere she did not feel safe, even if her sister told her to. She knows London—so we must find out where she would go willingly."

Miles frowned. "I don't think Burley will be in a mood to speak to us. We all but accused him of being a self-serving bastard in his desire to find Marianne."

Magda stared at him. "I agree that it was stupid of you." She stood up. "I will fix this. But before I go, I must see Lady Arabella if she is awake and can tell us anything that might help." I had never seen Magda in such a frenzy and wondered what she wasn't telling us.

Miles shook his head. "I just spoke to Jefferson. She's still unconscious."

"That may be Wicker, but there are other ways she can talk to me."

Then she turned to me, "Where are her clothes?"

"In her room. I will come with you."

Nodding, she made for the door. "None of you leave. We may have need of you." Then, as we climbed the stairs, she asked me, "Has she been bathed?"

"No, Matthew said it was best not to move her too much for the sake of her eye and any underlying brain injury she might have."

On entering Arabella's room, we found Matthew leaning over her, taking a pulse and frowning. "Is there anything wrong, Matthew?"

"I had hoped to see some improvement today, but there's been none." He looked frustrated as he continued to study her.

I headed for the chest where we had put her clothes. Pulling them out, I laid them on a fainting couch. Matthew looked up and asked, "What are you looking for?"

Magda answered, "Clues, this might be the same dress and cloak she wore when she removed her sister from the hospital where she had been admitted."

Matthew was gobsmacked. "She freed her sister?"

"Yes, why?"

Matthew arched a brow and licked his lips with hands on his hips, "The last time I saw Lady Marianne, she was highly suicidal. After what she's been through, I doubt that would have changed."

I sighed, looking down at her dress, underclothes, petticoats, and cloak laid out before me. "Then we'd best find her soon."

Dr Jefferson came to my side and stood looking down at them. "It's been over two weeks now, Lissa. Those clothes aren't going to show you anything."

I peered up at him. "You're right, but Arabella would have had to visit her sister frequently. I doubt Marianne is capable of caring for herself."

I sighed, looking back at the clothes after seeing the scepticism written on his features. I was flustered. "What motivated the beating? She must have been returning from somewhere since these are carriage clothes. I have seen her drive a Cabriolet alone in the Park. Wherever she went, she wouldn't have taken a groom with her. She would never put her staff in harm's way."

Matthew pursed his lips. "It would be nice if we could speak to the staff and examine her Cabriolet, but it has probably been cleaned by now."

Magda, in the meantime, was going through her pockets. Then she sniffed at a brown stain on the hem of her dress. Closing her eyes, she inhaled again. "This is not blood." She pushed it toward me. "Smell."

I took the hem in hand and breathed in. "No, it isn't blood. There's none of the usual coppery smell."

Matthew took it in hand, then nodded and sniffed. "You are right."

I glanced at Magda. "What is it?"

"Mud—there is an earthy smell."

Matthew offered, "From the Thames?"

Magda shook her head. "No, this smells like freshwater, no salt. There is nothing rotten in this mud. She was not in London when she collected this mud."

I found her reticule and rummaged through it. There was nothing out of the ordinary in it except a rosebud. I pulled out the picture I had taken from Blane House out of my pocket. There was a pastoral scene behind a portrait of Arabella framed on one side by roses. I passed it to Matthew and Magda to look at. "Do either of you recognise this place?" Both shook their heads no.

We continued examining her clothes until there was an audible catch in Arabella's breathing. Dr Jefferson rushed to her side. Magda and I followed. Her one eye was open and glistened with pain. She opened her mouth and whispered something none of us could hear. Matthew leaned close. "Can you repeat that, Lady Arabella?"

She licked her lips. "Water, please—"

Matthew reached for a nearby glass and helped her take a sip or two of water, then she sighed and laid back, closing her eye and whispering again so only Matthew could hear. Then she was gone again, asleep or unconscious.

"What did she say, Matthew?"

"Brown and something that sounded like capable."

Magda shook her head. "What is brown—the mud?"

Dr Jefferson interjected, "You said it was mud from freshwater?"

Magda stared at him like he was simple, "Yes—why?"

He grinned. "Capability Brown was a famous gardener from the last century and created some of the most beautiful gardens in the country with extensive water elements."

I glanced at him in disbelief. "There must be dozens of his gardens within a reasonable distance of London."

Dr Jefferson made a face as if calculating the odds, "I wouldn't doubt it."

I sighed in disgust. "It's impossible to determine where unless Lord Burley can make sense of this drawing."

Magda was mumbling to herself and went to shake Lady Arabella. Dr Jefferson took exception to her action. "Magda, stop that!"

She peered at him over her shoulder and frowned. "She is too deep and will not tell us more. Demons are battling for her life. Kezia and I will care for her."

Matthew glared at her and said, "No, you won't."

Magda glowered and spat out, "Yes, we will."

He crossed his arms. "No, I will not allow you to care for her. Not after your treatment of my patient just now."

Magda crossed her arms, and they stood there, staring at each other. I knew trying to mediate this standoff would be useless, so I watched this battle of wills. Surprisingly, it was Magda who gave in. "Fine—this time, you win, Dr Matthew Jefferson. I have much to do anyway."

She moved towards the door, saying over her shoulder. "Come, Little One, we must convince the others that we need to find the garden." She moved with a determined stride to the stairway, then spun around and pointed back the way we had come. "He is a stubborn man—I like him."

Then she continued down the stairs calling back to me, "Who hides a person in a garden if they are not dead." We both stopped simultaneously.

She looked back at me, and I said with all my heart, "No, she wouldn't kill her sister; they only have each other."

Magda started back down the stairs, "But they have a brother. Who may not care about them as he should." I had to acknowledge that she could be right and thought back to the man the Nun had seen in the garden.

We found Kezia and Judith standing in the hallway. Judith looked tired as she hugged me, "Lissa, I am exhausted, and the Inspector is done with me, so I am going home. Magda, are you coming?"

Magda glanced at me, then at the library door. She appeared to mull it over, then nodded. "Yes, I think it best. I have nothing to add that the Little One can't attest to."

Then I asked, "And you, Sister Bride?"

Kezia smiled. "I am off to the school. I miss the children, and only the Lord knows how long Father Kelly will be able to watch over them." I saw them off and then returned to the library.

The Hamiltons had gone home, but Inspector Fry sat with Jibben while Miles stood by the window. We greeted each other, and I sat down after calling for refreshments. "Well, Inspector Fry, how might we help you?"

He was looking about the room taking everything in. "I believe, Lady Tinley, you may have left out some details of your visit to Blane House. Unfortunately, Lady Hamilton left shortly after I arrived. Her excuse was something about an important dinner engagement, and she was in a hurry. She seemed to have very little information that she was willing to part with."

I smiled at him. "Perhaps you didn't ask Lady Hamilton the

right questions."

He scratched at his jaw. "Fair enough, Lady Tinley. I remember you from the warehouse murder and how adept you were at avoiding being too thorough in your answers. You and your friend seem to share that talent."

I smiled at him. "Thank you! I will take that as a compliment Inspector. What do you think I withheld from you at Blane House?"

"The drawing that you took with you by saying it was paramount to national security. Yet I saw only a beautiful lady surrounded by a pleasant vista from Broadlands gardens."

I was astonished that he had recognised the scene. "What gardens?"

"Broadlands. It is a country estate with beautiful expansive gardens by the River Test. There are several follies that seem to pop up as you walk along. The owner opens it to the public when he's not in residence."

Miles looked to Jibben. "Who owns Broadlands?"

"I have no idea, old man."

Inspector Fry was stymied, "Can you possibly focus on the issue at hand, gentlemen? Can someone please tell me what this has to do with the murder of the child at Blane House?"

I bit my lower lip and glanced at Miles, who nodded for me to go ahead. "It has nothing to do with her murder. But we have been asked by a family friend to look into the disappearance of a young woman from Blane House, she seems to have run away, and her family is desperate to find her."

He mulled this over, then said, "They locked her up to prevent an unsuitable liaison, perhaps?"

He was entirely off the mark, but I agreed, "Her reputation is already ruined.

He nodded. "Gretna Green is a bit far to travel, but the weather is fair. Yet you say her family still want her back?"

"They are hoping to keep it quiet for the family's sake. However, they are wealthy enough to take her away and find her a foreign husband for the right price."

He shook his head. "There's enough young bucks here that lack funds. So why take a foreigner into the family?"

I looked down my nose at him. "Inspector Fry, I am surprised. I never thought you to be biased."

He blushed with shame. "I fear it's leftover from the war. I wasn't more than a child then, but I still remember people's unpleasant feelings regarding foreigners. But you are right, Lady Tinley. You might say London is a major city at the crossroads of the world. We must adjust and give up our fears and prejudices. Not so easy, but we need to try."

"That's very astute of you, Inspector."

He blushed again, then returned to business. "So, this young woman who ran away was a resident in Blane House—but she's not a madwoman?"

Rennie, our maid, arrived with the tea giving me time to think, but I was at a loss for what to say. Finally, I threw up my hands. "Fine, Inspector, you have me. A madwoman is in possession of state secrets that would bring down the government and ruin many of the country's leading families. We must find her before some Russian agents do and use that information against us."

He sat there looking at me, holding his cup of tea halfway to his mouth, and then gradually, he started to sputter, chuckle, and burst out laughing. "Alright, Lady Tinley, have it your way. All I need to know is, did this madwoman murder that young girl?"

I shook my head. "No, of course not. She's been missing for over a fortnight. But it could have been the Russian Nun, Sister Mary."

He looked at me in amazement and arched his brows, fighting not to laugh again. "You should write one of those Penny fictions. So you are saying that a Russian Nun killed the maid?"

Miles shrugged when I looked at him, so I smiled. "It's a possibility, Inspector."

Inspector Fry's expression changed quickly, and he became serious. "Inspector Stewart told me once that I could trust you if anything should ever happen to him and that I should take your word as truth, realising that sometimes you wouldn't tell me everything. But you would never impede my investigations. I respect him. He helped me become the officer I am, so I will take him at his word until you prove him wrong." He pulled out his pad of paper. "Now, can you give me a description of this Russian Nun?"

Miles moved to sit, "Inspector Fry, I don't think you're going to want this case. The Nun is Irina Ivanov Bagration. Her Uncle is Prince Andre Gregor. He's with the Russian Embassy."

Fry's face drained of all colour. "Well, I've stepped in it, haven't I? Superintendent Lord Ross will want an explanation on this one—what do I tell him?"

Miles smiled. "Tell him to apply to Sir Thomas Wiseman for the answers he wants."

Inspector Fry whistled, then looked at Jibben. "You part of this too?"

Jibben grinned. "That I am ."

Fry shook his head. "I am glad I'm just a simple policeman." He glanced at Jibben, then back at Miles in consternation. "So, this murderer will go without punishment because her Uncle is a diplomat?"

"It would seem so unless we can convince her own country to turn her over to us. But I wouldn't hold out any hope of that happening."

"I hope the child's death is worth it."

His comment stunned me, and my response prickled with remorse and guilt. "No, Inspector, nothing is worth the loss of Milly's life. Nothing would assuage my conscience if my questions were partly responsible for her death."

He wiped a hand over his face. "I beg your pardon, Lady Tinley. I know you lost your ward to violence not that long ago. That was unfeeling of me."

I sat up straight and said to him, "This has nothing to do with Peter. It is about common decency Inspector."

He put his cup aside and rose. "I think I should give ground before shoving my foot further into my mouth."

I smiled and rose, extending my hand to him. "Don't let my prickliness bother you, Inspector. You will soon get used to us. I imagine this won't be the last time our paths will cross."

He smiled kindly. "Thank you, Lady Tinley. But I would not want to be in your position for all the tea in China." He bowed to us and left.

Jibben grinned. "Well done, Lissa, you distracted him from the drawing."

Miles shook his head. "I seriously doubt it. Remember, Stewart trained him—I doubt this is the last we have seen of Inspector Fry. Perhaps I should speak to Stewart about his ambitious former protégé."

I picked up Marianne's drawing and surveyed it. "The Broadlands, if I remember correctly, is in Hampshire—but who owns the property?"

Mr Malcom came to the door to announce, "Sir Thomas Wiseman is here to see you, Lord Tinley."

I rose to leave, as did Jibben, but Miles waved us down. "Thank you, Mr Malcom. Please show him in."

Sir Thomas joined us and surveyed the room. "The others have

101

left?"

Miles' brow furrowed. "Excuse me?"

Sir Thomas glared at him. "Don't play dumb with me, Tinley! You people are on the brink of causing an international incident. I knew I shouldn't have approved Madam Magda's crazy scheme. How dare you implicate the daughter of a diplomatic attaché in a tawdry murder in some home in St. John's Wood! What were you thinking, letting your ladies even enter such a neighbourhood?"

Then Sir Thomas glared at me. "Is that tea still hot?" I nodded as he snapped as if I didn't know, "Two sugars and lemon— please." I poured and handed him the cup.

"The Prime Minister, Lord Melbourne, called me to his office. He was furious!"

"When?"

He glowered at me. "What has that to do with it?"

"It has only been a few hours since everything transpired; nevertheless, it seems that Irina Bagration wasted no time reporting to her uncle."

Sir Thomas was stunned. "How did you know the Russians went to Melbourne?"

"Aunt Mary recognised her. Her name is Irina Bagration, the niece of Prince Andre Gregor. She might be posing as, or is, a Benedictine Nun, who may or may not have been involved in the death of a servant girl."

"What are you talking about?"

Miles was very calm and controlled in his response, "Perhaps you would like to listen to what happened since your information seems somewhat skewed."

"Fine, Tinley, I am listening."

Miles, Jibben and I explained what had happened today. When we stopped, Sir Thomas looked utterly confused. "So, none of you accused this Countess Irina Bagration of murder?"

I arched a brow in curiosity. "We didn't have the opportunity. Magda found evidence of a conveyance and a struggle in the lane behind the house, but we have no idea if she was the murderer or an inconvenient witness."

"So, you believe Blackburn and his assertion that the Russians are hoping to obtain this document that Burley said his sister complied about their late Father's assets and connections?"

Miles nodded, steepling his fingers. "It seems as likely as the Brocklehurst Group. We don't know, but they may even be working together, but we have no proof. The Russians are only a link at this point."

Sir Thomas was becoming impatient. "What link! If the Russians placed this woman there, why didn't she take the document before Lady Marianne was spirited away by her sister?"

I couldn't believe he ignored the obvious "How many people would think to look at her drawings? If the Reverend Mother hadn't described them to us, we would never have thought to ask Milly about them or even look for them."

Sir Thomas sipped his tea. "Drawings? Do you think she

recompiled her Father's ledgers and contacts from memory into drawings? I've never heard of anything so ridiculous in my life. I handed him the picture we had found in Milly's room and encouraged him to examine it closely. He studied it, then looked up. "A clever trick, but it means nothing—who could make any sense of this?"

I licked my lips, "Only Lady Marianne and perhaps her sister."

"Then we need to speak with Lady Arabella." He glanced at all three of us in the room. When no one answered, his eyes narrowed, and he hissed, "What aren't you telling me?" I bit my finger waiting for someone to say something. "Well?"

Miles sighed. "Perhaps you should come with us."

Sir Thomas arched a brow as Miles opened the door. He glanced at me, and I smiled, then followed my husband as I heard Jibben say behind me, "You had better come, Sir Thomas—you wouldn't believe this without seeing it."

I heard them coming behind me, and as I passed the General's portrait, I said to myself, '*If you ever cared for me, help me protect Arabella and her sister.*'

Miles stood, waiting outside Lady Arabella's door. He was speaking to Dr Jefferson as I approached. They nodded at me. "Is she any better, Matthew?"

"Not that you would notice. She's no worse, so I am cautiously hopeful at this point."

Sir Thomas came even with us and stood with his hands behind his back, "Cautiously hopeful about what, Matthew?"

Dr Jefferson nodded. "Sir. It's not my story to tell, so if you will excuse me." He opened the door and went back into the sick room.

Sir Thomas stared at Miles. "What is going on?"

I opened the door wider and walked in; Matthew was taking Arabella's pulse as he looked up and said, "I expect all of you to be quiet and respectful."

Sir Thomas gasped and then asked, "My God—what kind of accident was she in."

Matthew scowled at his Father-in-law and pulled the bed sheets back enough to see the bruising on her throat, the imprints that were clearly those of a man's hands. "It was no accident, sir. It was a brutal beating."

"Does her husband know what happened?"

I added, "This happened possibly at the hands of her husband. Before she lost consciousness, she wasn't quite clear on that point except that he was there. She suspects that her maid is dead for helping her escape."

He stared at me in disbelief. "You are serious, aren't you."

"Yes, I am."

Sir Thomas gestured for us to come out of the room. When the door closed, he spun on us. "Does her husband know that she's here?"

I took exception to his tone, "Of course not!"

He inhaled. "May I ask why not?"

I threw a hand towards the door. "Because he possibly did that to her! She may lose the use of an eye if she even recovers!"

He stared down at me. "Do I need to acquaint you with the law?"

"That she is his chattel, property, and he can beat her at will, is that the law?" He looked affronted at my response. "I will not contact him, and I will not allow him in my home even if you tell him. And if you do, I will sever my relationship with the Agency and appeal to the King on her behalf."

He arched his brow and stared down his nose at me. "Well played, Lady Tinley. I have sometimes wondered if you had the famous Turner backbone. I see that you do and have adopted Lord Tinley's attitude towards inconvenient laws." He paused to see if I would back down, but I stared right back. "Fine, I won't tell anyone of Lady Arabella's presence here for the time being, but I don't know how you expect to keep it a secret. Does her brother know?"

I pursed my lips, "No."

"Shouldn't he?"

I sighed. "No, Lady Arabella said it was safer for him if he didn't know."

He mashed his lips together and pulled at his chin. "You agreed with her?"

"I think we should respect her wishes until we have more

information."

He nodded. "Then I suggest we determine how to approach this problem."

We returned to the library, where he picked up the drawing again and looked at it closely

"Tinley, do you have a magnifying device?

Miles went to his desk, opened a lower drawer, pulled out a magnifying glass and handed it to him as Sir Thomas sat to examine the drawing closely. "Hmmph, this is very clever. It has me stymied, though." He tossed it onto the table beside him and placed the glass on top of it. "Should we ask her brother about this code his sister developed?"

Miles stared out the window. "It would be a risk—but we might have to. I think we should speak to Colin about this first. What about Jean Campeau?"

Then Sir Thomas appeared deep in thought, but finally, he glanced at Jibben. "You have worked closely with him, Locke. What do you think?"

"I don't know if he's a code breaker, but the numbers might mean something to him. May I take it with me?" he pointed to the drawing.

Sir Thomas frowned. "I am still unsure about Campeau, but if you think he can be trusted, all right. Just don't tell him too much about why we are interested."

I thought back to Emilie and the codebook she had been

creating. "Emilie! She sees patterns where I don't. She has worked on developing several different codes. Which you have so far rejected. But it would be worth having her work with Campeau—except she's still in Northumberland."

Sir Thomas was deep in thought. "Yes, but you are familiar with her work. Locke, you and Campeau will work with Lady Tinley starting tomorrow."

I sucked in a breath. "Tomorrow is Lady Cowper's Ball."

"I think you can work on the drawing before needing to primp for a Ball, Lady Tinley. Now I must be on my way."

I scowled at him, but he wasn't the least disconcerted. So I asked, "Before you leave, Sir Thomas, we have been told that the drawing is of a Capability Brown garden which can be found at somewhere called the Broadlands. Do you know who owns that home?"

He smirked. "Palmerston does. Henry John Temple, the 3rd Viscount Palmerston. I think you might have found your link to the Russians, Lady Tinley. No one hates Russia more than our Foreign Secretary. You will probably have a chance to meet him at the Ball tomorrow since he and Lady Cowper have a special relationship."

I glanced at Miles, who gave nothing away in his expression. "I look forward to meeting the Foreign Secretary. It seems we might have some things to discuss."

Sir Thomas spun on his heel. "You will not involve him in this! Winkle information out of him if you must, but do not directly involve him. I don't need another summons from Lord Melbourne.

I expect you to watch your step, Tinley! Now I am off to meet with Blackburn. I will inform him of what we know from your sojourn at Blane House."

After he left, we all sat down and exhaled. Jibben was the first one to articulate our position. "To quote Inspector Fry, we have stepped in it this time."

I nodded. "Our objective must still be to find Marianne. Perhaps we can angle for an invitation to Broadlands."

Miles chuckled. "I will leave that to you, my love. But be careful with Lady Cowper, Melbourne is her brother, and we can't afford another *faux pas*."

Jibben put a finger up. "About Lady Cowper, there is another Russian connection."

I turned to him. "What?"

"The Russian Ambassador Carlo Andrea Pozzo di Borgo. Lady Cowper had an affair with him during the war, and it is rumoured that he even fathered one of her children."

Miles shook his head in dismay. "Jibben, you are right; we have stepped in it this time." He slid down in his chair and sighed, "Why does it have to be us?"

Jibben grinned. "Oh, come now, this is what we do, Tinley. Sir Thomas said winkle information out of people any way we can."

Miles glared at him. "I am fairly certain he didn't say in *any way we can*."

Jibben waved his hand in dismissal with a twinkle in his eye.

"Believe me, my friend, it was implied."

Miles placed a hand over his face and shook his head. "You have no ethics, do you?"

Jibben faked being affronted. "Moi! No, I beg to differ, my friend; I have exceptional ethics, but they are flexible."

Miles chuckled, then burst out laughing. He poured Jibben a whisky and handed me my lukewarm tea. "Here's too flexible ethics! Cheers"

Jibben and I raised our glass and cup, echoing, "Cheers."

Chapter 5

Flexible Ethics

While we sat at dinner the previous evening, Miles received a letter from Lord Melbourne. He was to appear in the morning at his office with Sir Thomas and Lord Blackburn. As a result, he spent a restless night and rose well before dawn. I got up with him and went to the kitchen, where I lit the stove and set the kettle to make tea while Miles fetched a seed cake and my pickled eggs from the pantry. As we sat at the table, I found that I had no appetite for the eggs, just looking at them turned my stomach.

Miles celebrated that our child had finally rejected my former treat. Interestingly, the seed cake made my mouth water, and while on my second piece, I finally asked him, "What could Melbourne possibly want that you needed to be there as well as Sir Thomas and my Father?"

"I have no idea—the Russians may be stirring up a diplomatic storm to keep us from investigating them while trying to find Marianne. I wonder why they would want what she knows so badly. The information is years out of date. Unless something implicates their people in schemes that are still active, I have to question if we are missing something?"

I took his hand in mine as I took a sip of my tea. "I do wonder what we have gotten into?"

He gazed into my eyes. "A war of sorts, where the battlefield is

111

of the mind, and we are the troops."

He arched a brow and pulled me to him, kissing my cheek. "I suppose."

As we finished our cake and tea Mrs Jonas and Kit entered the kitchen, yawning. The early dawn light was filtering through the windows as Mrs Jonas let out a squeak at our presence while Kit picked up a heavy skillet holding it threateningly until he realised who we were.

Finally, Mrs Jonas put her hands on her hips. "You two need to get yourselves back to bed. Breakfast isn't for some time yet. Kit and I only wanted to get a head start on the bread, you know how Sir Stephen likes my sweet rolls, and I suppose Mr Campeau will enjoy some fresh croissants.

Miles looked perplexed. "Why should you be up so early just for them?"

She grinned. "Sir Stephen sharpened my knives yesterday and told me he and Mr Campeau would be here for breakfast."

Miles rolled his eyes. "I see."

Looking at the large jar in front of me, I interrupted them, "Mrs Jonas, I think it is safe to get rid of the pickled eggs now. I seemed to have gotten over that craving."

She chuckled and nodded. "I'll see that someone deserving gets them, milady." Kit and Miles both coughed, trying to cover a chuckle. Miles then took my hand and helped me to stand. We wished them both well and left, climbing the stairs back to our room and falling into bed and back asleep.

It was much later when I woke to find Miles gone and Meg bustling around the room. "Time to get up, milady. Sir Stephen and Mr Campeau are on their second cup of coffee and a second basket of pastries."

I sighed and blinked, watching her lay out my day gown. "Lord Tinley is gone?"

"Yes, milady, he left to have breakfast with your Father." I sighed, knowing that would leave me to contend with Jibben and Mr Campeau alone.

Meg helped me dress after I washed, styled my hair and sent me on my way. Partway down the stairs, I stared at the General, asking, "What do you know about all of this? If you could—would you help?" Of course, I got no answer to those questions, but I wished he had left more information regarding his double dealings to help us at junctures like this.

I entered the breakfast room to find my two guests waiting patiently. Jibben grinned. "Thank God, you are here at last! Mr Malcom wouldn't allow us near the chaffing dishes until you arrived."

I waved my hand at Tyson. "You may remove the lids now. I should think, Jibben, that you both would be stuffed with the pastries you have consumed." Tyson grinned as he watched the gentlemen ready to make a sprint to the buffet. But they held back and waited for me to serve myself. Once I resumed my seat, they filled their plates, returned to their chairs, and quickly disposed of their meal while conversing.

When we were done, we retreated to the library and found

113

Marianne's drawing still lying where I had left it yesterday. Without explanation, I passed the picture to Mr Campeau, only asking, "Does this make any sense to you?"

He walked to the window, looking at it in the light and then, holding it up to the light, remarking. "This is genius!" Jibben jumped up and rushed to his side as Campeau said, "Can you see it?"

Jibben took it in hand and stared at it for what seemed like forever. Then he said, "My word." Then he looked at Campeau. "What does it mean?"

He piqued my interest. "What are you two talking about?"

Jibben sighed. "I am not sure, but this looks like elements of an accounting system and—what else, Campeau?"

Campeau grinned. "The letters are fragments of sentences. We will have to put in some work for it to make any sense out of it. The numbers may or may not be a page from an accounting book that might relate to the written information." His shoulders slumped. "This will take considerable time without a copy for each of us to work from."

I pulled out paper and pencils from the escritoire, then rummaged around and found a pair of scissors. Placing a chair on one side of the table and sat down. I cut the page into three pieces and said, "Draw up a chair, gentlemen." They both stared at me as if I had lost my mind. I stared back, waiting for them to join me. "I have no desire to lean over this table all day staring at this drawing, and we don't have copies, so it makes sense to divide it. Come now, let's get to work."

They came to the table and took a pencil and paper in hand, then their part of the drawing. Jibben looked at me. "Now what?"

Campeau smiled. "We strategise and copy out what we see line by line, then see if it makes any sense."

Jibben glowered at him, saying, "And what if this is merely a mad woman's reminiscences?" I glared at Jibben for giving away so much.

"Then we will discover that, my friend, or you will have a key to decipher any additional documents in your possession. So I take it that this is not just another exercise in trust for me? There must be an urgent reason for you to involve me." Campeau turned back to his page and, in a quiet voice full of speculation, asked, "Is the madwoman you mentioned Lady Marianne Braithwaite?"

My jaw must have dropped as he looked at me shyly. "Lady Tinley, I was my brother's accountant and secretary. As such, there was little that I didn't eventually come to know. I know that he sent Cooper once to Scotland to get information from her. But then she disappeared." Jean said nothing else and started copying from his drawing.

"Excuse me—you said she disappeared?"

Campeau stopped writing, "Yes, Cooper told Johnathan that her family had moved her. But, unfortunately for Johnathan, her doctors there had no idea where she had been taken."

I glanced at Jibben, who tried not to show how astonished he was. Then, finally, he croaked out, "Cooper was very loyal to your brother, wasn't he?"

Campeau had put down his pencil. "Not always. He had one failing as far as Johnathan was concerned—he had a conscience."

I stared at him in disbelief. "So he wouldn't have harmed a madwoman but would attempt to kill an old Gypsy woman?"

He sighed. "It is complicated. Cooper was born in a madhouse, and when his Mother died, he had to leave. That was when Johnathan found him, but he still felt for those incarcerated behind the walls of that place. They were truly his family."

He clasped his hands in front of him. Cooper and I didn't agree on much—but killing people unable to defend themselves was the one we both felt strongly about." Then his expression became suspicious as he looked at the drawing. "This is Lady Marianne's work, isn't it."

Jibben slammed his fist down on the table, glaring at me. "I am going to tell him, and damn Sir Thomas. This is like working with one arm tied behind our backs." He went ahead and told Jean Campeau all that we knew. I slumped in my chair, placing a hand over my face. This was already getting out of control, and Miles had yet to return from Melbourne's office.

We continued until it was time for luncheon. We had made no progress beyond filling page after page with sentence fragments and a series of numbers. None of which we could make out as a coherent message. I sighed and threw down my pencil. "Perhaps this was just what it looks like a drawing of Broadlands."

Campeau sat back, his brows knit in deep concentration. He pulled the pieces together again. "Who is this woman in the foreground?"

I sat up, "Lady Arabella Harris."

"Lord Rupert Harris's wife?"

"Yes, why?"

He studied the picture again. "You are sure this is Broadlands, and that is Lady Arabella?" I nodded, and then he sat back, biting his thumb in thought. I waited for him to say something, but he shook his head. "I can't think—it's right there." He tapped his head in frustration.

Mr Malcom came and announced luncheon, so we adjourned to the dining room. Shortly after sitting down, Miles and my Father joined us, throwing themselves into chairs and accepting wine and a soup plate. Both men looked flustered and angry.

My Father glared at us and said, "We have been told to cease all our investigations into what happened at Blane House and all matters associated with it, that includes Lady Marianne's disappearance though it was not specifically addressed."

I was gobsmacked, "But we are not obligated to the Prime Minister."

My Father nodded. "As such, Sir Thomas is seeking an audience with the King. But his Majesty has been busy with preparations for his birthday banquet. So he is not in a good mood. Moreover, the Duchess of Kent and her comptroller John Conroy are giving him headaches about Princess Alexandrina Victoria attending."

I shook my head. "That is such a fraught relationship. I feel sorry for the Princess."

"Indeed." My Father then asked, " But what have you achieved today?"

Jibben explained what little we had discovered about the drawing. Campeau added what he knew, and we discussed Cooper's possible role. Jean's thoughts that there was something about the picture of Lady Arabella was eluding him. At least, I hope he wasn't deliberately withholding information from us. He ended with, "It all is moot now that you have been told to stop your investigation."

My Father nodded, but I could tell he was thinking. He and Miles had exchanged several looks that seemed full of mute dialogue. The meal progressed at a leisurely pace until we arrived at the coffee. Then my Father said, looking at all of us. "What I am about to say stays in this room. I want you to continue to work on the drawing and the investigation, I am the leader of the Brotherhood, and I will not sit by and watch my country stumble blindly into the control of another."

Jibben frowned. "That is a bit of a chance, isn't Blackburn? We have been told to cease."My Father ignored his remark, seemingly deep in thought again.

Miles glared at Jibben. "He's right. Why should we stop an investigation into the disappearance and murder of our citizens?"

Jibben scowled at him. "If we ignore the Russian connection, that leaves us with nothing to pursue."

My Father grinned. "Not necessarily. We do as Lissa has suggested. We find Marianne Braithwaite first."

I smiled. "So we leave Blane House and the Russians out of the equation?"

"Yes, I'm not sure there's any more we could obtain from the Sisters anyway."

Jibben nodded, "Kezia will continue helping at Blane House when Father Kelly can spare her. So if she should find out anything, we can hardly ignore it; besides, she's not part of the Agency or the Brotherhood."

My Father looked sceptical. "Are you sure she is going to continue?"

Jibben smirked. "She will when I ask her." Then he slapped his head. "One other thing Grandmama can practically see inside my head; I cannot keep this from her."

I chuckled. "Remember, she is already off on some mission of her own, but I am sure our paths will cross again in this investigation."

Father sighed. "True, Magda always finds her way into our affairs." He paused, running a hand along the table's edge before saying, "Locke, you may tell her what we have planned. Her insights have always been helpful in the past." Then he looked at Miles. "What of Edward?"

Miles sighed and tapped the table in front of him. "He will never accept us stepping away from the investigation. He and Burley will barrel headlong into this and make a mess. I don't see how we can exclude them and maintain any kind of control over their actions."

I pursed my lips. "What of Hamilton? If the Home Office is investigating Lord Harris, he may want to be part of this."

Father ran a hand over his face. "We can't involve everyone."

I added, "You know he is observant enough and will guess we are up to something."

He took a few seconds, then bit his lip before saying, "We will proceed tonight as we had planned. Then tomorrow, we will meet here with everyone, extracting promises of secrecy and involving only those that can contribute. I don't want us falling all over each other's feet."

My Father left soon after, followed by Jibben and Campeau, who took parts of the drawing with them. Miles distracted me from working any more of the picture with the promise of a foot massage after a bath, in which he joined me. It was one of my favourite things we shared, but time could get away from us. Once we were out and my hair was dry, we spent time with the children before getting ready for the Ball.

Charlotte played with her dolls while Alex tossed blocks across the room at a pile of toy soldiers as if it were a game of skittles. Charlotte bounced up and ran to us while Alex remained intent on knocking down the last soldier. Then he pushed up and toddled over, grabbing Miles around the knee, saying, "Up, Papa." Miles bent and picked him up, and as soon as he was face to face with him, Alex seized his nose "Efalant Papa!"

Miles looked to me for an interpretation. "Remember the parade, and we saw the elephants."

He glanced down at his son. "That's not fair old man. My nose is not that big!" Alex giggled and blew on Miles' cheek, making a screeching sound, then laughed as Miles pulled out a handkerchief to wipe the drool off his face.

He ran with Alex over to his cot and began tickling him, so our son was crowing so loud that it brought Anne into the room. "My gosh, I thought someone was being murdered!"

Miles handed our gasping son over to Anne. "I think he wet himself." She eyed him, knowing full well that he was the cause of the accident. Anne changed Alex's nappy, after which we sat with both children while Charlotte read a story from her favourite picture book. Miles grinned when he interrupted her once, saying, "That's not how you told it last time."

She shook her head. "Silly Papa, the pictures look different every time I see them. So the story changes."

Anne was smiling as she tidied up. "She knows her numbers and letters and is doing well with her reading. She has an active imagination when it comes to storytime." She smiled at Alex, then looked at Charlotte. "Children, it's time for dinner."

Charlotte jumped down, yelling, "Pudding, Alex! If we eat all our vegetables, we get pudding." Anne put Alex down just as he wrinkled his nose at the word vegetables but toddled off with Charlotte to the schoolroom where Tyson waited with their dinner."

As we returned to our room, I stopped Miles, who looked down at me and asked. "What?"

"It was something that Anne and Charlotte had said that made me wonder about a couple of things. First, Anne thought you were murdering Alex. Second, at Blane House, Nell and I were just a short way down the hall from where Milly had gone, and we heard nothing until Mother Clare screamed. Yet Milly lay only a few stairs down from the doorway. Third, we thought we saw Sister Mary disappear around the corner of the hallway, but it was shortly before the scream if that was her. I am not sure that Sister Mary could have raced around and reached the child on the servant's stairs. Milly must have known and trusted her killer."

"Or the killer was lying in wait for her and surprised her. You don't think Mother Clare killed her?"

"I don't know, Miles. Seeing blood or a weapon with those black robes would be hard. But I didn't smell blood on the Reverend Mother. So perhaps Sister Mary left Blane House in fear for her life. It doesn't make any sense."

"And what did Charlotte say that got you thinking."

"That the pictures look different every time she looks at them. In the drawing of Marianne's, we saw things in the morning light that we didn't see in the afternoon. I need to look at it again."

"Darling, you cut it into three pieces."

"I know, but I need to look at my piece again before dressing." I ran down the stairs and into the library with Miles behind me. I picked up my part of the drawing, took it over to the window, looked at it again in the sun setting, and studied it closely. "Miles, hold this for me." He took the picture, and I stepped back. "The folly in the background. Someone is standing on the steps."

"What difference does that make?" I took the paper from him and angled it so the light shone on it. "What do you see?"

He stood there, contemplating the drawing "Lady Arabella."

I rolled my eyes. "In the distance, Miles."

He concentrated again, "It looks like a woman standing on the steps of the folly."

"Could it be Marianne?"

He shook his head, looking sceptical. "It's impossible to tell. But if she is the artist, she wouldn't be in the drawing."

"Unless it was a message to whoever found it telling them she was there. Milly said Marianne told her not to say anything except to the secret keepers."

He ran a finger down his nose. "We keep secrets, Miles. That is a farfetched assumption, Lissa."

My shoulders slumped. "I know, but this is a woman whose mind was broken the last time we saw her. She could be better and make a lucid choice to insert herself, or she is mad and still inserted herself."

"Or she only drew what she saw." I slapped his arm for being so rational.

"We need to think differently, Miles, especially since our usual avenues of investigation have been forbidden to us." I looked at the clock and sighed. "It's time to get ready for the Ball."

Meg and Robert were waiting for us in our room. On our bed

was a beautiful emerald green watered silk gown bereft of decoration, and on top of it was a gift box that I opened to find a diamond and emerald necklace, bracelet, and earbobs. "Miles, they are beautiful!"

"It wasn't my doing, love. They are from the Shellard collection. My Father wanted you to have them. Lady Jane says they are too heavy and all wrong for her colouring."

"You expect me to believe that after you heard me admire Judith's Emeralds."

He smiled shyly. "I knew Jane never wore them, and beautiful jewellery should be worn."

"And the gown?"

He blushed. "Oh yes. I am not a fan of all the bows and furbelows on Ballgowns, so I designed this one myself. Call it an early birthday present."

"Miles, my birthday is months away, and our child will be here by then."

I saw his face fall, but something other than my surprise made him emotional. Then it dawned on me, "Miles, I am fine, the baby is fine, and I will sail through this birth just like I did with Charlotte and Alex." I knew he feared losing me each time I entered my confinement. I went to him, cupping his face in my hands. "You can't do this every time, Miles—we will be fine."

He nodded, "I know that, and as such, there is an extra panel that Mrs Mac inserted to cover our child, but it can be easily removed to accommodate your own beautiful body after the birth." I kissed him gently because that was what he needed. It was my way of thanking him for caring so much, and he knew it.

Meg was smiling at our exchange. "It will look wonderful on you, milady. Now you need to hurry, or you will be late, and Lady Cowper doesn't tolerate such things from what I hear." I chuckled since the Beau Monde norm was no one ever arrived on time.

Once I was ready, Miles fastened on the necklace, kissing my neck and beaming like the day we had married. It made my heart race. I stood up, and he wrapped his arms around me, kissing me, then deepening it to the point I seriously considered if we should stay home. Miles grinned. "I think we should go before I take your dress off."

It was a warm evening, and I only required a light shawl as we climbed into our carriage. We were stopped half a block from the Cowper's home by the carriages waiting to disgorge their patrons. I would have insisted we walk to the entrance if it hadn't been for my silk slippers.

While we sat, I noticed the same older, heavy-set man with bushy side-whiskers and a long flowing moustache that I had seen on our way to Blane House standing on the walkway, pushing his way through the crush of people. He stared at us as he passed us with an expression of open hostility.

I reached for Miles to draw his attention and pointed out the window, but by the time he turned to look, the man had moved on and disappeared into the crowd. "That was odd. I just saw the older man I had mentioned while on our way to Blane House. I thought then that he and the younger man who blocked our carriage were together. But when both men realised they were

125

being observed, they left going in opposite directions."

Miles moved to jump out of the carriage, but I grabbed his arm. "Don't, Miles, that might be what he wants." He nodded, then sat back.

"Will you be able to draw his likeness when we return home?"

"I suppose so. I don't know how detailed it will be, but it should be enough to help identify him."

When we finally reached the head of the line and descended, I looked about for the man but didn't see him. So I took Miles' arm to walk in, saying, "We need to warn the others. Jibben saw the young man I thought was with him, so we should also keep an eye out for him."

The crowd pulled us into the entry hall and swept us up the stairs to greet our hostess Lady Cowper. Her husband was a retiring gentleman and not present, which was not unusual on such occasions. On the other hand, Lord Palmerston was close by but not intrusive. Once we finished speaking to Lady Cowper, we moved to the Ballroom, where the dancing had already commenced.

I scanned the room, looking for our companions and located Jibben and the Hamiltons on the far side and turned to find my Mother and Father, along with Edward and Fiona, moving toward us. We greeted each other, and Miles asked, "Where are Arthur and Aunt Mary?"

Mother laughed. "They are with your Father and Lady Jane in the card room, listening to the gossip for us and holding court."

Miles grinned, then chuckled. "Jane does like a rousing game of Whist." Then he asked my Father, "What is our plan of attack?"

My Father nodded behind him. "Our first victim is heading our way now." I glanced over Miles's shoulder to see Lord Palmerston walking toward us.

When he reached us, Palmerston bowed to Mother, Fiona and me and, after nodding to the men, asked, "To what do we owe the pleasure of not only the Johnson brothers and their lovely wives but the Blackburns company as well?" he casually peered about the room. "I see the rest of your party have strategically placed themselves already." No one said a word, and he chuckled. "Come now, people, everyone knows you were the victims of a Melbourne dressing down today. What was that about—some sensitive matter that you stepped in?"

He stood there, smiling conspiratorially. Then in a hushed voice, "I know you are looking at the Russians. All I can say is, if you ask me the right questions, I might be able to give you some illuminating answers." Then he bowed and walked away.

Father looked at Miles, who smirked, saying, "That news travelled quickly."

Miles and I watched Palmerston join a group that included the Home Secretary, Lord John Russell, who was watching our group intently. He raised his glass and nodded at us. I turned back to my parents, who had also seen the salute. "What did Palmerston mean by ask him the right questions?"

My Father focused on Miles. "I have no idea. Perhaps we should ask Hamilton if Russell and Palmerston are working around the Prime Minister. If they are, I would prefer not to get involved in a political chess game."

Miles agreed, "Yes, but we seem to have Palmerston's blessing to look into the Russians."

My Father took a glass of champagne from a passing footman's tray and wrinkled his brow after taking a sip. "Let's wait to see what Sir Thomas has to say. His Majesty has no love for Russell; he disapproves of what he considers his radical politics."

Miles chuckled. "He also has a contentious relationship with Melbourne at best."

Mother smiled. "Then we had better hope that his Majesty will support our investigation."

Hamilton and Nell joined us with Jibben, who responded to her comment, "Hear, hear."

Hamilton looked perturbed, staring at the wall behind us. I glanced at Nell, who giggled, "Brian was called to Lord Russel's home today and told that he had his blessing to assist in your investigation. But if it all goes to hell, he would deny all knowledge of his involvement."

Hamilton peered at her frowning. "Those weren't his exact words, but it was implied."

Father shook his head. "I don't like being used as political pawns. Therefore, I suggest that we work on this in our usual way. Tomorrow I want to meet with any of our Irregulars who speak or at least understand Russian and determine if there is any potential for safely inserting one of them into the embassy. We also need to discover who these men are who seem to be following us."

That caused some consternation, particularly with Hamilton regarding Nell, for he tended to be overprotective of her.

Jibben had mentioned that he had seen the blonde young man today when riding with his son John and I admitted seeing the older man only a street away from Lady Cowper's home this evening.

Everyone looked around as if they expected to see these people lurking nearby. A shiver ran down my spine when I saw the older man walking through the crowd. But I lost sight of him as he disappeared near the terrace doors. Miles seemed to have followed my eye. "That's him?" he asked, and I nodded. "Locke, would you like to help me detain one of those men. they just went out on the terrace."

I moved to go with him, but he stopped me. "No, stay here in case he doubles back." I huffed but realised that he was right. He and Jibben weaved their way slowly through the pressing crowd and the dancers. I watched until I lost sight of them.

My Father turned to my Mother, "I just saw Sir Thomas arrive with Isabel and Jefferson. Stay here. I want to speak to him alone."

He walked away, greeting the Jeffersons as they passed. Matthew looked over his shoulder when he reached us. "What's that all about? Sir Thomas barely snarled at me all the way here, and Colin looks like he's eaten something disagreeable."

My Mother chuckled. "That's a good analogy, Matthew. He may have to swallow some of his words, and he won't like it, not one bit.'

I glanced around at the crowd before whispering, "The investigation seems to have the cautious backing of Lord Russell and Lord Palmerston without them knowing exactly what they are backing."

Nell scoffed, "It could be a political game to tweak the prime minister."

Hamilton glanced down at Nell. "That's an interesting thought, my love." He looked over his shoulder, where Palmerston and Russell were still in deep conversation. "And entirely possible."

We stood there as a group, and it became clear that we were becoming the focus of scrutiny. Finally, Mother whispered, "I think we need to break up and go separate ways. Lissa, are you coming with me to find your Father?"

"No, Mother, Miles asked me to wait here."

"Very well."

Hamilton asked Nell to dance, but she turned to me before accepting, "Do you want us to stay with you?"

"Heavens, no, go ahead and dance."

Matthew and Isabel stood at my side, looking about the room. Finally, Isabel touched her husband's arm. "There's Lady Emma. I must ask her about her musical next week. She wanted me to help select the pieces for her soprano soloist."

Matthew nodded. "Feel free, my love. I will wait here with Lady Tinley."

I smiled up at him. "Lady Emma, I take is not a favourite of yours?"

He rolled his eyes. "Lady Emma's husband is a hypochondriac. I would end up being cornered to discuss his dyspepsia and corns." I smiled at him then he asked. "Where is your husband?"

Judith came rushing through the crowd just then, short of breath, and gasped, "Matthew, thank God you are here—the terrace— someone is seriously hurt; they need your help."

Matthew dashed off without saying anything. I turned to a still gasping Judith with my heart in my throat. "Who is it?"

She shook her head. "I don't know, but someone called out for Dr Jefferson."

I swallowed hard. "Miles and Jibben went out to the terrace a few minutes ago, tracking that man I saw watching us on the way to Blane House."

She stopped her gasping and gapped at me. "My God, no!"

We both tried to rush towards the terrace but were held back by the press of people. Then I saw Miles' and Jibben's heads bobbing through the crowd toward us. Judith and I noticed them simultaneously, but following them closely were two military officers with very sour expressions. I reached out to touch Miles, but one of the red-coated officers pushed my hand away and said. "Stand back, Lady Tinley."

Judith looked to Jibben, "Stephen?"

He tried to smile. "A simple misunderstanding, my love, find Blackburn and Wiseman."

I heard behind me some grumbling as people were being pushed. "What's this all about!" Palmerston and the Home Secretary had made their way to us, glowering at the officers. Then, finally, one of the men answered, "Murder, sir."

Lord Russell growled, "Preposterous, follow me." I gasped and held onto Judith, and we followed our husbands, who were being marched off towards Lord Cowper's library.

Hamilton came to my side. "I will fetch Blackburn and Sir Thomas."

"Thank you, Brian."

Nell took my hand as we followed in the wake of the officers and two of the most powerful men in government. Judith pushed us forward and stormed into the library, glaring at the two officers who would bar our way and snapped at them, "You will bring Lady Tinley a chair. She is with child, in case you hadn't noticed."

Lord Russell leaned against a large mahogany desk. "Who wants to explain to me what happened?"

There was a knock at the door, and Dr Jefferson came in. "There has been no murder, gentlemen."

Everyone looked at him as if he had lost his mind. "It was murder but not by these gentlemen. There were powder burns on the victim's fingers, and a spent pistol was beside his body. But there was no blood on the terrace, and rigour mortis was setting in, gentlemen."

He was met with blank stares. Matthew sighed, adding, "He has been dead for at least two hours."

Russell glowered at him. "You are sure of that, Jefferson?"

"Yes, sir. I would swear to it in court."

His eyes veered back to Jibben and Miles. "Would either of you care to explain why Major Brooks and Smythe would feel it necessary to arrest you?"

The way the two men glanced at each other made me shiver. Then the one addressed as Brooks said, "They were leaning over the body and acting suspiciously."

Miles rolled his eyes. Russell looked directly at him but ignored the expression. Then he turned to concentrate on the officers in their scarlet tunics. "How so, gentlemen? What was suspicious?"

They looked at each other, and Smythe spoke up. "Lord Tinley was poking at his neck, sir, and was trying to stop his breathing while Sir Stephen was restraining the man's free arm."

Russell looked at Miles and Jibben. "Well?"

But it was Matthew who spoke up. "They were checking his pulse. When it is faint in the wrist, you check the larger vessels in the neck."

Russell looked back at the Majors. "Well, gentlemen, is that what they were doing?"

Smythe snorted, "Jefferson is their friend. What else would he say."

Russell nodded. "He is a reputable physician who has served his country well. Hence, he is Sir Matthew Jefferson, not just doctor Jefferson." Neither man said anything. "Very well, that seems to have been cleared up. Now, who is the man?"

Everyone looked at each other and shook their heads, even Jibben and Miles looked perplexed. Lord Russell glared at all of them. "Come now, gentlemen, it's not a trick question."

Miles spoke up, "I have never seen him before."

Jibben shrugged his shoulder. "Neither have I."

Lord Russell pursed his lips and addressed his next question to Matthew. "Is it possible that he was forced to kill himself, or it was made to look like a suicide?"

Matthew looked perplexed. "I wouldn't be able to answer your questions until after a thorough autopsy."

The general expression around the room was one of distaste. "Cutting into a man will tell you if he killed himself or not?"

Matthew smirked. "An autopsy requires a thorough examination of his body and examination of his personal effects, not just cutting into him. Many things can be gleaned from an autopsy Lord Russell that can be invaluable in preventing the rush to judgement against an innocent man."

Russell sucked on his lower lip, then nodded. "Fine, you may conduct your autopsy, Sir Matthew. I will have the body delivered to your surgery, but the autopsy must be conducted discreetly."

Matthew stared at him in disbelief. "Sir, the entire company in the Ballroom know that something untoward happened."

Miles intervened since Matthew and Lord Russell started raising their voices, "Might I suggest you contact Inspector Stewart of the River Police? He knows how to be discreet."

Lord Russell looked perturbed. "This is hardly in the River Police jurisdiction."

"No, but you are in charge of the country's policing and internal affairs, and this seems to be an internal affair which gives you the right to appoint whoever you like to investigate the matter—discreetly."

Lord Russell stared at Miles with a look of displeasure. "Are you instructing me in my duties, Lord Tinley?"

"Never, Lord Russel, just reminding you that you have a choice in the matter."

"Fine, I will send for him, but he is to work with Sir Thomas Wiseman on this matter."

The two majors appeared to be less than pleased with this pronouncement, having lost their opportunity to be the heroes of the hour. Lord Russell left with them, saying, "Not a word about what has transpired here tonight, gentlemen, or I will have your guts for garters."

Everyone else, including my parents and Sir Thomas, who had just arrived with Isabel, gathered around as Miles looked at

Matthew curiously and asked, "Do you think suicide is possible?"

I noticed Matthew was perspiring freely now and seemed exasperated as he sat down. "Of course, he didn't commit suicide! But those two dunderheads that caught you would have had you and Locke in Newgate before we could hear your story. So, what happened? I just laid my career on the line with that lie." He flicked some lint off his leg and then smirked. "Lord Russell seems to have caught on and given me the out with a forced or staged suicide."

Sir Thomas was frowning. "Lord Tinley, Sir Stephen, your wives are looking weary. I suggest you take them home immediately. I will send Inspector Stewart to interview you at the Tinley's. After all, Lady Tinley's condition is delicate, so you should take your family doctor with you." I grimaced at him as he pointed at me, "Do not argue with me on this one, Lady Tinley. I want you, your husband and the Lockes to stay here until the rest of us leave this room in a more orderly fashion. Then you will depart with Matthew and Isabel."

Jibben swallowed. "You don't want to know what happened?"

"No, I do not! At least the rest of us can then answer any questions truthfully."

Isabel Jefferson slipped into the room then. "Matthew, Father, what's going on?"

Her Father turned to her, "You are leaving with your husband, Tinley, Locke and their wives. They will catch you up on what's going on."

Isabel fishmouthed and looked about to refuse when she glanced at her husband and saw how distressed he appeared. Finally, she went to him and took his hand, "All right then, Father, I assume we are going back to the Tinley residence?"

Miles answered in a somewhat disgruntled voice, "Correct."

He opened the door to find Lady Cowper and Palmerston standing there. Lady Cowper looked over her shoulder. "Your carriages are out front. I am so sorry you must leave so soon." She smiled and then giggled. "At least I am now assured that the Ball will be the talk of the town tomorrow. Thanks to all of you. You do make things interesting."

Palmerston scrutinised all of us. "Hopefully, Sir Matthew's public findings will be congruent with one of Lord Russell's hypotheses. But I suggest you leave the story as to why up to us." He focused on Sir Thomas. "Thomas, I think you should come with me to determine what that story should be. Blackburn, circulate with your lovely wife and spread the story that the shock was too much for your daughter. She is leaving with her husband and physician, and that Lady Locke swooned and is being taken home by Sir Stephen."

Judith opened her mouth and said, "I never swoon."

Palmerston smiled. "There is a first time for everything, my dear." Then he looked at Hamilton. "I am sure Russell will want to have a word with you, Hamilton. Perhaps you and your beautiful wife should return to the dance."

Then he took up Nell's dance card, "Ah, you have a waltz open." He signed his name. "Please don't leave before I can claim

137

my dance, my dear." It was a command and not a request.

Mother and Father hugged me, saying they would come as soon as it seemed appropriate to leave. Miles took my arm and whispered, "Look, frail."

"What?"

He snickered, "Look fragile, like you are about to faint."

I grasped his arm tightly and feigned being overcome with emotion. "This is beyond ridiculous."

"Consider it an opportunity to practice your acting skills." I slapped his arm.

Jibben turned to Judith. "Should I carry you?"

She glowered at him. "You wouldn't dare."

He stepped forward to pick her up. She stepped back and broke a heel on her slipper. He grinned. "Now, I will have to carry you, my dear." He swung her up in his arms, and we moved out of the room and down a side corridor.

Once outside, we climbed into our carriages and left. I kept an eye on the window, looking for anyone watching us, but it was quiet. When we arrived home, Mr Malcom greeted us without raising an eyebrow. I smiled and told him, "Everyone will arrive within the hour, Mr Malcom. Can I count on you and Mrs Jonas for a cold supper?"

He bowed. "Of course, milady." and disappeared through the green baize door.

I saw out of the corner of my eye that Tyson was taking charge of our wraps, cloaks, hats, and gloves while smirking. He caught me watching him and wiped the smirk from his face immediately. "It is all right, Tyson. By the end of this night, I am sure you will know everything."

"Yes, milady." he blushed, saying hurriedly, "I mean no, milady!" We all chuckled as Tyson's blush deepened, and then he rushed to put our things away.

We made for the library, which seemed to be where we did our best thinking. I picked up our cat Patches and sat down in the chair she had occupied, placing her on my lap. She didn't seem to like the silk of my gown and leapt down to leave just as Bard, our dog, scooted through the open door to lay by the hearth. Miles took the seat beside mine, and the other couples sat looking dejected. Judith fussed with her gown, saying. "I had this specially made for tonight, and you two had to go looking for a body."

Jibben looked at his wife in disbelief. "We did not go looking for one, my love—we merely found it."

I pursed my lips as I watched Matthew. He was deeply disturbed, finally leaning forward and focused on Jibben, then Miles, he asked. "Please tell me that neither of you killed him?"

Miles was shocked by the question, "Of course not!"

Jibben was indignant. "You thought that we did?"

Matthew shook his head. "No, but then who did? Did you see or hear anyone?"

"I thought you said rigour was setting in."

"I lied, but it will be by the time Stewart sees the body."

Miles suddenly looked confused. "I didn't hear a shot." Then looking at Jibben and asked, "Did you?"

Jibben shook his head. "Now that I think about it, no, I didn't."

Judith gasped. "Then how did the dead man get shot on the terrace, yet no one heard or saw it happen?"

It suddenly hit me. "The man on the street, Miles, this was orchestrated. He knew that one of us would follow him to the terrace where a body had been placed. You were supposed to have been taken into custody for murder."

Matthew rubbed his eyes and snapped. "You had better work out what happened and let me know! I am going up to check on Lady Arabella. Feel free to keep speculating without me."

Isabel took his hand to stop him. "Look at them, Matthew. This isn't speculation. They are serious. Lissa told me about the man she saw on the way to Blane House and how he watched them with such clear hostility."

He cupped his wife's cheek. "I know they are serious, darling. I am just concerned that I might not be able to find what I need to prove them innocent in the autopsy."

She smiled up at him. "You will." He patted her hand and left to go upstairs.

Then she looked back at us. "Matthew could lose his right to practise if he lied to keep you out of prison."

Miles nodded. "We won't let that happen, Isabel, I promise

140

you."

My eyes snapped to him, "You would go to prison for a crime you didn't commit?"

He took my hand in his "I won't let Matthew lie for us. We didn't do anything, and we will prove it."

Mr Malcom came to the door, "Inspector Stewart is here, milord."

"Show him in, Mr Malcom."

He stepped aside to let the Inspector walk in. Then Stewart pointed at Jibben and Miles. "You two! If you ever leave a crime scene again before I arrive, I will arrest you for obstructing an investigation."

Miles poured him a whisky and then passed it to him. "I suggest that you take a seat Inspector. We were ordered to leave by your superior, Lord Russell.

He took a sip smacking his lips. "By the way, you didn't murder the fellow, so Dr Jefferson won't have to lie for you."

All eyes were on him as he enjoyed another sip of his whisky. "The dead man was dragged through the garden and placed on the terrace. Obviously, he left there with the intent to ensnare you or someone in a murder. The two majors agreed that the man appeared dead when you found him."

Miles sighed. "Thank you, Stewart."

He waved a hand. "Now, do you mind filling me in on what has been happening? I will have a lot of explaining to do when Lord

Ross asks why I was called into an investigation outside of my jurisdiction."

My Father answered as he entered the room without my Mother and the Hamiltons. "You won't have to. Lord Russell has seconded you to conduct this investigation."

Stewart sat back, studying all of us. "So, this is how it starts? Getting sucked into your world of secret dealings for the Crown to save the country from embarrassment?"

Jibben laughed. "Excellent summation Stewart, except you have been part of this world for some time. You just haven't realised it."

Stewart rubbed his neck. "Am I to be compensated differently?"

My Father laughed, "Yes, and handsomely."

Stewart waved a hand. "Not too handsomely. I don't want to try and explain it to the wife. But if you cover all my expenses and a bit more over my regular pay, I will be happy to assist."

I realised then there was little that I knew about Stewart personally. I didn't know if he had a wife and wondered if he had children. Where did he live? But I didn't ask those questions. Instead, I invited him to share our cold supper, which Mr Malcom had just signalled at the door was ready. "Would you care to join us for a bite to eat, Inspector?"

"I would like that, Lady Tinley. Thank you very much."

We adjourned to the dining room, where we helped ourselves

and ate while my Father filled in Inspector Stewart about our investigation. It seemed to make Miles uncomfortable, but he accepted it as inevitable. Dr Jefferson joined us, only nodding at me, indicating that Arabella was unchanged.

My Father finished bringing the Inspector up on everything except Lady Arabella. Then Miles spoke up, "I like you, Stewart, but you don't have to work on this. Our work is dangerous, and you have a family to look out for."

Stewart laughed. "It's a little late for that now, Lord Tinley. But I imagine the river underbelly will applaud this move. I will be out of their hair for a while. I wish I had Fry back as my second."

I interjected, "Speaking of Inspector Fry, he became involved with the murder of a young servant girl at Blane House. He will have been warned off the case by now, as we were."

Stewart chuckled. "That is not going to deter Fry. He is tenacious, and ignoring the murder of an innocent young woman will not sit well with him. He may not be pursuing it officially, but I can guarantee he has not given it up. I will speak to him; I assume these cases are part of the same overall investigation."

Father chewed on his lower lip. "I would prefer you not share anything you have heard tonight."

Stewart smiled, but there was no warmth in it. "I know how to be discreet, milord."

My Father steepled his hands. "I meant no offence Inspector. It's a habit." Stewart nodded, but otherwise, he did not respond.

Jibben commented, "It's getting a touch prickly in here. But I can assure you, Stewart, that Lord Blackburn is usually even more annoying when giving offence." Everyone chuckled and agreed, much to my Father's chagrin.

Dr Jefferson and Stewart made an appointment to review the autopsy results once he was done the next day. Then he rose wearily from his seat. "It has been a long day for me. If you will excuse me, I am going home. I will see you tomorrow Sir Matthew." He nodded and left.

Once I heard the door close, I looked at my Father. "Why didn't you tell him about Lady Arabella lying upstairs?"

"Until we have more information about her part in all of this, there was no reason to. And it is safer for her and him." He sat back with a glass of port and said, "Now, who is going to Hampshire to follow up on this drawing?" He peered at me and asked, "You honestly think that the second person in the picture is a clue to where Lady Marianne can be found?"

"I am not sure, papa, but it is all we have so far."

"Regardless of what I say, I know you would only go anyway."

Judith grinned and glanced at Jibben before saying, "I found out from Lady Cowper that Lord Palmerston is hosting a retreat at Broadlands next week." Then she looked at my Father. "I suppose we can count on you to secure an invitation." She stated it as a fact, not a question.

My Father cleared his throat. "I suppose I must."

Chapter 6

Clues?

The Invitation to Broadlands arrived before we had even finished breakfast. Knowing how this precipitous timing would throw the household into a flurry of activity, my shoulders slumped. Moreover, I was concerned about Meg's condition, with the travelling and the work it would entail.

I spoke to Miles, and we determined now was the time to send Meg and Robert on holiday. We called them to the library and talked to them as friends, not employers. In truth, Robert looked relieved. Meg, however, argued, as I knew she would until Robert said he would like to go to the seaside because it would be good for little Jack. Eventually, Meg capitulated, seemingly pleased by the idea of relaxing, and agreed to leave the next day. We notified Rennie and Tyson that they would replace Meg and Robert at Broadlands.

Judith, Nell, Mother, and I went shopping for last-minute things and a gift for our host from de Bearne and DuQuenoy. When we were done, we stopped at Gunter's for an ice. As we sat chatting, the attractive young blonde man who had held up our carriage on our way to Blane House pulled a chair up to our table. He took the spoon I had halfway to my mouth and gulped down the ice. "Ah, most refreshing." His accent was engaging but barely noticeable. He grinned at me. "My name is Urie Vasiliev, ladies, and it is a pleasure to meet you all finally." Then he went around the table and named each of us, which was unsettling.

My Mother's expression was one of cool disdain as she said, "What can we do for you, Mr Vasiliev."

He waved a finger, "Not, Mister. Count, Count Urie Vasiliev."

She nodded. "Very well, Count Vasiliev—what can we do for you."

He grinned, took another spoonful of my ice, and sucked it back. "I wish to make a suggestion." Then he scowled, "Stay out of this—you and your husbands." He stood, bowed as he clicked his heels together, and walked away nonchalantly out the door.

I pushed my dish away and stared at my companions. "Well, that was unpleasant."

Judith leaned forward. "Stay out of what? We have two murders, a beating and one missing person on our hands. If he was going to threaten us, he could have been more specific."

Mother shuddered and spat out, "I hate trumped-up little toads like that. Counts in the Russian court are as numerous as fleas on a dog, and most haven't two pence between them." She waved to our server and paid our bill. "I think we should leave. We need to tell Colin about this intrusion."

We returned to my home, where all the men were gathered, waiting for Dr Jefferson and Inspector Stewart to arrive with the autopsy results.

Mother was in high dudgeon when we entered the house, throwing her hat to Mr Malcom and demanding, "Where is Lord

Blackburn?"

Mr Malcom pointed to Mile's study directly across from us. She marched to the door and threw it open. "A Russian lapdog harassed us at Gunter's."

The men had all turned and were staring at my Mother, not saying a word, so I added, "It was the young man who stopped our carriage on our way to Blane House."

Jibben growled, "That pipsqueak! Where?"

Judith sighed. "She told you, Gunter's."

Hamilton's reaction was a surprise. He barely glanced at Nell and calmly asked, "Did he tell you his name?"

Mother spat out, "Count Urie Vasiliev."

Hamilton groaned, "He's an attaché with the Russian Embassy."

Nell stared at him in surprise and asked, "How do you know him?"

"I have been following him for Lord Russell, but he's a slippery fellow. It's like he knows he's being watched."

Nell gasped. "Does he know it's you?"

"I doubt it, darling—but he seems to have a sixth sense about it." Hamilton sighed. "This investigation is not going to be easy."

Father was rubbing his chin. "Palmerston has invited some of the Russians to his house party."

I whipped around. "I thought you said he hated the Russians?"

He smirked. "That might be, but he believes in getting to know potential adversaries. That's his job as Foreign Secretary."

Miles was quiet. "Are we still going to Hampshire under the circumstances?"

Father leaned back. "We have twenty Irregulars in the area, and Montgomery is back now and can watch things here."

Jibben grinned. "Jean should come with us."

I was surprised. "Campeau—Is that wise?"

He waved his hand. "How many times must I tell you that he is trustworthy? Besides, the Russians often speak French, and Jean is fluent."

Judith gawked at him. "As are you and everyone in this room."

Jibben nodded. "Yes, but he has a French name too." Jibben could never pass up a time when he could insert his odd sense of the absurd. Judith reached out and slapped him on the back of the head.

He glowered at her and then scrutinised our gathering before saying, "Then I suggest that we have concealed weapons on us at all times."

My Father nodded. "Regrettably, I agree, Locke."

We divested ourselves of shawls, bonnets, gloves and parasols while I sent for tea. The following discussion was about other safety measures we would need to take.

Magda arrived partway through with Dr Jefferson and Inspector Stewart. All eyes were on Matthew. He sighed as I poured them tea and said, "Magda was waiting in my surgery when I arrived to do the autopsy."

Jibben huffed at her, "You should tell someone where you are going when you leave the house."

"I did, I told Mugs."

Judith giggled, and Jibben rolled his eyes. "You told the dog?"

"He was the only one awake. I needed to ask someone about the dead man's clothes."

"Grandmama—did you take someone into Dr Jefferson's surgery?"

"No, I took the clothes, then returned them." She selected a strawberry tart and took a bite.

"Where did you take the clothes?"

"To Andreas—you know him. He's a respected tailor in the Polish community."

My Father leaned forward. "Are you telling us that the dead man was a Pole?"

"Yes, he was Antoni Gzowski."

Hamilton groaned. "He's a known political activist and only recently arrived here from France."

Miles asked, "France?"

"He's one of the lesser-known political elites forced into exile in France when the Polish-Lithuanian Commonwealth collapsed and was divided up between Prussia, Austria and —Russia."

Miles sighed, "The Russians again—Melbourne will be furious."

Father shifted in his chair and glanced out the window to the garden. "What else did you discover, Magda?"

"He has no family here but has some unsavoury friends. That is all I know, Colin Turner."

She turned her gaze to Dr Jefferson. "Matthew, did you learn anything illuminating?"

Matthew inhaled deeply and then blew it out. Whoever killed him tried to make it look like a suicide. However, there were threads and a small feather embedded in the wound, and though there were powder burns on his right hand, he was shot in the left side of his head."

Father chewed on his lower lip. "Meaning?"

Stewart sat up, hissing. "Someone held a cushion to his head and shot him."

Jefferson put up a finger. "But he was already dead when he was shot, the small blood vessels in his eyes were ruptured, and his neck was broken."

Stewart looked puzzled. "There were no signs of restraints, so he must have been surprised."

Jibben frowned. "How did he get the powder burns on his hands?"

Stewart leaned forward. "I would say he was involved in a firefight before being captured and killed."

"Why would they bring him to Lady Cowper's Ball if there was so much obvious evidence that he had not been murdered on the terrace?"

Stewart puckered his lips, looking about the room. "My best guess would be that it was a warning, but to who and why is still a question, but I don't have the answer. I plan to search his lodgings after I leave here."

"You should probably know, Inspector, that Count Urie Vasiliev accosted us in Gunter's today."

Stewart stared at us and groaned. "He's quite the troublesome young man taking advantage of his diplomatic status to get out of any number of petty crimes. So what did he want?"

Mother answered, "It was all rather obscure. He told us to *'stay out of this.'*

Stewart chuckled. "Could he have been any more ambiguous? Stay out of what? You have been involved in two murders, and you have a missing person. Except you seem to believe they are linked."

Judith nodded. "Precisely—but you forgot the beating and Lord Harris selling secrets to the Russians." Then she slammed a hand over her mouth. "Oh my God, I am sorry, Lissa!"

Stewart glared at her, "What beating? I don't have all the facts. I can't help you!"

I rubbed my temple feeling like a headache was coming on and sighed, "Lord Harris's wife came to me a few days ago. She was savagely beaten and terrified, but she couldn't tell me much before losing consciousness. I accepted that her husband had beaten her, but it is unclear if that is true. Except she did say that he witnessed it." I explained the details of her arrival and about Capability Brown, the drawing and how it was tied to Palmerston, the Russians, and possibly the Brocklehurst Group.

Stewart ran a hand across his face. "Fry, I suppose, knows nothing about Lady Arabella? You never do things by halves, do you? I spoke to Fry today, and you were right; he has been warned off the murder at Blane House, but he is sure you were hiding something from him. You have put me in a difficult position with my colleague."

My Father leaned forward, his hands clasped between his knees. "You can leave now and forget what you have heard today if you want to, and we can take it from here."

Stewart shook his head. "I couldn't, not now." Then he smiled. "I understand this can be dangerous, but it's more interesting than chasing my usual clientele. So, you are leaving for Hampshire soon? How should I contact you if I need you?"

My Father stood up and strode to the window. "You will be coming with us, Inspector Stewart."

He quirked a brow, "Lord Blackburn, I will not be a valet."

"I didn't say you would be, Sir Reginald Stewart; you are my son-in-law's new personal secretary."

My Mother glanced at him, then my Father. "You are about the same size as Colin. I think we can put together a wardrobe for you."

Stewart shook his head. "No, thank you, Lady Blackburn. I will wear my own kit. I have the clothes I need to fit in like a knight who needs to make a living at your behest."

Judith's brow furrowed. "That sounds so sad."

Stewart said, "Yes, but effective. The ladies will love me, the servants won't be so standoffish, and the toffs tend to forget me like the furniture. Yet I will have the run of the house."

Jibben burst out laughing. "How long have you been doing this sort of thing?"

Stewart chuckled. "How do you think I got to the Bywater's murder so quickly? I was already there without an invitation, but I was on another case that night. I heard Sir Thomas order his groom to send for me, so I stepped forward and told the man I was the Inspector, and he was just as happy not to have to race along the waterfront looking for me."

He stood and then asked, "When do we leave? I must tell the missus I will be out of town for a few days and arrange things at my station."

"Monday morning Inspector, where shall we collect you?"

He shook his head. "I can't have people know that I have left town with the likes of you—it would compromise my position. I will meet you on the road before your first stop on the way to Hampshire." He nodded to all of us and left.

Jibben arched a brow, focusing on my Father. "Was that wise to include him?"

Father turned back from the window. "Possibly not, but I took a chance on you, which was a bigger risk than Stewart. Besides, he was right. He will be able to go into places at Broadlands that we can't."

Jibben laughed. "Very true, Blackburn, on both counts."

Magda, who had sat quietly munching on tarts and sipping tea, snorted, "We took the chance on you, *Gadjos*. You are very entertaining, which was hard to resist."

She put her cup down, saying, "Now we must go to see Lady Arabella. She is awake."

Just then, Dolly came to the door. "I thought you should know that Lady Arabella is awake, milady."

Dr Jefferson was on his feet at once. "Let me examine her first. Then I will let you know if you can come in."

Magda rose with him. "I will come with you." He glared at her, and she put a hand palm out. "I promise I won't poke her again." Matthew rolled his eyes and followed her out.

The rest of us waited for Matthew's affirmation. When he returned, he sat. "Magda is sitting with her. But she is highly emotional right now." He seemed to struggle with his next words, "I had to tell her that I couldn't save her eye. She will be blind in that one eye for the rest of her life." He rubbed a hand across his face. "The orbital bone was shattered, and that side of her face will be slightly disfigured, but she will still be a beautiful woman."

He sighed, sitting back. "I want you to find the person that did that to her, and however you can manage it, make them pay."

I felt tears sliding down my cheeks and reached for Miles' hand. Matthew looked at me. "She would like to speak to you and Miles."

I glanced at Miles as he helped me up. Then, in the entry hall, I stopped. "I don't know if I can do this, Miles."

"Lissa, you are the strongest person I know, and Lady Arabella will need our support. We won't let the person who did this to her go unpunished, even if we can't do any more than make them a social pariah. I will speak to Locke about ruining them financially."

I chuckled. "Would Jibben do that?"

Miles cupped my cheek and whispered. "Without a doubt."

We reached her room and knocked on the door. Magda opened it and said, as she stepped aside to let us in. I was surprised that the curtains were open and a mountain of pillows propped up Lady Arabella. Her face was a mass of bruises, and though her eye was still slightly swollen, I could see that it was a blood-tinged milky white. She watched us approach with her good eye and tried to smile. I sat in the chair on her good side, and Miles stood behind me. She tried to speak, but her voice was raspy and barely above a whisper.

She licked her lips and looked at the glass of water mixed with a bit of wine on the bedside table. I picked it up and presented the glass tube for her to suck on. She closed her eye to take a sip, then coughed and sputtered a bit. I realised then her throat tissues would still be swollen from being strangled. She smiled, took a couple of deep breaths, and said, "I can never thank you enough for taking me in and not sending for my husband."

Miles was behind me, I couldn't see his face, but he said in a gentle, concerned voice. "Who did this to you, Lady Arabella?"

She closed her good eye, took a deep breath, and tried to chuckle, but it came out as a sob. "Not Rupert—he wouldn't want to bruise his hands." She took another deep breath before continuing. "He prefers a riding crop for a good beating," which explained the old scars on her lower back and legs. "He had his valet Anderson beat me this time."

A single tear ran down her cheek. "While he watched and gave direction." She sighed. "My Father made terrible matches for his daughters." Her mouth turned up into a smirk. "Marianne always thought I had married for love. I was simply better at hiding my misery while she wore hers on her sleeve."

I leaned forward and took her hand. "I am so sorry." I felt reluctant to ask her while she was in such pain, but I had to broach the subject. "We know that you helped Marianne leave Blane House. Where is she?"

"Before I tell you anything, you must promise me—you won't take her back—someone there terrifies her; she believes they were put there to watch her. Milly was her only friend—the only person she trusted. Didn't she give you the picture we left for you?"

I didn't want to tell her about Milly, so I looked up at Miles, who asked, "How did you know we would come?"

"You were kind to Marianne once." She coughed, and I helped her drink some more. "I knew Justin would go to Edward at the very least when he found out she was missing. He was livid when he heard Rupert had Marianne moved to London."

Miles nodded. "My brother and yours were ready to tear London apart looking for her. He's not happy we are keeping him out of the investigation."

She smiled. "That sounds like Justin and Edward, for that matter."

I pursed my lips and asked, "The drawing is of Broadlands, correct?"

She smiled. "I knew Broadlands well as a child and visited there a few times after my marriage. Lady Cowper knew of my scars and told me I would find refuge at Broadlands if I were ever in need."

I was shocked. "Lady Cowper and Lord Palmerston know about Marianne?"

She coughed, then whispered, "No—I couldn't trust anyone."

Miles asked, "Then, where is she?"

"You must realise that if you go to help her, Edward is the only person likely to gain Marianne's trust besides me." She waited for us to respond.

It was Miles who nodded, saying, "We understand."

She smiled. "Thank you, Miles." Then she sighed and continued, "Mariane and I would visit the Broadlands as children when my Father was still a man of substance and was respected.

There is a ruined folly by the river. Underneath it is a couple of small rooms that are furnished and dry."

"Surely Lord Palmerston would know about them."

"No, I don't think so. There are indications that the last people in those rooms were from the previous century when it belonged to the St. Barbe family. That's why I selected it; it hadn't changed since we were children."

"But you said Capability Brown."

She smiled. "I don't believe it's a Brown folly. It looks older, much older. It was rumoured to be part of an old abbey that was thought to have stood on the sight." She took a deep breath before continuing, "The entrance is still there." Suddenly she looked fatigued, and her good eye was closed while the white one was eerily semi-open.

The hand that I was holding relaxed and let go of mine. I panicked and leaned forward. "Arabella." Her eyelid fluttered but didn't open. Miles leaned over me. "It's all right. She's asleep, Lissa." He pointed at the just perceptible rhythmic movement of the bedcovers. "See, she's still breathing."

I sighed and leaned back against the chair. "What a horrible life she must have had. I just can't imagine. Yet, she remained silent all these years. I wonder if that's why she never had any children."

Miles looked perturbed as he said, "Her inability to produce an heir could have been what started the beatings." He glanced down at me. I was angry that he would even suggest such a thing. "Yet it might be Harris's fault they have no offspring."

158

I rose and took his arm, leaning against him. "I am aware of that. But it doesn't make it any easier to understand or accept. The laws must change, Miles. It is reprehensible that a man can beat his wife without repercussions."

"I agree, my love."

Miles cupped my face as we closed the door behind us. "I never want you to doubt my love for you—." He sealed this declaration with a kiss, full of unexpressed emotion."

I gazed into his face, and with as much love as I could infuse into my voice, I told him, "I love you more than life itself, my darling." He hugged me tight, kissing the top of my head.

When we stepped apart, I asked him, "There is something I don't understand. Why would someone kill that Polish man and leave him on Lady Cowper's terrace? How does he fit into our investigation?"

"I agree with Stewart that it was a warning, but I have no idea why or to whom it was directed. Unless it was for Palmerston or Russell."

I added in a whisper, "Or us." Then a thought struck me. "Perhaps he was placed there not as a warning but as a clue to something else."

Miles arched a brow. "You think someone other than his murderers placed him there to draw attention to Poland's plight?"

"It is possible. Otherwise, why bring the issues between Poland and potentially Russia to anyone's attention? It might be a political matter that doesn't directly threaten British national

159

security."

"As far as we can see."

"I am inclined to agree, but if you hadn't seen that older man from your journey to Blane House at the Ball, we might not have been the ones to discover the body. There's nothing to tie us to him."

"Miles, I didn't see the man on the terrace, and neither you, Jibben or Matthew could describe him. What if he was the man I saw on the street? Matthew did say he hadn't been dead long."

"Darling, think about it; you saw the man exit through the terrace doors, Jibben and I gave chase right away. We didn't hear a shot or an altercation. So it couldn't be him."

"I need to be sure; I have to go to Matthew's surgery."

Miles took my hand and pulled me to a stop as I started to rush off. "No, you are not." I glowered at him, and then he offered, "Why don't you draw his likeness? If you can do that, then Matthew, Locke and I can confirm his identity."

I nodded and walked downstairs to collect my drawing materials while Miles disclosed to the others what Lady Arabella had told us. I sat near the window, closing my eyes to think about the older man. I had only seen him briefly twice but found his likeness indelibly marked in my memory. I opened my eyes and began my sketch. It wasn't long before I was satisfied that I had captured his likeness."

I passed it to Miles, and then he handed it to Jibben and Matthew. They all agreed, "That's not him."

Nell took the page from me. "That's the man Lissa and I saw on the way to Blane House. At the time, I thought he was staring at the young Russian Jibben was dealing with."

I gasped. "I hadn't considered that."

My Father shrugged, which surprised me. "Stewart will locate the dead man's lodgings and inspect them. I would rather not have anyone suspect that we are suspicious or directly involved in investigating the man's death."

We fell quiet; everyone seemed wrapped up in their thoughts when Hamilton asked, "To change the subject back to our original motivation in launching this investigation. Since Lady Arabella indicated that Marianne would only trust Edward, I think it is paramount that you take Edward and Fiona to Broadlands. Nell and I will give up our invitation to them and stay here and look further into the Russian and Polish connection, which I can do best here in London."

Nell frowned, but she nodded. "I have friends in the Polish and Russian communities. You would be surprised what the lower class know about what is going on behind the scenes that we can't penetrate."

I glanced at Miles. "We should speak to Edward in person. He doesn't know about Arabella, and I don't think we can keep it a secret and involve him."

My Father cleared his throat. "I suppose I should enquire about Burley and see where he is and what he's doing. If he remains in London, you will need to watch him. Hamilton, I had better assign you a few Irregulars to Nell and the children to guard your home."

Hamilton jerked back. "You think that's necessary?"

Father looked down his nose at Hamilton. "You are investigating a murder that may have been politically motivated. So yes, I think it is necessary."

Hamilton nodded. "There is a great deal of work to be done."

Father nodded. "I will have Stewart tell whoever is taking on this case and have them report to you while he's gone. Then, you can coordinate with him and the Irregulars."

Hamilton agreed, and then they left. Miles and I followed, only to find them waiting outside for us. Hamilton stepped forward, his expression full of concern, "Watch your back, Miles. I don't trust anyone involved in this mess, including Palmerston."

Miles grinned. "Take care, my friend, and keep the Irregulars close." Nell and I hugged, the men shook hands, and the two of them left. Then Miles called for our carriage.

Chapter 7

Brothers

We arrived at Edward and Fiona's and noted that Lord Burley was waiting on the steps while Mr Gordon held open the door. Miles sighed as we climbed down from our carriage. "I suppose it was inevitable that we would run into him at some point."

"Miles, we can't tell him about Arabella."

"I don't see how we can avoid it." We smiled and joined Lord Burley as he ushered me through the door. Mr Gordon welcomed us, but he seemed to sense our discomfort. "Lady Johnson is in the small drawing room, Lady Tinley. Then he turned to the gentlemen, and Sir Edward is in his study."

I waved them on and went to the small drawing room. Fiona looked up from some needlework, "Lissa, what a surprise!"

I exhaled and plopped down in a chair. "Oh, Fiona, it is such a mess."

She put aside her needlework. "Is this to do with Lady Marianne's disappearance?"

"Yes and no. Miles is walking a tightrope right now. But we need your help." So I explained everything we knew and what we had found out about Marianne. I even included Arabella's beating and that we were harbouring her secretly.

Fiona's eyes got bigger and bigger as her eyebrows arched higher. "Miles is trying to explain this to Edward?"

"Edward and Lord Burley."

Both of us were at a loss for words until we heard the shouting, then Fiona quickly jumped to her feet. "We had better intervene before someone gets hurt."

Voices from the study reverberated through the hallway while the footmen tried to look as if they hadn't heard a word. Finally, Fiona noticed them and said. "Nathan, Jason, you might as well go and have tea. I doubt this will end any time soon." They both nodded and rushed for the green baize door.

Fiona marched to the study door, flung it open and yelled, "Stop this right now!" All three men spun around to face her with their mouths open, and then she continued, "Now sit!" She huffed and waved me to a seat. "Lissa has explained everything to me, and I want you to pay attention, and until I am done, there will be no questions, no yelling, no walking out or making baseless threats."

She stared at Lord Burley, who was still red with indignation. "I hardly think this is a discussion that ladies should participate in."

Glaring at him, she said. "This is my home Lord Burley, and I will not be silenced by any man. You will sit and listen, or you may lose both your sisters." When his demeanour didn't change, she threw at him, "That is if you ever cared for them to begin with."

Burley wouldn't go as far as to insult a lady in her own home, but he was not pleased and appeared poised to storm out until

Miles moved to stand between him and the door. "I think you should take my sister-in-law's advice and sit down, Justin."

Once everyone had taken a seat, Miles and I explained what we knew and assumed, swearing them to secrecy. Lady Arabella's story was left for me to explain, and as I went into the detail of her injuries, Lord Burley's expression changed to one of disbelief. Then, finally, the horror of it all set in, and his shoulders slumped, his head bowed, and he covered his face with both hands. "Why didn't she come to me."

I looked at him with sympathy. "What would you have done, Lord Burley? The law is on her husband's side. You signed away your guardianship of Marianne, and it would take time to prove it was forged and would jeopardise your sister's safety.

"I would have found some way to protect them."

"In fairness to them, they had no way of knowing that you weren't the same kind of man that your Father was."

"I am nothing like my Father!"

I waited for him to calm down. "On the face of it, I would agree, Lord Burley. But if you intend to help us, you must do what we tell you. The lives of Marianne and Arabella count on you being in control of your emotions and your willingness to work with us."

He looked about the room, not focusing on anyone or anything as if he was making a calculation. I trembled as I watched him. "Lord Burley, if you are determining how to elude us or interfere, I can guarantee you that the repercussions to you will not be pleasant."

Burley scowled at me. "I thought there were to be no baseless threats made in this room."

"It is not a threat Lord Burley merely a friendly warning, but I assure you that it will likely become a threat if you continue with your current attitude."

"I don't have to sit here and take this kind of abuse from a woman!"

Miles glared at him and grabbed his arm, which he shook off as he tried to pass him. "I think it's time you visit with Arabella. If your attitude hasn't changed after seeing her, Burley, you will spend the investigation's duration in my wine cellar."

Lord Burley straightened his coat sleeves in a huff and turned to Edward. "Are you with me on this, Johnson?"

Edward looked at Miles, then me and finally at Burley. "They mean it, Justin, and you would do well to heed their warnings and advice when it comes to such things."

Burley threw himself into a chair and glowered at us. "I take it that Harris doesn't know where she is?"

"No, and likely her maid was killed while facilitating Arabella's escape."

Burley's face fell. "Brewster? My God, she's been with the family—well, you might say she grew up with us. She's only a few years my senior." He bit his lip. "I will have to check on her somehow."

Miles shook his head. "You can't. It would only draw any suspicion that you know what has happened to your sister. Besides, Lord Blackburn has already put a man onto it."

"Do you take care of everything like this?"

Miles' face was full of compassion and understanding. "We try, and if Brewster is still alive, we will protect her. It's what we do. So now I suggest you pull yourself together and join us at our home."

Fiona had decided to ride with us while Burley and Edward waited for their mounts to be brought around, yet they still beat us there. Magda had refused to allow them past the entry hall, much to Mr Malcom's amusement.

I handed our Butler my hat and gloves. "Mr Malcom, please see that tea is brought to the library."

"Yes, milady."

Miles asked, "Are the children back from the park?"

He nodded. "Yes, milord, along with the small army of Irregulars that Lord Blackburn saw fit to send with them."

I smiled and thanked my Father silently for thinking of the children. "Thank you, Mr Malcom."

He smiled and went off to see to the tea. Edward and Burley waited impatiently for Miles, Fiona and me to join them, and then Magda led the way up the stairs. Once outside the door, Magda stopped baring our way and hissed, "She is awake but fragile." She pointed at Edward and Burley, "You two will not upset her or ask questions to which you already know the answers."

Edward nodded, but Burley stubbornly said, "I need to hear it from her own lips."

Magda shook her head and gave him a disgusted look. "When you see her, you may change your mind. If not, you will regret it." Then she pulled out her Templar knife, flipping it end over end while staring at Burley. "Do we understand each other, Lord Justin Burley?"

Edward had watched this with interest and some amusement. He pulled on Burley's arm to gain his attention, then arched his eyebrows. "Justin—she means it."

Burley looked at him in disbelief. "Edward, she's an old woman." He took a step toward her, but Magda sliced off his cravat and caught his stick pin in her hand before he knew what had happened.

Edward chuckled. "I warned you."

Magda looked at Edward. "You have become a good boy, Edward Johnson."

Burley was perplexed as he glanced at Edward, then Magda. "What does that mean?"

Magda chuckled. "It's simple—once, he was not so good."

Edward laughed, then covered his mouth as Magda's hissed, "Shush, we are standing outside a sick room, have some respect." She looked back at Lord Burley. "Are we in agreement now?"

Burley swallowed as she handed him the stick pin, and he

nodded. "Yes, we are in agreement."

She turned to open the door we entered and found Dolly sitting at her bedside knitting. She looked up, smiled, and then rose, whispering, "Lady Arabella has had a much better afternoon. Dr Jefferson is incredibly pleased with her progress."

I looked back to see Burley frozen to the spot. "My God, Arabella?"

Her one eye opened, and she tried to smile. "Justin? It's so nice to see you."

He slowly slid into Dolly's vacated seat and took her hand. She gripped his, then looked over his shoulder. "Edward, it's good to see you too."

She refocused on Burley. "I am sorry to disappoint you, brother. But when Rupert had Marianne moved, I had to act quickly. I think he is working for the Russians—and he wants what she knows about papa's," she swallowed, and one tear slid out of her good eye "secrets."

"Where is Marianne?"

She gripped his hand. "I can't tell you, Justin. I can't trust that you won't tell Rupert. You always seemed such good friends."

He gasped, and she shook her head slightly. "I don't think you would do it to hurt me. But perhaps you would in order to save the family name from further scandal; I am not sure."

His brow was furrowed with concern and confusion. "I would never hurt you or Marianne."

"Justin, I have seen you work hard to re-establish the family name. I am sorry, but I can't believe you wouldn't give us up to protect that name." He touched his forehead to the bed, and she reached out a hand, resting it on his head. "I am sorry, Justin, I truly am. But, let these people do what they do best."

I heard a sob come from Burley and saw his shoulders tremble. I turned to Fiona and the other men. "Magda and I will stay with him." They nodded and left while we sat beside the window, looking out onto the street below.

The sobbing continued for a bit, and then there was some quiet conversation, but nothing to upset Arabella. Finally, her brother rose and came to us. "She is asleep."

The highly emotional Burley leaned against the far wall as we stepped out the door. "I swear I never knew about Harris. He always told me how happy he and Arabella were. But after almost ten years of marriage, they never had any children, so I wondered if that was true. But Arabella never said a word."

Magda stood with her arms crossed as he sniffed and pulled a handkerchief from his pocket. He stared at her. "I know I should have asked her. My only defence is that an unfeeling man raised me. My Mother was a loving woman, but I think you know the story about how she died."

I stepped up to him and linked my arm with his "Come, Lord Burley, the tea should be ready."

He guffawed, "I believe I need something stronger than a cup of tea, Lady Tinley."

I smiled up at him. "I think we can manage that."

I heard the door behind us open and close. He peered back over his shoulder. "Is it safe to leave Arabella with that woman?"

I arched a brow in surprise. "Magda? There's no one better to watch over her. She is an exceptional healer and rather handy with a blade."

He pursed his lips. "Will she be coming to Hampshire with us?"

"With us?"

"Yes, I thought you already knew I have been invited to Broadlands. Palmerston has been trying to get me involved in politics. An ardent Tory raised me, but I must admit that the Whigs have some attractive policy ideas."

I stopped. I was dumbfounded. "I had no idea that you were politically minded?"

"Neither did I. It was Edward's suggestion. He said he knew the signs of someone bored with life and told me that I needed to find a passion, and since I love to argue, he thought politics would be a good fit. Then his Father introduced me to Palmerston as a potential protege."

"How interesting, I didn't know."

He smiled down at me. "Really? Your family has a reputation for being nosy—" he blanched, then added, "but helpful."

I laughed. "I think you phrased that far too politely, Lord Burley."

We finally reached the stairs and started down them until he stopped at the General's portrait. "I am surprised you have the General so prominently displayed."

"I was tempted to burn it a year ago, but I have found that things and people are not always as they seem. He did a great deal that was wrong, but he also tried to make amends. If he had lived, he might have had a second chance to set things right."

He nodded, "My Father and brothers cut his life short. I wouldn't blame you if you held it against me."

I took his arm again as we started down the rest of the stairs. "How biblical of you, Lord Burley, visiting the sins of the Father on the son? It wouldn't change anything. I might even grow to like you."

He arched a brow in surprise. "I would be honoured, Lady Tinley."

I chuckled. "Well, Edward likes you, and he doesn't suffer fools lightly."

"His wife doesn't care for me."

"She will come around once you can show her that you are open to the idea that women are more than breeders and decorative."

He blushed from his neck to the roots of his hair. "The truth is, Lady Tinley, women like you and Lady Johnson scare the hell out of me."

"We are not so different from other people, Lord Burley. We

have a variety of interests and skills, and we worry and rejoice about the same things."

He snorted, "You are also Agents for the Crown and highly opinionated."

I laughed. "Yes, there is that."

We had reached the library as Mr Malcom arrived, pushing the tea trolley with his usual impeccable timing. I glanced at Lord Burley. "A good butler is worth his weight in gold—you should interview your staff and find out what hidden gems you might have."

He nodded. "That might be an idea at my country estate, I inherited them from my Father, and I am not sure that they aren't robbing me blind, but it seems like a monumental task. But I spend more time here in London than in the country."

"If you want to get on Fiona's good side, ask her to help. She's a good judge of people and runs an exceptionally efficient household."

"I will consider it. Thank you."

We entered the library to find Edward sipping on a whisky as Miles turned with a glass in hand and offered it to Burley, "Here, you look like you need this more than I do." Justine took it, but rather than gulping it back as I expected, he sat and stared into the glass.

Miles arched a brow in question, but I shook my head, indicating we would talk later. Miles nodded and ventured to start a conversation, "So, Burley, Edward told me you had been invited to Palmerston's. I suggest we make up a party of it, along with the Lockes, Edward and Fiona, and my in-laws."

I glanced at Fiona, wrinkled her nose but said, "You might as well come with us, Lord Burley. We have plenty of room."

Burley nodded at her and smiled. "I would like that, Lady Johnson. It will allow me a chance to get to know you better." Fiona looked amused, but she peeked at me with astonishment, and I knew I would have to explain later.

I watched Burley closely as I poured the tea and provided everyone with a selection of sandwiches and cakes. His expression was full of agony when not engaged in speaking. When Magda entered the room, he jerked back from what seemed to be a particularly painful thought.

She took a seat directly across from him, which, not surprisingly, he seemed to find unsettling. Magda leaned forward. I feared she was about to chastise him until she said, "It is not your fault Lord Burley. Young men are often stupid and do not see what is plainly before their eyes. You are starting to question things you have long accepted to be true. The eyes can deceive us when we choose not to look deeply."

Burley looked at me in dismay. I smiled and said, "She's starting to like you, Lord Burley." He leaned back, peering at Magda in disbelief, and she gave him one of her most winning smiles.

Edward burst out laughing. "Now you have done it, old man. If Magda is willing to accept you, your life will never be the same."

He raised his hands. "I don't want to be an agent."

Magda shook her head. "You would make a terrible agent. I think, though, you need a wife. A Member of Parliament should have a wife—but a smart wife, not a wallflower for decoration." I almost bit my tongue thinking about my conversation with Burley just a short while ago.

Burley sat up, "Madam, I cannot run for Parliament. I am a peer of the realm and have a seat in the House of Lords."

Magda tipped her head, scrutinising him. "Then you should sit in it—or go to work as Lord Shellard does in an important office. You have a good brain, but it needs exercise."

He bowed his head. "I will consider your advice, Madam Magda. Once I have cared for my sisters properly."

She reared back in surprise. "You have priorities and scruples— I am impressed."

He chuckled. "I only wish I could lay my hands on Harris."

Magda smiled at him. "I will help you if he does not pay for what he has done soon."

Lord Burley looked shocked, then smiled and thanked her. "I might take you up on that, Madam."

Miles turned to Edward and Fiona regarding our trip, "We leave for Hampshire on Monday. I am sorry I couldn't give you more notice."

Fiona waved him off. "It is more than enough time. Jilly is extremely efficient."

I blinked several times, thinking I had heard wrong, "Jilly?"

Fiona giggled. "Aye, Deborah ran off to marry her beau and returned to Germany. Jilly has stepped in and has turned out to be a gem, and instead of continuing to use one of the footmen, Rabby is now Edward's valet. Jilly will be so excited it will give her a chance to show off her skills in another house."

Miles smiled. "I thought she wanted to be a housekeeper?"

Edward chuckled. "She likes travelling and realised that she wouldn't travel very often as a housekeeper."

Burley looked puzzled and asked, "You know intimate details about your servants?"

I answered him, "Our servants mean as much to us as family. Jilly and Rabby have saved our lives more than once. You would be surprised who we consider as friends and family, Lord Burley."

"You most certainly are unusual people."

Miles had been leaning back, listening, "We may be unique amongst our class, but you will find that people, regardless of social class, are the same. We have the same struggles and aspirations, for the most part. The only thing that separates us is an accident of birth."

Burley shook his head. "I can't see my valet and me being confidantes."

Miles laughed. "Your valet probably knows more about you than your best friend or any family member. So it would serve you well to stay on his good side and the same for your butler. Never ignore the staff—they know almost everything going on in your homes." Burley looked horrified. "You need to find out who they are and support them. They are not furniture."

"I feel like I need a whole domestic education."

Magda shook her head. "You need a good woman and make her your wife; we will work on it."

Miles laughed at Burley's expression, then cleared his throat. "I suggest we get down to business and discuss our route and plans to travel to Broadlands. Perhaps it would be a mistake for you to ride with any of us. It would look suspicious, considering our history with your family. We have guards accompanying us and others that will meet us along the way, such as my new secretary Sir Reginald Stewart."

Burley's brow wrinkled. "A Scot?"

Miles quickly glanced at me. "He was raised in London—but he needs to earn his way."

"How did he get his knighthood?"

"A family connection—hoping it would attract a wealthy divorcée or tradesman's daughter."

"Poor sod, they are a dime a dozen these days, having to look for work or an heiress to marry despite coming from respectable families."

Edward was staring at Miles like he had lost his mind. But, of course, he knew Reginald Stewart and that Miles already had a secretary, so he asked, "Is he related to the Inspector?"

Miles' clenched his jaw. "You would think so. They look very much alike—but no, there's no real relationship."

Edward rolled his eyes, then closed them, understanding Miles' hidden meaning. "I think I remember meeting the fellow."

Miles nodded. "Yes, you have." Edward shook his head before saying, "Fiona, I think we need to go home and prepare for the journey.

Fiona shook her head. "I have been thinking about this. I can't go, I need to be here for Elspeth, and I won't leave her with a wet nurse. But you should go. Marianne will need someone she trusts, and from what Arabella has said, that's you."

Mr Malcom came in with a note and passed it to Miles. He opened it and moved to the window.

Edward looked unhappy and stared at Fiona before answering, "I can't leave you alone here."

Fiona smiled at him. "Yes, you can, Edward; I am secure in the knowledge that you love me and only me. If you like, the children and I will stay with your Father and Lady Jane."

He smiled. "That would make me feel better."

Burley rose. "I suppose I should go as well." Then he turned to me, "If you are leaving, who will be watching over Arabella." Magda's head snapped up from the tea trolley, selecting another tart. "Dr Jefferson will watch over her as well as the staff here. No harm will come to her."

Burley ignored her but looked at Miles. "What of Arabella's

husband? Rupert may come here. They can't stop him."

Miles grinned, holding up the note. "Palmerston will see to it that Lord Harris will join us in Hampshire."

Burley glowered. "You will have to keep him away from me."

Miles stared at him. "We can't, so you must act as you normally would around him. You cannot let Harris know about Arabella. Can you do that?"

Burley huffed and walked around his chair, stopping to grasp onto the back. "If Marianne is there, she will need me, and I won't fail her again. I promise to be my usual aloof self."

Edward put his hand on his shoulder. "He means it. You can't let Harris know anything, Justin. It could mean Arabella and Marianne's life if you do."

Burley then turned to me, "You may be right. Considering our family's animosity, I doubt Harris would consider looking here for her. Thank you for the hospitality to my sister, Lady Tinley."

I smiled at him. "I believe you are right, Lord Burley. I look forward to seeing you in Hampshire." He nodded and left.

Chapter 8

Warning Signs

It was Sunday, and we were on our way out of Church when I saw the Russian who accosted us in Gunter's standing near our carriage, trying to engage our grooms, Jackson and Martin, in conversation. Then, he disappeared into the crowd coming through the church gates as we approached.

I glanced at Miles and saw him peering toward where Count Vasiliev had gone as he helped me into the carriage. Then he turned to my Father and Edward, whispering something.

I nodded, "I assume you saw Count Vasiliev?"

He nodded. "He's following us, but your Father assures me that McClintock and Raymond are following him in return

"I leaned back into the squabs and kept my eye on the street. My parent's carriage was three ahead of us, and Edward was somewhere behind. Three riders appeared out of the crush of people and stopped our carriage. Our coachman Sean yelled at them to move on, but suddenly, with pistols drawn, they fired into our carriage just as Miles pulled me to the floor. Jackson and Mark returned fire at the men as they spurred their horses and rode off.

The people around us were swarming our carriage and yelling at the shooters charging their way through the traffic surrounding the church. Jackson yanked open the door as Miles pulled me onto the seat. "We got one of them, milord. Mark is holding onto him."

Miles looked around. "Bring him here. We had better take him back to the house."

Edward came racing up to my side of the carriage. "My God, are you all right ?"

"Yes, thank you." I was flustered by his appearance and had my pistol in hand before it registered that it was Edward. The thought so shook me that I could have shot him that I snapped, "You and Fiona should go home. We will see you at luncheon."

He glanced Miles way, who was concentrating on the retreating figure of Jackson as he said. "I take it there will be an unexpected guest at the table?"

Miles nodded. "Very likely, if he's not too badly wounded."

Edward patted my hand. "You are sure that you are all right ?"

I took a deep breath to steady my nerves and smiled. "Yes, Edward. I appreciate your concern." Miles turned back to look at him. They nodded to each other, and then Edward disappeared back into the crowd.

Jackson and Mark returned with the wounded man. I was able to get a good look at him—but he wasn't familiar. The man was neither a ruffian nor a gentleman. He stared straight ahead and ignored me and his captors. Miles had turned the man and signalled for Jackson to assist him into the carriage. His arm was bleeding slightly, but he ignored it and glared at Miles. Once the grooms were back in their seats, the carriage started forward with a jerk, gradually picking up speed. Miles yawned, stretched out his legs and examined the man slumped on the facing seat. "Does your arm hurt?"

The man turned his face away to stare out the window. Miles asked him the same question in French, German, and Italian, and then he turned to me, "How is your Russian, my dear."

I almost laughed. I didn't know a single word of Russian. "Don't their aristocrats usually speak French?"

Miles nodded. "True." and laid his pistol casually across his lap, keeping a hand on it and an eye on the man across from us who still hadn't moved. I tried to reassure the injured man, "We have a healer and a doctor we can call to care for your arm." He turned slightly to glare at me. So, I sighed, not knowing if he understood me, as he turned back to stare out the window.

The rest of our short journey was silent. When we arrived, Mark and Jackson jumped down to take charge of our unwanted companion and followed us through the door. Mr Malcom was there to take our hats and gloves as he scrutinised the silent man with us. "Should I ask Madam Magda to come to tend to your guest?"

"If you please, Mr Malcom. And would you ask Mrs Jonas to hold luncheon? Sir Edward and Lady Johnson will be joining us along with my parents."

"Yes, milady, I will see that she's informed." He nodded at our footman Howard who disappeared through the green baize door and dispatched Jane, our upstairs maid, to find Magda. "May I bring you some refreshment in the meantime, milady?"

"Tea would be welcomed, Mr Malcom. Thank you."

I followed Miles and our guest into the library. Before I could even think of closing the door, Magda came in with her bag and thumped it down. Then, staring at the man before her, she stepped forward, cupping his face, "Misha—Misha Andropov?"

Miles rubbed his forehead, groaned, and looked from her to our guest, exclaiming, "This is Colonel Misha Andropov of the Russian Secret Police?" She nodded.

I was confused. "Who—what?"

Miles took my hand, "Colonel Andropov is somewhat like—one of us, only Russian. Your Father sent to him requesting his assistance, but I had no idea he would answer the call so quickly."

Misha grimaced as Magda removed his jacket and opened his shirt. He was stoic through the entire process, and not until she finished bandaging his arm did he say anything. In perfect English with only a hint of an accent. "Thank you, Mama Magda."

I was shocked when he called her Mama. He turned to study Miles and me before saying, "You must be the Tinleys." Miles nodded as the man grinned, saying, "You need to train your men to shoot the right people."

"You shot at us first?"

His expression darkened as he barked out, "I did not! I have been following those men who did. I had no idea why they targeted you unless it was a distraction so that they could confuse and lose me."

Miles was perplexed. "So, you are not here responding to Lord Blackburn's request?"

"No, I have been in London for months. I followed Count Urie Vasiliev here. He is a dangerous man. We received information that he came here to obtain papers that could upset the balance of power and ruin the alliance between our two countries."

"Then who were those men you were following?"

"They are Vasiliev's men, his personal guard. I didn't know they were tracking you. I saw the Count outside your church with them and knew it meant trouble."

Miles chewed on his lower lip. "I apologise for interfering."

Mr Andropov stood and slipped on his coat with Magda's help. "Thank you for the care, Mama, but I think it's time I left."

Miles stepped in front of him. "I am sorry, but I must insist you stay and speak to Lord Blackburn."

Andropov looked irritated and sounded exasperated. "I do not answer to him. You should know that each country's Brotherhood is responsible only to their own leadership."

Miles nodded. "But there are cooperation agreements between the different countries."

"Which we never signed, Lord Tinley. We have remained pure in our objectives. Europe and Britain stepped away from the original order. They don't even call themselves Templars anymore."

Miles pursed his lips. "For good reason. Might I point out that you have become as secular as we have here? I understand that you take wives and have businesses."

Andropov glared at him. "We are still devout to the one church and our faith."

"You can hardly reduce your argument to one of religion. The Knights survived a purge and the protestant reformation in Britain while your fellow knights hid behind the Russian Orthodox Catholic Church."

Misha cut the air with his hand. "Arguing about the past doesn't change who we are today."

Miles crossed his arms. "I am not a knight Mr Andropov."

"I have heard of the perverted alliance of the Brotherhood with the British spymaster; they are now the toadies of the Crown."

Miles bristled and took a step forward, but Magda stood between them. "Stop this! Sit down, both of you. Misha, you will stay and speak to Lord Blackburn."

Andropov looked like a stubborn little boy "Mama, this is not the Steppes of Russia, and you are not caring for a lost boy."

Magda rolled her eyes. "You have never seen the Steppes, Misha. I found you starving in the streets of St. Petersburg, then found you a papa and mama to care for you."

"Yes, and I can never thank you enough for taking me to Ivan and Mikka. They saved my soul, and you saved my life."

This was a story I would love to hear, but just then, I heard voices in the entry hall. The door opened, and my Father and Mother entered, followed by Edward and Fiona. Their eyes focused on Andropov with keen interest.

He clicked his heels together and bowed to my Father, "Lord Blackburn, Colonel Misha Andropov at your service."

My Father arched a brow looking at Miles, who said, "He doesn't actually mean it. He has been in London on official business for some time."

Father extended his hand, which Andropov took reluctantly. "Mr Andropov, did my daughter or son-in-law shoot you?"

"Neither, sir. I believe it was a groom named Jackson—he only scratched me."

Miles rolled his eyes. "Which was a good enough shot to knock you off your horse." Misha glowered but nodded. "Believe me, if Jackson had wanted to kill you, he would have."

Andropov chewed on his lip and grudgingly replied, "Fair enough. He did laugh at me when I suggested that he missed."

Miles added, "Mr Andropov was following Count Vasiliev's two henchmen who fired into our landau."

Mother came to my side. "Are you all right, Lissa—should we call for Matthew?"

"I am fine, mama." She studied me until she was satisfied that I was telling the truth.

Howard brought the tea, my Mother sat beside me, and she poured. Mr Andropov stared at the cup with something akin to horror—Edward laughed, took the cup, and then poured it into a potted fern. Miles went to the decanters and poured a large measure of whisky into the cup. "It is not vodka, but I think you will find it acceptable."

Andropov took the cup casting a suspicious glance at its contents; he sniffed it, then hesitantly took a sip. He took his time rolling it around his mouth, then swallowed. In the end, he stared at Edward and shrugged, saying, "It is good. It is a Scots brew?"

Edward smiled. "Yes, it's from our cousin's distillery."

Andropov settled back slowly, enjoying his drink while the rest sipped our tea. I offered him a selection of cakes, but he shook his head no. Instead, he selected a small dish of fish eggs nestled in shaved ice. He beamed when he spied it, took a small spoon, scooped it up, and swallowed, followed by a sip of whisky. He smiled as if eating ambrosia. I wondered how Kit or Mrs Jonas had thought to add caviar to the tea tray and where they had found it on such short notice.

My Father had waited patiently for the customary conversation to lag. "So, Mr Andropov, would you care to tell us why you are following Count Vasiliev?"

His expression was stoic as he said bluntly, "No."

My Father glared at him. "Might I remind you that you are working as a Russian operative on British soil—without my permission?"

Andropov's expression didn't change. "Yes, I am."

Father took a deep breath and said, "Miles, I think we will need to convince Mr Andropov that his cooperation is required."

Miles rose, followed by Andropov—they stood glaring at each other until my Father waved at them both. "Sit down! I meant we should consider informing Count Vasiliev that Mr Andropov is following him."

Andropov's eyes glinted like steel, and his lips compressed in a firm line of disdain. "Your threats mean nothing to me."

"It is not a threat Mr Andropov."

Magda snorted in disgust. "Misha, this is not a game. People's lives are at stake here."

He crossed his arms. "You must know, Lord Blackburn, that I cannot tell you anything without my superior's approval."

"Yet he sent you to my country without notifying me that you were coming here or for what purpose. That makes me unhappy, Mr Andropov, especially when you are following someone who has been stalking my family and agents."

Andropov sneered, "You call your knights agents? You have no respect for the old ways."

"I respect the old ways, but they don't always work in the present. If knights do not adapt, they are left behind and will disappear as a relic of the past."

Our guest squirmed in his seat. I believe he may have agreed with the wisdom of my Father's words but was hesitant to go against his own country's rules and traditions. "My superior is in St. Petersburgh. I cannot possibly communicate with him fast enough to obtain direction. But you have yet to identify yourself as a knight, Lord Blackburn."

My Father felt in his pocket and pulled out his Templar coin. He tossed it to Andropov, who examined it closely and tossed the coin back. My Father smiled. "Now, may I see yours?"

Misha fished his out and passed it to my Father, who barely looked at it. "Your reputation precedes you. Last year, I met your master in France, where we discussed a cooperation agreement. Unfortunately, we could not agree on what that meant and left it agreeing that we would, as a courtesy, be made aware of anyone we sent into each other's regions. Therefore, since I have received no such communique, I can only assume that you are here for a purpose that threatens Britain's best interests."

Andropov wiped a hand across his face. "You would throw me into your Tower of London as a spy?"

Father chuckled. "No, I would lock you in Lord Tinley's wine cellar and leave you there until you came to your senses."

Andropov looked confused. "A wine cellar?"

Magda laughed. "They are quite effective but have proven lethal to several." Andropov mistook her remarks which I believe was her intent and looked horrified.

He recovered quickly and said to my Father, "I take your meaning, Lord Blackburn. I can only tell you that Count Vasiliev is looking for a document that could affect my country and yours adversely. We need to know what is contained in that document and prevent it from causing embarrassment to Russia. Not everyone associated with my government agrees, though. Some people would use that information to manipulate the most powerful in our countries. So it was decided that rather than going through diplomatic channels, we would deal with this in our way."

My Father snorted, "For someone who ridiculed us for working in the best interests of our government, you seem to be doing the same thing, but without consideration for how your actions would affect the people of Russia. You cannot serve two masters. The needs and safety of the people are always our first consideration."

Our guest seemed to ponder what my Father said and pursed his lips. "I agree, Lord Blackburn. But these are powerful people that could do great harm. We must ensure that they work for the common good, not self-interest; acquiring these documents gives us leverage. I know that the document was created by a woman, the daughter of the late Lord Burley. She was intimate with the details of her Father's criminal activity. A woman of interest followed her from Scotland to London and is now suspected of murder."

I focused on him and asked, "Sister Mary?"

He chuckled. "Yes, but her real name is Countess Irina Ivanov Bagration. Her uncle is—"

"Yes, we know he's Prince Andre Gregor with the Russian Embassy."

He smirked, "Correct, though the Prince appears to be unaware of his niece's involvement."

"Is she a nun?"

"She once was but became discouraged by the church's restrictive doctrine. Her motivation to involve herself, in this case, is suspect."

My Father ran a finger along his jaw and pursed his lips. "It seems that we are working with the same objective in mind. But I don't believe the Countess is on our side in this."

Andropov was scrutinising my Father suspiciously. "Would you be willing to share information with us if you obtain it first?"

I watched my Father closely. This could be a mistake if he agreed. "Mr Andropov, this is a delicate situation. Our focus is on finding Mrs Braithwaite and any documents she has produced. However, she will not be sacrificed for the sake of those documents. If you interfere with that objective, you will pay for it." I was surprised that my Father brazenly threatened Misha.

Mr Andropov sat back, studying my Father. Then he glanced about the room at our impassive faces. "I can see that you people are of one mind. But I have no idea what the Countess and her companions are planning."

Edward chuckled. "Then we will just have to get to Marianne first."

Andropov said, "You are going to Palmerston's house party, correct? The Countess and Vasiliev will be there as well."My Father only nodded. Andropov added, "I will be close by, but I am only one man, and I will not be at Broadlands."

Father had been concentrating on the bookcase across from

him when he asked him. "Do you understand Gaelic, Mr Andropov?" He walked to the bookshelves and pulled out a Gaelic grammar book I had borrowed from the Bruce library ages ago to learn the dialect.

He looked taken aback. "The Scots language?"

He tossed him the book, which made me cringe. "Yes, I assume you have spent some time in the country since you could tell the whisky was Scots and not Irish."

He was cautious in his response as he flipped through the book. "Why would that be necessary?"

"Because if I were to send you a message, I would prefer that it was difficult for others to understand."

He grinned. "Interesting—I believe it could work since we seem to be allies for the moment. May I leave now? I want to be in Hampshire before you arrive. One other thing, I don't suppose you would tell me where Lady Marianne is hiding."

My Father chuckled. "You suppose correctly. I am willing to work with you, but that doesn't mean I trust you."

He went to hand the book back to my Father. "Keep it for the time being. I will collect it before you leave Britain." Andropov nodded, bowed to the rest of us and left.

Miles sat back and stretched his legs out. "You think he will be of assistance?"

"Perhaps, but if Count Vasiliev and Countess Irina are aware of his scrutiny, it might be a distraction we can use to our advantage."

Edward snorted, "How can you be sure he isn't working with the Russians he says he's following."

My Father was pacing, "We can't, but I would rather have him where I can see him then working behind the scenes and unknown to us."

Fiona watched my Father for a bit, then took Edward's hand, saying, "I expect you to return to me in one piece, Edward Johnson. I wish I were going with you. It all sounds rather exciting."

My Mother patted her hand. "I will tell you all about it when we return home."

Miles pulled his legs back. "I think if we hold back luncheon any longer, we will be eating only sandwiches."

As he rose to ring for him, Mr Malcom appeared at the door, "Luncheon is ready, milord."

Chapter 9

From London to the Halfway Point

Our journey started without a hitch, and we even managed to find Inspector Stewart waiting for us as he promised with his baggage on the roadside.

He climbed in and leaned back with a sigh. "I believe we will have some interesting company at our first stop. Several Russians rode by with a fairly large entourage."

I asked him, "How do you know they were Russians?"

"I work on the Thames, Lady Tinley. I have heard dozens of different languages and learned a great many. The Russians are talented smugglers and impressive fighters, whether they have been born high or low."

Sighing, I said, "Wonderful. So now we have to watch our backs night and day—we will need to warn the staff, Miles."

"Murphy and your Father have already thought of it, my love. They will all have quarters near ours at Broadlands."

I arched a brow. "How did he manage that?"

"Seems it was Palmerston's idea to have our trained staff closer to where trouble might occur and a buffer between those that might cause it on behalf of their masters."

"That was very intuitive of him."

"He considered it wise since Melbourne will be attending as well."

He looked at Stewart. "Our Irregulars are also in place around Broadlands. But I had a visit from your former protégé Inspector Fry. It appears he's not comfortable leaving a murder unsolved and says he is following a lead that might take him out of the city."

Stewart cursed quietly under his breath. "He will get himself killed one day, too damned nosy for his own good."

Miles chuckled. "Remind you of anyone?"

Stewart flushed but was quick with a retort. "Yes, he does—all of you." They both barked out a laugh. Then he continued, "I saw Sir Stephen drive by and noticed several colourful boxes among his baggage. I assumed those would be his Grandmother's. How is he going to account for Magda's presence?"

Miles' eyes twinkled. "She volunteered to be the entertainment, telling fortunes and drawing up astrological charts." Stewart's mystified expression showed his disbelief. "I can assure you the woman is a chameleon, and since she is known to be a confidant of our group, it gives her the distinction of being exotically eccentric and therefore acceptable in society." He chuckled. "She's quite the rage among hostesses looking to stand out."

Stewart shook his head. "I hope she understands the seriousness of what she's walking into."

"Magda is more than capable of handling herself, believe me."

Stewart pursed his lips. "And what of your brother and Lord Burley?"

"Edward is very capable. Burley, on the other hand, I don't know well enough to say, but he bears watching."

"You think he would betray you?"

Miles appeared to give it some thought before answering, "I don't believe he would, at least not intentionally. But he is consumed with the need to protect his family and regain their former place in society."

"Have they slid so far?"

I nodded, "Far enough that he would have trouble contracting a respectable marriage within the Beau Monde."

Miles seemed surprised, "How do you know that?"

"Making calls with Mother and Aunt Mary. Lady Edith, Lord Tomlinson's eldest daughter, is enamoured of Lord Burley. He is good enough to be invited to dinner parties, balls and soirees, but Justin doesn't meet Lord Tomlinson's exacting standards for a son-in-law."

Stewart snorted, "He does aim high, doesn't he, the daughter of a war hero and one of the country's richest, most influential men."

I glanced at Miles and took his hand. "The heart wants what it wants."

Stewart gawped at him. "I suppose you're right."

I chuckled. "Not all members of the upper class marry for money or position, Sir Reginald."

He grimaced at me using his assumed name, then nodded, relaxed back into the seat, and closed his eyes, saying, "So, I have noticed." I glanced at Miles, who had adopted a similar position and admired their ability to sleep in a moving vehicle.

I turned to watch the countryside as we passed through it, and at some point, I fell asleep and woke to someone rummaging through one of the baskets that sat on the floor near Inspector Stewart. I opened an eye to find him rifling through the contents, finally selecting a thick roast beef sandwich, then sinking his teeth into it with a look of deep satisfaction. I smiled. "There are bottles of ale in the other basket. They may still be cold." He coughed when I spoke as he hurriedly tried to swallow. "It is all right, Sir Reginald, that's what the food is for—help yourself. I am sorry not to have offered it before."

He grinned. "I left without breakfast."

"No need to explain. Would you please pass me a scone? They are on the left-hand side of the basket."

He pulled one out, handing it to me just as my husband's hand shot out, taking it from me. "Dr Jefferson said you shouldn't eat between meals. We will be at our Inn for luncheon before too long, and unlike Sir Reginald, you had breakfast." Miles then bit into the scone and swallowed it in three bites.

Stewart held back a chuckle. "I don't know if I can get used to being called Sir Reginald."

Miles waved him off. "Not to worry, we will use it only when you are formally introduced. After that, they will either call you Stewart or Reggie."

He glared at Miles. "Anyone who calls me Reggie may find themselves on the floor nursing a sore jaw."

Miles smiled. "I will let that be known, Stewart it is."

"And how exactly did I come by my knighthood?"

"Services to the Crown, but you are not allowed to talk about it. They will assume you helped quash some royal scandal."

Rather than scoffing Stewart nodded, "I can work with that." Then he grinned and asked unexpectedly, "Tell me, Tinley, what do you think of railway expansion? If what I have heard is true, they will soon connect every city in the country."

Miles brushed the crumbs off his trousers. Then he looked at Stewart. "I wish there was more regulation. Investment currently is chancy with so many competing companies. I have invested conservatively but don't plan to keep a stake in them for too long. Such burgeoning building and competition are fraught with the potential for collapse."

Stewart nodded and looked disappointed. "I had hoped to make a small investment myself."

Miles smiled. "Then speak to Locke. He is a financial genius who will steer you in the right direction to make you some money safely."

"Thank you."

I watched Miles trying to puzzle out this exchange. "Why so interested in railway investment, Inspector?"

"A nest egg for the family in case something happens to me. Police work isn't exactly safe, and our police pensions aren't that much or reliable depending on who's in government. I guess, at times, I feel my mortality."

Miles nodded. "Sound reasoning Stewart. As to the pensions, I will speak to my Father. But, I promise if anything were to happen to you, we would see that your family are taken care of."

Stewart looked gobsmacked. His eyes glistened. "Thank you, Lord Tinley. I can rest easier now."

Miles smiled. "You are welcome, Reggie."

Stewart chuckled. "You get that one for free, Tinley." Miles laughed along with the Inspector. I shook my head at them; men could be such children.

We rode on for a time and finally came to a small village with a large Coaching Inn named the Bell. Everyone in our party was happy to descend and walk about the courtyard. Then we adjourned to the common room for luncheon.

"Some foreigners have claimed the private parlour." the Innkeeper grumbled. "They even brought their own food as if decent English fare wasn't good enough for them." Then he realised he might have made a mistake making such a complaint and asked what he could do for us.

Miles put him at ease by inhaling, "It smells wonderful in here to me—what do you think, Colin."

My Father grinned. "Indeed, and I am peckish."

Just then, my stomach growled loudly, and the Innkeeper beamed, "Right away, milords." He rushed off, calling to his wife, "Bess! Only the best for our guests!" She turned to survey us and nodded with a smile as she disappeared into the kitchen, and he went through his cellar door.

A serving girl showed us to a secluded corner where a window overlooked the village green and duck pond. The window was open, and a refreshing breeze fluttered the curtains. She took our drink order, and though they didn't have pomegranate juice for me, they did have a mild apple cider which was deliciously cool. The meal was delicious, and a cherry tart was the highlight. I ate two pieces, much to Miles' amusement.

As we paid the bill and rose to leave, we heard yelling from above, followed by someone falling down the stairs. Edward and Stewart were the nearest and rushed along with the Innkeeper to see what had happened. The rest of us walked closer out of curiosity, and just as we reached the stairs, a scream emanated from above, followed by only one word from a female voice calling out, "Urie!" Sitting at the bottom of the stairs was the blonde man who had harassed us in London.

He was laughing at a dark, heavyset man storming down the stairs yelling in a heavily accented voice as he pointed at Count Vasiliev, "You! You will stay away from Irina!" Then he continued mumbling in Russian as he stomped back up the stairs.

Edward was staring at the man on the floor with disgust, and Stewart looked conflicted about whether he should ignore him or arrest him. Ultimately, the man picked himself up and bowed to us as if he had just put on a great show.

Then his eyes landed on my Mother and me. "Ladies—these must be your honourable husbands and friends." His grin was even slimier as he said, "Broadlands just became more interesting."

Then he dusted off his clothes and casually walked out the front door. Not soon after, the woman I had known as Sister Mary came rushing down the stairs in a beautiful blue carriage dress, followed by an older woman with steel grey hair and a face etched with deep frown lines. Then additional men came clambering down, followed by the older gentleman who had chastised Count Vasiliev. They milled about the entry hall while he paid their reckoning. It was then that I caught the former Sister Mary's eye. She turned away, so the brim of her bonnet hid most of her face, spoke quietly to the older woman who shot us a look of pure vitriol, and then pulled her by the arm out the door.

My Mother leaned into me. "What was that about?"

"Her look or Vasiliev's remark?"

"Both."

"I have no idea, but it proves this week could be interesting or dangerous."

Mother turned to my Father as the older Russian, and his entourage left. "Colin, do you have any idea who that gentleman was?"

"That is Sergei Popov. He is tentatively referred to as a trade attaché at the embassy. But from what Sir Thomas and I have found out, he has no official status in the Russian government and is not part of the nobility."

She arched a brow. "Popov seems very possessive of Countess Irina."

Jibben nodded. "I would say it's a match in the making."

Judith shook her head. "I almost feel sorry for her."

Magda was glaring at the door. I wanted to ask her what had angered her but felt it was best left alone as she shuffled Judith out the door. I watched her stand outside, staring at the Russian carriage as it pulled out with numerous outriders. When she looked back at me, she asked, "Do you still have the talisman I gave you long ago?"

"Yes."

"Good, I will make more for the others. We will need them to fight that witch." She spun on her heel and walked back to her carriage before I could ask her to explain.

Jibben and Miles came up beside me. Jibben was frowning. "Grandmama has caught the scent of an ancient evil in that group."

I nodded. "The grey-haired woman."

He shook his head in denial, and his eyes got a faraway look as if reliving a memory. "No—it's the fallen nun. She has made bargains with the devil. Grandmama can smell it on her." Then he headed off to follow Magda.

I walked with Miles to our carriage, where Stewart had already installed himself. I glanced at both before saying, "Magda will be making everyone a talisman, and I suggest you keep it with you when she gives it to you. Don't ask why. Just accept it."

Stewart raised an eyebrow but didn't disparage the idea, thankfully. He only changed the conversation. "So where and when are Andropov and Lord Burley supposed to appear."

Miles pulled his hat off, ran a hand through his hair, and then left the hat on the seat beside him. "Andropov will be in the nearby town of Romsey, and it was felt best that Lord Burley arrive on his own. So as not to draw attention to our alliance."

Stewart nodded. "Do you trust either of them?"

Miles snorted in derision, "Not in the least."

Stewart sighed. "That's a relief. Does Burley know who I am ?"

"No, and we intend to keep it that way."

Miles then asked him, "How's your Gaelic?"

Stewart laughed. "Gaelic—you're jesting, of course."

"Hmmph—your story then is that you were raised by your English Mother in London and had nothing to do with your Scottish relatives."

"That's a relief—I couldn't mimic a Scots accent to save my life. They sound like they've swallowed marbles on their best day."

Miles laughed. "Only when they want to confound an Englishman."

"I will keep that in mind. My current Sergeant is a Scot. Perhaps I should ask him for lessons."

I nodded. "I have often thought Scots Gaelic would be perfect to use as a code when you want to speak freely to another operative."

Stewart gave me a puzzled glance. Miles groaned. "She's very serious."

I slapped his arm. "You even agreed the idea had merit."

He smirked, "I did; that's true."

The carriage started moving forward, and Miles pulled pistols out from under the seat. He checked that they were loaded and handed one to me and another to Stewart, who didn't seem surprised as he asked. "I take it you are expecting trouble?"

"I think the Count's falling down the stairs was to draw our attention so they could assess the strength of our party. So yes, I expect trouble."

He banged on the roof, and the carriage stopped, as did all the others when we did. He and Stewart got out, and all the men talked, then he came back and climbed in. "Stewart is riding with Edward from here on out. There is a rise ahead, and a copse of trees obscures the view. I think they will try to attack there as we descend. The coachmen are checking the traces and equipage for any sabotage. We are going to take a running start at this, so be prepared for a bumpy ride."

The carriages started towards the incline. As we raced ahead, the countryside was a blur, and then suddenly, there was an explosion of sound as men on horseback burst through the copse of trees, firing their weapons, and we returned fire on both sides.

At the top of the rise, a carriage stood in the middle of the road Miles leaned out and fired at the conveyance spooking the horses, which sent them into a wild charge down the other side of the rise. A scream came from inside as it veered off the road, coming to rest against a tree. Our carriages raced past, careening downward and onward. We didn't slow until we came to a crossroads and made our turn. Miles tapped the carriage roof, and we stopped in a village at a small Inn to rest the horses. We gathered ourselves and reloaded our weapons as a precaution.

Miles and Jibben searched for the local constable and laid a complaint against highwaymen on the road behind us. Surprisingly, he was a man who took his job seriously and immediately rounded up a few men to return to the sight of the attack to investigate. Several men turned to nod when we entered the common room as we walked past them. My Father smiled and returned their greetings.

In the far corner sat Mr Andropov, who rose and joined us. "I see you escaped a direct assault."

Jibben glowered at him. "You knew, yet you did nothing?"

"It was a guess. I had no way of knowing if or when they might try it, and I am but one man." He looked about the room. "And your men here would not have aided me to mount a rescue."

Jibben growled, backing Andropov up against a table. "Fortunately, your countrymen weren't very subtle in their intent, and we were well prepared."

Andropov arched a brow. "Such hostility is not becoming Locke."

Magda hissed, "Misha, you cannot always wait to see which side will win. You must pick one and fight."

He glanced at Magda with saddened eyes. "I have no desire to die for a lost cause, Mama Magda."

She shook her head, reached into her ever-present satchel, pulled out what I recognised as the talismans she had promised, and passed them about the table. "Put these in your pockets and keep them with you always. They will provide you with some protection by alerting you to danger."

Andropov twirled his, then laid it down, reaching into his pocket, pulling out a rather dilapidated twin of the one in front of him. Magda smiled and pushed the new one towards him. "Double protection Misha—it was destined."

He smiled at her. "Thank you, Mama."

Edward picked his up and examined it closely. "Is that some of Fiona's hair?" Magda only smiled as he said, "You stole a hair from my wife's head."

Magda looked amused. "She gave it to me, Sir Edward—she's a Scot. They know the value of protection."

"You mean they are a superstitious lot."

"And when you Englishmen throw salt over your shoulder or cross your fingers, is that not superstition?"

Edward lowered his head and chuckled, "I should know better

than question your intentions." He tossed it up, caught it, slipped it into an inside pocket, and patted it. "I will feel closer to Fiona with this."

She smiled and said, "There is a kiss from Vincent and a giggle from Elspeth in it as well."

Edward grinned. "Thank you, Magda."

The rest of us didn't question her and slipped our talisman into our pockets, except for Stewart. He studied it closely as if looking for something specific. Magda leaned over, tapped his hand, and, in a quiet voice, said, "Every one of them is there, Inspec—I mean Sir Reginald."

"But how?

"The park when you took your family on a picnic."

He looked perplexed as he examined it closer, then smiled. Finally, he glanced up at Magda. "May I ask why?"

As if she was speaking to a child, she sighed and said, "Because love is the greatest protection you can have. And you have that in abundance, like the others here." He nodded, slipped it into his inner pocket, and, like Edward, laid his hand on it for comfort. No one questioned that she must have collected these items long before knowing we would need them.

The Russians stormed in while we took refreshments, waiting for the horses to recover. I noted that there were fewer of them this time. Perhaps we were more successful in halting their attack than I realised. They were followed by the constable, who looked flustered and enraged simultaneously. He came to my Father and bowed; my Father raised his hand to stop the constable from speaking. "They claimed their diplomatic status protected them from arrest and prosecution."

The constable glared over his shoulder at the waiting delegation of Russians. "No, milord, they claimed that you attacked them."

Jibben made to stand glaring at the Russians, but Miles stayed him with a hand. He peered up at the constable. "I assume they underestimated your ability to tell the difference."

"Aye, milord—damn foreigners think we Englishmen would bow to the likes of them. Besides, they tried to bribe me when they saw I wasn't buying their story. Bribe me! Can you imagine? Like I would turn against me own people, not bloody likely." He nodded to the ladies at the table. "Sorry, ladies, for the swearing, but I have never been so insulted." He doffed his hat and walked away, stomping past the Russians while glaring at them indignantly.

They took seats across the room from us and glared in our direction. Jibben, for some reason, seemed to find this amusing and began making faces at them until Magda smacked the back of his head. "You are a Knight of the Realm and the Brotherhood—behave."

Then she snickered at the shocked look she had earned from the Russians. Jibben sat back complacent, smirking at them and seemingly enjoying their confusion. The constable chuckled at the bar where my Father had gone to offer him a purse for his services. He gladly took it, then purchased a round of ale for his helpers and passed out the coin they had earned.

The older Russian came to our table and stood looking down at my Father. "Lord Blackburn, I am —"

My Father interrupted him, "Yes, we know who you are, Sergi Popov, a trade attaché to the Russian Ambassador."

He didn't appear surprised. "And you are Sir Thomas Wiseman's favourite Agent."

My Father tipped his head to the side, not bothering to acknowledge the statement as he asked, "Is there something we can do for you, Mr Popov?" He emphasised the mister as if Popov was beneath us, and he hit the mark.

Popov recoiled and frowned before responding, "I wish to apologise for what happened earlier. It was merely a case of mistaken identity."

My Father snickered. "Yes, I am sure it was."

Popov glared at my Father and Andropov; hostility sparked in his eyes. "Yes." He bowed stiffly and returned to his group.

The entire time the older woman watched us with veiled eyes and a hard mouth. Judith leaned into me. "That old hag gives me the shivers."

I turned to watch Countess Irina, who seemed flustered as she watched Popov. While Count Vasiliev was sitting back, sipping on a dark ale and laughing. When Popov returned to their table, he barked something in Russian to the Count, who frowned, slammed down his pint and left. Then Irina stood and faced the older man, slapping him, then left the table to follow the Count out the door.

Judith touched my arm. "I would love to know what that was about."

"So, would I?"

Andropov had disappeared at some point when our attention had been drawn to the drama at their table. I looked about, but he seemed to have disappeared. "Would you like to take a walk and stretch your legs?"

Judith grinned. "Definitely."

As we excused ourselves, I invited my Mother to join us, but she declined, claiming to have a headache and that Magda was preparing a headache powder for her. Miles took my hand as I rose. "I will come with you."

"Is that necessary?"

"Yes."

I nodded, and Jibben stood as well to accompany us. Judith and I both sighed, but we were resigned to their company. Once outside, we saw that Countess Irina and Count Vasiliev were in a heated argument in their native language. When he reached out to cup her cheek, she slapped his hand away and stormed off towards the stables. Judith arched a brow and whispered, "Lovers quarrel?"

I shook my head. "I don't know. The Count seems to have little if any control over his behaviour." I turned to my husband as the Count approached us. "Judith and I will see if the Countess needs any assistance."

As we passed Vasiliev, I heard rather than saw him turn to watch us and in a voice loud enough to be heard, he said, "Lord Tinley is it true that making love to a woman with child is highly erotic?"

I clenched my jaw and waited for Miles' response. Instead, I saw Countess Irina turn around with a horrified expression. I peered over my shoulder in time to see Miles lay the Count out with one punch. He shook his hand and swore, then stared down at the man in the dust at his feet. The Countess ran past us and knelt by the Count, attempting to help him to his feet. After the second attempt, he found his feet shook her off, spat at Miles' boots, and stormed off. The Countess turned to me, bit her lip, then said, taking a deep breath. "I am sorry for the insult he gave you. Urie is not happy here in England. He wants to go home."

Judith looked sceptical. "Homesickness is his excuse for being uncouth?"

The Countess' face flushed. "No, of course not. All I can do is sincerely apologise on his behalf."

Miles stared at her, "Vasiliev owes us an apology, Countess, not you."

She sighed and stared down at Miles' hand. "I hope you are uninjured, Lord Tinley."

"I am fine, Countess; thank you for asking." Then she shamelessly fluttered her lashes at him and smiled like a shy schoolgirl. I glared at her, ready to put her in her place, when I saw the Count watching her intently. Finally, she nodded, walked off to join Vasiliev, and continued their conversation in a less heated vein.

I glanced up at Miles' bemused expression. "You can wipe that smile off your face, husband. She was flirting with you for the benefit of her vanquished hero."

Miles peered over his shoulder at them. "She's not my type, too skinny and pale. Besides, the type that plays shy and retiring tends to be dreadfully dull."

I slapped his arm, then took his hand in mine to examine the damage done by the altercation with the Count. Two knuckles were skinned but not bleeding. He was watching me and smiling. When I let go of his hand, he pulled me into a hug and whispered, "I love you and making love to you any time is quite erotic."

Andropov had come up behind us. "That was impressive, Tinley, but he will try and make you pay for it."

"I have no doubt that he will—try. I am looking forward to it. I could use the practice."

Andropov snorted, "You English are so bizarre. You show such little emotion in public but can explode at any moment, catching others like myself and the Count unawares. But watch your back. I doubt it will be a face-to-face confrontation the next time since only your women and Locke witnessed his humiliation. If any of his party had been out here, I imagine you would have been called out."

Miles snickered. "Again, I could use the practice," Andropov laughed, then strolled off.

I pulled Miles to the well, dipped my handkerchief into the icy water in the bucket, and then wrapped it around his knuckles. He placed a hand over it and bent down to kiss me. "Miles, you didn't have to hit him."

"Yes, I did!"

We returned to the Inn's common room, ordered another drink, and waited until my parent's coachman Mr Cripps came to tell us that the horses were ready to move on. As we pulled away, the Russians were still there, seemingly a show of good faith to demonstrate that we would not clash again. At least not before we reached Broadlands.

Chapter 10

Overnight then Onto Broadlands

We arrived in Hook, a small town halfway between London and Romsey Hampshire, where Broadlands was located. Dalton and Murphy had secured our rooms at the White Hart, a respectable and well-established Inn. As we entered the Inn, it was comforting to see the likes of Murphy and Lettie, my parent's old friends and valuable retainers, smiling and welcoming us as they introduced us to Mr Pipps, the Innkeeper.

Murphy announced to my Father, "There seems to have been an issue with our rooms. Some Russian diplomats wanted us turned out, but Mr Pipps was firm that our arrangements had been made well before they had arrived." The men in question stood to the side, scowling. I recognised them as having been with the Russians who attacked us.

My Father stepped forward, offering his hand to Mr Pipps. "It's good to see you again, Tam. It's been some time, but I see the life of innkeeper suits you." He focused on Mr Pipp's burgeoning belly.

The man chuckled. "Aye, it has, milord." Patting his abdomen, he then said. "The last time I saw you, your name was plain Turner. Now you be Lord Blackburn. I was sorry to hear of the death of your Grandfather. He was a fine man if a touch old-fashioned in his ways." It was then I realised that he was a member of the Brotherhood. This exchange obviously had the

214

Russians confused as they listened in.

"Thank you, Tam. Now perhaps we can work out this dilemma with the rooms. Did your brother ever buy the Blue Boar?"

"Yes, milord he did, and a fine place it is, just down the high road from here. We can't thank you enough for helping out with that."

"It was my pleasure. Do you think he could accommodate these gentlemen and their party?"

He grinned. "Without a doubt, milord."

My Father then spoke to the Russians to make the arrangements. Both men glanced at each other, then nodded with barely contained disdain. Then, Mr Pipps called out, "Harry lad, take these two gentlemen down the road to the Blue Boar and tell Hank I have sent them. They be—" he looked at my Father, who nodded. "important people and Lord Blackburn will be paying their bill for the inconvenience." That seemed to please the Russians, and they left with Harry.

Mr Pipps sighed. "Thank you, milord. I thought I might have an international incident on my hands. Hank will love the custom they'll bring. He's just getting Boar on its feet. His wife is as good a cook as my Ruby, and he's made several improvements. They will be as comfortable there as I could make them here. Now Ruby has your rooms waiting for you to freshen up, and the private parlour will be ready for your meal in about half an hour.

My Father nodded. "I would like our servants to dine with us and be accommodated as close to us as possible."

"Aye, milord, Mr Murphy and I have arranged all that, not to worry, milord." My Father nodded his appreciation, then clapped Murphy on the back, causing him to smirk and blush as Lettie looked on with immense pride. Then she stepped up beside me. "Meg and Robert are off on holiday?"

"Robert finally convinced her it would be good for little Jack. She's been looking exhausted, so we felt they needed to get away for a time."

She nodded. "I am so glad you aren't looking to replace them."

"Whatever gave you that idea?"

She arched a brow and chuckled. "Meg did—she worries that she isn't as flexible as she should be with a family."

I laughed. "I told Meg she had nothing to worry about, but I will speak to her again when they return."

Then she patted her flat belly and said, "Aedan and I are finally expecting again." I leaned in and gave her a hug congratulating her.

"And Murphy allowed you to come along on this trip."

"Aedan's learned a thing or two since we married and Acton was born." Then she chuckled, "Now I must be off. I promised to help Rennie sort out life at an Inn—she is a bit nervous."

I reached out to touch her arm. "Thank you, Lettie." She nodded and walked off to assist Rennie and the others in finding the correct rooms.

My Mother came to my side. "How are you feeling, darling?"

216

I looked down at my increasing belly and smiled, placing a hand there. "Surprisingly well, mama, this one differs from Charlotte or Alex. He's active but not annoyingly so. It's like he's trying to let me know he's there and comfortable." She put her arm around my shoulders and kissed my cheek. Then she went to speak to Ruby Pipps about our meal.

Miles and I found our room. He looked about, then stared at me, "You should lay down and rest, Lissa. Dinner won't be ready for a while."

I sighed, looking at my concerned husband. "Let me look at your knuckles."

"You are going to ignore me, aren't you."

"Miles, we made it here, and we are safe. I intend to relax, but I don't need to lie down."

There was a knock at the door, and Rennie entered with a pitcher of hot water, followed by Tyson, who carried the small baggage we would need for the night. Rennie was grinning from ear to ear as she bustled about, and Tyson glowered. Then, he asked to speak to Miles in the corridor. They weren't gone long when Miles returned. "Rennie?"

She turned, smiling. Then her eyes fell when she saw the disapproval on Miles' face. "Is it true that you spoke to the Russians at our last stop?"

Her eyes were huge, and she bit her lip. "Just one of the groom's milord."

Miles nodded. "I don't like to be harsh, Rennie, but I won't

217

tolerate such behaviour in our servants. If you have ambitions to be a lady's maid, that is a lesson you must learn. If you make such a mistake again, I will be forced to send you back to London."

Her eyes glistened, but she was wise enough not to protest. "Yes, milord."

I took pity on her, "Rennie. I suggest you speak to Lettie about what is expected of a lady's maid when travelling. I understand that it can be a daunting experience."

Rennie bobbed her head. "Yes, milady, I will."

"You may go now. I can manage." She made her escape but not before I heard her sniffle, fighting back the tears that had glistened in her eyes before she left.

"Miles, was it necessary to be so harsh?"

"Yes, it was—she was not only flirting. Tyson heard her answering the young man's questions about us."

"Could Tyson just be jealous?"

Miles shook his head. "I thought that might be the case, but when I challenged him, he assured me that he has no romantic intentions towards Rennie. Instead, he has ambitions to become a butler eventually and says he has no time for skirts." He chuckled. "He poured it on a bit thick, but I believe his overall assertions."

"I would hate to send her home—I am sure that Lettie will take her in hand, and your threat will probably resonate with her for years to come."

Miles and I washed and changed out of our travelling clothes,

218

leaving them for Tyson and Rennie to brush down later."

After we had changed, we sat together before the empty hearth leaning against each other and discussing our dreams for our future and our children until there was a rap at the door, and Tyson came in to announce that dinner was ready. So we adjourned to the private parlour, where we found the rest of our company.

Jibben was laughing at something Edward had said. Then, between guffaws, he said, "Yes, but I wish Hamilton was here. He gets himself tied into knots so easily." I was intrigued to know what they had been discussing, but they didn't appear inclined to share.

Miles chuckled. "Hamilton's lost a lot in his life, Jibben, and I can't say I blame him for being overly cautious sometimes." As he gave me a knowing look, I realised they must have been talking about how protective he could be of Nell.

My Father and Mother entered with Judith, who went to Jibben, glaring suspiciously at his smile. "What mischief have you been up to?"

His superficial expression became contrite, but his eyes still glistened with amusement. "Nothing, my love, nothing at all."

She shook her head and asked him to fetch her a glass of wine. He bowed regally and moved to the bottles on the sideboard. His back was turned as Magda came in on Inspector Stewart's arm. I was astounded at his transformation as we progressed on our journey. He had increasingly taken on the persona of a gentleman born to the position. When Jibben turned around, he almost dropped his glass, "Stewart, what on earth happened to you?"

He chuckled. "Mr Murphy happened to me. He's an excellent teacher."

I smiled at him. "I doubt he's that good, Sir Reginald. I believe you've always had a latent knight hiding under the façade of being a hardened River Policeman." He chuckled and blushed as he showed Magda to her seat and offered to fetch her a glass of wine.

We had just settled to eat our sweet when there was a knock at the door. Miles opened, and we all turned to find Countess Irina Bagration standing there. "I must speak to you."

My Father rose and waved her to come in, then had Tyson close the door behind her. "Countess, what can we do for you." He offered her the chair next to my Mother.

She sighed, staring at me, then blinked several times while seemingly collecting her thoughts. Then her eyes shifted to Magda and widened with fear. Finally, she swallowed and addressed Magda. "You will know if I lie."

Magda scowled at her. "Let go of your glamour, and I will see if I can believe you." Suddenly Irina's countenance shifted, her shoulders slumped, and I could see worry lines about her mouth and eyes, and she appeared genuinely fearful.

Magda watched her closely and seemed satisfied as she said, "Speak."

She looked at Miles. "You broke Urie's nose. I thought to warn you that he will kill you now."

220

Miles smirked, "I seriously doubt that."

She looked disappointed. "You don't understand. Urie is one of the Tsar's elite assassins. You will not see him coming." She turned to watch me as I glanced at Miles. He still appeared unconcerned. She was watching him intently. Her expression was full of anguish and panic as she said. "You must believe me!"

My Father had been watching the exchange, and though he knew why Miles had hit the Count, he was perturbed by her assertion, "Why should we believe you?"

She glanced at Stewart, her brow furrowed, and she frowned. I wondered if she was trying to place him, but then she gave up and sighed, "Because he saw the one who killed the serving girl at Blane House, Mother Clare."

My Father grew impatient and snapped, "I will ask you again. Why should we believe you? You could have just as easily killed the girl in the guise of Sister Mary."

She hung her head. "I was the one who let him into Blane House. He was to search the girl's room, but the Reverend Mother saw him, so I had to flee. She knew Urie as the one who brought me to Blane House, so she would have known I was the only one who could have let him in."

I was shocked that Mother Clare had anything to do with Milly's murder. My Father rubbed his ear, glancing at Stewart, who sat ramrod straight on his chair's edge as if ready to pounce. Then he looked back at her. "Why tells us now?"

"Because I need you to believe me! I don't want you to kill

Urie. He was sent by my Father to protect me from Popov. If you kill him, no one will keep Popov from forcing himself on me and compelling me to marry him."

My brow wrinkled as I stared at her. "One would have thought Urie was the predator, not Popov."

She sighed. "I travel with him and Urie at my Father's request to see if I can discover Palmerston's intentions towards Russia. He is known to be attracted to beautiful women, but my charms have been to no avail."

Jibben snorted, "That's easy to sort out. You need a wig. Palmerston's attracted to brunettes, not blondes."

She quirked an irritated brow at him. "I doubt that a man of his reputation has one type he is attracted to."

Jibben shrugged his shoulders and assumed a bored expression. "If Lady Cowper catches you at it, I suggest you watch your back." She didn't respond but turned to my Father.

Miles scrutinised her and asked, "Then why kill Antoni Gzowski?"

"Who?"

"He was one of the Polish political elite forced into exile in France after the Polish-Lithuanian Commonwealth collapsed. He saw his country parcelled out to Prussia, Austria, and Russia."

She frowned. "I had nothing to do with Gzowski's death—" She hesitated before adding, "nor did Urie. I have no idea why he was killed or who killed him. You must understand that Russian politics are extremely complicated, Lord Tinley."

I was shocked when Miles asked, "Then who is Misha Andropov." Magda glared at him but said nothing

Her eyes narrowed, and she hissed, "I have seen him speaking to you. I suggest you beware. He is from a rival sect of knights."

He pressed her. "Rival to who?"

She grimaced, "Urie's sect, they are both Templars."

He smirked. "Two branches of the same tree?"

She bit her lip. "Yes, you could say that; you have your own here in England though they have a different name here and in Europe." Then, she sneered, "They hide in the shadows."

Stewart smiled. "Interesting theory Countess. Any idea who they are here in England?"

She stared down the length of the table, scrutinising all of us. "If I didn't know that you already worked for your King, I would have said that Sir Stephen most assuredly worked for the renegades."

Jibben only smiled, but I knew him well enough to see the tension about the eyes that her guess had been too close for comfort. He rubbed his eyes and then began chuckling. Edward quickly joined, followed by my Father and Stewart. Only Miles remained stalwart in keeping his expression neutral.

Irina turned to Judith, "Tell me, Lady Lock is your husband one of them?"

She laughed out loud, "Far from it, Countess."

"Are you so sure?"

Miles seemed to have had enough. "That is a fascinating story Countess, but I am afraid the Templars were branded heretics centuries ago and disbanded after their leaders were slaughtered. So even if England did have remnants of them, in the years after the Protestant Reformation here, they would have been eradicated as Catholic heretics."

She shook her head. "Believe what you like, but it is all true."

My Father had been tapping a finger against his lips until he rose, "Thank you for coming to us, Countess. Sir Reginald will escort you back to the Blue Boar."

"No, thank you. I have one of my men waiting for me below."

She stood and walked to the door, where she stopped looking back to stare at Magda. "You know what I have said is true." Then she turned and left.

As the door closed, Jibben arched a brow and poured himself another glass of port. "How much do you think they know?"

Father leaned back and crossed his arms. "I think this was a fact-gathering attempt; fortunately, she gave away more than she got from us."

I had been thinking back to Blane House. "Do you think she was telling the truth about Mother Clare and Blane House?"

Miles rubbed his forehead and sighed. "You ladies were there. What do you think?"

I glanced at my Mother, who shook her head. "I don't know. Maybe that was the intent to plant a seed of doubt."

Judith nodded. "I agree with Irene."

Magda glanced at me; I was at a loss now. "Mother Clare was exactly as she appeared, a pious harmless woman who knew nothing about who murdered Milly." Magda sighed, saying, "This person succeeded in planting the seed of doubt. I know that the Reverend Mother is a good woman. However, that person who just left us is not good—she is evil."

Judith looked confused. "The Countess said you would know if she told the truth. Why would she say that?"

"To make you doubt me." She watched our confused faces. "She comes from a place that does not recognise my people as human. Their beliefs are contrary to everything you believe about the lesser classes. She is a member of the Russian ruling class. Their beliefs and rules are centuries old and ingrained. They hold onto them as lifelines—if they do not change, they are doomed."

Jibben grimaced. "How did she know about the Brocklehurst Group and me."

Magda patted his cheek. "She didn't, Jibben, she was stabbing in the dark, hoping to hit something, but you did well not to react." Then she chuckled, "You Englishmen must be very frustrating to her kind; you keep your emotions tightly under control, so stoic."

Jibben laughed. "The infamous British aloofness. So now what? There are no other precautions we can take. We have a mad assassin after Tinley and a Russian witch trying to befuddle our minds."

I chuckled. "Yes, but at Broadlands, we will be among those infamously staunch and aloof British, with their famous distrust of foreigners. They have only one Russian witch with them. I hardly think she will be enough distraction to influence the important men attending this house party."

Magda snorted, "Do not underestimate her power, Little One. But our mission is to find Lady Marianne and her drawings, nothing else."

I nodded, leading to my next question, "When is Burley due to arrive?"

My Father answered, "Not until well after we have arrived at Broadlands."

"Do you think he will remain indifferent toward us?"

Jibben smirked. "An angry Burley might be a better cover. Edward and I plan to poke that bear to keep his ire stoked towards us."

My Father snorted. "On that note, then I suggest we all retire. I want to arrive at Broadlands before the sun sets tomorrow."

We all rose and said goodnight retiring to our rooms. A contrite Rennie and a triumphant Tyson were both waiting for us. Rennie went about her duties with quiet efficiency. I thought about reaching out to her, but I knew she needed to understand the expectations for a lady's maid and that what she had done was wrong. Furthermore, she needed to know that she would incur my displeasure when she failed and must earn back my trust. Therefore, Miles and I remained reserved in our dealings with Tyson and Rennie.

As we lay together in bed, I turned to look at him. "I wonder what Marianne will be like when we find her without her sister for guidance and companionship."

He closed his eyes in thought. When he opened them, I saw the pain I hadn't seen since our first days at Samuel and Emilie's Chateau when he had contemplated taking his own life. "You said that Milly seemed to think Marianne was quite sane if a touch eccentric. Burley wrote to the doctors in Scotland when he found out she had been moved. They told him she had periods when she was lucid and carried on a normal life in the hospital, even helping the other patients reach their good memories. I don't know what to expect, but we can't forget she was severely traumatised by her experiences, and her family had essentially abandoned her to strangers."

I sighed. "Yet Marianne still made progress."

He nodded. "Burley told me she still had terrible dreams, and sometimes she wouldn't sleep for days until they finally had to sedate her."

I cupped his cheek. "You know what that feeling of abandonment is like, alone and caught in horrifying circumstances."

"Yes, but I had you and my family around me. Even when I went off with Grimes to Cornwall, I had him. I could tell him things I couldn't share with the rest of you because he had also seen true horror in his life. I don't know what I would have done if I hadn't had that. Even knowing that you loved me."

"I think I understand, Miles. You could talk to Dr Grimes, a relative stranger and bare your soul because he could go into the darkness with you—where we could not. You would never want us to know the depth of your pain." He smiled and leaned in to kiss me with a passion that pushed his pain away from our love, but I knew it was something he would always carry within him.

He leaned back and brushed a stray curl from my face. "I don't know which Marianne we will find, Lissa. I hope she is surrounded by light and airy open spaces."

"What if she has run off again?"

"Then we will help Burley find her."

I nodded, wrapping my arms around him. "Yes, we will."

In the morning, I awoke to light tapping on the door. It was Rennie with the water for me to wash. I had decided to forgo a bath until we reached Broadlands, where I intended to luxuriate in a full-size bath, not the tiny hip baths generally available at country inns. Miles was already up and gone, so once I had washed, I went to the private parlour where everyone was sitting for breakfast.

Jibben gave me a cheeky grin as he passed me, coming from the buffet, "Good Morning, sleepyhead." Just before popping a hot fried potato into his mouth without thinking and quickly spat it back out, exclaiming, "Hot!"

I giggled at his desperate and unsuccessful grab for my glass, which I had in my hand. "I always tell Charlotte and Alex to blow on hot food before putting it in their mouth." I finished my juice as he glared at me and stomped back to his seat, seizing a glass of small beer and guzzling it down to cool off his burnt tongue.

Judith could hardly suppress her giggles, so she tried chiding him to hide her mirth, "That's what you get for being cheeky."

Miles poured me a glass of cider while I filled my plate. The country air had made me ravenous, and I ate like I didn't know when another meal was coming my way."

Miles watched at first with amusement and then concern. "Are you supposed to be eating so much? I thought Dr Jefferson told you you needed to watch your weight."

The other men at the table all gasped, and it was Stewart who voiced their thoughts. "Are you insane, man? Never, ever question a woman's weight, especially when they are—when they are in a certain condition."

I smiled at Stewart and glared at Miles. "My husband has always been a touch mad when it comes to me in this condition, Sir Reginald."

Everyone laughed. Miles, however, grimaced, and I wondered if he had harkened back to our talk last night. It was then that I realised the power of words to hurt just as they had at that moment. I took his hand and squeezed it, drawing his attention to me, and I mouthed, '*I love you.*'

After breakfast, we found our carriages ready for the trip's final leg just as Murphy rode up to my Father. "They have left already,

229

milord."

"Thank you, Murphy. There is no good place to have the Russians. Behind us or ahead of us, we can hope they won't try anything again before we reach Broadlands."

Miles and I climbed into our carriage, and he pulled out the pistols. He checked them and then laid them on the seat beside him. He didn't look at me, but he answered my unasked question, "It never hurts to be prepared."

It was late afternoon by the time we crested the hill looking down into the valley where the River Test flowed, overlooking the river sat the beautiful Palladian mansion of Lord Palmerston, its buttery yellow brick gleaming in the setting sun. We stopped in front of the East Portico with its massive pillars, descended from our carriages, and passed through into an imposing domed entrance hall. Everything about it was grand and made to impress. It was a home fit for a King. The Russians had arrived well before us and were busy perusing the Sculpture Gallery containing parts of the previous Lord Palmerston's collection.

Lady Emily Cowper and Lord Palmerston greeted us. Emily had graciously consented to play hostess for Palmerston with her husband's permission, even though he was not in attendance. After being shown to our rooms, Rennie and Tyson informed us that baths had already been prepared. Miles and I glanced at each other, realising that neither knew our habit of sharing a bath.

In truth, I was tired, so the thought of relaxing in a hot bath alone was appealing. The full-sized copper-lined tubs were set up in our adjoining dressing rooms. The hot water lapping over me as I climbed in was heavenly. I lay there listening to Miles splashing about in his bath next door. He was rarely one to stay long in a tub unless I was his companion. And I knew that shortly he would come to me wrapped in a towel with his banyan thrown over his shoulders to wash my back and rub my aching feet.

As I waited, I dozed and was awakened when I heard the door click open. I opened an eye expecting to see my delicious husband. But, instead, Count Vasiliev stood there, leering at me. I was on the verge of screaming when my husband appeared behind him with a pistol placed behind the Count's ear. "I told you once before to stay away from my wife."

The Count chuckled. "Your memory is faulty, Lord Tinley. You said nothing of the kind."

Miles tapped the pistol's barrel on the bruised side of the Count's jaw. "That's a shame. I thought I had made myself perfectly clear when I knocked you on your arse."

He pulled back the hammer on the pistol, and whatever retort the Count had ready died on his lips, and he froze before ultimately saying, "You are unusual for an Englishman. I thought you took more interest in your horses and brandy than your women."

"Then you would be wrong—and I prefer a single malt Whisky to Brandy, preferably Scottish, but the Irish make a passable one." He pushed the pistol back under the Count's ear. "Now, I suggest you apologise to my wife, then leave before I blow your brains out."

The Count tried to sneer as he said, "In front of your wife?" but his voice trembled.

"Oh, believe me, my wife is not squeamish and just as capable of blowing your brains out as I am ." I smiled at my husband before covering my mouth as I tried not to giggle, which unsettled the Count even more as he gawked at me with horror.

"You people are—"

Miles finished his sentence, "Exceptionally good at what we do. Something that you should remember."

He took one step back from the Count, but the pistol remained cocked. "I suggest you leave before I change my mind and use this. But you would do well to remember our little chat; I would prefer not to ruin our host's party with an untimely death."

The Count stepped back from Miles glaring at him, "You people are insane."

As he turned, I could see by the cant of his shoulders that it was all he could do to keep from running out of the room. When he closed the door behind him, Miles released the hammer, set the pistol aside, and came to my side to massage my shoulders. I shook my head. "He is right, you know. That was a foolish thing to do."

"No, my dear, Vasiliev is foolish. I intend to speak to Palmerston, and he can then admonish him in private or public. It's his choice. But I think I made myself clear to the Count, so I don't anticipate him trying anything so overt again. However, when you are alone, I want you to lock the doors, and I would prefer that you did not walk about alone, my love. I know that makes you angry, but—"

I put a finger to his lips. "No, Miles, I think it's wise advice, but might I ask the same of you?" He arched a brow and stared at me with an incredulous expression, so I added, "He could just as easily shoot you in your bath, my love."

He smirked. "Agreed, we will stay in company or behind locked doors."

Miles helped me out of the bath and then rang for Rennie and Tyson, and we dressed for the evening. I chose an aubergine gown paired with my blue diamond necklace, and Rennie wove ribbons of silver and plum through my hair. Miles looked exceptionally handsome in his dark evening kit, exchanging the traditional black for a deep, almost black forest green with pristine white linen. In his cravat was a sapphire stick pin I had given him. I smiled. "Aren't you quite the rake tonight." He chuckled as he pulled at his cuffs, preening for my benefit.

We found the rest of our party in the gilded salon with its ornate plaster panelling. The room was furnished with soft Aubusson carpets on which sat groupings of classic Adams sofas and chairs, all with gilt trim. It was a room that harkened back to the previous century but was beautiful.

Miles stepped aside to have a word with Palmerston before we moved to where my parents were standing with the Prime Minister, Lord Melbourne. He glared at us and, without preamble, hissed, "Tinley, are you trying to create an international incident?" Miles' brow furrowed, but he didn't respond. "Do you have no defence, sir?"

"I am merely trying to think of which incident. The one where Count Vasiliev asked me an inappropriate question about my wife

233

and our intimacy or when I found him entering our suite to ogle my defenceless wife in her bath."

Melbourne's face coloured, whether from temper or embarrassment. " I had no idea." But he sputtered while taking in my apparent state of being enceinte and nodded. "Yes—well, I can see that you had no choice. The Russians tend to, ah—."

My Father offered, "Lie?"

Melbourne glared at my Father. "Yes, but I would rather put it down to misunderstanding our customs. They are a backward nation."

My Father snorted, "Forgive me, sir, but their court is more European than ours. I doubt they would send a delegation unaware of our social customs and that a man's wife is sacrosanct, especially when with child."

Melbourne huffed, he hated being challenged, and he casually glanced at me before saying, "From what I have heard, I would think that Lady Tinley was able to take care of herself."

Miles smirked. "She is, but that doesn't preclude me from exercising my rights as her husband. You can take heart that I didn't challenge the Count to a duel. Imagine the scandal of having the son of one of the Lords of the Exchequer arrested for protecting his wife by challenging a foreigner."

Melbourne glared at him. "Point taken, Tinley. I hope you and your wife will take the appropriate precautions to avoid making such a scenario possible."

Miles nodded. "Of course, my Lord."

Palmerston and Lady Cowper came to join our group. He smiled at Melbourne's obvious discomfort. "I see that you have heard the latest complaint of abuse from the Russians."

Melbourne huffed, "I have."

"And Tinley's rebuttal?"

He sighed. "His actions were perfectly reasonable under the circumstances. I am impressed by his restraint."

Palmerston chuckled. "I thank you for not killing the peacock, Tinley. Lady Cowper informed me that blood is extremely difficult to remove from carpets."

Miles looked over his shoulder at the Russians, where Count Vasiliev and Countess Irina watched us with disdain. "I hope the other party has been duly warned about his behaviour?"

Palmerston slapped him on the back. "To right, Tinley, come along Melbourne, and let us teach my guests a lesson in British etiquette."

As they walked off, Lady Cowper turned to us. "Not that we don't love having you here, but would you like to tell me why it was so important for you to be here this week? Surely it wasn't just to irritate the Russians."

My Father pursed his lips. "It is essentially the same reason why the Russians are here; to find something that is missing."

Lady Cowper tipped her head to the side and smiled. "You mean Marianne Braithwaite." I was stunned, and the rest of us were noticeably quiet. "Come now, people, I was a close friend of her Mother's and have always taken an interest in the girls. But unfortunately, I couldn't convince Burley that the matches he made for his daughters were terrible choices. However, I have kept in touch. Arabella reached out to me about Marianne some time ago, and I suggested she could come here."

I suddenly took a deep breath. "So she hasn't been left alone."

Emily shook her head. "I don't know. Arabella never brought her here. But the girl's old nurse lives nearby. She may be caring for her." Emily pursed her lips. "Does Burley know that she might be in the neighbourhood?"

My Father responded, "Not that we know of, so I ask you to exercise caution about mentioning it to her brother or anyone else." My Father just lied to our hostess. Of course, Burley knew Marianne might be here.

Mother interjected quickly, "Does Lord Palmerston know that you suggested Arabella bring Marianne here?"

Emily pulled at her earbob. "No, I know he wants whatever Marianne has hidden and would do anything to get his hands on it. But I also understand that it would cause many people a great deal of difficulty. In my opinion, politics and personal blackmail should never mix. So it would be better for everyone concerned if those documents never saw the light of day."

My Father nodded his head. "I agree that the information could be extremely damaging, and some people would use it for nefarious reasons, but I cannot agree that it should be destroyed."

She shrugged. "Yes, but your code of honour differs significantly from most others, Lord Blackburn. In truth, if it came into your hands, I would feel better knowing that it would not be used to harm innocent people inadvertently. But I cannot say the same about Sir Thomas Wiseman."

Miles nodded to her. "You seem to know a great deal about us, Lady Cowper."

"I am a keen student of humanity Lord Tinley, and you are good people. You have proven it time and again. I would dearly love to know why and where that code of conduct comes from."

I relaxed. Lady Cowper didn't know about the Brotherhood and was merely fishing for information but was it for herself and the welfare of those she would help, or was it for Palmerston's benefit? She smiled knowingly. "Now, if you will excuse me, I must see to my other guests."

Jibben, Judith and Magda strolled over to us, and Jibben said, "You look a tad green, Blackburn."

My Father snapped back, "Nonsense."

Mother rolled her eyes. "Lady Cowper might be aware of Marianne's hiding place and may have facilitated it, but I am not sure. I can't believe that Arabella would have confided in Emily, considering her relationship with Palmerston. Yet she assures us that Marianne has a friendly face in the neighbourhood that could be looking out for her."

Jibben peered over his shoulder. "Hmmph—" He turned back to our group. "Melbourne looks like he swallowed something extremely distasteful."

My Father chuckled. "Miles acquainted him with why the Count is not dead."

Jibben looked at me with interest as Miles asked, "The Count tried to make it personal again?"

Jibben scrutinised me. "You are a minx, Lissa." I opened my mouth to chastise him when he raised his hands and rushed on to say with a tad too much delight, "I will be your second Tinley."

I finally snapped at him, "Miles will not be fighting a duel—we intend to avoid them and not be caught alone with any of them."

Jibben nodded. "That's wise, but lock your doors too."

Judith stared at him. "That's all you have to offer, is lock your doors?"

Jibben shrugged, raising a finger and smiled, saying, "Keep Grandmama's talisman with you." He winked at me, and I couldn't help but giggle.

Miles shook his head. "I expect you to be an extra pair of eyes, Locke."

"Of course, my friend." He looked over his shoulder and asked, "Has anyone seen Burley yet?"

I replied, "No, but I thought I saw someone arriving just as we were coming down."

As if my words conjured him, Burley walked into the room with Edward at his side. My brother-in-law came toward us, but Burley stopped to speak to Sir Nigel Worth, a Member of Parliament from Devon, where Burley had his country residence. He looked irritated and was abrupt in his response to Sir Nigel, which earned him a rebuke for rudeness, but Burley ignored it as he moved our way. Edward reached us first, warning, "He's in a temper and testy that you are in here and aren't actively out looking for his sister."

Burley reached us and hissed, "What are you doing here drinking champagne when my sister is somewhere out there."

After all, we had been through, I was on edge and snapped back, "No one is drinking champagne, and the whole idea was not to be obvious!"

He glared at me. Then his expression changed to one of confusion as he looked about the room. "What's happened?"

I was surprised that he was so attuned to the charged atmosphere around him. "The Russians have been making a nuisance of themselves. And your arguing with Sir Nigel is bad form, Lord Burley, especially when we're trying not to draw attention to ourselves. So I suggest you go back and politely listen to what Sir Nigel has to say. For heaven's sake, he's your Member of Parliament and may want your assistance or opinion."

He peered back at a glowering Sir Nigel and huffed, "You're right, Lady Tinley. So if you will excuse me, Edward, would you care to join me? Your Father's country property is in Devon, as well as yours, so we might as well try to look interested."

Edward put a hand on his shoulder. "Let's get this out of the way, Sir Nigel is a bore, but he is effective in the Commons." They both turned back with smiles plastered on their faces. Burley made an effort to apologise to the man while being supported by Edward. Our group broke up and mingled with the other guests maintaining our distance from the Russians. They, by choice, seemed to remain a tight-knit group accepting only highly placed British government functionaries into their circle.

Before we had gone our separate ways, Mother noted, "Lady Cowper will have to be creative with her seating arrangements. It will be interesting to see what she manages."

Miles and I stopped to speak to Lady Angela and her husband, Lord Lange, our nearest neighbours in Dorset. So I was facing the door when Lord Harris, Lady Arabella's husband, entered, still in his travelling clothes. My heart sank when I saw him looking about the room, and I tightened my grip on Miles' arm. He glanced at me and then followed my eyes, stiffening. Palmerston had already noticed his arrival and went to him, taking him by his arm and pulling him out of the room. Miles returned to the conversation with Lord Lange drawing my attention back to them as we made superficial promises of dinner invitations once we returned to London.

We continued to circulate about the room playing a delicate dance of avoiding the Russians without making it obvious. Fortunately, they made it almost redundant since they rudely rebuffed most people who approached them.

Dinner was finally announced, and we found there were no place cards. The room was set up with several small tables like a restaurant. Palmerston's table was set on a raised dais, and we were encouraged to sit with who we liked and where we liked. It was a novel idea but shocking to many of the guests. Lady Cowper explained that she didn't want us to feel constricted by normal conventions during our visit to Broadlands. My Mother grinned, saying, "Emily is definitely creative. She is assured that this party will be the talk of the Beau Monde for months to come."

Judith nodded. "Or until the next scandal comes to light."

Dinner was a pleasant meal and quite animated. Lady Cowper looked pleased with herself, and Melbourne looked relieved. I bent towards my Father. "Where is Lord Russell? I thought he was supposed to be here?"

"He begged off at the last moment."

I glanced to see Lord Harris sitting at Palmerston's table. "Do you think he relinquished his place to Harris?"

Father pursed his lips, then shrugging, said, "It's possible. Who knows what game Russell and Palmerston are playing? I intend to stay out of the politics of this situation."

"What do you think of Lady Cowper's opinion that the information should be destroyed."

He shook his head. "It's naïve, but I agree it shouldn't be turned over to the government for political blackmail."

I sat back. "If we find it, do you plan on turning it over?"

"I need to see and decipher it before making such a decision."

Magda smiled as she looked suspiciously at the fish on her plate. "This is not good—don't eat it. She slapped Judith's hand. "It has been tampered with."

I put my fork down and signalled for the footman who had served us. "Has anyone but you and the Cook handled this fish?"

He blanched and whispered. "I saw the Russian lady's maid add some seasoning behind Cook's back." I scanned the room to see that many people had already taken a bite.

Magda stood up and admonished the footmen to remove the fish. Emily Cowper rose, grasping that something was wrong and apologised that the fish had turned while waiting for everyone to arrive. The footmen then retrieved the plates of those that had accepted fish, replacing them with soup plates offering a flavourful consommé. The rest of the meal proceeded without further incident. Countess Irina seemed as shocked as anyone in the room over the fish, but I still didn't trust her.

After dinner, the evening proceeded with the usual entertainment of music, cards, and some dancing. Nothing else untoward occurred. At one point, Mr Murphy and Sir Reginald appeared with what seemed to be urgent correspondence for my Father and Miles. Both men got up and left the room. Lord Burley was sitting near me and asked, "What is that about."

I glanced at him. "How could I possibly know?"

He huffed and began tapping the arm of his chair as we listened to Lady Angela play Moonlight Sonata. "This waiting is ridiculous. We should be out searching the grounds for my sister."

I tapped him lightly with my fan, "Shush!" He frowned but turned his attention back to Lady Angela. Then I saw his head swivel as Lord Tomlinson came from the card room to sit near Lord Harris.

Burley bit his lip and glowered at them, not behaviour that would make his case for his daughter's hand if Lord Tomlinson caught him. I leaned over and said, "Lady Edith is not here, Lord Burley. However, if you intend to impress her Father while you are here, I suggest you stop glaring at him."

He grimaced. "I saw Lady Edith before I left. That was the reason why I was late." I heard the hurt in his voice and felt for him at that moment.

When Miles returned without my Father, he leaned over me to whisper, "Your Father wants to talk to all of us." It wasn't long before we adjourned to wait in my parent's room. Sir Reginald and Mr Murphy checked the room for hiding places before the other members of our party gradually arrived.

The last to enter was Burley, who immediately went on the attack, pointing towards the window and the grounds beyond. "Why are we not out there searching for my sister!"

My Father looked at him like he was indulging a child. "Because it's nighttime. I will not have my people out there banging about in unknown territory. And secondly, I will not frighten your sister, nor will I put her or us in danger by drawing attention to such bizarre behaviour."

Stewart then pulled up a chair along with Murphy as he reported, "None of the staff here are assigned to care for the Russians; they brought all their own people. Their staff are not liked, so they have taken over the second staff dining room as their own. Cook has forbidden them to touch the food since the fish incident, and the butler has agreed that none of them will be allowed to serve even if the regular staff must do double duty.

Lady Cowper has approved."

I leaned forward. "Did anyone say anything about Lady Marianne?"

Murphy nodded. "The Cook remembered her from when she was a child, and she used to come to Broadlands, but no one else seemed to know her, nor did the Cook admit to having seen her recently. I doubt then that Marianne is getting foodstuffs from the house."

Stewart chuckled. "To my never-ending shame, I even asked if anyone had seen any ghosts on the grounds. I was assured they do not have ghosts at Broadlands, not even an errant monk from the reformation."

Murphy nodded. "Same with the outside staff, though the head gardener had left for his own home before I could speak to him, he doesn't live on the estate. None of the people I spoke to are aware of any hidden tunnels. The master of the dogs said there had been rumours since he was a boy that there were cellars from an old monastery still somewhere on the property, but he had no idea where they were located."

Father ran a hand through his hair and strode to the window to look out into the darkness. "It seems we will have to rely on the one drawing we have from Marianne and potentially the head gardener. Have you any idea how long he's been here?"

"He started here as a boy when Palmerston's Father was the Viscount."

None of us had any further information, but it was early days yet, so we adjourned and retired for the night.

Chapter 11

A Gardening Lesson

In the morning, it was arranged that those who wanted would ride. At the same time, the rest of us, including Judith, Mother and I, with Sir Reginald and a handful of others, would be taken on a tour of the gardens by the Head Gardener, Mr Byron Raynor.

After going through the formal gardens, many of the party returned to the house. While the four of us stood on the lawn before the house, looking down on the River Test. Mr Raynor had noticed as we had hoped he would and followed us to look out over the valley and the gently sloping manicured lawn that led down to the river bank. He smiled as he noticed our admiration. Then, in his raspy voice, he shared, "Capability Brown made this a masterpiece of the garden."

I smiled at him. "It is beautiful. Tell me, Mr Raynor, I understand that the house was once part of a monastery."

"Nay, milady, that be a story some locals made up. These lands once belonged to a Benedictine Nunnery that was in Romsey. But there be no ruins here. However, the former Lord Palmerston and Capability Brown built several follies along the river that appear to be convincing ruins. One or two of them are even older."

"So, there are no hidden secrets out there?"

"I didn't say that, milady. Every garden has its secrets." His eyes twinkled as he grinned at me.

"Now you are making fun of me."

His expression changed suddenly and was profoundly serious. "Never, milady."

I glanced at my Mother, who nodded, so I decided to push my luck. "Do you know Lady Marianne and Lady Arabella Browne? I understand, as children, they spent a great deal of time here."

He pulled at his ear. "Their Father once had a place on the other side of Romsey, and their Mother's parents used to live just the other side of that rise. The place has gone to ruin since they died. No one goes there anymore. It's a shame, really. It's on some of the best land in the county. Lord Palmerston has been trying to buy it, but he can't find out who the heirs were."

I was stunned. "Didn't their son inherit?"

He nodded. "He did, but he died at Waterloo. He and his wife never had children, and she returned to her people. Weren't no one else that took up residence? So I'm not sure who owns it now."

"Is it possible that it went to the granddaughters?"

"I suppose, but I have never seen them since they married. No one goes there anymore."

"Thank you, Mr Raynor. Is it possible to visit the follies?"

"Aye, milady, they are nice and dry this time of year."

"Are there any hidden secrets in them?

"He chuckled. No, milady, they are just wee stone buildings with a bench or two where you can sit and admire the view. Well, enjoy your walk but be careful. The path next to the oldest folly is a tad overgrown. It's not been used for years, so I wouldn't go that way. It only leads to that ruined house."

We strolled down the lawn and along the river. "Why did Arabella lead us astray about the follies?"

Judith pursed her lips, looking to her left at the small Grecian-style building. "Maybe she didn't. As a child, what she would remember as large dry rooms may not be more than a small storage space where furniture used in the folly might be stored in the winter. Mr Raynor may not even be aware of them if the family had used them before his time here."

I pursed my lips. "Emily Cowper said their old Nurse might be caring for Marianne. If she were coming and going at Broadlands, surely someone would have seen her."

My Mother touched my elbow. "What are you thinking?"

"I think that Arabella may have very well brought her sister here and hid her in the folly temporarily." Then, glancing back over my shoulder, "Look, you can see this stretch of the lawns from the two front reception rooms and probably even further from the upper stories."

"So, the nurse might have moved her?"

I shook my head. "It's possible, I suppose, but I doubt it."

Judith grinned. "Moved where, to the nurse's home?

Stewart shook his head. "No, she wouldn't take her to her own home. That would be too easy a trail to follow." He looked out at the panorama in front of us, then whispered as if thinking out loud, "The grandparents abandoned home." Finally, he echoed Mr Raynor's words, "No one goes there anymore."

Mother looked out over the river. "You think Mr Raynor knows, and he was telling us without telling us."

Stewart stared at her. "Why would he do that?"

"Plausible deniability, Inspector."

Judith huffed. "So, do we pay a visit to the ruin?"

I shook my head. "Let's go to the folly first and see if we can find these hidden rooms, then leave a message."

Stewart's head snapped back to look at me. "A message? Just leave a note and hope someone drops by to see it?" He shook his head. "Let me go to this ruin of a house and investigate."

I shook my head. "Let's not get ahead of ourselves. If Marianne is there, we can't risk scaring her into moving again."

Mother threw up her hands. "I still don't understand how you intend to leave her a message that wouldn't alert someone watching us to her presence."

"A puzzle, Mother—in Gaelic, just like Marianne did in a drawing."

Judith asked, "How do you know that she understands Gaelic?"

"I don't, but I hope she would have learned it from the other

249

patients and perhaps staff after several years in Scotland."

My Mother huffed, "You are taking a great deal on conjecture, Lissa."

"I know, but we can't afford to scare her—it's all we have at this moment."

We continued our walk as we went over what I should say in the message. We arrived at the folly and looked for an entrance to a secret passage. I stood thinking back to my conversation with Arabella, but she had never told me how to find the hidden rooms.

Mr Raynor, though, had told us about the path behind the folly that was a tad overgrown. I walked out of the folly and around behind it and found that some prickly holly bushes were hiding what looked like a door if you looked closely. Except for the faint outline in the stonework where the lichen had fallen off, we would have missed its clear, crisp edges. I pushed, but nothing happened. The Inspector threw his total weight against it, but nothing moved.

Then, Judith leaned on a decorative cherub that moved inward, and the door opened enough for Stewart to get his hands into the crevice. Then pulling, he fell forward as the door slid open easily. The air that escaped was not musty or stale, and the smell of woodsmoke and fish emanated from the interior. Stewart warned us back as he pulled his pistol, proceeded cautiously down the stairs, and disappeared. Then he called back, "It's clear."

Judith took a rock and propped the door open for safety's sake. Then we scrambled down a short flight of stairs. Inside, the rooms were dry and furnished just as Arabella had described, but they would be cramped quarters for an adult. On a table lay pencils, paper, and a partially completed portrait in Marianne's style. It took some time for me to remember enough Gaelic to compose our message and draw Edward's likeness standing by the folly. Mother arched a brow "Why Edward and not her brother?"

"She knows and trusts Edward. The folly hopefully indicates that he's here at Broadlands."

I left it on the table and placed an onyx paperweight on it. Then we left, erasing any sign of having found the entrance as best we could. As we walked back along the river, I asked Judith, "Where did Magda get to this morning?"

Judith sighed. "She rose early and was gone before breakfast. Something about the woods holding secrets she needed to discover."

Stewart looked worried. "I thought we were supposed to stay together?"

Judith chuckled. "You know Grandmama; she is a law onto herself."

Stewart seemed to take umbrage and snapped, "Are you not worried about her?"

Judith took exception to his tone. "Of course, I am concerned! But it won't change anything. Magda will still do what she wants."

He shook his head. "You people are remarkably odd." We all stopped and looked at him, then chuckled. I took his arm and remarked, "We will grow on you, Sir Reginald." Then he laughed

251

as well, and we climbed the gentle slope leading up to the house.

High on the second floor, I saw the outline of a woman standing in one of the windows watching us. When she realised I had caught sight of her, she jerked the curtains closed. I was sure it was Countess Irina. My Mother walked beside me and leaned in to whisper, "I saw her too."

I whispered back, "Was it Irina?"

She shrugged. "I am not sure."

"At least she couldn't see the folly's hidden entrance from there, and we had been gone long enough that we might have just been walking in the woodland."

Stewart whispered to us while looking ahead, "Don't worry, milady. I covered our tracks as we came out, let her guess. By the way, you were right. It was the Countess at the window."

I didn't look at him but asked as I trudged up the hill holding my skirts up ever so slightly, "How could you possibly know that from this distance?"

Eventually, we crested the slope, and he stopped turning around as if taking in the view again. "I have to be able to identify people at a distance. You get to know body types and stances, plus I could see the glint of her blonde hair."

I was amazed. "You have astounding eyesight, Sir Reginald."

"Aye, milady, it's a family trait." He chuckled. "My mum had it too. It got my brothers and me into a mite of trouble when we were boys. I swear she had eyes in the back of her head too. She always knew when we got into difficulty."

My Mother laughed. "That's not simply good eyesight Sir Reginald. It's a Mother's innate ability to read her children."

"You may be right, Lady Blackburn. She always seemed to know things."

We turned back and walked into the house. Stewart bowed to us and walked towards the back of the house as Countess Irina came down the stairs. I watched her as her eyes followed him as if calculating how she could approach him for information. I chuckled inside, knowing she would find that an impossible task. If nothing else, Inspector Stewart was focused on his duty to his family and his profession.

When he passed out of sight, she continued down the stairs leisurely and came to our group as we divested ourselves of bonnets, gloves, and shawls. "Your husband's secretary is an interesting man and rather handsome in a rugged way with his bronzed skin. Is he recently returned from the Indies?"

I smiled serenely. "Sir Reginald? No—he spends a great deal of time on the water."

"Oh really, does he sail in the regatta?"

I gave her what I hoped was a detached smile. "Sir Reginald is a secretary Countess. He could hardly afford a yacht."

I started to walk away. "Is he married?"

I stopped and turned around. "Yes, she is a lovely woman, and he is devoted to her."

"Interesting."

I looked down and clasped my hands in front of me. "Leave him alone, Countess. You will only embarrass yourself in pursuing him."

Her expression clouded as she frowned. "I do not dally with workers or bastards, Lady Tinley, unlike some people."

I laughed. "You are missing out on a great deal, Countess. Some of my best friends are bastards and from the working class."

I moved on with my Mother and Judith, who were tittering at the Countess's expense. I could feel the Countess' eyes burning into my back. Still, I wouldn't give her the satisfaction of a reaction and ignored her gasp of indignation as we turned into the drawing room where Lady Cowper was gathered with the other ladies who had returned from their ride.

I had just taken a cup of tea from Emily when Rabby, Edward's new valet, came into the room. He bowed and then came to me. "Sir Edward and Lord Tinley would like to speak with you, milady. They are in the library with Lord Melbourne and Lord Burley."

I raised an eyebrow and looked about the room. Everyone within hearing had stopped to watch my response. I calmly placed my cup on the table near me and accompanied Rabby out of the room. I smiled at his discomfort, he had only recently returned to Edward's employ, so I tried to put him at ease. "How are you adjusting to being back in Sir Edward's household?"

Rabby grinned. "Sir Edward is a good master—much better than Sir Albert."

"I seem to recall that you once had ambitions to be a groom. Have you given that up now?"

"I still like the horse's milady, but being a valet is a might easier, and I get to travel places I never would as a groom. Also, it's nice being treated with some respect by others."

"How is Jilly?"

He blushed. "She be Jilly still, opinionated and waspish at times. But she's a fine lady's maid."

"Nothing further between you two?"

He blushed again. "Not yet, milady, she still be three years younger than me."

I chuckled. "Rabby, she will always be three years younger than you." He nodded self-consciously just as we reached the library, where he knocked on the door for me, opening and closing it behind me.

I looked over my shoulder, but Rabby hadn't joined us. I examined the four gentlemen in the room as I walked to my husband's side. Miles and Edward looked amused, Melbourne appeared confused, and Burley was obviously angry. I slipped my hand into Miles' and smiled at him. "What can I do for you, gentlemen?"

Melbourne licked his lips and then clasped his hands behind his back. "You have been out walking, Lady Tinley. Did you find anything interesting?"

"I found the gardens and the aspects enchanting, as did my

companions."

Burley looked about, ready to explode. "I saw you returning. You were flushed and animated."

I glanced at him. "I was walking uphill after a long walk on the grounds. So it is only natural that I was flushed."

"You were staring at me—I mean at the house."

"At first, I was enjoying the beauty of the building. But it wasn't you that I saw. It was Countess Irina who I saw watching us. I am sure you know that we are not exactly on friendly terms. I take exception to being spied on."

Melbourne arched a brow. "Spied on milady?"

"Yes, Lord Melbourne, I have been the victim of two incidents of abuse from her companion, Count Vasiliev. Each time my husband has come to my defence. In turn, she defends her companion's shameful behaviour."

Lord Melbourne took in my condition and sighed, turning to Miles. "Fine, Tinley, I accept that you were justified in your reactions to the Count. However, I don't need the details of what took place, and I am satisfied that Lady Tinley did nothing to warrant such attention."

I gasped, glaring at him. Then, I said, "You actually entertained the idea that I would have welcomed his attention?"

He flushed and glanced down. "I am not proud of it, milady, but as Prime Minister, I must walk a fine line when I listen to the complaints of foreign guests. I assure you I did not find them the least credible knowing your impeccable reputation, not to say your service to our country."

"Thank you for that, at least, Lord Melbourne. Though I suppose it would be too much to ask that a politician defend my good name without question."

Melbourne glared at me. "Yes, well, sometimes good manners must be sacrificed in the name of diplomacy."

I stared at him, my blood boiling, but the only retort I could manage was, "Fascinating." Miles rubbed his nose and turned his head to the side, obviously trying to control his amusement. I glanced at Edward, who looked less than pleased with Melbourne.

Lord Burley, however, had no concern for me and exploded, "What did you find!"

I turned to look at him directly and frowned. "I don't know what you are referring to, Lord Burley."

He was frightfully worked up and hissed at me, "You agreed to look for my sister Marianne! She's here somewhere, and you've done nothing to find her. Nothing!"

Miles shifted his focus to Burley, and his expression was cold and steely. "Burley, you need to control yourself and stop yelling at my wife."

"What are you going to do—strike me?"

Miles took a step forward, but Edward moved between them. Melbourne was thunderous as he yelled, "What is this all about!"

The door opened, and Palmerston, the Foreign Secretary, my

Father, Jibben and Lord Russell, the Home Secretary, who appeared to have just arrived, walked in, closing the door behind them. Palmerston stared at Lord Burley. "Sit down and shut up, Justin."

Burley reared back affronted but took a seat, as did everyone else. My Father had remained standing and cast a smile in my direction. Then, out of his inside pocket, he pulled the Templar coin. He placed it on the table in front of everyone. Russell, Palmerston, and Melbourne all leaned in to examine it. Burley sat sulking with his arms crossed, glaring out the window.

"What is said here, gentlemen, stays here. There will be dire consequences if it doesn't. Melbourne sat up, completely indignant "Here now, are you threatening the three most senior members of the government?"

My Father tipped his head back and sighed. "If I am forced to, then yes. But I would rather not."

"On whose authority do you act?"

My Father took a seat and crossed his legs. His expression was serious, and one could almost say regal, "We are called the Brotherhood, and we act in the people's best interests, as our organisation has since its inception."

Melbourne waved a hand. "Nonsense, you are Wiseman's operative and have been since the war."

Father sighed. "I was until my Grandfather died, and I inherited his title, property and the leadership of a secret organisation that protects the interests of the people of Britain. We are autonomous, Lord Melbourne. We answer to no one."

Melbourne opened his mouth to speak, but Palmerston held up a hand. "Don't embarrass yourself any further, William. I knew the late Lord Blackburn. While he may have hidden away in Wales, he worked quietly in the people's best interests, just as his grandson said. It is not a political organisation. These people don't care about government or their policies."

It was interesting how he had phrased his understanding of the Brotherhood, that its purview could also include government policies that hurt the people. Jibben was sitting in the window seat, and Burley was now drumming his fingers annoyingly on the arm of his chair. Melbourne glanced at him. "What has this all to do with Burley's sister?"

My Father stared at Burley. "Justin—may I explain?"

Burley glowered at my Father but ultimately nodded. "Fine, but as you said, what is said here, stays here."

"Are we in agreement on that gentleman? If not, then I will go no further." Lord Burley finally relaxed and nodded. The other three took longer to come to terms with such an agreement. The Brotherhood had never been so exposed until now, which concerned me greatly.

Melbourne looked at me, then at my Father. "You mean to tell me that your daughter is one of your operatives."

He looked at me, smiled, and said without hesitation, "She is one of my best."

Russell glared at Miles. "And you, Tinley, are you part of this organisation?"

"I suppose you could say yes. I take on assignments from Sir Thomas and Lord Blackburn. In addition, my wife and I often work together." He chuckled, looking at Edward, then Jibben. "You could say it's a family business."

Melbourne looked at Jibben. "Locke?"

Jibben covered his heart and seemed ready to launch into one of his self-deprecating speeches, but he didn't. "We are of one mind and one heart. The British people's welfare comes first and always will. I work with them because they believe in that and work for it. We are family" I smiled at him; it warmed my heart to know that was how he truly felt.

Melbourne looked astounded. "I have always considered you a brilliant financial manager but a man of shallow character. I am glad to see I have been proven wrong."

Then he focused on Edward. "You are one of them as well?"

Edward smirked. "I offer my services and expertise when it seems appropriate, but I am not officially one of their group, but I am family."

Melbourne shook his head, then turned his attention to Palmerston. "You knew about this all this time?"

Palmerston shook his head. "Not everything, and I doubt that will ever change."

Melbourne waved his hand. "Very well, but what has this to do with Burley's sister?"

My Father explained, leaving out where I thought Marianne was hiding or that the documents she had created of her Father's accounts and journals were possibly in the form of pictures. It took considerable effort to answer their questions without giving everything away. Eventually, the three government officials though not satisfied, knew they wouldn't get any more.

I rose, and all of them stood with me. "Now, gentlemen, if you will excuse me, I need to change. Luncheon should be announced shortly."

Miles and Edward followed me out and up the stairs. Once we reached our room. Edward followed us in, and Miles asked, "Are you lost, brother?"

He closed the door and leaned against it. "I know Lissa well enough that she discovered something today on her walk. What was it?"

I motioned for him to take a seat and explained what we had discovered and assumed. He listened carefully and didn't interrupt. Then, when I finished, he sighed, "When do we go after Marianne ?"

I shook my head. "We don't—she trusts you, Edward. She may panic and run if forced to face too many of us."

Edward bit his lower lip. "Fine, then you will come with me. I can't face her alone; I won't know what to do, Lissa. I love Fiona more than life itself. I know that what I once felt for Marianne was pity, and she will see it in my face. It will only hurt her more. Please, come with me?"

I looked at Miles, glaring at his brother, "Miles?"

He peered at me sideways. "I am going at least part of the way with you, and I will wait for you at the folly."

I sighed. "You can't stay there alone."

"Then I will bring Stewart or Locke with me."

I threw up my hands. "Then all of us might as well go. Then, if Marianne tries to run, we will at least have a chance of catching her."

Edward grinned. "That's a wonderful idea."

I placed a hand on my back, stretching. "Get out, Edward, I need to change, or we will be late for luncheon."

Edward chuckled and left smiling, having gotten his way. Miles came to rub my shoulders. "Shall I send for Rennie?"

"Heavens, no—you can fill in for her."

He chuckled. "Yes, milady, what would you like to wear this afternoon." I sighed as he stopped the massage and walked into the wardrobe.

"The peach one."

Miles called back to me, "Which one? You have three."

I sighed. "I do not. I have one in peach and one in apricot. The other is a ball gown, not an afternoon gown, and I didn't bring it."

I sat down at the dressing table, examined my hair, tucked in a few curls, and re-pinned them with Miles' assistance. Then he helped me out of my walking gown and into the peach dress. Once I was ready, we went to join the others in the drawing room. Lord Burley was off by himself sulking when Edward came to me, "Burley is anxious. He thinks you know where Marianne is."

"I might, but I am not about to tell him."

Edward peered over his shoulder. "He is her brother Lissa."

"And Arabella doesn't trust him."

Edward nodded. "Then you two can deal with him." I looked over his shoulder to see Burley bearing down on us.

I glanced up at Miles, sighed, and then waited as Burley stopped at my side. "I want to know what you discovered about Marianne's whereabouts."

Before Miles could say anything, I decided to be honest. "Arabella asked me not to tell you."

From behind me, a voice said, "I didn't know you were on speaking terms with my wife, Lady Tinley."

I stepped aside and closer to Miles as Arabella's husband joined our circle. "We have met occasionally, Lord Harris. She has an appreciation for my brother-in-law's art."

He didn't even blink and brushed aside what I said by bluntly asking, "What did she ask you not to tell Burley?"

Edward stepped in on this one, "We might as well tell him, Lissa." He smiled at Burley, saying, "I am to paint your Earl portrait, Justin. She told us that you hadn't done one yet and have been putting her off."

Burley frowned. "She knows I hate the fuss and don't have the time."

I interjected, "Edward can do the preliminary sketches here, can't you?" It wasn't how he liked to work, but he nodded. "Yes, I can take your likeness. Then you can sit for me in your robes and coronet."

Burley scowled. "I don't care what Arabella wants. I am not wearing that damn coronet." He gave Edward a scathing look. "How were you supposed to do this without my knowledge?"

He looked at Miles. "My brother is the same size as you, and our Father has the requisite robes. He could stand in for you, and I would put your face in place of his."

Miles scowled at Edward and said, "We look nothing alike."

Burley nodded. "At least we can agree on that much."

Harris had looked sceptical during the conversation until Burley decided to play along. "Very well. I will sit for you. We can make the arrangements later" Then he took Harris by the arm and walked away with him, surprisingly not exposing us to further questioning.

Edward glared at me. "Now, what am I supposed to do?"

Miles stared at him, perplexed. "What do you mean?"

Edward rolled his eyes. "His portrait!"

I smiled. "You will paint him, and it will be brilliant."

He ran a hand through his hair. "I don't even like him!"

I continued to smile. "You don't have to. It's a commission."

He shook his head. "If I don't get paid for it, I am sending the bill to your wife, Miles." Then he wandered off.

Shortly after Judith and Jibben came to our side, Jibben grinned. "Seems like Burley saved your stones from the fire, Tinley. Harris is an aggressive basta—person." I smiled when he caught himself before saying, bastard.

Miles nodded. "I know it. I have to say Burley surprised me, but I am still not sure we can trust him."

Judith tipped her head to the side, then looked back at Burley talking to Lady Angela. "Guilty by association?" She stared at Miles' blank face. "The family name is Browne. How many of them have you killed or been involved in their deaths? Their name has a bad association for you."

Miles smiled. "I agree, Judith."

Jibben leaned in. "So, what's the plan?"

I glanced up at Miles, "Tomorrow, we see about approaching Marianne."

Judith chewed on her lower lip before saying, "If she is still there, Lissa."

"Why wouldn't she be?"

"I don't know. I felt like we were being watched and not by anyone here. We may have already scared Marianne off." I had to nod in agreement that Marianne may very well have left.

That unsettled me, but I hoped that she was wrong. There was nothing else to say, so I changed the subject and asked, "Where is Magda? I haven't seen her today."

Jibben sucked in his lower lip. "She came in a while ago muddy and miserable and is taking a bath."

I felt my heart sink. "Would Magda have known about the derelict house?"

Judith shook her head. "I don't see how. But you're right. If she did, that might have frightened Marianne into leaving. After all, she doesn't know Magda."

Jibben screwed up his face. "But where would she go?"

Miles looked about the room, lighting on the Russians. "I suggest that we stop talking about this in the open." He pulled me along to where my parents were standing, with Jibben and Judith following.

My Mother glanced at me. "What's wrong, darling?"

I stared at Miles as he said, "She and Judith think Marianne might have flown the coup."

"What on earth gave you that idea?"

Jibben interjected, "They think Grandmama did it inadvertently."

My Father frowned. "I am not sure I understand, but we can't discuss this now, so I suggest we go for a walk in the gardens after we eat."

As I scanned the room for Edward, the butler had come to announce luncheon. Then I saw my brother-in-law walking towards us with Burley. Elsewhere Lord Harris, Lord Melbourne, and the Russians were staring at us from the opposite side of the room."

Edward and Burley stood by while those around us started to file out. Justin was staring at us and approached, asking, "What's happened? You all look ill."

My Father smiled and slapped him on the shoulder as the Russians walked by. "I hear Edward is going to paint your portrait. You are lucky. I am still waiting for him to do mine." Of course, it was a lie, but the Russians wouldn't know that.

Burley shrugged. "Yes—it should be an experience." Then, as the final Russian passed us, he hissed, "What is wrong?"

"Take a walk with us after luncheon; we will meet you in the orangery."

Burley arched a brow. "Very well." Then he put out his arm. "Lady Blackburn, may I escort you into luncheon."

Mother smiled at him. "It would be my pleasure, Lord Burley."

My Father extended his arm to me. Judith took Miles, leaving Edward and Jibben with the two dowagers making their way out the door. They sighed and went to do their duty.

I sat by Lord Burley, waiting to be hit with a barrage of questions but instead, Justin expressed concern for my safety. "I would ask to have my room changed if I were you and find a new lady's maid. I saw that Count Vasiliev following your maid out of your room."

I felt my face blanch. I looked at Miles; he was staring at the Count, who had raised a glass to him. I wanted to shake Rennie and find out what she had been doing. From the Count's look, it was not good. I ate sparingly, and when we were done, I asked my Mother to find Lettie and meet me in my room as Miles accompanied me up the stairs. "Take a deep breath, Lissa. We don't know that Rennie told him anything."

I squeezed his arm in panic. "And we don't know that she didn't."

On entering my room, I found that everything had been overturned, clothes were strewn all over the floor, and even my jewellery box had been ransacked. I choked back a sob and sat down. Tears were welling up in my eyes. "I don't understand why—why would she betray us like this?"

Miles picked up my jewellery box, "Nothing's missing."

Mother arrived with Lettie, "My God, what on earth happened?"

I was too upset to speak, so Miles explained what Burley had seen. Then Jibben and my Father arrived. "Burley told us, good Lord—did they do this?"

I sucked back another sob. "I don't know. Where is Rennie?"

Lettie pursed her lips. "She wasn't at luncheon, milady."

Burley and Edward then came in, and I asked him, "Tell them what you told me."

Burley looked contrite. "I thought the woman with the Count was your lady's maid, but it seems I was wrong. The woman with the Count was much older than the person Johnson described."

I glanced up at Lettie. "Can you and Murphy find Rennie?"

"Yes, milady—right away." She spun around and left at a run.

My Father was examining the lock on our door. "It was picked, Miles—not expertly, but you would still have to know what to look for to notice."

Lettie returned, "Rennie is missing, milady. One of the kitchen maids saw her go out shortly after you went for your walk this morning, but no one saw her return."

Tyson came in with Murphy, who turned to him, saying, "Tell them what you saw."

He coughed to clear his throat. "Rennie was speaking to that Russian groom again. So I went over and told her she'd lose her position if anyone saw her."

I asked, "What did she do then?"

Tyson shrugged. "She told me to mind my business, and she headed back towards the house and went in through the scullery."

He was staring at the floor, "What else, Tyson."

"I told the groom to leave her alone. He told me that he wasn't interested in a pale English girl. That they are too haughty."

"And she didn't come back out?"

"Not that I saw, milady?"

I glanced at Miles. "Then, where is she?"

Just as I asked, a key rattled in the closed door and swung open. Rennie came shuffling in with a stack of bed linen that blocked her view of all of us. She dropped them on the bed and screeched when she saw us and the state of the room, "My God, milady—what happened? Are you all right?" She looked about her and saw Tyson, and her face fell. "I can explain, milady. I told Anton to leave the other maids and me alone and that we weren't interested in his kind."

Everyone stared at her in disbelief, "It's God's truth, milady. Tyson heard me tell him to leave me alone. They're not nice people. They think they're better than everyone else. I caught him trying to kiss Polly, one of the milkmaids; she didn't want any of it. Being from London, my mouth got ahead of my brain. I shouldn't have said anything."

I glanced at Tyson. "Did you hear any of this conversation?"

Tyson pursed his lips in annoyance, "Yes, milady, just as she said."

Miles sighed. "But you weren't willing to share that part with us?" Tyson lowered his head as Miles continued, "I don't know what's the problem between you two, but you had better work it out before we return to London, or you will not be filling in for Meg and Robert again."

They both nodded in agreement and whispered, "Yes, milord."

I turned to Rennie. "Can you tell me why you are bringing in the bed linen, Rennie? That isn't your job here."

"No, milady, it isn't, but the maids were behind up here, and I thought you'd want to rest after luncheon, so I decided to help out. But I didn't make this mess, milady." She looked daunted as she stared at the disarray, then started picking things up.

Lettie bent down. "I'll give you a hand. We'll have things set to rights in no time."

Rennie smiled and mouthed a *'thank you.'*

I went to Rennie and took her by the shoulders. "It was good of you to stand up for the other maids and offer to help out."

Lettie chuckled. "It has been sixes and sevens downstairs, milady, what with so many foreigners and competing requests. Country staff always find it a strain to host big parties."

"Wise words, Lettie. I will have to keep that in mind when we entertain at the Rambles."

Then everyone dispersed to change. Rennie helped me into my forest green walking dress and half-boots. Miles changed into a more relaxed attired for a stroll. We met in the Orangery as arranged, and as we walked out, we kept checking our surroundings for anyone following us. As we moved past the formal gardens, our conversation turned to Judith's and my suspicion that Marianne may have left the area already.

Burley shook his head. "Why would she do that?"

"I don't know. It's just a feeling I have. Perhaps she found out who was on Palmerston's guest list. I think the old nurse might know since she lives in the area. Perhaps she found out and told her." I shrugged, "Judith said she felt like we were being watched. If it was Marianne, we might have frightened her, and she could be anywhere now."

Lord Burley growled, "Ridiculous! She hasn't any resources."

"We don't know what Arabella left for her maintenance. I can't see your sister returning to London and not providing for Marianne's comfort."

He grunted reluctantly in agreement but still asked. "Then why make a drawing of the folly?"

"For her safety's sake, in case someone such as the Russians or Lord Harris found it instead of us." I paused as I thought of something that made my heart skip. "There wouldn't be any way they could make an association with your grandparent's home, is there?"

Burley chuckled. "No, even Harris didn't know about my Mother's family owning property around here. It was left to my Mother. She, in turn, left it to Arabella and Marianne in a sealed codicil. I only found out about it after my Father died. Arabella told me she and Marianne wanted me to have it if anything happened to them and had my solicitor draw up the paperwork." I glared at him suspiciously. If he knew this much, what else did he know? He caught me scrutinising him and stated emphatically, "I would never hurt my sisters! I don't want to be alone in this world! My brother Alexander and sisters are all I have that is good in this family."

I felt for him suddenly, "You don't consider yourself good, Lord

272

Burley?"

He looked up at the sky and swiped a hand across his leg. "It's a struggle every day Lady Tinley. Associates of my Father approach me frequently, wishing to do business. It's difficult not to follow my Father's path to wealth. But, so far, I have resisted."

I nodded. "And marrying Lady Edith would make things easier?"

He snorted and shook his head. "I would not be the first peer to marry to save the family fortunes by a fortuitous marriage, but I genuinely care for Edith."

"How much does she know about your family."

He sighed. "Everything—I couldn't in good conscience court her and hide behind the lies that you people and the Crown put out to lessen the blow of my Father's treachery."

"You didn't have to do that."

"I couldn't risk the loss of her affections if someone came forward and told her."

"Does her Father know?"

He nodded. "He does. He was a close friend and business partner of my Father's at one time and has tried to distance himself from the association. Yet, he didn't suffer financially. I assume that her Father looks at me and sees Randall, Julian and my Father." He stared at me and said, "Society is a spiteful bitch."

Miles chuckled. "That she is, Burley."

Judith looked perplexed when she asked, "Why is it that society, storms, and ships are always considered female?"

Jibben barked a laugh. "That's easy. They all share the trait of unpredictability."

Judith, Mother and I glared at him while he grinned. Then his face fell as he looked into the distance. "Here comes Grandmama, and she looks to be in a temper."

Magda stomped up to us, waving her arms. "She has fled! How many of you went to the folly?" All of us put up a hand. Finally, she spat out, "Fools!"

Judith was perturbed by her attitude and hissed, "If you had told us what you had planned, maybe we wouldn't have been fools!"

Magda glared at her, then shook her head. "We have all been fools." Then, in Romani, she mumbled something like a curse before saying, "I found her nurse, but Marianne was gone."

Judith huffed with exasperation, "Where did she go?"

"The Nurse said she went off into the woods but never returned."

"Didn't she look for her?"

Magda glared at me askance, "She is old and frail, barely able to care for herself, let alone Lady Marianne."

Then she turned her fury on Burley. "You are the cause of this! She must have seen you and ran."

Burley's hands were clenched in fists. "Gone where! Old Nan must know something. I will go and speak to her."

Magda stepped up and poked him in the chest. "No, you won't! She doesn't know anything and is already fretting over your sister's disappearance and that Arabella has not returned as promised. I told her that we would find her and protect her. Don't make me a liar."

Burley growled, "Damnit, what am I supposed to do then!"

Magda lowered her voice. "Where would she go?"

He removed his hat and pulled at his hair, "I don't know!"

Edward stood back, speaking quietly to Miles and my Father, and then he said, "Why don't we just go to town and ask if anyone has seen her?"

Burley frowned. "Where would she go from there?"

No one spoke until my Mother suggested, "The hospital in Edinburgh?"

I shook my head. "Not if she thought Harris or the infamous Dr Cooper would find her there."

Miles sighed. "The only other possibility is London. If I wanted to hide, that's where I would go."

Burley nodded eagerly. "She knows the city, and perhaps she went to one of her friends."

Edward glowered at him. "What, friends, everyone knew that she was in a mental hospital; you think they will let her into one of their houses."

Judith offered, "Blane House?"

I shook my head. "No, she fled there. I can't see her returning, especially since Lord Harris had her admitted there."

Burley was highly agitated. "Then, where? I sold our mausoleum of a London townhouse, and she wouldn't go to Arabella's home." Everyone nodded. "What about your home Tinley?"

Jibben said, "Tinley doesn't live on Cornwall Terrace anymore. It's the Agency headquarters now, and she would notice the strange people coming and going."

Miles ran a hand through his hair. "My parents aren't in London. They have gone to see John off on his first voyage."

Edward's head snapped up. "They what?"

Miles glanced at him. "You knew about it."

"I thought that was next month."

"No, brother dear, it's this month, they were to see him off, and we are to fetch him home next month so that he can share all the sordid details with us about his journey to Naples."

Edward sucked in a breath, saying, "Fiona was supposed to stay with them while we are down here. Oh God, I think I know where Marianne would have gone. He blanched and whispered, "My home—it's the only one she would think of as friendly."

Burley smiled. "That's wonderful! It's perfect."

Edward shook his head. "No, it is not—I am married, Justin. You once told me that the one thing that kept her alive was that she and I would marry someday. Don't you see, my wife and children are in that house."

Miles interjected, "Fiona may have gone with Father and Lady Jane."

Edward shook his head. "Not with two children, especially with Elspeth still needing frequent feeding. No, she would stay home."

Burley ran a hand through his hair and paced in a circle. "The doctor told us that challenging her delusions could prove dangerous and that we should just let them play out."

Edward paced back and forth. "You haven't met my wife. She is very possessive of me."

I interjected, "Fiona is also compassionate and intelligent, Edward; she wouldn't hurt Marianne."

He crossed his arms. "What if Marianne tries to hurt Fiona or the children."

Burley recoiled, "She wouldn't do something like that."

Edward turned on him. "For God's Sake, man, she's mad!" He inhaled deeply, then said more calmly, "You don't know what she might do—none of us does."

Burley didn't respond to his outburst but looked at my Father. "So now we leave for London?"

My Father inhaled, "We should, but that would alert all the interested parties here. Seeing John off is as good an excuse as we have for the Johnson brothers to leave. Miles, Lissa, and Edward should go. I will speak to Palmerston, and he will cover for them as two forgetful brothers who were supposed to see their brother off on his maiden voyage. Leave Rennie and Tyson here with most of your baggage. That will make it look like you will only be gone for a day or two."

Miles asked, "What if it's longer?"

"Send me word. I will make the excuse that Lissa is not well."

Jibben nodded. "In case you haven't noticed, the Russians watch our every move. They will send someone to follow."

Miles frowned. "Then we will have to stop them. We can't return to London the way we came."

Jibben snapped his fingers. "Go to Portsmouth. Hire a boat to take you to London."

Miles smiled. "Any boat in particular?"

He grinned from ear to ear. "The Pelican, I will give you a good deal."

Edward stared at him. "Is this one of your coastal runners."

Jibben reared, "I do not smuggle if that is what you infer. With a good wind and tides, you can be in London the same day."

Miles looked at me, then Edward. We both nodded in agreement that it was the best idea, and then Burley said, "I am coming with you."

Edward stood in front of him. "No—you won't. It will give us

278

away. If you do, you will jeopardise our lives, Marianne's and Arabella's. You don't want that."

Burley was furious. "I can't sit here and pretend I am enjoying myself."

Jibben snorted, "You are not fooling anyone now as it is. If you leave, you know Harris will follow you."

Burley looked defeated. "God, what a mess this is. If my Father weren't already dead, I would kill him."

My Father placed a hand on his shoulder. "We will save your sister, Justin. Just be patient."

Jibben then patted him on the back. "You and I will ride to Romsey and ask about Marianne. Then, if you like, we can drop in on the old nurse. She should at least be able to tell you what Marianne was like, but no tormenting her, or you and I will have a problem."

Magda huffed and said sternly, "Jibben, you can't do that!"

Jibben looked down at Magda. His eyes were deadly serious, and he said quietly but with conviction, "Grandmama, you are often right—but not this time. This man needs to be doing something constructive, not playing billiards or chess and walking old ladies into dinner."

Magda grimaced at the criticism; she reached up to smack Jibben but then dropped her hand and conceded, "You may be right, Jibben."

Lord Burley smiled. "How can we let you know if we find

anything, Tinley?"

Jibben answered. "We have operatives in Romsey that can get a message to him. Then my friend, in a day or two, I think you will be unwell and need to seek the aid of your personal physician in London. Judith, Grandmama and I will take you in our carriage. Grandmama is a renowned healer, but she cannot travel alone with you, and I will not leave my wife behind."

Burley grinned. "You people have an answer for everything."

Jibben chuckled. "Yes, but you aren't a convincing actor Burley. So Grandmama will have to dose you with Ipecacuanha—it will be uncomfortable, but no one will doubt that you are ill." Everyone but Burley laughed as Magda scrutinised him, seemingly calculating his required dose. He already looked sick at the thought.

We continued our walk toward the woods when my Father suddenly called out, "Down!" Everyone but Burley ducked as the crack of a rifle being fired rang in the still air.

Miles and Jibben had run off in the direction of where the shot came from, while Edward caught Burley as he started to fall. He had been hit in the leg. Magda looked down at him before kneeling at his side. He glanced at her and chuckled, "You won't have to dose me now."

She nodded. "No, but neither will you be able to travel. You would be extremely uncomfortable travelling in a coach, Lord Burley. So I am afraid you will have to stay here.

My Father shook his head. "No, he should see Matthew. So,

280

Burley, you will return to London after all and by boat with the others."

Magda nodded, smiling. "Yes, that would be better." Then she looked up at Edward. "Will you please go back to the house and ask for a litter and men to carry him back? He nodded and ran off. The building was visible from where we stood, so I wondered who had sent the shooter after us and if Burley was the intended target.

My Father kept watching over us with pistol drawn. "Why would someone want to shoot Burley?"

Burley shook his head and grimaced in pain as Magda ripped his trousers open to get to his wound, and he said through a clenched jaw, "If you hadn't yelled, I believe that you or Tinley would have gotten it in the head." Then, as Burley added, my Father glanced down at him and then back to where the shot had come from. "Your shout must have unnerved them, and they shot low, trying to adjust the trajectory for when you ducked." Then he screeched, "Christ woman, what are you doing!"

Magda pulled at some weeds nearby and crushed them up in her hands. "Stop being a baby. These herbs will help until I clean the wound and remove the bullet."

Edward returned with several men, a litter, and a furious Palmerston. "I was insane to invite you, people here when you are in the middle of—" He stopped before he went on, noticing that he had been followed out by Sergi Popov, huffing and puffing and glaring at all of us.

He looked down at Burley and frowned as if confused, then up at my Father, saying with a heavy accent, "What is the meaning of this Blackburn!" he pointed at my Father's pistol, and his eyes lit up. "You shot Lord Burley?"

Palmerston glanced at him with disgust. "Don't be an idiot, Popov. You think he would still be standing here with Burley conscious."

I looked over their shoulders and groaned, "Here comes Lord Melbourne."

The Prime Minister took in his surroundings. Then I saw Miles and Jibben coming out of the woods dragging one of the Russian grooms with them. A rifle was slung over Miles' shoulder, and a huge bruise was blossoming over the right side of his face, where he must have been hit with the butt of the rifle, no doubt. "I think you have a great deal of explaining to do, Mr Popov. Shooting a peer is a serious offence, and as this man is one of your party, you will be held accountable for his actions."

Popov sputtered in a rage. "He is not one of mine! He is one of Countess Irina's men."

The men from the house loaded Burley onto the litter and started back with him, Magda at his side. She called back over her shoulder, "She is a witch."

Melbourne frowned. "What does she mean by that?"

I sighed. "Trouble."

Miles and Jibben dragged the groom forward. Jibben glared at the man. "He doesn't appear to speak English or French."

Popov snorted, "That's because he's Georgian they do not even speak Russian and are uneducated clods."

My Father raised an eyebrow. "Yet the Countess employs them?"

"She is a Bagration." As if that was to mean something to us. He hissed at our blank faces. "The Countess's family were once the Georgian Royal family, immensely wealthy and powerful before Russia annexed Georgia." Then, he turned and stormed off towards the house, and over his shoulder, he shouted, "Shoot the bastard. He will not be travelling with my party any longer."

The young man seemed to have understood that as he broke free from Jibben and Miles long enough to make it no more than six feet away when another shot echoed in the air, dropping the man. Count Vasiliev stepped out from the trees, grinning. He walked up to the body and, with the toe of his boot, pushed him over onto his back. His eyes were open to the sky; he was dead. Edward had returned and pointed a loaded pistol at the Count, who grinned while saying, "Put your pistol away, Sir Edward. Unlike him, I am part of Popov's party and have diplomatic immunity. Besides, you would have hanged him anyway for shooting Lord Burley—I saved you the cost of a trial. Send someone to pick him up and feed him to the pigs."

He started to walk away, with Melbourne glaring at him. "The bastard's right—christ, what is going on here."

My Father arched a brow. "I can only speculate on what they are up to."

Miles and Edward were whispering off to the side, and it

283

continued to get louder and louder, with Edward finally barking, "I tell you, it is not until next month!"

"He's leaving tomorrow, and we promised to see him off; why do you think I agreed to come here? It puts us that much closer to Portsmouth!"

Palmerston was standing there with clenched fists, glaring at my Father, when he shifted his focus to them and snapped, "What are you two harping about!"

Miles looked at Palmerston calmly. "Our younger brother is in the Royal Navy and is going off on his first cruise to Naples, and we promised to see him off."

Palmerston wiped a hand across his brow. "By all means, leave. With fewer of you here, it might be calmer. In fact, why don't you all go!"

My Father grinned. "Capital idea, sir. Lissa hasn't been well on this trip. Her Mother and I would like to have our physician examine her."

Palmerston then Melbourne glowered at me as Melbourne said, "She looks healthy enough to me. But something tells me you now believe you need to be in London."

My Father pursed his lips. "Do you wish me to confirm that, sir?"

Melbourne glared at him. "Blackburn, you walk a fine line—but I don't want to know. I will sleep better at night. Just try not to get yourselves killed. I would never hear the end of it between your Mother and Shellard."

My Father choked back a cough. "What about the Russians, sir?"

He huffed and looked back, watching the fading figure of Count Vasiliev. "Palmerston and I will delay them, but I can't give you more than a day."

"A day is enough, sir. Now, if you will excuse us, we need to pack."

Palmerston and Melbourne waved us off, promising to stay until someone came for the dead groom. We reached the house and went immediately to Burley's room. His valet was there, along with Magda, who was busy dressing his leg and said. "The bullet is out and packed with my salve. Dr Jefferson will stitch it closed once he sees him."

Miles nodded, then looked to the valet. "We are leaving. Pack up your master's things; you will be coming with us.

The valet looked relieved and quickly agreed, "Yes, milord." He immediately spun around and entered the dressing room. I could see him pulling down cases and humming.

Lord Burley was sitting in bed and glowering at Magda, but he heard the valet's humming. "My man Sorely doesn't like nor trust the Russians either." Then he swore as Magda finished off the bandage. She took out a vial of laudanum, and he croaked, "No, not until we are out of here. I want my wits about me."

Magda arched a brow, then conceded, "As you wish."

She cleaned and packed up her things and walked out with us. We left Lord Burley with his valet and went to our room to call

Rennie and Tyson to pack. Everything had been set to rights when we entered, but Rennie sat at my dressing table crying while holding my midnight blue gown with the silver trim; she looked up and cried out, "Oh, milady, someone's cut a piece out of your gown."

Magda took the garment out of her hands and growled, "It is from the bodice— over the heart."

She set down her bag and pulled out her templar knife. "I will be right back. Rennie, make up the fire." She left and returned within minutes with a piece of lemon-yellow silk about six inches square. She took her bag over to the hearth, pulled out various herbs, wrapped the silk around them, and then burnt the edges of the silk. Then she moved away from the fire, tied a red string around the bundle, dipped it into her small bottle of aqueous vitriol and carried it out of the room.

When she came back, she smiled at me. "She will never wear that shade of yellow again. Rennie, you are to burn Lady Tinley's gown, now." Rennie was packing but nodded as Magda left.

Miles stared at the gown, "Why?"

Rennie stopped to pick up the gown, glancing down at the midnight silk, heartbroken as she fingered the gown, but she looked up and answered my question, "It's a warning and a curse, milord. If the person who owns that yellow gown touches that bundle and doesn't burn up, it's a warning. If it burns up, it's a curse. That one that Madam Magda made will burn up. The person it's intended for will never come at you again."

I took my gown from Rennie's hand, stuffed it into the fire, and

286

then stood and watched it catch fire. Miles came to my side, took the poker and pushed the gown deeper into the hearth. I glanced at him as he said, "I won't take any chances. Magda's been right too many times for comfort. I nodded in agreement, and we watched my gown burn while Rennie and Tyson packed behind us.

Rennie approached us when there was nothing more left of it but ash, "Time to change, milady."

Miles nodded and went into the dressing room where Tyson was waiting.

Chapter 12

Down the Rabbit Hole

Burley held up well on the journey to Portsmouth. But once onboard the Pelican, he begged for the laudanum after being gingerly placed in his bunk. Then he promptly fell asleep.

Out on the open sea, I climbed to the deck with Judith and my Mother. They both took a deep breath. Mother said, "I love sailing."

Judith nodded. "It is exhilarating. I am so glad that Jibben bought this yacht. It's lovely for coastal trips. It's fast too. He is even thinking of entering her into the Regatta next year."

I was leaning against the railing, looking at the coastline. "I wonder how Palmerston kept the Russians from noticing all of us leaving."

Mother sighed. "I doubt he could, but at least we should have a head start."

I heard Jibben and Miles come to join us, so I asked them what they thought our hosts could do to delay the Russians from following us. Jibben laughed. "Our coachmen took care of that before we took to the road."

"How?"

"The Russians will find that most of their tracings have been tampered with; it will be difficult to mend them and get on the road quickly."

I glanced at Miles. "Will our men be all right heading back to London alone?"

"Your Father made sure that Murphy, Stewart and Andropov returned with four heavily armed irregulars for each carriage. Don't worry, love. They will be fine."

I nodded but still felt unsettled, knowing I would be until we were home. The yacht was swift and as the sun set, we entered the pool of London and disembarked, then found conveyances to take us home. The Lockes escorted Burley and his valet to their home while Edward came with us. We stopped at Edward's first and alighted to ensure that Fiona was safe.

The lights were on, but the door was locked, and only after considerable knocking did the footman, Jason, finally answer. He ignored Edward and said, "It is good to see you, Lord Tinley, but I am afraid Sir Edward is out of town."

Miles nodded. Edward stepped forward to say something, but Miles pulled him back into the dark behind him before he could utter a word. "Thank you, Jason. I am sure he will be in touch when he returns. I hope the young ones are fine."

"Yes, milord Miss Elspeth is well and is constantly with her Mother and Lady Marianne. Even Master Vincent is behaving very well."

Edward pushed at Miles' back, but Jason's eyes were fearful as Miles shook his head no and hissed at his brother, "Stop it!"

Edward relented, knowing that Fiona was in an awkward, if not dangerous, situation. Jason closed the door and locked it again. At least we knew that Marianne was there, seemingly dangerous and delusional.

Miles pulled Edward back into our carriage as Edward was grousing, "Why hasn't Gordon put an end to this, and where is he?"

Miles leaned forward. "Did you not hear Jason? She has Elspeth with her constantly."

Edward spat back, "Well, of course she does. Fiona has to feed her!" Edward slammed a fist against the carriage door. "I want my wife and children out of there!"

Miles moved to sit beside him. "We will get them, Edward—be patient. Perhaps someone got information out to Mr Malcom or Sir Thomas."

Edward's next question was reasonable, "Then why haven't they done something."

"Marianne couldn't have arrived much earlier than we did. They may have just found out."

Edward swiped a hand through his hair. "I suppose you are right, but what are we going to do?"

Miles grinned. "Reconnaissance. Let me send for Jibben and Magda. Hopefully, Marianne won't remember them."

We arrived at our home within a few minutes. Edward and Miles jumped down, then assisted me to alight. The door was opened immediately by Mr Malcom. "I am glad to see you, milord. Miss Jilly is here and in a rare state."

I nodded. "Mr Malcom, will you ask Sir Edward's valet Rabby to join us as soon as possible."

"Yes, milady, you will find Miss Jilly in the library wearing a hole in the carpet."

I peeled off my gloves, removed my bonnet and passed them along with my wrap to our footman Howard. Then I marched to the library, with Edward and Miles following me. I opened the door and found a tearful Jilly pacing back and forth, who jumped at the door opening. "Thank God you have come; I can't find Sir Thomas anywhere. So I sent Uncle Jacob to look for him. She sobbed before adding, "A madman has taken the house hostage!"

Mr Malcom entered the room, "Lord Tinley, Sir Stephen is here with Mr Thornton. Unfortunately, there is a problem."

"Send them in."

Jibben and Thornton came in and paused, looking at each other, then Jacob said, "I am not telling them—you tell them."

Jibben glared at Thornton. "You came for me, not the other way around."

"You live next door to the man! It seemed the smart thing to do. His staff ain't gonna listen to me, and the police are as likely to arrest me for it."

Jilly was chewing on her fingernails and then screeched, "What are you talking about, Uncle!"

Thornton crossed his arms, and Jibben sighed, "Sir Thomas is dead, bludgeoned to death."

I sat down abruptly. "Where?"

Thornton's stubborn expression melted away as he watched me. "He were at the Agency like he was on his way out. I found him just inside the door. No one else was there. So I went looking for Dr Jefferson, but I can't find him anywhere."

Just then, Matthew came walking in. He had his medical bag in hand and must have been here to see Lady Arabella. "What do you need, Jacob?"

Thornton sat down and swallowed hard, Jilly was bouncing on her toes, and Jibben looked sick. Miles gestured to a chair. "Sit down, Matthew."

His face drained of colour. "What's happened? Is it Isabel?"

Miles asked, "No, but where is Isabel?"

"We were to have dinner with Fiona. I came here first to check on Lady Arabella. Then I was to join them." He finally noticed Edward and asked, "Why are you here and not at home."

Edward dropped into a chair and waved a hand at Miles to answer. He glanced at Jilly. "Please, Jilly, sit." She glared at him but sat. Then we launched into what had happened in Hampshire and here. He looked stunned. "Thomas—is dead? And my wife—no one knows!" What are we going to do?"

Miles sucked in his lower lip and rubbed an eye. "Let me think."

I leaned forward. "Should I send for Father?"

Jibben shook his head. "I already sent him a message to explain and asked him to go to the Agency to handle the police."

Jefferson was sitting there, staring at his hands. So I went to the drinks cabinet and poured all the men a whisky." Jilly shook her head when I offered her lemonade or tea.

Miles tossed back his drink and then set the glass aside. "There's nothing we can do about Sir Thomas. Let Colin deal with it. Right now, we need to rescue Fiona and Isabel."

Suddenly there was pounding at the door. Then Lord Hamilton came racing into the room ahead of Mr Malcom. "What in hell happened? I just came from the Agency. I was scheduled to meet with Sir Thomas about the dead Pole Antoni Gzowski, and the place was swarming with Scotland Yard constables. Colin was there. He said you could fill me in that it was too sensitive to discuss in front of the police." He glanced at Matthew, who was staring into his glass. He hadn't looked up or moved since I gave it to him. Then it dawned on him, "It's Sir Thomas. Oh God, Jefferson, I am sorry."

Jefferson chuckled. "He'd probably rather die in his Agency office than in his bed." He wiped a tear from his eye. But I don't know what I'll do if I lose Isabel too."

Hamilton was jolted. "What the hell is going on? What do you mean, lose Isabel too?"

I went and knelt by the doctor's chair. "Matthew, where are your children." He looked at me blankly. "Matthew, where are

Jean and little Thomas."

He stared up at me. "Oh my God—they are with Isabel."

I glance up at Miles. He sucked in a breath, then turned to look out the window. I called out to him, "Miles?" he didn't move. "Miles, what are we going to do?"

There was a commotion in the hallway, and my Mother came in with Isabel Jefferson. Matthew fell to his knees and sobbed. Isabel went to him and knelt, pulling him into her arms. "Irene came and told me about Father." Her eyes were puffy, and her face was tear-stained. "Matthew—"

He sobbed, "Thank God, you are all right. The children, are they home?"

"Yes, of course, darling Jean complained of a tummy ache, so I begged off dinner with Fiona. I didn't want to leave her alone." He stood and pulled her up and into his arms. "Perhaps we should go home. There are things we need to discuss." He turned and looked about at us. "I am sorry, but I don't think I will be much help to you right now. Lady Arabella is doing well, and there's nothing else I can do for her. I will have Grimes look in on her."

I walked to them, hugging Isabel. "Of course, you need to go home. Let us know if there is anything we can do for you."

Isabel nodded. Tears were streaming down her face again. Matthew had pulled himself together as my Mother said, "Take my carriage, Matthew. Colin will be here before too much longer."

He nodded, and with his arm around Isabel, they walked out.

My heart went out to them, and there was now the question facing us of who had killed Sir Thomas. Was it Marianne, the Russians, or someone else? I glanced at Miles. My Mother watched him closely as she said, "Miles, you have made problematic decisions before, and now your family needs you. Fiona and the children need you and Edward to rescue them."

Miles nodded. "I am going to need all of you then. Irene, you and Lissa need to pay a visit and don't let Jason turn you away this time." Then he turned to Jilly, "What room is Marianne holding the children in?"

Jilly's expression was one of confusion. "They be in the guest room next to Lady Johnson's sitting room. But Lady Marianne isn't holding anyone Lord Tinley. It's the man—Anderson who's holding them. He keeps harping at her about journals. He even threatened to kill her. Lady Johnson told me to hide with that tapping code you all use. So, I listened in. I think Lady Marianne is playing at being a madwoman."

Edward rubbed his face. "She is a madwoman."

Jilly shook her head. "Not that I could see Sir Edward. She came to the house and had tea and admired the children. She was happy that you were married and with a family. Then, she left, saying she was going away for a time. Lady Johnson tried to convince her to stay, but she said she couldn't put your family at risk."

Then she comes back almost immediately with this Anderson person holding a pistol on her. Mr Gordon tried to wrestle it from him, but he pounded him to the ground. He's in a bad way. Mrs Gillis is caring for him in the kitchen larder where Anderson locked

295

up all the staff."

Miles asked, "How did you get out?

She glanced at Edward, who looked on the verge of a breakdown. "Out the window in Sir Edward's studio. Down the trees Lord Hamilton said our neighbour should prune back, well they never did, and now they're touching the house."

Edward's head snapped up. "Jilly, you could have fallen and died."

She cocked her head to the side and stared at him. "I've been climbing up and down things harder than trees and the like for years."

He stared at her in disbelief. "In skirts?"

She nodded her head. "There be ways, but I am not about to show yee."

Rabby came into the room then, and Jilly ran to him, wrapping her arms around him and sobbing. He looked at me, lost for what he should do. I motioned for him to hug her back, and he smiled. Rabby didn't know why she was upset, but he took her to a corner settee and sat with her while she explained all that had happened.

I glanced at Hamilton, who seemed flabbergasted, but he finally asked, "Then what is our plan?"

Miles looked at his brother. "Edward, are you ready for this?" He nodded. "I need to hear you say it, Edward. You can't put the rest of us at risk by freezing or bowling in with disregard for the plan."

He glared at Miles. "I am ready, and I can do this."

"Good—now, who here is good at climbing?"

All four men looked at him like he was insane. Rabby spoke up, "Jilly and I can get in if that's what you need."

Miles nodded. "Fine, I need you to open the conservatory doors. Then you are to leave the house and come back here."

Jilly shook her head. "No, we won't—we will head for the larder and let everyone out. You must be incredibly quiet, Lord Tinley, or he will kill them."

Miles nodded. "I understand, Jilly."

Thornton was quietly sipping his whisky. Then he interjected, "Now, just a minute! With Mave not here, Jilly is my responsibility. I am not sure I should let her get mixed up in business like this—it sounds dangerous."

Miles arched a brow, but before he could say anything, Jilly spoke up, "Uncle Jacob—I am of an age now and don't need you telling me what I can and can't do."

Jacob mumbled, "No one ever could—yur just like yur mum."

Jilly smiled. "Thank you, Uncle."

He scowled at her. "That wasn't meant as a compliment."

Jilly ignored him and took Rabby's hand. "We'll unlock the conservatory door for you, Lord Tinley. Give us at least five minutes once we are inside, milord."

Jacob got up. "No need to be climbing any trees. I can pick the lock to the garden door in Sir Edward's study. Then yee can go and unlock the conservatory. I'll go to the larder. I want yee children to nip out the conservatory door and wait in the mews."

I stood. "I am coming with you."

Miles glowered at me. Then behind me, I heard a cough. "I am coming too."

Lady Arabella stood in the doorway. "I am sorry. I was eavesdropping. But I saw Dr Jefferson leave with his wife, and they looked incredibly distressed. So I came down to see what the problem was and if I could help. Then I heard you talking about Marianne." She glanced at Edward. "I am so sorry, Edward, to bring this on you."

Edward offered her his seat. She took his hand as she gingerly lowered herself into it. "It is not your doing, Arabella. Marianne is as much a hostage as my wife and children. We will save them all. I promise."

She smiled and patted his cheek. "You have always been the knight errant Edward. But Anderson is a heartless killer. I can be the distraction you need."

I asked her, "What makes you think that?"

"Because I got away. I can only assume that Anderson would hate it when he cannot complete a job. He's the type that likes to extend the pain for as long as he can, and I got away during one of his rest periods. Brewster would have taken my place, God rest

298

her soul, but he would still think of me as unfinished business."

"I don't understand how he knew Marianne had gone there."

She sniffed. "Harris probably set him to watch people's homes where she would likely go. Marianne and I had very few faithful friends. Edward was one of them."

Miles bit his lower lip and asked, "Has Marianne ever been violent?"

"No. Why do you ask?"

"Sir Thomas was found murdered in our previous home on Cornwall Terrace. It's a suite of offices now."

She nodded. "I am aware of the Agency, Lord Tinley. Rupert often talked about wanting to blow it up, but it was all talk."

Miles nodded, and then Hamilton interrupted, "Can you tell us how long your husband has been passing information to the Russians."

She chuckled. "So you know about that too." She took a deep breath. Until then, she had turned her face away, not showing her blind eye. Now she faced us. Its milky whiteness was unsettling. Now that the swelling had subsided, you could barely notice that one cheekbone was slightly depressed from having been fractured.

She smiled at my pursual. "I am getting used to it, Lady Tinley. Your housekeeper has set herself the task of making eyepatches, several to be exact. She's a sweet and thoughtful girl."

Then she sighed and licked her lips. "As to your question Lord

Hamilton. My husband has been going to his club once a week for over two years to attend political meetings. I followed him once." She chuckled. "I thought he had a mistress, but he went to the Russian Embassy. I discovered from the local constable that he was a regular visitor once a week in the evening like clockwork."

Hamilton rubbed his chin. "Do you know an Antoni Gzowski?"

"Yes, he was an associate of my Father's and yours, a political activist that went into exile in France."

"May I ask what he had in common with our Fathers?"

"I have no idea, but it must have been profitable, or my Father would not have remained friends with him even after you people ruined him."

Hamilton grimaced at her words. "Thank you, Lady Arabella."

"I didn't mean to insult you, Lord Hamilton. I am merely stating facts."

He bowed his head, "No offence taken."

She looked about the room. "I think I should be the one to confront Anderson. May I have a pistol, Lord Tinley?"

Jibben coughed and cleared his throat. "You must excuse my rudeness, but one eye will change your depth perception, and you may not be able to hit a target accurately."

She sighed. "I hadn't thought of that. Would you accompany me then, Sir Stephen and be my eyes?"

Jibben bowed. "I would be delighted, milady."

Jilly was up and bouncing on her heels. "Can you stop patting each other on the back and get moving?"

Miles nodded. "Good advice, Jilly. Let's get ready. He called Mr Malcom, told him our plan, and then asked my Mother to explain it to my Father when he arrived. Then he opened a weapons cache he had behind a bookcase and passed them out. Jilly and Rabby waved their knives at Miles. "This be all we need, milord." Then they disappeared out the door with Thornton.

I took Lady Arabella upstairs and had Rennie and Dolly help us dress in men's clothing. Once we reached the garden terrace, the men were already waiting for us, and we slipped out the garden gate. When we arrived at Edward's home, all the rooms on the ground floor were lit, and I could hear Elspeth crying. Then I saw a shadow pass a drawing room window. It was Fiona, and she came out onto the terrace and called out, "Edward!"

Edward ran forward and grabbed his wife as we moved quickly into the house. We could see in the light that she had been crying. He hugged her closely, saying, "Oh, thank God, you are all right. What of the children?"

"They are fine. Gena is putting them to bed. Lady Marianne was so brave she kept them safe anytime that man Anderson threatened them. She would put herself between him and them."

"Where is she?"

Fiona gulped. "I don't know. We both attacked Anderson at the same time. I hit him over the head with a candlestick, and she cut him with a letter opener. The blood seemed to send her into a frenzy, and she ran from the house. I sent Jason after her, but he lost her in the park."

Thornton came into the room, looking pale. "It's a slaughterhouse in there."

Miles focused on Fiona, who was now sobbing on Edward's shoulder. It was then I noticed her gown was covered in blood. Miles patted his brother's back, "I will go." Edward nodded.

I grabbed his arm. "I am coming with you."

Jibben and Lady Arabella stood side by side as she said, "I need to see that he's dead."

He took her arm, and they walked beside Miles and me out of the room and up the stairs. Jilly was sitting on the stairs with Rabby. Both looked sick, but they ignored us. We walked partway down the hall to a door that was standing wide open.

Gena was walking down the hall towards us with Vincent and Elspeth. She looked haunted. "I can't get them to settle." Tears were streaming down her face. Miles stood in front of the door as Vincent ran to him. "Unca Mils." Miles lifted him up, hugging him tightly as he buried his head into Miles' shoulder.

I reached out and ruffled his hair. He opened his eyes and looked at me. Then, he said, "Hello, Aunny Liss."

I smiled at him. "Miles, you should go with Gena. Take the children down to Fiona and Edward. They need you. We can deal with this."

He glanced at me, unsure. "I know what to expect. Remember I saw those rooms in Somerset where Marianne was forced to watch those people being murdered."

He nodded and walked off with Gena carrying Elspeth as Vincent asked, "Badman gone?"

Miles spoke honestly, "Yes, he's gone."

"Good." Then they disappeared down the stairs.

I stepped in front of the open doorway and addressed Lady Arabella. "I believe you know the horrors that Marianne was exposed to in Somerset." She nodded. "You need to know that conceptually understanding and seeing it is very different."

She nodded again and held onto Jibben's arm tighter. I stood aside and then followed them into the room. It was not as bad as the rooms in the Young's house had been, but it was still a horror."

Lady Arabella gasped, "My God!"

Anderson's body lay before us, one side of his head was caved in, and his throat was slit. Blood was everywhere. Jibben unwrapped Lady Arabella's arm, walked to the bed, pulled off the counterpane, and threw it over the body. "There's nothing else to be done. The Police will need to be called, and we need to get our story straight."

Arabella grabbed his sleeve. "We can't tell them about Marianne. They will notify Rupert about her and me."

He nodded. "We will think of something."

"Can't we dump his body in the river? No one will care."

Jibben shook his head. "We don't do things that way, milady."

She was panic-stricken. "I can't have Rupert know where I am
."

He patted her hand. "He won't, I promise."

We closed and locked the door and found our way back to the drawing room, where Edward held Vincent and spoke to him quietly. I think he was telling him a story. While Fiona was at his side, feeding Elspeth. Gena was sitting near the hearth—she looked shattered. I went to her side. "Gena?" she looked up at me. I had forgotten how young she was, so I opened my arms, and she came to me. "It's all right, Gena. Go ahead and cry."

And cry she did until Mrs Gillis, the cook, came in and took charge of her. "Come now, girl, I've got the kettle on. You come with me, and I will tell you about my time in Devon when I was a girl. My, I was an adventuress then."

Gena sniffed, then giggled. The young were so resilient, which was good, as I heard her say to Gena, "Now Jilly will need you to be strong for her. She's terribly upset, and she's downstairs with Rabby. Come along, and let's see if we can't cheer them up."

I turned to Miles, who was smiling at his brother and his family. Jibben was poised by the terrace doors speaking to Jacob, who nodded, then spun on his heels and trotted off. Arabella stood close by, gazing out the door.

I walked over to watch Jacob disappear into the night. "Where have you sent Jacob?"

"To muster his sources and start looking for Marianne."

I arched a brow. "You think he can find her?"

"If she has had a mental break, she will likely run through the streets. So we need to find her before someone coshes her or she goes into hiding."

Arabella was staring at him, horrified. "You sent that man after my sister?"

Jibben nodded. "He and his mates are more likely to find her than we are."

She became angry. "You, stupid man! She doesn't know him. And you expect her to go willingly with them?"

Jibben had his back up at being called stupid "She is a wild thing right now, milady, and Jacob is very good at taming wild things without hurting them. We don't know how she will react if anyone looking like us were to approach her."

"What do you mean looking like us?"

"Gentlemen and Ladies. Think about it, who has harmed her the most? It was not the likes of Jacob that betrayed her but the people she should have been able to trust. Believe me, Lady Arabella, I know what I am talking about."

She looked sceptical but nodded. "I will have to trust you, Sir Stephen, since I have no other allies."

He chuckled. "Better us than nothing, eh?"

She smiled. "I am a bit of a snob, aren't I."

Miles came over to join us. "It is hard to trust people you once believed were your enemies."

She arched a brow, "You are very different from what I remember, Miles."

He laughed. "Yes, I am not as angry."

Edward came behind him and added, "But he is still just as stubborn."

I smiled. "That's a family trait that you share with Miles."

Edward smirked. "You have the same trait, dear sister."

Miles chuckled and said, "More so, actually." I rolled my eyes until I noticed Arabella watching us with an expression of longing.

She clasped her hands before her. "I have never seen family interaction so intimate. My brothers were always in competition with each other."

Miles nodded. "Speaking of brothers. Justin is back in London. He should be ensconced in his townhouse by now." From the look on her face, she was confused. He added, trying to make it sound trivial. "He was wounded in the leg by a Russian at Broadlands."

"Should I go to him!"

I took her hand. "You have only just risen from your sickbed. Lord Burley is wounded. He wouldn't be able to protect you if you stayed with him. But do you want to see him?"

But she shook her head. "No—no, I can't trust him yet. Rupert will go to him. You said my husband was in Hampshire. I know him; he will return here now that you have left. I can't let him find

Marianne or me."

Edward rose and came to us. "Arabella, you can stay here with us. Rupert needn't know."

She glanced at me. "No, not after what you have already been through." She turned to me and pleaded, "May I remain with you, Lady Tinley? He will not think to look for me there."

I glanced at Miles, who said, "I think that's an excellent idea. Edward, you, Fiona, and the children are welcome to stay with us. I will send for Dr Archer, and until he arrives, I will ask Dr Grimes and Magda to take care of Mr Gordon."

Fiona had finished feeding Elspeth and joined us. "I would like that, Miles, but only for one night; the children would benefit from being with Charlotte and Alex."

Edward called Jason, "Tell Gena, Rabby and Jilly to pack enough for a few days and have the carriage brought around." Fiona glared at him but did not challenge him. "After that, find the local constable and send him for the police and Dr Grimes. Then off to bed with you."

Jason nodded. "Yes, milord." He could barely hide a yawn but waited until the carriage came to the front entrance. Then, as Edward took his hat from him, Jason said, "Nathan and I will make sure everything is locked up tight, sir."

Edward nodded. "Make sure the grooms lock up the mews too, and keep your weapons close."

"Yes, Sir Edward." Then he went off to find the constable.

Gena and Jilly waited in the entry hall while Rabby and Nathan clambered down the stairs with all the children's things and cases for Fiona and Edward. Then Jilly and Rabby jumped into the second carriage, which led off.

Miles helped me into the landau after the others climbed in, saying. "Edward and I will stay until the police and Grimes arrive. I will ask him to have a look at Gordon."

Then he stepped back, and the carriage moved off the short distance to our home. When we arrived home, we were greeted by Lord Hamilton and my Mother and Father.

Fiona and I went up with Gena to see the children to bed. I spoke to Anne about the trauma Gena had been through. Then I showed Fiona to her and Edward's room, where Jilly was already putting out her things for the night. She looked at Jilly and said, "Off to bed with you, lass. I can manage from here." Jilly bit her lip and looked like she would argue, but she nodded and left.

"Fiona, you are exhausted. You should go to bed."

"I should, but I don't think I could sleep a wink."

She looked at my face as I said, "Think of Elspeth."

She understood my meaning and said, "I know the stress could dry up my milk, so I will get ready for bed and try to rest." I smiled, hugged her, and left her sitting at the dressing table, removing her hairpins.

I returned to the drawing room, where Jibben yawned and looked at Hamilton. "I am for home; I need to be with Judith. I think it's time we leave, Hamilton. It's been a long day. I will let

Magda know that she needs to look in on Gordon tomorrow." They both waved and nodded, then left.

Edward and Miles arrived shortly after they departed. "Grimes and the police arrived fairly quickly and have taken things in hand." He glanced at Lady Arabella. "I didn't tell them that Marianne was a mad woman. The police listened to Jason and Nathan's story, which bears that out. They examined Mr Gordon and agreed that Anderson's death was self-defence." Then he looked at me. "Have you told your Father that Marianne is gone?" I shook my head. I hadn't told them anything.

My Father looked defeated. "Wonderful."

Miles nodded. "Locke sent Thornton and his people out looking for her. That's all we can do for now unless you have any better ideas, Colin."

Father rubbed his temples as if he had a headache. "No, that was sound thinking. With Samuel in the north, you will have to step up and take charge, Miles."

My husband's face clouded with doubt. "I am an agent Colin, not a leader. We should send for Samuel. He's your second. Or perhaps you should take over responsibility for the Agency."

My Father rubbed his forehead. "We can wait on that decision until I can talk to Samuel. But Miles, while you might be impulsive, you have excellent instincts. I would recommend you to the King as Sir Thomas's replacement if Samuel doesn't want it."

Miles shook his head. "What of Hamilton or Locke?"

"My Father chuckled. "Hamilton is a good agent but not as

creative as you; besides, he still has ties to the Home Office. As far as Locke goes, if you're impulsive, then Locke is reckless."

Miles chuckled. "True, but it's a moot point right now. I suggest that we all retire and wait for Thornton to report. I doubt we will hear from him before morning." My Father yawned and agreed. He took my Mother's arm, and they left. Lady Arabella excused herself and climbed the stairs wearily while Miles and I adjourned to his study. I watched him pace the room. "Miles, please sit down. You are making me dizzy."

He came to sit beside me. "You should retire too."

"Not if you are not coming with me." His brow was furrowed, and his lips were pressed tightly together. "If the Agency leadership is bothering you, just refuse it, Miles."

He sighed. "It is not that. A small part of me wants the leadership role. I have felt for some time that Wiseman wasn't as progressive as he could be." He bowed his head and clasped his hands in front of him. "But now is hardly the time to discuss this: the poor man lost his life, and we have no idea why. That should be a priority."

"Do you think his death is connected to the Russians?"

"I wouldn't be surprised, but I honestly don't know. I believe Sir Thomas' and Gzowski's deaths are related. He and Hamilton were working on Gzowski's death. I will have to speak to him tomorrow about what they found out."

"Perhaps you should go to Sir Thomas' office and see if he left any clues about what he found that might get him killed."

Miles nodded. "I will speak to your Father about it. In the meantime, I will put a few irregulars on Hamilton tomorrow to watch his back."

"He won't like that."

He grinned. "No, he won't. But if you tell Nell, she will convince him it's the right thing to do."

"You think he could be in danger?"

"Yes—but it depends on what he knows."

I nodded. "Or what someone thinks he knows."

"Exactly. Now love, I think we should both go to bed. You need your rest, and I am suddenly feeling exhausted."

Mr Malcom was waiting in the entry hall for us. "We are locked up tight as we can be milord."

Miles patted him on the back and told him about his friend Mr Gordon. Our butler nodded. "Gordon is a tough fellow and has fought back from worse. Thank you for telling me, and if you don't mind, I will drop by and see him tomorrow."

"Of course, Mr Malcom. Now goodnight to you."

Chapter 13

More Questions than Answers?

A full day had come and gone without a word from Thornton.

Edward had a crew of men into his house to rip out the room of carnage. It was to be redesigned entirely. Then he secretly had Father Kelly come as he said to set any restless spirits to rest. Miles teased him that he was a latent Catholic, knowing he had no love for our Vicar Strom, who would undoubtedly cast aspersions on Edward for conducting pagan rites in his home. Fortunately for the family, the vicar liked Fiona despite her upbringing in the Church of Scotland.

Lady Arabella was restless and concerned about her brother, so I decided to accompany her on a visit to his home. His new townhouse was on the edge of Mayfair and just qualified for respectability. Arabella was shocked. She had been unaware that he had sold their Father's townhouse and other properties to cover the mountain of debt he had inherited. He lived modestly with just his valet, a maid of all work and a cook.

"I had no idea that Justin had come down so low."

I smiled at her. "It's not so bad. He has economised to pay down his debt quickly."

She sighed. "I wish I could help him."

A thought came to me then, "I think you can."

"How?"

"Your grandparent's property must be worth a considerable amount. The house might be a ruin, but I understand that the land is extensive and some of the county's best, and according to a reliable source, Lord Palmerston's is eager to discuss purchasing it."

She smiled. "I think that would be an exceptional idea."

Miles had been kind enough to send Dr Grimes around, and we found him tending to Burley. I waited downstairs while Arabella went up to see Justin. His maid of all work brought tea and biscuits after Dr Grimes joined me. "It was good that Grandmama acted so quickly to care for him. Since he returned, he hasn't seen a doctor, and some infection has set in. It is not bad, but I will have Grandmama make up some of her potion for him."

Grimes nervously crumbled a biscuit over his plate before speaking again, "Could I ask a favour of you? Would you send for Archer? Jefferson has asked me to look in on his patients since Isabel is a wreck, and he needs to spend some time with her."

I nodded. "Miles already anticipated the need and sent an express to Archer this morning."

"Thank you." He looked about the room and sighed, "How the mighty have fallen. I never expected to see a Browne living in such meagre circumstances."

I nodded. "It's hardly meagre, but Lord Burley has his eyes and heart set on an heiress. I believe he's trying to prove his worth to her Father by not living above his means and paying down his debt to the exclusion of the usual creature comforts of our class."

He chuckled. "Is it working?"

"The lady is enamoured, but the Father is not impressed so far."

"Too bad this place could use a woman's touch. Perhaps Lady Arabella could stay with him."

I shook my head. "Not while her husband is alive and has the law on his side."

"He did that to her?" he pointed to his eye.

"He had his valet do it while he watched and made suggestions."

Grimes dropped his plate onto the table, staring at his hands. "God knows I am far from a perfect husband. I could never raise a hand to Mina like that or order anyone else to do it. I can't comprehend what kind of man does that."

"Neither can I, Peter, neither can I."

He licked his lips as if thinking about something difficult that he wanted to say. "I have completed the autopsy on Sir Thomas and know the weapon used to bludgeon him."

"Was it left behind?"

"No, it wasn't. But I am positive it was an Imperial Field Marshall's baton."

"How could you tell?"

He grimaced, "The inscription on it left an imprint on his brain tissue read *'Terror belli, decus pacis'*, in English that means *terror in war, ornament in peace.*"

I shook my head. "Are you telling me a Frenchman killed him?"

"Yes, or someone who wants us to believe so."

I clutched at my throat as I thought, "Oh God—Johnathan Campeau's Father was a French Field Marshall, but they are both dead."

Grimes stared out the window. "It might have been someone associated with the family or wanting you to believe it was—Jean Campeau."

"That's possible. However, it couldn't be Jean. He should be in Wales by now."

"You hope."

I was impatient, waiting for Arabella to finish her visit so I could tell Miles what the doctor had discovered. Then, finally, Grimes stood up, brushed down his trousers, and straightened his waistcoat. "I am off to the hospital now. I should be there most of the day if you require me."

I thanked him, sent him on his way, and sat there in a quandary as I tried not to think of Jean Campeau betraying our trust, but it was difficult to resist.

Arabella came down, smiling. "He's asleep now. Sorley is sitting with him. I am glad to see that he is so devoted to my brother."

315

She chuckled. "Living with you has made me look at servants with different eyes."

I smiled and offered her tea which she refused. Now that she had seen her brother, she was anxious to return to our home. She was incredibly nervous about being out and about. Pulling her heavy veil down over her face, we went out to our waiting carriage. As we climbed in, I saw Lord Harris riding past. He gave me a sharp disdainful look. Fortunately, he didn't stop, but I wasn't sure that he hadn't seen Arabella despite her veil. So, I asked Sean to drive about for a bit and had Mark and Jackson keep an eye out for his lordship.

I didn't tell Arabella I had seen her husband and only explained that I thought she would like to take the air even though we were enclosed in the carriage. She didn't question me and seemed to relax against the squabs, but she didn't lift her veil. After a brief time, Sean headed back in the direction of our home, finally pulling into the mews at my request rather than letting us out at the front door. Lady Arabella looked at me, saying, "Thank you for ensuring my husband didn't see me. I appreciate your efforts not to lead him back here as well."

I nodded so she had seen him after all. I should have known that she would be wary, "I hope you don't mind coming in through the kitchen."

She chuckled. "You know I haven't been in one since I was a little girl, and my Mother was alive. So this will be an experience."

I was surprised to hear that she had never been in her kitchen, but at least she wouldn't have anything to compare ours to since Kit, our young assistant cook, was an unusual addition to a traditional London kitchen.

He and Mrs Jonas were busy putting the finishing touches to luncheon when Mrs Jonas looked up and smiled. "Lady Tinley, aren't you just glowing? I've made that cock-a-leekie soup you developed a taste for when in Scotland."

"Mrs Jonas, you are a wonder and is that a chocolate tart I spy over there?"

"Aye, milady, for the pudding tonight." She smiled at Lady Arabella and then looked back at me. "I've still got to make the dinner rolls. Would you like to help?"

"I'd love to." I glanced at Lady Arabella. "It is great fun and wonderful therapy to help a body forget its problems."

She didn't look convinced until Kit came out with an armload of ingredients saying, "Come, Lady Arabella, it'll do you good. I'll help you." He gave her a winning smile even though he couldn't see her expression.

She pulled off her bonnet with its heavy veil and set it aside. Dolly was still working on the eye patches for her, so the eye was in full view. Neither Kit nor Mrs Jonas reacted other than Kit saying, "That's more like it, milady. Now let me get you an apron. He set aside his armload of ingredients and took her bonnet and shawl while handing her an apron. I took care of myself while Kit helped Lady Arabella, teaching her the rudiments of baking bread and rolls while chatting about his life as a cook. He soon had her laughing as he instructed her. Afterwards, we sat and had tea. It was then time for us to change for luncheon, and we left them with promises to return for additional lessons.

Lady Arabella chuckled. "I don't think I have ever enjoyed anything so much." She concentrated on climbing the stairs but asked me, "Do you often do that?"

"Oh my, yes, as I said, it is very therapeutic. Kneading bread is wonderful when you are in a temper." I laughed, and she chuckled along with me. "But honestly, learning cookery has been a boon at times when we have been stranded without the usual amenities."

She stopped and looked up at the General's portrait. "I don't suppose he would approve."

"No, I don't suppose he would have."

"I am surprised you have his portrait hanging here, considering your history?"

I chuckled. "I was surprised as well, but he serves his purpose and reminds me of how far I have come." We continued up the stairs and went to change.

As Rennie was fixing my hair, Miles came in. "Where is Arabella?

"In her room, Dolly is helping her to change into one of my day dresses."

He screwed up his face. "You had better take her up to the nursery. Lord Harris is here with Edward."

"What!"

"He insists that he saw you and Arabella at Burley's home."

"Burley told him you came to see him to assure yourself that Dr Grimes had been there and he was being cared for appropriately."

"And he's not convinced?"

"He said he saw another woman with you, and he's convinced it was Arabella. Edward is trying to persuade him that he was wrong that the woman with you was Fiona since you would never go to a single man's home alone."

I grimaced. "He must know that Anderson is dead and is grasping at straws."

He nodded. "I need you to convince him."

"Is Fiona here?"

"No, she went home with the children. She insisted she would not be driven from her home by one bad memory."

I nodded and looked at Rennie. "I need you to explain all this to Lady Arabella and take her to the nursery. Do not let her leave under any circumstances."

Rennie nodded. "Yes, milady."

I stood up and took a deep breath. "I am ready."

Lord Harris was arguing with Edward when we entered Miles' study. Harris came at me shaking his fist. "Where is she!"

I glanced at Edward, hoping I looked perplexed as I focused back on Harris. "Who?"

He clenched and unclenched his fist as he raised it toward me,

Miles growled and stepped forward. Harris was wise enough to lower it. "My wife! I saw her with you at Burley's house. Don't deny that you were there."

"Of course, I was there. After all, we brought Burley back to London and had a physician of our acquaintance see to him. He lives with minimal staff, and I wanted to ensure he had all he needed. My sister-in-law Lady Johnson was with me as a chaperon."

He snapped back at me, "Come now, you are hardly friends with Burley."

I nodded. "True, but he doesn't have many, does he? He was injured while with our party at Broadlands, and we felt a responsibility towards him." Then I wrinkled my brow, hoping I looked perplexed. "I thought your wife was in the country for her health."

He ground his teeth, "She, she—" he now looked doubtful that he should give voice to his lie. "Yes, she was—or should be, I mean. I was just startled seeing you at Burley's home. I must have been mistaken."

"I feel sorry for Lord Burley. He's lost a great deal over the years. But he is an enterprising young man with a good plan to recoup his fortune and regain his family's place in society."

Harris's eyes gleamed. "Really?" He half-smiled, "His Father had a talent for making money."

I glared at him. "His Father was a criminal in every sense of the word. The current Lord Burley is nothing of the kind."

Harris sneered, "You are mistaken, Lady Tinley. The apple never falls far from the tree."

I shook my head. "Believe what you like, Lord Harris, but I will reserve judgment until he proves me wrong."

He made for the door, then spun on his heel. "Why was your sister-in-law wearing a heavy veil?"

I pointed to the window where the sun was shining brightly. "She is a redhead, Lord Harris, it was a sunny day, and her skin is very fair. Freckles are never in fashion." He glared at me but made no rebuttal and stormed out with Edward following.

We waited to hear the door close. My hands were shaking from our encounter. I still wasn't sure if Lord Harris believed me. "Now what? Lady Arabella can't stay here."

Miles ran a hand through his hair, "We will need to get her out of London somehow." I nodded. Then he asked me, "How was your visit with Burley?"

Then, I remembered what Dr Grimes told me about the murder weapon used on Sir Thomas. I shuddered as I told them what he had found and shared my suspicion that the murderer might have been Jean Campeau.

He shook his head, "It's not Campeau. Your Father was here earlier. He received a letter from Montgomery written just yesterday. It came with the dispatches from Wales. He and Campeau arrived without incident, and he's settled in." He glanced down at his desk, where papers were scattered all over the top. "Then someone is sending a message to us that the

Brocklehurst organisation still has us in their sights."

"But why kill Sir Thomas?"

He shrugged. "Revenge for us killing Johnathan Campeau? Perhaps they hope to cause disorder at the Agency by removing him, or he surprised them. It is impossible to say."

"Have you heard anything from Matthew and Isabel?"

"Just that the funeral is set for Sunday."

I nodded. "I should go to Isabel.

"I wouldn't do that right now. She's holding the Agency responsible for his death, which means everyone associated with it."

"She's in pain, Miles—she will understand eventually that her Father was the Agency."

He looked down at his hands. "You might be right. I suppose time will tell, but I still wouldn't go there yet."

"Very well." I sighed and gazed out the window. "Miles, I just had a thought. What about Wales—we could send Lady Arabella there. She would be safe and out of the way there."

He pulled on his ear and cocked his head. "That might work. We will need to consult with your Father and Lady Arabella."

"Consult with me about what?" Lady Arabella was standing in the doorway. "I saw Rupert ride away, and I eluded your maid."

I chuckled. "We have been talking that it might be prudent to get you out of London. The Blackburn seat is in Wales. It's a vast property by the sea and out of the way."

She smiled. "You want me to leave you to find Marianne on your own?"

I frowned. "Realistically, there's nothing much you can do, Arabella."

She sighed. "But you will need someone she trusts when you find her."

"We have Edward and Fiona with us, and she trusted me once before. Perhaps she will again."

She sighed, and the light in her good eye dimmed in defeat. "I should probably argue more, but I don't have your tenacity, Lady Tinley. I am not brave."

"You are brave, Lady Arabella, in so many ways. But you will need to leave London. So let us take care of you."

She nodded, clasping her hands in front of her. "When do I leave."

Miles smiled. "Let me make the arrangements. Do you mind sailing?"

She grinned. "I have never been on the sea, but I look forward to it."

My stomach suddenly grumbled, and I blushed while Miles snickered, saying, "Shall we see to luncheon? I understand there is cock-a-leekie soup on the menu." Lady Arabella and I giggled as he took our arms and escorted us to the dining room.

Miles was on his second bowl of soup when we told him that Arabella had made the rolls. He stopped chewing, looked closely at the bread, and grinned, "Well done, milady. It took Lissa at least three tries before she got them right."

I was astonished that he would say such a thing about me, no matter how true it was. Lady Arabella peered at me in shock until I burst out laughing, tore off a bit of bread, and threw it at him. He laughed and called for our dog Bard to eat the crumbs on the floor, but Bard took the roll Miles had been eating right out of his hand instead. Arabella started to titter, then laughed at Miles' dumbfounded expression that the dog had snatched his roll. She finally choked off the laugh and said, "Is this what family life is supposed to be like?"

Miles shrugged. "I can't speak for anyone else, but this is our family life."

She smiled softly, and I could see the longing for a different future in her eye. "I have never been to Wales. What is it like?"

I said the first thing that came into my head, "Beautiful, haunting, and when a storm comes in from the sea, it is a beast but still beautiful."

"It sounds wonderful."

Miles looked at her frankly. "I will start making the appropriate arrangements after luncheon."

"Thank you."

Once we finished, Lady Arabella and I selected a book from the library, then went to the terrace and watched Mr Jonas putter about the garden.

About an hour later, after entering the drawing room, Miles joined us to sit in front of a chess problem. Arabella wandered over to scrutinise the board and asked if he wanted to play a game. He agreed, and it turned into an intense match. Both players were highly competitive. They were engrossed in their game when Jacob Thornton came strolling through the garden and up to the terrace. I motioned for him to come in, which he did, closing the door behind him and sitting down. "I am a mite parched milady, do you think—"

I looked at Miles, who was chuckling as he said, "I will get it, my dear."

Thornton smacked his lips. "A large one will save you another trip, milord."

Miles nodded just as Thornton noticed Lady Arabella, he didn't rise, but he nodded, smiled, and said, "Milady."

She, in turn, acknowledged him with a simple bob of her head, "Mr Thornton."

Miles returned with the decanter and glasses. I arched a brow as Jacob took a deep quaff of the glass of whisky Miles offered him, and then I asked, "Well?"

He cleared his throat and sat up straight. "Yes, well—you'd be shocked at the number of mad women there be in London that ain't in madhouses. By the way, Father Kelly told me that Blane House had burnt down. The nuns and most of the patients got out. They be staying at the school until they can find another place. One person died, someone named Mrs Danvers. She was seen dancing in flames." He shook his head. "Sad thing."

Miles was losing patience, but Jacob was either terribly blunt or a storyteller. Unfortunately, there was nothing in the middle, so I interrupted his narrative, "What of Lady Marianne?"

"Yes, now she is a tricky one, never stays in one place for long, is highly adaptable and good at stealing food. By the way, yee owe me half a crown. I paid the vendor for the carrots she stole in the market and the clothing she nicked in Petticoat Lane."

Miles rubbed a hand over his face. "Done, now where is she, Jacob?"

"As I said, she don't stay put for long. So Rabby got leave from Mr Edward to follow her; he and his friends are trying to herd her back this way."

I was concerned about the safety of Rabby and the others. Before Sir Thomas was murdered, he had approved employing men, women, and children from the rookeries as Irregulars in London's rougher areas. They had the survival skills that we didn't and could operate with impunity in and around the rookeries and the docks where we couldn't.

Arabella frowned. "You are herding my sister like she's some animal."

"I am sorry, milady, but she's as skittish as a starving cat. Sister Bride is out there looking too, and she may be able to win her trust if anyone can. She's used to dealing with wary people. Your sister, by the way, seems to have a soft spot for the disabled, giving them the food and clothes she steals. But aye, milady, she'll come this way eventually. As I said, she's skittish." He drank back the contents of his glass and set it down. "Now I've got to go see about me, boys."

Arabella "You're supervising them personally?"

He looked taken aback. "Of course—it's me job." He rose then and left.

She watched him walk through the garden, then turned to me, "He is dedicated."

I smiled. "When he talks about his boys, it's his ferrets, not the Irregulars he's referring to."

She swallowed hard and coughed while staring at me. "His ferrets? Is he the famous ferret man that his Majesty has spoken about?"

I nodded. "Yes, That's Jacob Thornton, the Rat Catcher to the Crown."

She giggled just as Dolly knocked and entered through the open door to the hallway. "Excuse me, milady, milord, but Lady Arabella's new clothes have arrived."

"Thank you, Dolly." I glanced at her. "Shall we?"

She was gobsmacked. "But how?"

Miles smiled. "Mrs Mac took your things that you wore here and was able to recreate your measurements. If anything needs alterations before you leave, Dolly can help. She's incredibly talented."

Dolly blushed. "I have also finished your eyepatches, milady."

Arabella looked at Miles, then me. "I don't know when I will be able to pay you back."

Miles waved his hand. "It's nothing, Lady Arabella. We are glad to help."

She stood up and went with Dolly. After they left, I went to my husband and kissed him. "You are a sweet man."

He chuckled. "You have always told me how a new frock could lift your spirits."

I kissed him again, then went to Arabella's room, where I found Jane, Rennie and Dolly with her. They were unpacking all manner of clothing. Arabella turned to me with a tear rolling down her cheek. How could you know what colours and styles?"

I smiled, saying, "It was my husband. He's very observant and has an exceptional eye for style and colour."

"Lord Tinley is responsible for all of this?"

I nodded. "Yes."

"Oh my—I've never known a man who is interested in what I like or has such exquisite taste."

I snorted, "It runs in the family. Actually, most of the men I know are creative and observant in one way or another."

She was like a young woman looking at her first Ball Gown, and as if reading my mind, Jane pulled out a fabulous turquoise silk gown that would be perfect at any Ball. Arabella fingered the material smiling, so I suggested, "Why don't you try them all on, so Dolly and the girls will know which ones need alteration."

She stood up and turned to me, looking like the haughty Arabella I had previously known. "I can't accept this."

I sighed and clasped my hands in front of me. "Of course, if you wish. Then I will also take back my dresses that we altered for you. But you will look odd walking about naked."

Her mouth fell open in shock. "What?"

"Lady Arabella, my husband did this because he is a kind and compassionate man. You will need clothes, and you will need to dress like the lady you are. If you want to repay him at a later date, you can try. But I warn you, it will be impossible. So please accept our gift." She nodded and went back to admiring the clothing.

I turned to leave and said, "Enjoy." I decided to visit with my children once I was out in the hallway, and after walking to the nursery door, I heard Alex's high-pitched squeal. I opened the door to find my husband, with his coat off, lying on the floor, dangling Alex above his head and Charlotte sitting on her Father's chest, bouncing up and down, calling out, "Horsey, horsey!"

Miles laughed but could barely catch his breath as Charlotte bounced up and down. I reached down to take Alex from him so he could wrestle our eldest off him and tickle her into submission, to her great delight. Alex was kicking to be let down just as Miles flipped over onto his knees, so I placed Alex on his back, holding him while Miles scampered about pretending to be a horse. Charlotte waited patiently for her turn, and once she traded places with her brother, she dug her heels into Miles' sides, causing him to exhale loudly and collapse. She seemed delighted as if he had galloped around the room. "Papa—you promised me a pony. When do I get a pony?"

He rolled over and sat up, pulling her to his chest. "On your next birthday, my dear. How old will you be then?"

"That's easy, papa. I'll be six."

Alex crowed, "Me six, six— six."

Charlotte laughed at her brother. "No, silly, I'll be six. You are two, almost three."

I put Alex down beside them. "Me tree!"

Miles laughed. "You have to enunciate, old man. It is three, not tree."

Alex frowned at his Father, grabbed his nose, then leaned in and screeched, "Tree! Papa!"

Miles covered his ears. "Tree it is, then." Charlotte and Alex were both laughing.

Anne came in just then and bobbed her head at Miles and me. Then put her hands on her hips "Miss Charlotte, Master Alex, look at your clothes. They are all mussed up. You'll have to change before we go to the park."

Alex frowned, looking down at his jumper. "No, Annie—no, change me."

She smiled. "We will see."

Charlotte came and hugged me, then patted my slightly rounded belly, "Hello, baby Crispin Corwin."

I arched a brow at Miles, then looked down at Charlotte "Crispin Corwin?"

She nodded. "Alex and I think you should call the baby Crispin or Corwin."

I smiled. "Alex thinks so, too?" she nodded so hard it set her curls bouncing.

Miles smiled. "Let Mama and I think about it."

Charlotte grinned, then took Alex's hand. "Come, Alex, let's go play in the park." Alex trundled off with his sister waving at us as Anne led them out of the playroom.

Miles smiled at me as I reached out a hand to pull him upright. He straightened his clothing, put his coat back on, and, taking my arm, we walked out and down the corridor. "What you did for Lady Arabella was remarkable. She wasn't sure if she should accept them at first. But I convinced her it was the lesser of two evils."

Miles stopped and drew back. "Two evils?"

"Yes, the first one being indebted to you, or the second, choosing to walk about naked."

He burst out laughing. "You rarely mince words, do you, my love."

I grinned. "I have my moments." We continued walking towards the stairs, and as we passed Lady Arabella's room, I could hear giggling. I pulled him back as we came to the head of the stairs. "Do you think Jacob will be able to drive Marianne here?"

Miles sighed. "It is hard to say, love—here or into the Thames is just as likely."

"I hope he finds her soon. It would be nice if she could travel to Wales with Arabella."

Miles grimaced. "I don't think that would be such a clever idea, my love. She will need the care of a physician."

"Terrance Stockton is in Wales now and practising medicine again. We could ask Magda to go with her. We can't send her back to Scotland, Miles."

"I suppose it's possible."

I sighed. "Perhaps you should consult with my Father. He may have some ideas."

Miles scowled, "If I am to take over Sir Thomas's role in the Agency even temporarily, I have to be able to make the problematic decisions, Lissa." I knew that he was resisting the idea of becoming one of the Agency's leaders. Though I thought him more than capable, he just needed to believe in himself.

He walked into his study, peering over his shoulder. "I need to be alone to think, Lissa. I hope you don't mind."

I shook my head. "Not at all, my love."

I collected my book from the drawing room and retired to the library sitting in one of the large leather chairs, kicking my shoes off and pulling my feet up under me. Then I became lost in the story. I read for about an hour, then relaxed deeper into the chair and dozed as the sun shone on me, and I finally fell asleep.

I was awakened by pounding on the front door. I walked to the doorway to see Howard running down the corridor and sliding to a halt to open the door. Outside stood Father Kelly. "I must speak with Lord Tinley. Jacob Thornton sent me."

Miles came out of his study and invited Father Kelly in. "Howard, will you please get Father Kelly something to drink."

The priest waved him off. "No, thank you, milord. I came only to deliver Thornton's message."

Miles nodded. "Go ahead then."

Father Kelly cleared his throat. "The Lady Marianne is hiding amongst the docks and warehouses. He has her corralled in the Limehouse district. As you know, it's a warren of foreign communities. Between the canal boats, the merchant ships and the private yachts, it will be nigh impossible to suss her out without more men."

Miles groaned. "What is the woman doing wandering about in Limehouse? She should stick out like a sore thumb and will get herself killed."

Father Kelly nodded. "It's getting late, milord. You can't afford to waste time. Limehouse at night is a vastly different animal from the district during the day. If you are going to rescue her, time is running out."

"Thank you, Father Kelly."

Miles glanced at me. "I need to contact Hamilton and Locke. Then, we need to go down to Limehouse."

"If you will excuse me, Father, I will send the message now." So I found our footman and sent him after Hamilton and Jibben, explaining what he needed to tell them. When I returned, Miles was alone, and Father Kelly had left.

He was biting the end of his pen and staring out the window. "Miles, what are you plotting?"

He chuckled, "I am trying to think like a frightened gentlewoman in a dangerous and unfamiliar area of London."

I smiled. "And how is that going?"

He scratched his head. "It isn't."

I sat and tapped the desk. "There must be something familiar in Limehouse, or she wouldn't go there. Somewhere that she would feel she could hide."

"What could she possibly know of Limehouse." I shrugged, and we sat lost in our thoughts.

Suddenly he snapped his fingers. "It's not Limehouse. It's the West India Docks—her Father's warehouse was there."

"Do you know which one belonged to him?"

"No, but perhaps her brother does."

"What about Lady Arabella? I will ask her, Miles."

He nodded. "I will send a message to Justin to see what he

knows."

I went back upstairs to question Arabella when she met me at the head of the stairs with her hair redone, an eye patch in place and dressed in a beautiful blue primrose afternoon dress. I smiled at her. "You look lovely."

"Thanks to you and Lord Tinley, I feel like I might be able to find a new life eventually." Then she stared at me, and her face fell. "What's wrong—is it Marianne? Have they found her?"

I sighed. "Come, let's not discuss this on the stairs."

She came down the stairs to join me and grasped my arm firmly. "Tell me!"

I stared at her hand, which she removed. "We think she may have fled to your Father's warehouse on the West India Docks."

Arabella bit her lip. "I have no idea where it is specifically. I don't think even Justin knows; the warehouse was part of our Father's criminal activities." I sighed, thinking this became tougher than we had hoped as she said, "But I can help."

I shook my head. "I am sorry, but you aren't used to this type of work, and the docks are nowhere to take a lady."

She pouted, then added, "Marianne will know me. She trusts me."

I shook my head again. "We don't know her state of mind. She might not recognise you. It is too dangerous."

Arabella looked defeated. "Then what can I do?"

"Help us work out a plan. You can at least be part of that." She agreed, and we went to Miles' study to wait for Hamilton and Jibben.

Arabella paced while Miles sat, staring out into the garden. I watched them, thinking about the possibilities until I asked, "Miles, is it possible that all those involved in the smuggling operations would have their various warehouses together?"

He turned back to look at me. "I have considered that, but I wondered if it would be too obvious."

I glanced down at my clasped hands. "Yet I can't help thinking that the General and Old Burley may have started smuggling together before being seconded into a larger organisation. Is it possible that they shared mutual warehouses or had them close to each other?"

He ran a hand through his hair. "It's possible. But I need to think, Lissa."

Lady Arabella glowered at him. "It's almost dark out there, and you need to think!"

"Yes. We can't just charge onto the docks. There is a subculture which comes out at night, and they are intolerant of interlopers, especially people like us who have no business being down there. I am concerned about Marianne's safety and the men and women I have sent there."

"Why aren't you going there yourself?"

Miles closed his eyes. He was losing patience and trying not to snap. "I am going, and my wife will be going with me, as will many of our friends."

She frowned, then said, "You make friends amongst the rabble and your servants. What kind of people are you?"

He barked back at her, "Is that so surprising? The only thing separating us from them is an accident of birth, milady."

She snorted, "I am nothing like them."

Miles waved a hand at her. "You need to make up your mind. Are you part of humanity, or are you one of those that can't see past the end of your nose? I judge people by their actions, not their purse size or pedigree. Though you would be surprised by how many of them have illustrious sires. Their misfortune was being born on the wrong side of the blanket and ignored by those Fathers."

She threw herself into a chair. "It is heredity and our upbringing Lord Tinley that makes us different—you and me and your family. I was not allowed to think of myself as anything other than superior to those people."

He laughed. "Our assistant cook has a noble Father. He is one of the brightest young men I have met. Yet his Father's legitimate son is slothful and doesn't apply himself to anything other than enjoying his position's advantages. If we lived in a different world and inheritance was based on intelligence, then the cook would be his Father's heir."

She sighed. "I have tried, but I don't understand you people. I baked bread today, for heaven's sake, yet I can't imagine ever doing that in my kitchen. I laughed with a housekeeper and shared intimate concerns with a maid. For a time, I forgot who they really were."

I smiled, "It's your decision about what you want to make of your life and who to include." ."

She nodded. "I see I have a fair amount to learn. If I am ever to make a new life for myself."

"Your brother could use your help."

"No, Lady Tinley, my brother needs a wife and family. I have no desire to host parties or visit the opera. I want a welcoming quiet community, not the conniving Beau Monde. I desire only peace and quiet."

Miles smiled at her. "I think you will find that in Wales. The arrangements should be finalised any day now. Then you can retire to Wales for as long as you'd like."

It wasn't long before Hamilton arrived with Nell, then behind them came Jibben, Magda, my Father, and Edward, all dressed in clothes better suited to be found in the second-hand shops of Petticoat Lane. I stared at my Father while Miles appeared gobsmacked as he addressed him and Edward, "What are you two doing here?"

My Father spoke first. "Thornton sent word to me that all hands were needed, that they had trapped Lady Marianne in the area of Limehouse and the Isle of Dogs."

Miles tossed his pen aside, scooped up a map, walked it over to a table, and spread it out. "I believe she's hiding in one of the warehouses on the West India Docks."

My Father looked at the map, then at Miles. "How did you come to that determination?"

Miles inhaled, "It was a matter of deduction after reviewing the facts that we know." He explained how we had focused on the possibility that she might be hiding in her Father's warehouse.

I waited for my Father to countermand his assumption. Instead, he said. "I agree. I suggest we get there as soon as possible before Thornton loses her."

Chapter 14

Come Out, Come Out

We arrived on the docks in the back of a wagon that Thornton had sent for us. Miles helped me down and admonished us to stay close to our partners. The streets were pitch black, damp, and musty smelling. The warehouses in the area sat dark and foreboding, looming over the docks and the sounds of water slapping against the wooden pilings and the sides of moored boats echoed off the buildings.

In the distance, you could hear music, laughter and shouting coming from the chophouses and pubs that attracted the dockworkers and sailors in the evening hours. The signs of human habitation where we stood were almost non-existent.

The occasional drunk stumbled past, ignoring us. Until we heard something that sent a shiver down my spine, someone nearby spoke in hurried Russian.

Then the cultured voice of Lord Harris cut them off. "She has to be around here. We have looked everywhere except at her blasted brother's residence." There was a pause, and then he sneered, "That bloody doctor forbids Burley any visitors or excitement. Yet that bitch of Tinley's was there." He didn't mention his suspicion that Arabella had been there as well.

Then, the other person spoke with slightly accented English. I recognised Count Vasiliev's oily voice. "Yes, the Tinleys. I would like to have them removed, especially his wife. She sees too much and doesn't know any humility." I glanced at my companions to see if they heard them. Miles motioned us to move closer together and back further into the shadows.

Lord Harris laughed. "English women are not the wallflowers they once were. My wife had denied me an heir because she discovered shortly after we married that I had a mistress and a by-blow. I don't know how she does it, but I gave up ploughing that barren field. Besides, she's as cold as ice in the marriage bed."

The Count snorted, "You Englishmen have no idea how to woo a woman in bed. You look only to satisfy yourselves."

Another gruff, heavily accented voice that I think was Popov hissed, "Stop this foolishness—where is this warehouse, Harris?"

"How should I know? The old man never let me in on his schemes. He took my money but never included me."

Popov growled, "Yet he made you money—it's a shame that he became suspicious of your motives. But he was wise never to trust you."

Harris laughed. "Yet you trust me."

Popov snickered. "Not really." The report of a pistol firing followed.

"You damn fool, Vasiliev! Now we will never know where to look." Then I thought I heard a grunt, followed by a splash.

Vasiliev chuckled. "He said he didn't know where it was. Harris had reached the end of his usefulness. You said so yourself."

Popov grumbled, "I said I didn't trust him—but I suppose you are right. Lord Russell and Palmerston are already suspicious of him. So tell me, why did you have to kill Gzowski?

"Gzowski was going to Palmerston with what he knew. I had no choice but to kill him!"

"We could have mitigated what he told him by going to Melbourne. He and Palmerston are not friends."

"They seemed friendly these last few days—and with Tinley and Blackburn."

Popov snorted in disgust. "And Wiseman—why kill him?"

"That meddling Sir Thomas found out what Harris was doing while looking into Gzowski's death. It was only a matter of time before he went to the King and the Tsar. We are safe from scrutiny. I made it look like the French killed him."

Popov spoke again, "We no longer have time to discuss this. Get the men and have them spread out. We need to search all the warehouses."

Vasiliev chuckled, "Not necessarily. My contact has narrowed it down for us."

That was the last I heard though they continued to mumble. I tried to take a deep breath when they moved on, but the smells of dead fish, rotting timbers, and the urine-soaked alleyway we were standing in made me gag. I only managed to stifle the urge by burying my face in my sleeve.

Miles pulled me into a hug, and everyone held their breath until the sounds of the others vanished into the night. When

Miles let me go, I looked up at him. "We have to move quickly and find Marianne before they do."

My Father hissed, "I would like to know how they thought of the docks."

Miles interjected, "The only reasonable conclusion is they have a source. The other possibility is that given her Father's business, they assumed the location of his warehouse was a natural hiding place."

Jibben added, "She believes she's safe because no one else knows what she knows."

Hamilton huffed, "I want that Count—he killed Gzowski and Wiseman!"

Miles hushed us as we got louder and whispered, "We will get him and Popov, I promise." Everyone was incensed by the Count's admission.

My Father blocked us from moving out of the alleyway. "Be careful what you promise, Miles. They are Russian diplomats, and our laws do not apply to them."

I could see Hamilton's grin as the moon came from behind a cloud. "There are other ways, Blackburn."

No one else spoke until a drunkard stumbled into the alleyway. He glanced up at us and said in a clear and distinct voice, "And when were you planning on inviting me to the party?"

Miles grinned. "Stewart, what are you doing down here?"

"Andropov and I have been following the Russians."

My Father spoke in a hushed voice and asked, "Where is Andropov?"

"As I said, he's down here following the Russians." Then he frowned, "Unfortunately, he doesn't understand the spirit of cooperation and has gone off on his own."

Edward and Jibben said in tandem, "Wonderful, everyone's here!"

Stewart ignored them. "Andropov believes that Vasiliev killed Sir Thomas. He was supposed to meet with Hamilton and Wiseman, he saw the Count in the vicinity and followed him, but it must have been after the murder that he didn't see what happened, only the police arriving."

My Father nodded. "He was right. We just heard Vasiliev admit to killing the Polish man Gzowski and Wiseman.

Stewart swore, then added, "I suppose you are down here for another reason other than a late-night stroll. Looking for Lady Marianne?"

Miles answered, "We think she might be hiding in her Father's warehouse."

Stewart sighed. "Well, you are in the wrong place for one. It's on the other side of the wharf."

"I thought it would be beside my Grandfather's?"

"No, Lady Tinley, your Grandfather was the importer, and old Lord Burley was the exporter. His warehouse is about half the size of your Grandfather's." He glanced around at us, then chuckled, taking in our costumes. "I suppose you will pass muster, but if anyone does any talking in this group, leave it to me, Lady Hamilton, Sir Stephen and Lord Tinley." Everyone nodded, and we filed out behind him.

At one point, he turned and shook his head. "Stop following me. I am not a Mother duck." He stopped and told us where the warehouse was. "Now spread out. I need to find Thornton. I hear he's down here with his bunch." He shook his head and muttered, "Amateurs."

Everyone roused themselves and went off in a different direction but within calling distance. Jibben, Magda, Miles, and I moved off in one group. Edward, my Father, Nell, and Hamilton moved off in another. At the same time, Stewart went in search of Thornton.

Magda was grumbling under her breath, so I leaned toward her. "What's wrong?"

"That Russian kills without reason, so I am cursing him. Do you still have your talisman?"

"Yes, you admonished us to carry them always."

"Good, that Russian witch is nearby. I feel her. She will extend the hand of friendship, but it's poison. We must stop her and that thrall of hers before they find Marianne."

"What will they do to her?"

She took my hand a squeezed it. "They will kill her—after they torture her for the information."

I sighed and grasped Miles' hand, and he whispered, "I know, my love." Then he whispered something to Jibben, and we increased our pace.

We finally reached our objective, but the immediate area was alive, with men loading a sloop that was obviously a smuggler at this hour. We moved away so as not to garner their attention. There was no time for an altercation. Further down the dock, we backtracked to hide behind some bales until the men all went aboard their ship, waiting for the early morning tide to change in their favour. Once things quieted again, we moved out and down towards the Burley warehouse. It looked dilapidated and deserted. I hurried to Miles' side. "It looks like it has been neglected for years."

We inched forward, listening to every little sound. Cats fighting rang out over the water nearby to the right. There was also the sound of someone urinating off the side of one of the large merchant ships anchored in the South Dock. Sound travelled remarkably well in this walled basin. Once the person had finished, they returned below decks, and we crept forward. I was wary of any noise around us and strained to hear any other movement in our vicinity.

As we came closer to the derelict building, the smell of rot reached us. It was a mixture of wood, fish, and carrion. Miles held us up when the sound of voices approached from our left. They were speaking in Russian, but one was undoubtedly a woman. It had to be Countess Irina.

Magda sniffed. "The witch is here." confirming my assumption that the Countess was in the group approaching our hiding place.

Miles grimaced, looked about, and said, "We will have to run for it." He stared at me. I know he was wondering if I was up to it. I glared at him and nodded for him to move out.

Everyone ducked and raced across the open space to the warehouse. A shout went up, but it was a thick Cockney accent. Perhaps it was one of the guards that patrolled the West India Docks. The barking of dogs followed his angry shout, and I could hear the scrabbling of the claws eating up the distance between us and the building.

Then I heard another voice call out in Dials cant, and I could tell it was Nell from the inflexion. Their group must be nearby and trying to distract our pursuers. Suddenly there was a high-pitched whistle, and the dogs stopped. I could just make out the outline of three dogs looking back over their shoulder the way they had come, and then they raced off away from us. Nell's ploy seemed to have worked. Hopefully, it didn't put them in jeopardy. Jibben and Miles threw themselves against a small door to access the warehouse.

They forced the door open, and my husband hissed, "Everyone in, now!"

Magda raced ahead of me and had disappeared by the time I entered. Jibben found a lantern next to the door and lit it, shutting all but one side. Miles growled, "Douse that light."

Jibben shut the open side. "I am keeping this with us. It's as dark as pitch in here, and I don't have the eyes of a cat!"

The only windows were high above the floor and were grimy with soot and years of neglect. Many of them were broken, yet hardly any light penetrated the gloom. Miles held my arm. "Where's Magda?"

"I don't know. She raced ahead of me and disappeared."

Jibben growled in a whisper, "God damn it, Grandmama!"

Miles let go. "We can't look for her now—let's move before we have company."

We cautiously moved forward, sensitive to any movement or noise in the cavernous building. Miles sucked in a breath as he banged his shin against an old crate. "Christ, I can't see a blessed thing. Open the lantern, Jibben, before we kill ourselves."

Jibben opened the shutters on two sides of the lantern, spilling light across the grit and debris cluttered floor. Raising it higher, we could see only a few stacks of broken crates, shards of broken pottery beneath our feet and the lingering scents of wool and cotton. The sound of the door behind us opening sent us ducking behind one of the stacks of crates.

Jibben shuttered the lantern, putting us at a disadvantage until our eyes adjusted. Just then, the moonlight shone through the many shattered windows above and lit up the faces of Count Vasiliev and Countess Irina. They stepped in, looking about, and the moon went behind a cloud. I heard the Countess say, "Find a light. I am not going to break an ankle in here for nothing."

The Count chuckled, but I heard his cautious footsteps move back to the doorway. He found another lantern and lit it, leaving all its shutters open. The light was shining brightly. Fortunately, it fell just short of our hiding place. In his other hand, he had a cocked pistol. The Countess hissed, "It's too bright."

The Count snorted, "It is this or nothing."

"Fine, but let's move quickly. I feel like we are being watched."

They walked to the opposite side of the building and moved ahead of us, holding close to the wall. Miles pushed Jibben forward, adding, "Quickly and quietly." He took my hand and pulled me along, trying to be as silent as possible. Jibben headed for the stairs while the Russians seemed to go deeper into the building.

Once on the stairs, Miles chose speed rather than caution, "Hurry!" Jibben seemed to agree as he led the way up. On the second floor was additional storage space. The smells of lavender, rose oil, and spirits, such as whisky, permeated the air. Three corridors ran off this space, leading to smaller storage rooms and offices.

In the back corner, I could hear voices whispering. But Miles moved us to the rooms closest to us. The first three were empty. The fourth and final one showed evidence of human habitation, but it did not appear to have been recent. The blanket left behind was mouldy and covered in a thick layer of dust. We moved onto the second corridor; it was more of the same. The final room had been cleaned, and an empty chamber pot was in the corner. Two blankets were neatly folded and stacked in the corner and behind the door hung a dress made of durable grey fustian. The petticoats were patched but clean. I had to wonder if these were Marianne's. But where was she, and how had she washed and mended her clothes? Before we could look further, Magda walked in.

I whispered, "Magda." She was followed in by a haggard-looking woman that was not Marianne.

Magda frowned. "She is gone."

Jibben hissed, "Who is this person?"

Magda ignored him. "This is Lady Arabella's maid, Brewster. She sent her to care for Lady Marianne and bring her to London." I was shocked to see the maid we had presumed dead and wondered why Lady Arabella had lied to us. It didn't make any sense. Something was wrong. But I decided this was not the place or time to voice my concerns.

Magda continued, "They intended to find passage to Canada, but Lord Harris stopped his wife from leaving. Arabella was the only one with money, so Marianne brought them here to hide." Yet Arabella had nothing when she came to us and told us she was more or less destitute. Why would she lie?

"Where is Marianne?"

Brewster's shoulders slumped. "I have no idea. She became frantic, saying they were coming, and ran off. I couldn't contain her. She gets like that sometimes, but she always comes back."

Miles bit his thumb. "I am afraid we don't have time to wait; others are looking for her."

Brewster whimpered, "I should never have left Lady Arabella. We could have found some way to escape together."

Miles glared at the maid before saying, "She did escape. She's staying at our home."

Brewster cast a suspicious eye his way, then whispered, "Thank God." But her assertion lacked any emotion. Perhaps it was only her fatigue and fear, for we still weren't out of danger yet.

Miles ignored her, turning to the rest of us. "Now we have to find Lady Marianne." He glanced back at Brewster. "When she's run off before, where has she gone?"

Brewster screwed up her face. "I've never been able to follow her. She's a sly one she is. But I think she goes to the market. She always returns with clothing or food."

Miles frowned and asked, "She has money?"

Brewster shook her head. "What little we had was used to leave Hampshire."

"Why did she leave there?"

Brewster sighed. "I told her about her sister being beaten, and she said she had to get back to London and find her. Lady Marianne sometimes dresses up like an old woman and stalks Lord Harris."

Jibben rubbed a hand across his face. "She using disguises? That's just brilliant; now it will be even harder to find her."

Miles put a finger to his lips "Hush." The sound of slow, measured footsteps was coming closer. He glanced around the room, pointing to a shadowy corner. "What's behind that door." Brewster bit a fingernail. "Quick, woman, what is it."

Brewster looked over her shoulder and hissed quickly, "Lady Marianne's dressing room," Then she huffed, "and Lady

Marianne."

Miles glared at her. "In there?"

"She's sick milord—in her mind. She whimpers that people searching for her are going to hurt her. It paralyzes her sometimes."

Jibben went to cover the door to the corridor while Magda and I opened the other door. The clothing there was neatly folded and arranged. Surrounded by a jumble of rags in the corner, cowered Lady Marianne Braithwaite. The light of the lantern Magda had taken from Jibben caught her alert eyes. I went down on my knees in the doorway and smiled. "Lady Marianne, you might not remember me—"

She stared at me as she responded, "I know you, Lady Tinley. Have you come to save me once again?"

"I would like to take you to your sister."

Her brow furrowed with confusion. "Brewster said Rupert had his valet beat her to death. They are both out to capture me."

"No, she escaped. You helped my sister-in-law kill Anderson, and someone killed Lord Harris. They are both dead, Lady Marianne."

She slapped her hands together, "God has answered my prayers. I wasn't sure, I had never killed anyone before, but he threatened Edward's children. I could never let Edward be hurt like that. He has a courageous wife, though—I think it must be the red hair." Then she giggled.

Magda hissed behind me, "Miles wants us to leave now!"

Marianne looked over my shoulder. "You are the Gypsy woman who makes potions and tells fortunes on the heath. You are a good person. My sister said you saved her from having Rupert's baby after they married."

I looked back at Magda in astonishment. Then her expression changed to one of sadness. "That was long ago, and she had been badly abused." My heart ached for what these women had suffered at the hands of the men in their lives.

I held out my hand. "Come, let's go."

She shook her head at first and dropped my hand, then asked, "You truly know where Arabella is?"

"Yes, but we must hurry. Others are looking for you, and they are not good people."

She chuckled. "I know. There are always people looking for me. If I could remove my brain and give it to them, I would. I want to be left alone."

I extended my hand once again. "Then come with me."

She nodded and reached out, taking my hand. I pulled her up and pulled her into a hug which she returned. We walked out to where Miles and Jibben were pacing the floor, and Brewster was chewing on her fingers. Marianne looked about and smiled at my husband. "Miles, it is good of you to come for me once again. I suppose Edward is about somewhere."

He nodded, then hissed, "Quiet!"

Everyone froze. Someone was coming down the hallway, opening and closing doors. The one to this room stood wide open. Magda had shuttered the lantern, and we stood in the dark. I stood with Marianne's hand in mine. A darker shadow appeared in the doorway, and I heard a sigh. "I found them." It was Edward's voice. Miles was one step away from stabbing his brother in the heart when Magda un-shuttered the lantern."

Miles swore, "Christ, Edward, I could have killed you!"

Edward smirked. "But you didn't. We will have time for a chat later. Right now, we need to move. Stewart and Andropov are keeping the Russians busy, but they won't follow them for long."

My Father, Hamilton, and Nell peeked into the room. Father nodded. "Lady Marianne, it's good to see you again. Now may I escort you out of here."

She smiled at him. "You were always a charming man Colin Turner.

He offered her his arm. She walked toward him and brushed a hand across Edward's cheek as she passed him. "You have a lovely family, Edward. I am so happy for you."

He smiled at her. "Thank you for taking care of them, Marianne."

She smiled and took my Father's arm when he said, "We need to get out of here; now." We all filed out of the room and started to walk back the way we had come, but she baulked, "No, not that way. I have a secret way. Come with me."

She led us into the last room in the corridor. It was an old-fashioned jakes that stank to high heaven, causing my gorge to rise. I could barely keep from heaving up the contents of my stomach at the smell. She looked at me with sympathy. "I am sorry, Lady Tinley. I know your sense of smell must be extremely sensitive in your condition, but it is the safest way out."

I only nodded, breathing through my mouth, hoping to mitigate the odour. She flipped up the bench lid, which surprisingly showed a ladder below. Miles grinned. "Very inventive of you, Lady Marianne."

She smirked. "It wasn't my doing. I found it like that already. You must be careful, though. Some of the rungs are loose or missing. My Father's men must have used this whenever the River Police got too close." Then she lifted her skirt and pulled out a knife gripping it tightly with her teeth.

Miles hushed us again. "Quick, someone is coming!" He had Magda shutter the lantern again, then gently closed the door. We descended the ladder as quickly as possible, my Father leading, followed by Lady Marianne, with the rest following. Miles and Jibben were the last to climb down, pulling the bench lid closed. Once we were down, Magda opened the lantern and moved forward. We walked through a few inches of running water when Miles noticed someone was missing. "Where is Brewster?"

I looked over my shoulder, and Brewster came out of the dark behind us. "Sorry, milord, but my skirt caught on a nail. It took me a bit to get it loose." He frowned. Having been one of the last people down, he would have passed her if she had indeed been caught, but I could tell he was sceptical, and rightly so. Her story about Lady Arabella didn't add up.

We followed the water for a few minutes before coming to an open space full of wine casks and spirits that appeared to be full. Marianne grinned. "It's French and of excellent quality. Justin should sell it—I will have to make him aware of it if I ever see him again."

Jibben tapped a barrel. "I can help him with that, it doesn't have a customs stamp, but we can work around that little issue."

My Father sucked in an irritated breath. "Can we please get moving?"

Lady Marianne nodded, and we headed towards a doorway at the far end. Marianne jerked it open to face an unknown man, who swore in Russian, but Marianne stabbed him in the throat before they could say anything. We watched him grab her knife as he fell to his knees, gasping for a breath—that would never come."

Jibben stepped forward, pulled the knife loose, wiped it off on his trousers, and then passed it back to Lady Marianne as he said, "Impressive."

Marianne grimaced. "I am not proud of what I have had to do to survive. But I found that a knife closeup is effective."

Hamilton and Edward pulled the body into the room behind us, and we continued into the night. The moon came out from behind some clouds to light our way, helping us find the exit out of the Dock complex before disappearing again behind a cloud.

We walked as quickly as possible toward the chophouses and pubs we heard in the distance. Finally, we found our way to a street where a ruckus of flying fists and screaming had broken out.

Jibben chuckled. "I bet you this is Thornton's doing." We ducked through the crowd, not garnering any attention and continued to walk until we came to a place where we could flag down hackneys to escape the area.

The ride home was slow, and my heart was beating with a staccato of anxiety, hoping we were not followed. I couldn't help but wonder what had happened to Count Vasiliev and Countess Irina. It must have been them that Miles had heard coming as we escaped through the jakes, and I worried they might have followed us.

We arrived home to find our friend Dr Archer ensconced in the library, speaking to Lady Arabella. They both jumped up as we entered. When Lady Arabella saw Brewster, she gasped. I showed her my displeasure as I challenged her, "You lied to us and abused our hospitality by sending us on a wild goose chase to Hampshire, putting our lives at risk."

Brewster, not Arabella, responded, "No, Lady Tinley, we had agreed that I would wait in Hampshire for Lady Arabella. When she didn't come, I thought she was dead. Then Lady Marianne wanted to leave and find her brother. But I wasn't sure where he was, and I couldn't approach him directly and jeopardise her safety." Her story had changed but was she lying, and if she was, why?

I stared at Arabella to see her reaction. She seemed pleased to see Brewster but perplexed by what her maid had said. Perhaps her head injury had impaired her recollection of events. She said nothing until Marianne entered the room, and they raced to each other as Arabella said, "My God, Marianne, why did you come back to London!"

Marianne seemed perfectly lucid now as she said, "I saw Rupert in Hampshire; he was searching for old Alma. You know that she wouldn't have been able to lie to him convincingly. Her mind is not as sound as it once was. I didn't want him hurting her."

Marianne's story differed from Brewster's, but we knew her mind wasn't sound. I suppose she might have seen Harris in Hampshire. Yet, I knew I must never forget that a consummate liar had raised these two women. I just had to determine who was lying and why.

"Did you tell Alma where you were going?"

Marianne started to shake. "I don't recall—she could have guessed, I suppose!" She started pulling at her hair.

I stepped beside her, "Lady Marianne, you did the right thing to protect your old nurse." She glanced at me with a trembling lip. I smiled and nodded as I continued to reassure her. "You did the right thing."

She took a deep breath, and her shaking stopped. Arabella looked concerned but seemed lost in how to treat her sister. I spoke loud enough for both of them to hear me as I ran my hand over Marianne's hair. "You know you remind me of my daughter. She's smart as a whip but not quite trusting of strangers. You can trust us, Marianne. We won't let anyone hurt you again."

She giggled, "I would like that."

Arabella stepped forward again and took her sister's hand. "We will both be free soon, Marianne."

Marianne touched the eye patch over her sister's eye. "He did that to you, didn't he? He can't hurt you anymore, Arabella. Lady Tinley assures me that Rupert is dead, and I helped kill Anderson."

Then she started to shake again. "There was so much blood— just like at the Young's—so much blood." I motioned to her sister to run her hand over her hair. She mimicked me, making soothing noises, and they went and sat down together in the far corner.

Edward observed them and leaned into Dr Archer. "Can you say for sure that her mind is not sound?"

Dr Archer smiled. "Very few of us can make that claim. At a conference in France, a doctor spoke about a nervous condition many people suffer after traumatic events. It's not that they are insane. But they need a peaceful, loving environment and avoid anything that caused them to relive the trauma."

He watched the sisters closely. "It would take some time for me to evaluate her, but I think Lady Marianne could live peacefully in society, perhaps not in London, but a quiet, supportive country setting would be perfect."

Lady Arabella had been listening and smiled at Dr Archer. "I hope we can call on your services in the future Dr Archer." He made no verbal commitment but nodded.

Marianne watched Edward and finally pushed Arabella's hands aside and walked up to Edward, who was standing self-consciously by the door. She smiled at him and cupped his cheek. "It was thoughts of you that helped me get through those first months in Scotland. So when Justin wrote and told me you had married a fiery Scottish lady, I was genuinely happy for you."

She lowered her hand but still stared at him. "The way Arabella and I treated you and Miles when we were young was deplorable. Can you imagine a marriage between us? It would have been disastrous. I could never have tolerated you giving up the Tinley title or working as an architect back then. Now I see things through clearer eyes. I wish I could have been the woman to win your heart, but I am happy for you. Fiona is the better match. I would like to get to know her and your children. Vincent is such a handsome and bright little boy, and Elspeth will be as beautiful as her Mother."

Edward laughed. "I hope she is blessed with my temperament and not her Mother's."

Miles groaned, saying, "God help us all."

I moved to sit by my Father to watch them banter. Then I leaned in to whisper, "Papa, something is bothering me about their stories." I glanced at him to see if he had heard me, but he wasn't paying attention. Instead, he seemed lost in thought, so I asked. "What are you thinking?"

"When we came in, I noticed a couple of men across the street watching the house that were not our Irregulars. I would rather not leave you alone here."

Hamilton came to his side. "Nell and I could stay."

My Father nodded. "I will feel better when we get the sisters out of London."

Suddenly there was the sound of rain lashing against the garden window. It had come out of nowhere, and the wind picked up. Then the skies seemed to open in a deluge, and the thunder rolled. "I think all of you should spend the night."

My Father nodded. "Your Mother will know I am here."

Jibben nodded. "I warned Judith I could be very late."

Only Edward looked concerned. "I need to go home."

Miles nodded. "Out the back way and through the mews. You can ride Saint. He knows you."

Edward arched a brow, "I would rather walk. That horse is a killer."

Miles smiled. "Exactly, so no one will try and stop him."

Edward sighed. "Fine, but you're coming to talk that monster into letting me ride him."

The two were laughing when they left. Marianne and Dr Archer talked about the therapies she had undergone in Scotland. She spoke of Dr Cooper, and no one mentioned that he was not a doctor. Archer assured her that she would not have to return to Scotland, which appeased her.

Unexpectedly I heard Miles' voice screaming for Dr Archer and Mr Malcom one after the other. I rushed out of the library to see him half dragging, half carrying Edward. He had been shot in the chest. Dr Archer called Tyson and Howard, "Clear the table in the breakfast room and light all the lamps and candles."

Magda grabbed my arm. "Get linens. I will get everything else."

I made for the stairs, but halfway up, I had to stop with a stitch in my side. Nell came up beside me. "Go sit down. I will get the linens.

Rennie and Jane came running down the stairs in their wrappers and hair curlers. "Someone's on the roof."

Mark, Jackson, and Sean came in from the back carrying weapons. Mark was bleeding from the shoulder. I sent him to the breakfast room to be tended to while Miles and Mr Malcom organised everyone else. With a glance to my right, I saw Brewster standing with Marianne. Arabella was staring at the commotion with horrified. I had to think of where I could put them where they would be safe. I pointed to the green baize door. "The kitchens! Now! Mrs Jonas and Kit will know what to do."

They raced across the hallway just as a rock was hurtled through the fan window above the door. They looked back, and I yelled, "GO!" they did what I told them with one look back before there was an incessant pounding on the front door.

Tyson raced to make sure the locks were sound just when I heard rifle fire from outside, and then I heard Stewart's voice yell, "For God's sake, open up!"

I screamed at Tyson, "Let him in!"

Tyson threw open the door, Stewart and Andropov hurtled threw the door, and just as they fell to the floor, rifle fire pinged off the door jam where Stewart's head had been just moments ago. Tyson slammed the door, shot the bolts through, and pulled the entryway table with its marble top in front of it, wedging it under the handle.

I turned to see Anne and Dolly at the top of the stairs with the children. I motioned for them to come down. Charlotte's eyes were huge with fear, and her lower lip trembled, but Alex only seemed curious. Charlotte reached out to me, and I took her in my arms. "Are the bad men going to hurt us, Mama?" I kissed her, handing her back to Anne. "Don't be afraid, darling. Papa will stop the bad men." She nodded, and Alex smiled. Then I sent them to the kitchen along with Howard and Jackson.

I looked about, but Miles was nowhere to be seen. Then I heard shots coming from above, and I knew he was upstairs fighting whoever had gained entry from the roof. I looked toward the stairs and then back at Stewart and Andropov. Both were lying expended on the floor, trying to catch their breath. I glanced at Tyson, and he nodded. "I will get more whisky, water and bandages, milady. I nodded my thanks. I went to the men and grabbed at a stitch in my side again. Stewart was watching me. "Sit, Lady Tinley, tell me where the doctor is. We only have a few scratches." I pointed to the breakfast room, and he nodded.

Magda came through the green baize door as Tyson went to enter. He whispered something to her. She nodded, then took her armload of equipment to the breakfast room. She came back to me. "You must lay down."

I nodded. "We have three more wounded, but they don't look bad."

She nodded. "Nell will help, now go back to the library and lie down."

I looked up the stairs. "Miles—"

"He will be fine." I nodded. Then she added, "Pray for him."

Suddenly I was drained of all energy and dragged myself to the library. I walked through the door and felt the breeze from an open window. I turned to call for help, as a hand covered my mouth, and I was pulled towards the window. I tried kicking when suddenly I was flung back, falling onto a fainting couch near the window.

I heard scuffling and saw the flash of a blade in the ambient light coming from the hallway. It was Marianne. She slashed downwards, and the man slumped half in and half out of the window, the blood pouring from his neck onto the vase of blue hydrangea beneath the windowsill. She pushed the man out the window, slammed it shut, locked it, and grabbed my hand. "Come with me." She dragged me into the hallway, through the green baize door, down the stairs, and into Dolly's quarters. "You and I will stay here, lay down, and I will tell the others where we are."

Eventually, she returned with Dolly, Anne, my children, and Jackson, who sat alert and armed in the corridor. "Where are the others?"

Marianne smiled. "In the kitchen, my sister and your cook are making soup and bread, if you can believe it."

I nodded. "That sounds like Mrs Jonas." Then a thought struck me, "Mr Jonas?"

She shook her head. Dolly answered, "Kit and Mr Jonas have gone for help."

"God, they will be slaughtered."

Dolly shook her head. "Not Kit. This summer, he and Mr Jonas dug an escape tunnel under the potting shed at Lord Tinely's suggestion. It gets them into Sir Stephen's yard. They'll get help; wait and see."

I had to wonder if the noise here had disturbed the Locke household. Though we were neighbours, it was extremely late at night, and with the rain and the thunder, it might mask the sounds of a fight."

I lay back on Dolly's bed and listened to the rain pelting against the window. Then I wondered who they could go to. Sir Thomas was dead, Dr Grimes was most likely at the hospital, and my Father and Inspector Stewart were here. So the only other possible contenders for help would be Jacob Thornton and Inspector Fry, who didn't seem particularly charitable towards us at the moment.

So, we waited. I couldn't hear anything but my pounding heart as I stared at Mrs Jonas in disbelief when she came in with a tea trolley. She smirked, saying with her hands on her hips, "We're English, milady. We drink tea when things become difficult."

She passed me a plate of lemon biscuits. "Here, you barely touched your dinner before you went out." She made it sound like we had gone out to a Ball which made me laugh despite my mood. I accepted the plate of biscuits and the cup of tea and enjoyed them despite how worried I was.

When satisfied that I was eating, she returned to the kitchen, saying, "I need to supervise Lady Arabella. She's a tad enthusiastic when chopping the vegetables."

Marianne chuckled. "I never thought I would see my sister in a kitchen, let alone being domestic. After our Mother passed away, my Father had stringent rules about contact with the servants. Arabella was lucky that he allowed her to keep Brewster."

I smiled "Working in the kitchen is very therapeutic. Besides, Miles and I find that if you want an efficient household, you need to know your staff on a personal level. You can only do that by working with them. I have even turned out beds and beat carpets."

"That seems to be sound advice." She then sat beside me, took my hand and closed her eyes. I saw her lips moving and was surprised to think she was praying. I had never thought of the Browne family as being religious. But it was comforting.

I closed my eyes with the intent to pray, but instead, I fell asleep. My dreams started as nightmares about the possible carnage upstairs. Then they were a replay of the blood bath we had found in the Young's home in Somerset several years ago. Finally, they turned to Dorset, my children and the Rambles, and I relaxed into my exhaustion.

Chapter 15

Time to Redecorate and Prepare to Run

I awoke to Charlotte's butterfly kisses. On opening my eyes, I saw her leaning over me, smiling. Miles stood behind her, holding Alex, he looked terrible, and then my thoughts shot straight to his brother. "Edward, is he alive?"

Miles nodded. "He's too stubborn to die." He paused and frowned before saying, "Fiona is with him." He sat down and took my hand. "How are you feeling? Magda told me you had some pains."

I nodded. "I did, but I am fine now, Miles. It wasn't the baby, my love. I know what that feels like."

He frowned. "Are you sure?"

"Yes, my love, I am sure." We both knew the anguish of losing a child. So to change the subject, I asked, "Who came to our rescue?"

"Kit and Thornton were able to rally the rookery Irregulars. Mr Jonas got Inspector Fry to come with half a dozen constables. There are six dead attackers. The wounded on our side included Mark's shoulder and Tyson, who took a slice across the ribs. The other injuries our people sustained were minor. I am thinking of closing the house and sending the staff to the Rambles to rest and recuperate. We can deal with the mess upstairs when we get back."

"Get back from where?"

"Wales. My Father arrived with Jane this morning —we leave as soon as he speaks to Captain Bruce, who has one of his vessels in London. Your Father is meeting with Palmerston, Russell and Melbourne to tell them what happened here and our latest plan."

I sat up quickly, setting my head to spinning. "How long have I been asleep?

"It's not quite noon. Mrs Jonas has invited us to join the staff for luncheon since the dining room and breakfast room are currently unusable."

I sighed. "Is it that bad?"

"Well, you know how you weren't satisfied with the colours we chose for most of the public rooms—you will have the opportunity to redecorate them now. I believe you will even be able to replace some of the furniture." I groaned. "Nell said, not to worry. She will have her brother Ryan take care of what can be mended and repaired while we are gone."

"Has he added painter and glazer to his many talents?"

He snickered. "No, he only does furniture. Josiah Pickard will take care of the rest. He runs Edward's crews here in London when not busy as the Tower Mason." Meg and Robert are back and will be coming with us to Wales. Meg looks brilliant, by the way. The rest did her a wonder, according to Robert."

Something was wrong, though. Miles was talking too quickly.

"Before we came down, Charlotte was regaling Jack with her version of the altercation above stairs." I was shocked, and he chuckled. "Most of it was made up, but our daughter is extremely observant about the details she got right." Anne came into the room then and took charge of the children taking them to their luncheon in the nursery.

"When are we likely to leave?"

"After Sir Thomas's funeral tomorrow."

"So soon? Do Matthew and Isabel know?"

He nodded at me. "They were here exceedingly early this morning. They are staying at Sir Thomas's home to go through his papers. Isabel knew something was wrong when she awoke to see lights moving about our house and the gardens."

"Did you tell them that we know who killed Sir Thomas?"

"Your Father told them." I nodded, feeling so deeply sad for them.

"Nell and Hamilton left a few hours ago. Isabel and Matthew stayed for a brief time before leaving just as Judith arrived to help care for our wounded. She and Jibben are still here. Come then, let's get some breakfast into you."

"I would like to see Edward."

Miles paused and in a firm voice, said, "Not until you have eaten." I knew better than to challenge him when he used that tone.

"Where are Marianne and Arabella?"

"Asleep upstairs."

We went to the kitchen where everyone seemed to be gathered, I hugged Judith, and when Jibben threw open his arms, I shook my head smiling, then sidestepped him to stand on tiptoe and kiss him on the cheek.

We sat down to a mountain of food, stew, porridge, scones, eggs, bacon, ham, potatoes, fish pie, tea, and coffee. The conversation was regarding the individual fights, each story becoming more outrageous than the last. Miles smiled but did not contribute anything.

When they finally settled down and the meal was complete, he stood up and said to our staff, "The family is going away for a time, so we would like to treat you all to a holiday in Dorset at our home there, at least until this place has been repaired and set to rights. Many of you have been there before. Some of you haven't. It is not a matter that you must go there. It's merely an offer." There were smiles all around and many nodding heads.

Mark, who sat there with his arm in a sling, said, "Begging your pardon, milord, if we'd rather not go can we stay here? I want to care for the horses that you leave behind. Then there's Bard and Patches. They don't travel so well."

Miles grinned. "You are welcome to stay, Mark. I doubt once we leave that our attackers will return here."

He grinned. "Thank you, milord."

Jackson laughed. "I am sure that will make Cathrine happy." Mark blushed and nodded while Jackson slapped him on the back and said, "I had best stay with Mark milord, he won't be worth much with one arm, and he will need a chaperon."

Mrs Jonas sighed. "Horace wouldn't rest a day with workers traipsing about his garden. Besides, those two staying here will likely eat us out of the house and home or die of starvation."

Mr Jonas nodded. "Aye, she's right, milord. Workmen have no respect for a flowerbed."

Dolly agreed, adding, "I'd rather stay here milord and clean up after the workers every day than come home to a pile of work." Jane and Rennie nodded their agreement.

Tyson and Howard looked at each other "If everyone is staying, we will too."

Miles shook his head as the rest of the staff said they would stay behind, agreeing it would be easier to stay and work daily to remain on top of things. Mr Malcom was the last to speak up. "I think the staff have made wise choices, milord, and I shall remain with them to help Dolly supervise and watch over your valuables."

Miles laughed. "I suspected nothing less from any of you. But the offer stands. There will be extra in your pay pack for setting this place to rights." Everyone smiled, nodding their thanks and bowed as they left one after another.

I looked at Judith, who was sipping a cup of coffee like it was ambrosia. "You should go home and get some rest."

She nodded. "I promised to wake Grandmama when we were ready to leave."

Judith and Jibben went to fetch Magda while Miles and I slipped upstairs to the breakfast room to see Edward. He lay on a feather bed on the table. His eyes were closed, and his breathing was shallow and rapid. Fiona sat beside him with her head resting beside the hand she held. She didn't even look up as we came in, but her voice was brittle as she said. "Hello, Miles, Lissa."

I walked to the other side to see her puffy tear-stained face. "How is he?"

"Dr Archer doesn't hold out much hope. I am having him moved to the hospital. I want him out of this house and away from you people. He is not an Agent and should never have been involved in all of this." Then she sat up and glared at Miles. "How could you let this happen to him? You are his brother. You should have protected him!"

I took exception to her tone. "Just a minute, Edward insisted that he return home to you because you had recently been traumatised and insisted on leaving here after spending only one night. So don't blame us for your husband wanting to leave the safety of our home."

She turned her focus on me and snorted, "Oh, yes, the Lady Agent speaks. It is unseemly how you skulk about the slums of London pretending to be a whore or simpleton. My husband may die because you made him feel guilty about Marianne Braithwaite, that he had married me instead of that madwoman. Now get out and leave us alone! We can't leave here soon enough."

I was shocked and hurt by her admonishment and turned to Miles, who didn't seem surprised by her outrage. I suppose that I

372

shouldn't be either. Dr Archer stood in the doorway and motioned for us to join him in the hallway. I asked him, "How is he doing?"

Archer shook his head. "Just as Lady Johnson said, his condition is very grave. You need to be prepared that he may not make it." I grasped Miles' arm and turned my head into his shoulder. The tears were welling up and spilling down my cheeks.

I choked back a sob. "Is it safe to move Edward?"

Archer shrugged. "He needs the care he can receive in a hospital." Then he pulled us aside. ". Magda has a quantity of her serum prepared. Fortunately, I brought it from Dorset. But Fiona has refused to allow him to be injected. Jefferson and I would like to administer it, but she is a stubborn woman. We need her to change her mind."

Behind us, a voice rough with emotion said, "I will get her to change her mind." We turned to find Lord Shellard standing there with Lady Jane. He looked haggard and angry. "He is still my son, and when he is incapacitated, I become the guardian of his family. She will submit to the treatment. I suggest you get it prepared, Dr Archer."

Archer looked uncomfortable, but he nodded. What my Father-in-law had said was true. He could override any decisions she made, accrediting them to English law. I knew he would be reluctant to force her hand, but he would do anything to save his son's life. He marched into the room, and a few minutes later, he came out with a distraught Fiona and pushed her into Lady Jane's arms. "Take her home, Jane. I will be along as soon as Edward is moved safely."

Jane walked with Fiona towards the door, trying to get her to focus on Elspeth and Vincent's well-being. Lord Shellard glared at Miles. "Would you explain why I am on the verge of losing one of my sons yet again?"

Miles swallowed hard and ran a hand through his hair. "Come with me."

Before Jane and Fiona left, Fiona turned and spat in our direction, "I will never forgive either of you!" I saw Jibben, Judith and Magda standing at the top of the stairs, embarrassed at having witnessed such a moment.

Lord Shellard sighed. "She doesn't mean that, son."

Miles frowned. "She does right now. Let me take you to see Edward." Dr Archer moved along with us, bringing his bag as Magda, Judith and Jibben joined us.

Inside the room, Archer pulled out a jar of cloudy liquid that I had seen save the lives of many of the people I loved. Miles spoke to his Father as Archer handed it to Magda. She took it to the window to examine and smiled. "It is still good. Its potency should be at its highest now."

Dr Archer took it back and prepared a syringe. He looked at Magda. "In the hip or the vein."

She walked over to Edward. Scrutinising his face and torso, she closed her eyes and placed her hands on his face. "His spirit is conflicted about whether to stay or go. We will need to help him decide to stay." Then she opened her eyes, looked at Archer, and, in a deadly serious voice, said, "The vein, every four hours."

The doctor arched his brow. "So, often?"

Magda expression was sombre. "We not only fight the infection, but we also fight for his life."

Archer applied a tourniquet so his veins stood out, then injected him with the fluid. He sighed as he removed the tourniquet, applied a plaster and sat back. "I will stay with him until a carriage can be made ready to take him to the hospital."

Lord Shellard nodded. "I am coming with you." He looked at Miles, then placed a hand on his shoulder. "Promise me you will get the ones that did this to him."

Miles clutched his hand tightly, he shouldn't make such a promise, but he did. "Every last one of them that had anything to do with this. I promise you and him."

His Father pulled him into his arms, hugging him desperately, then he stepped back and said, "Bruce has a schooner in the Pool of London. I left a message for him to contact you." He hugged Miles close again and said to me, "Take care of Miles and don't let him brood." Then he hugged me and kissed both my cheeks.

I nodded, then said, "Take care of Edward and Fiona." He only nodded.

Magda, Jibben and Judith had watched this painful exchange looking deeply troubled. Then Jibben said, "I will have Father Kelly and Aunt Kezia light candles and say prayers."

Miles' Father looked over at him and smiled. "We are not Catholic, Stephen."

Jibben cracked a slight smile. "Neither are we, but it can't hurt. After all, God listens to everyone, doesn't he?"

Lord Shellard nodded. "So we are taught."

Jibben then bowed to my Father-in-law. A rare occasion for Jibben to do that to anyone, even the King. At that moment, he looked like the eastern prince that he had been mistaken for once.

A door was brought into the room, and Edward was carefully moved onto it, then picked up by Lord Shellard, Miles, Dr Archer, and Jibben and carried out to the open Landau. The door was laid across the two seats. Lord Shellard and Dr Archer climbed up to sit on either side, lending a steadying hand to the door. Magda glanced up into the sun, then back at Archer. "Remember every four hours in the vein. Then, when he awakens, put some in his broth or water." Archer nodded.

Miles looked up at Sean. "Slow and easy, Sean."

"Yes, milord." and they moved off.

I took Miles' hand. "We can't go to Wales and leave Edward and Fiona."

He glared down and me; for some reason, he was enraged and snarled at me. "We are going to Wales! Those who did this will follow, and I will drop their dead bodies into the sea."

"Miles—we don't kill unless it's necessary."

"That changed with this attack on us."

I knew he was angry, and I could understand that he felt

responsible for Edward, but this was not my husband speaking. He turned me by the shoulders to look into my eyes. "Please understand, Lissa, this isn't just about Edward. It's about Gzowski, Mrs Danvers, and Sir Thomas."

I cupped his face with my hands. "Promise me you won't be judge, jury and executioner. It will change you fundamentally, and you won't be the man I married." He closed his eyes, and I caught a tear that slid down his cheek. "Miles?"

He opened his eyes and took a deep breath. "I don't want this leadership, Lissa. Samuel needs to return and take over. I can't do this."

"I know, my love, just don't make any rash decisions."

He leaned his forehead against mine with closed eyes taking deep breaths. "What would I do without you?"

I smiled. "You would still be Wicker in the Dials helping the downtrodden."

He laughed. "I am too old for that now."

I took his arm. "We should go and pay our respects to Isabel and Matthew."

We walked to the door with Howard handing us our hats and gloves. It was a warm day, and I waved away my shawl. Walking out the front door, we passed the Locke's home and then turned into the front garden of Sir Thomas's home. His summer roses were a riot of colour. It never ceased to amaze me that such a button-down and formal man would have such a riotous garden. It was reminiscent of a country cottage garden.

Isabel came out to join us dressed in unadorned black. She smiled at us and then looked around her. "He loved this garden, even though it is so out of place in Mayfair. He worked in it almost every day with our gardener, I think because my Mother planned it, but she never saw it realised."

I smiled. "It is beautiful. Will you keep it this way?"

"I am not sure if we will move in here. It's up to Matthew."

Matthew came out to stand behind her. "It will be a joint decision. I must admit that I have always admired his study."

She took his arm and chuckled. "Well, that settles it." She looked back at us. "You have to excuse us; we try to laugh so we don't cry."

She saw Miles' face turn away, looking out over the beds of flowers. "Miles?" he turned to look at her, but his expression was haunted. "There is something I think you need to see. We found it among my Father's papers."

Miles arched a brow and looked to Matthew, who exhaled loudly, "She's right. Please come in."

She brought us directly into the study and walked to the desk picking up one piece of paper and passing it to Matthew. "He wrote a letter, Miles. It is as if he expected that he wouldn't be with us for much longer."

Then Matthew and Isabel walked out and closed the door. Miles took the letter to stand by the window. I sat and waited for him to tell me what it contained. He read it through and then seemed to reread it. Then he sighed like the weight of the world

378

had been removed from his shoulders. He looked at me and smiled. "I am absolved of taking charge of the Crown Portion of the Agency. He didn't think I was ready." He chuckled. "He believed that I was still too young and had too much to contribute to the fieldwork, but he admonished both your Father and Samuel to consult me, that while I was impulsive, he thought I had good instincts."

He sat down beside me and passed me the letter. I read it through once and glanced up at him. "Are you relieved now?"

"Immensely." Behind us, the door had opened.

"Did he send this to Samuel and my Father?"

Matthew and Isabel came in. "According to Mrs Hillyard, he sent out several copies of that letter."

Miles nodded. "The King and Melbourne were probably among the others; they will sleep easier to know that I am not in charge."

Matthew wiped a hand across the back of his neck. "That's not exactly true. Samuel is in Northumberland, and you are here. Colin will look to you as his counterpart until that changes."

Miles' shoulders slumped before smiling, saying, "No—we are headed for Wales, and that's Colin's purview."

I shook my head. Isabel looked at him with sympathy. "You aren't upset at not taking my Father's place?"

"Far from it, just ask my Father. The thought of becoming Earl one day terrifies me. Can you see me in Parliament arguing a bill and not pummeling my opponent into the ground?"

We all chuckled, and Matthew smiled. "I have no doubt that you will rise to the occasion when the time comes."

Miles rolled his eyes. "Thank you, old man, and I will remind you of that when they boot me out of the House of Lords."

Matthew shook his head. "They don't boot people out of the House of Lords, Miles."

"That's a shame."

Isabel had called for tea, and as it arrived, she sat to pour, and then her hand started to shake. I moved to sit beside her and took over. She smiled. "It is silly, but everything reminds me of my Mother and Father."

Matthew took her hand. "That's why we haven't decided whether to sell the place or move here."

I smiled as I passed her a cup of tea. "We would love to have you as neighbours, but as your Father discovered, living beside Jibben is not easy." Isabel tittered nervously.

Miles crossed his legs. "I will share some advice my Father gave me for when he passes on." He paused to collect his thoughts. "He said, and I am paraphrasing, *'Take what I leave you and make it your own without erasing the memories.'* In my mind, that means redecorating to your taste. Leave your parent's portrait in the drawing room beside one of your own family." Then he chuckled. "Mind you. He was far more eloquent and verbose."

Isabel listened to him, her face clearing as she looked about the room. Matthew glanced down at her. "If we move here, this room stays just as it is."

She smiled. "The gardens are lovely and larger than we currently have. Jane and Warren would love it here. They would be so close to their playmates living here."

Matthew nodded, then asked, "How is Edward?"

Miles grimaced. "Archer says it's grave. He is giving him Magda's magic serum against Fiona's wishes which my Father overrode. They have taken him to the hospital."

"Edward is strong, Miles. He has a great deal to live for."

"I know." Miles' expression was glum, but he had no intention of elaborating on what was bothering him.

I took his hand and told them, "Fiona is holding us responsible for Edward being wounded and in such dire condition."

Matthew shook his head, and Isabel's brow furrowed before saying, "She doesn't mean it. I know when I found out about my Father. I blamed everyone involved with the Agency, but I realised that it could have been anyone of you. Terrible things happen to good people."

Miles groaned. "Yes, but Edward isn't an Agent. He is an artist and a designer."

Matthew had been staring at Miles. "And he will be again Miles—Archer is an excellent physician, and Grimes will be available to him."

Isabel squeezed his hand. "And if he needs Matthew, he will be there."

Dr Jefferson smiled at her and nodded. "Now then, when will

you be leaving for Wales?"

Miles was moved and coughed to clear his throat. "Tomorrow, after Sir Thomas is laid to rest."

Isabel reached forward and laid a hand on his knee. "Our prayers will go with you."

We spent as pleasant an hour together as we could under the circumstances before returning home.

We had only just returned when Josiah Pickard arrived to start taking stock of the repairs required. I was surprised to see him, and he grinned at my expression. "Thornton told me about the altercation and said my services would be needed."

Then his expression soured, "Lady Johnson wrote me as well, forbidding me to work on your home as a representative of Johnson and Bruce. But I doubt your cousin or brother would feel the same. Besides, you are an investor, and it would be bad for business should it get around if we didn't help." Miles clapped him on the back, thanking him. Mr Malcom appeared and offered to take Josiah to the rooms requiring repair and refurbishment.

They passed into the breakfast room just as Tyson opened the door again to Captain Bruce. "Miles, my boy!" He looked around and smirked, "Redecorating, I see." When he saw our sombre faces, his smile disappeared. "What's happened?"

I hugged the Captain and said, "I will check on our guests and the children."

Captain Bruce looked around him. "Guests?"

Miles nodded. "Yes, come, and I will tell you all about it."

The Captain tossed his hat to Tyson. "You do lead an interesting life, Miles, and here I always thought you landsmen were boring."

Miles snorted, "Far from it."

I headed up the stairs as the door to the study closed. Walking past the General's portrait, I glared at him. "A fat lot of good you have been."

I heard a giggle from above and looked up to see the sisters descending. Marianne came to my side and looked up at the General. "He wasn't so bad, you know."

I could feel the frown forming on my face. "I wouldn't know about that—we didn't have an amicable relationship."

Arabella came down to stand one stair above us. As she looked at the General's portrait, she shrugged. "Men of his ilk always have secrets."

"If you refer to his opium addiction. I am aware of it. We all are."

Marianne nodded. "That's how my Father entrapped him. He fed his addiction and at the same time threatened to make it public to ruin his family."

"Well, he escaped that shame with his death."

Marianne tipped her head from side to side like a bird. "Is that why you are involved with the Agency? To atone for the General's crimes?"

"No, I do it to right the wrongs that men like my Grandfather commit every day and, in the process hurting innocent people."

Arabella sniffed. "Seems much the same thing."

Then, Arabella made to move past us. She said, "We will be leaving shortly. Since my husband is undoubtedly dead, Marianne and I will retire to the country."

"That is not wise. The Russians are still looking for Marianne and will not give up. Who do you think attacked us last night?" I stared at two blank faces. "You should be coming to Wales with us."

Marianne asked, "Why, Wales?"

"It is safe and defensible, and we have a mathematical genius and code breaker there." I turned to focus on Marianne and asked. "Where are the rest of your drawings?"

Marianne sucked on her lower lip. "You mean Papa's journals and ledgers?"

"Yes."

She smiled. "Someplace no one would ever look."

I arched a brow. "Is that all you are going to tell me?"

She shook her head. "If it makes a difference the little I had with me, you will find in the Agency umbrella stand."

"What?"

"When Brewster came for me, she said the safest place for

384

them was the Agency. So, we came to London, and I retrieved them from the Blane House garden and stuffed them into a hollow umbrella handle. She took it there for me."

"When was this?"

"Wednesday. I retrieved them from Blane House that morning. Mrs Danvers had hidden them for me in a potted plant in the garden because she could easily get out of her room. I put them into the umbrella handle and told Brewster. Then she took it from me and went to the Agency."

I felt sick. "Where is Brewster?"

Arabella suddenly sounded panicked. "I don't know?"

"Oh my God—she must be working with the Russians."

I sat down on the stairs just as Mr Malcom and Mr Pickard came to the bottom. "Milady, are you all right ?"

"Please get my husband for me, Mr Malcom; he is in the study."

Miles came out at his request and kneeled in front of me. "What's wrong, Lissa."

It's been bothering me how the Russians knew where Marianne was. "It's Brewster. She's working for them. Brewster lied, not Lady Arabella, and it wasn't Marianne who insisted they come back to London. She likely set fire to Blane House to keep Mrs Danvers from talking to us again." I started to shake. "She was complicit in killing Sir Thomas."

Lady Arabella shook her head. "I can't believe it."

385

Brewster came through the green baize door and stood staring at us gathered on the stairs. She looked to one side to see Tyson standing in front of the door, and Howard was blocking any retreat down the hallway. She bit her lip and then sagged down to her knees.

"They were going to kill my daughter. I had to do what they told me to do." Lady Arabella took a step towards her and then stopped looking confused.

Miles' expression was impassive as Brewster continued in a panic. "I grew up in their household and remembered the folly where they hid at Broadlands as children. It wasn't difficult to believe that was where Lady Arabella had taken her. When I found Lady Marianne, I convinced her to fetch the drawings. They were damp and dirty, and some disintegrated in my hands. I hid what I had in an umbrella handle. I thought if I could get them to Sir Thomas, he could help Lady Marianne and me. But Lord Harris saw me on my way to the Agency. I was able to elude him. When I arrived there, the door was open. I slipped in and heard two people yelling at each. I dropped the umbrella and ran. Lord Harris must have had someone follow me back to the warehouses. I felt like I was being watched the whole time, but I can't say who it was."

Miles had moved to stand over her "Interesting story."

Brewster looked up at him, pleading in her eyes. Then, finally, she prostrated herself at his feet. "It's the truth, I swear!"

Miles stared at her. "It sounds very probable, but I don't trust you. Tell me what the umbrella looked like?"

She glanced up, and he extended his hand to pull her up. "It is ebony with a silver lion's head handle."

He motioned to Howard, "Yes, milord."

"Will you please go to the Agency, Howard, and fetch it for me."

Howard headed off as Miles said, "Take Jackson with you."

He yelled back, "Yes, milord."

Miles kept hold of Brewster's hand. "Who was Sir Thomas arguing with?"

Brewster shook her head. "I don't know. They were threatening each other."

"Was there only two of them?"

"All I heard was an Englishman and a man with an accent."

"What kind of accent?"

"I don't know."

Miles nodded. "You are sure that there were only two of them."

"I don't know. I was afraid and ran."

I walked down the stairs and came to his side as he asked, "Where is your daughter?"

"What?"

Miles insisted, "Your daughter, where is she?"

Brewster suddenly made a break for the back hallway where Howard had disappeared. But Howard stepped out from the back and grabbed her. I asked Miles, "How did you know?"

"Your Father found the umbrella—it had been opened. Anything in it was gone; coupled with Lady Arabella's reaction to her lie about the daughter, I could see that she was trying to determine when this could have happened. Burley told us that Brewster had practically grown up with them. They would have known about any scandal of her having a child."

I glanced back at Lady Arabella. "Brewster has been my maid since my Mother died and was a housemaid before then. In truth, I can't remember when she wasn't with us."

Brewster spat in her direction as Howard pulled her forward, but she refused to say anything else despite Miles and Lady Arabella's persistent questioning.

Lady Marianne suddenly started laughing to the point of being almost hysterical. She ran down the stairs and danced around Brewster. Then she sobered, "You think I never saw or heard you talking to my Father and sleeping in his bed? Did you honestly think I would trust you? You sent Anderson after me when I went to ask for Edward's help. He made me kill him. That is on your head, not mine. Then you found my Father's Russian contact, Vasiliev, at Cornwall Terrace. He killed Sir Thomas, and you gave him my worthless drawings; they are all meaningless. They were just drawings! I knew you would betray my whereabouts to him, but these people got there first. You didn't catch your skirt on the ladder in the warehouse. You were telling him where we were going." Then she leaned in and spat in Brewster's face jumping back when Brewster tried to lunge at her.

Brewster screamed, "Your Father owed me thousands of pounds. I wanted my money, the only way I could get it was to sell you—you lunatic."

Miles, to my surprise, slapped her face. "Shut it—NOW! Captain Bruce, would you please take the ladies into my study."

Bruce nodded. "Come, ladies." He stepped up to offer his arm to Lady Marianne and waited for Arabella to come down the stairs.

Miles glanced at me. "Please, Lissa, go with them."

"What are you going to do."

"Just go with them."

I crossed my arms and glared at him. "No!"

"I won't let you do something you will hate yourself for, for the rest of your life."

Tyson cleared his throat "Milord." Miles ignored him, and Tyson tried again. "Milord, Inspector Stewart is here." There in the doorway stood Miles' salvation.

I sighed with relief. "Welcome, Inspector. I think you will be interested in Miss Brewster. She was integral to the fire at Blane House, the murder of Sir Thomas Wiseman and most recently, the murder of Lord Harris on the West India Docks—which I believe is in your jurisdiction."

"And here I thought I was coming to arrest you, Lord Tinley, for

389

the murder of Lord Harris."

The shock on my face must have been considerable as Colonel Andropov and Inspector Fry came out from behind him, with Fry saying. "She must be the woman my Patrolman saw fleeing from the scene on the night when Sir Thomas was murdered." He smiled at me. "He was jesting about arresting you, Lord Tinley. But, as I understand it, Colonel Andropov saw the Count murder Lord Harris."

He gazed at the damage in the entry hall. "It looks worse here in the light of day."

Miles responded curtly, "Yes, the Russians gave my wife an excuse to redecorate." Neither Fry, Stewart, nor Andropov reacted. "Would you care to tell me why you are here?"

Fry flipped open the pad he held in his hand. "A Sergi Popov, it seems, is afraid for his life and feels threatened by your mere presence."

Miles was stunned. "He accused me of murder?"

Stewart nodded. "At first. Then when I told him that Andropov and I were at the scene, he broke down and asked for our protection from a woman named Brewster and Count Vasiliev."

Mile crossed his arms, "Not Countess Irina?"

Andropov snorted, "Prince Andre Gregor's niece? He wouldn't dare implicate her. But the Prince has made it known that he would not protect the Count, nor would he help us apprehend him. I believe he's waiting to see who comes out on top and how to take advantage of that. For him, it's strictly political survival."

Miles shook his head. "There may be forces at work here that you have no knowledge of, so I suggest you speak to Lord Blackburn, Colonel." Andropov looked puzzled but appeared to accept Miles' rather berserk statement.

Fry stepped outside and called for three men who joined him in the hallway directing them to take Brewster into custody. As they dragged her out screaming obscenities at us, Stewart said, "We will need you and the ladies to make a statement Lord Tinley, about that person's involvement in the deaths of Mrs Hilda Danvers, Lord Rupert Harris and Sir Thomas Wiseman."

Miles agreed, "Of course."

Miles came to me and kissed my forehead, whispering, "Press Marianne about those hidden drawings. I believe her when she says they aren't the documents we are looking for; she's too smart to give them to Brewster."

I nodded and reached up to kiss him on the cheek. "You go ahead, darling. Lady Arabella, Lady Marianne and I will wait for you to come to us in the small sitting room. I will order tea for you, gentlemen; our cook makes a fabulous seed cake and lemon tarts." They nodded and adjourned to Miles' study.

I turned towards the sitting room and saw Marianne standing in the doorway. Once I had ordered the tea and taken a seat, she told me. "Your husband is a very astute man. He's right that I would never have given Brewster my Father's journals and accounts."

"May I ask where they are?"

"You may ask."

Arabella huffed, "Marianne stop playing these stupid games. Where are Father's journals or these drawings to which Lady Tinley is alluding?"

Marianne stared at her sister and said, "If Rupert was still alive, would you give them to him or Justin?"

Arabella blanched but said nothing, so Marianne continued, "You have lived in luxury all your life. Do you expect me to believe that you would be willing to give all that up even as you are now? Your husband is dead, and you have no children. The title and estates go to his younger brother. Where will you go? How will you live? Do you honestly think Rupert left you anything of worth? Don't be a simpleton, Arabella. You would take the information I possess to one of our Father's old allies and sell it to them or use it yourself."

Arabella was gobsmacked, "Marianne, I rescued you from Blane House."

"Was that out of guilt or greed?" She bowed her head over clasped hands. "Father chose me to be his eyes and ears because I was stronger and smarter than you." Captain Bruce watched the sisters with intense interest.

I interrupted this sisterly exchange. "So you won't tell us where the documents are for fear that whoever has them will use them?"

Marianne sat upright and stared at the picture of Miles, Edward, and their Father. Then I had an idea, "You trust Edward, don't you?"

She tipped her head from side to side, smiling. "I have always trusted Edward. He has always kept my secrets."

"You went to him, but he was in Hampshire, and Anderson followed you, but you had time before he took you, prisoner. Fiona must have left the room at some time, and you hid them there in his house." I smiled at her "Jilly said she thought you were playing at being mad. She's right, isn't she."

Marianne's face sobered. "Jilly? Ah yes, the young lady's maid is a bright young woman." She sighed and sat back in her seat until the tea arrived, and I poured it. Once she had taken a sip, she puckered her lips. "Madness is like a warm blanket, Lady Tinley. You can pull it around you for protection from the cold. When you are complacently mad, people don't pay much attention to you."

Then she grimaced, "It was a hard journey back for me. The doctors at the hospital in Scotland were exceedingly kind and good. They helped me find my way. But they never knew how far and how fast I had come."

She took another sip of tea. "Then, Dr Cooper arrived to assess me for Rupert. The fools didn't realise I had seen Copper in my Father's home more than once. I knew then that I was potentially in a great deal of trouble, so feigning madness was on my side again, and I used it to my benefit. I don't think Cooper and Rupert believed my performance entirely, but Rupert felt it in their best interest to transfer me back to London. Something that I secretly wanted. I knew my life was probably forfeit, so I had to get the journals and accounts to someone I could trust who would understand what they represent."

I bit my lower lip. "Edward was concentrating on keeping Justin from tearing London apart looking for you."

She smiled. "That sounds like Edward." I offered her a tart which she took and seemed to relish. "The Scots are good plain cooks, but I missed these kinds of treats."

"So, you won't tell me where you hid them?" My shoulders slumped. "Edward may be dying."

Marianne looked me in the eye, convinced by what she said, "Your witch won't let that happen."

"Magda?" She nodded as if knowing something I didn't, which made me wonder how sane she was, really.

Mr Malcom came to the door, "Lady Tinley? Lord and Lady Blackburn are here." I smiled as they entered the room behind Mr Malcom, who glanced at the tea tray. "I will have it refreshed, milady." I smiled my thanks as he bowed out.

My Father nodded to the sisters, kissed my cheek, and then went to speak to Captain Bruce.

My Mother waited for me to introduce the sisters as she sat and scrutinised them. "You both look very much like your Mother. But with different colouring."

Marianne laughed. "Mother used to call us night and day."

"I met her once when I was in London. My Aunt Mary introduced us. Lady Burley was charming but always had an aura of sadness about her."

Arabella cleared her throat, her eye glistening with unshed

tears. "She was the best for us."

My Mother looked at them with compassion. "What do you intend to do now?"

"I don't know, Lady Blackburn. My sister pointed out that I lived in luxury all my life and wouldn't know how to live without it." She glanced at Marianne, "But our Mother once told me that I should never expect life to remain the same, that love and riches could come and go at a whim. I should have listened to her."

Marianne chuckled, ignoring the pathos in her sister's words as she addressed my Father. "Lord Blackburn, I met your Grandfather once when he came to see my Father."

My Father didn't seem surprised, but I saw his fists clench. "Don't worry, milord. He was there to warn my Father that he was on the verge of reaching the point of no return in his activities and that something called the Brotherhood would intervene to stop him. Regrettably, he became ill after that visit. I often wondered what would have happened if your Grandfather had been able to follow through on his threat."

Miles and his three companions joined us just as the fresh tea arrived. I poured out for everyone and offered selections from the cake trays. Andropov seemed most appreciative of Mrs Jonas' seed cake and groaned with pleasure, making my Mother and I chuckle.

While we sipped tea, we discussed what had transpired here with Brewster. I didn't say anything about Marianne's revelations, nor did Miles share what we had discovered in Sir Thomas' study regarding the transition of power or his place in the Agency.

Stewart seemed to be aware of an undercurrent, just as Andropov was. On the other hand, Captain Bruce sat with arms crossed and a bemused expression.

Inspector Fry seemed satisfied with what little Arabella, Marianne, and I could tell him about what had happened here and on the docks. He rose to leave, expecting the other two to follow, and when they didn't, he sat back down.

Stewart coughed and stared at my Father. "I suppose it is useless to warn you that it's dangerous to have further involvement with the Russians."

Andropov agreed, "Yes, I would prefer you leave them to me."

My Father examined them as if he had no idea what they meant. "I understand. Rest assured, we are all leaving for a holiday in Wales. It is beautiful this time of year and will be very restful for Lady Arabella and Lady Marianne, who will be coming with us."

Andropov wasted no time rejoining. "As bait Lord Blackburn?" he looked at the sisters.

They were staring at my Father, who flicked some lint off his pant leg. "You gentlemen need to realise that they are bait wherever they go. Wales is my choice, where I will have my people around us capable of caring for their safety and dealing with an action the Russians might take."

Andropov nodded. "I would like to come with you."

Father rubbed his nose and surprisingly said, "If you must, and admittedly I would rather have you with us than wandering about alone." Then he looked at Stewart and Fry. "Are you coming as well?"

Both men shook their heads, with Stewart answering, "No, I think you have left us both more than enough to deal with here in London."

Andropov then asked, "When do we leave?"

My Father sighed. "Tomorrow after Sir Thomas' funeral, where can we pick you up?"

He smiled. "I will meet you on the dock." He looked at the captain, "We are leaving on Captain Bruce's ship, the Morgana, I believe?"

Father inhaled deeply as if to control his temper. "Yes—the Morgana. We will see you there."

Then the three men rose and left. Miles waited to hear the door close, looked at my Father, and bluntly asked, "Did you recently receive a letter from Sir Thomas?"

My Father smiled. "The one where he thought you were too young and impulsive to take his place?"

Miles chuckled. "Yes, that one."

"It was one of the reasons I went to speak to Melbourne, Palmerston and Russell. I assured them that you were not interested in the position. They were relieved, shall we say." Miles snorted, but he noticed that my Father's expression had changed.

"The King is not well, and he and the Duchess of Kent are not on good terms. He doesn't want the Duchess as a Regent with that sycophant Conroy at her side. He is determined to survive until Princess Alexandrina Victoria reaches her majority in nine months. Melbourne made it clear that his Majesty does not want us ruining his birthday banquet by causing an international incident here in London next week."

Miles rubbed his neck. "What if we cause one in Wales? Can we keep it secret until after his birthday?"

My Father smirked, "We can try." He bit his lip, then added, "I know how you feel about what happened to Edward, Miles, but you can't let that consume you and lead you to make bad decisions."

Miles stared at him. "I promised my Father and Edward that I would make them pay, and they will." I grasped his hand and held on tightly. He peered at me, then refocused on my Father, "I can't let this go, Colin. Don't ask me to."

Father sat back, crossed his legs, and then tapped his lip. "I agree, Miles—we will make them pay."

Captain Bruce grinned. "Aye, then we are of one mind."

It was time for me to tell them about Marianne's drawings. "We have one problem. Marianne may have hidden her drawings somewhere in Edward's house, and she isn't prepared to tell us where. She doesn't trust us not to use the information in them for the wrong reason. She only trusts Edward."

Marianne raised a finger. "I am not as mad as I once was, Lord Blackburn."

My Father smiled at her. "Young Jilly already made us aware of that fact."

Arabella was uncomfortable and screwed her face up after glancing at her sister and then looking down at her hands. "She believes I would take them and use them for personal gain. That I couldn't resist the temptation since she pointed out that my life from here on out would be considerably different from what I have ever known."

Chapter 16

Wales and Conflict

Sir Thomas' funeral was a well attended sombre affair. I looked for the Russians at several points during the service and surprisingly saw none.

I was staggered to see Fiona come with Lord Shellard and Lady Jane, but she refused to speak to us, and when it was over, she retreated to their carriage with Lady Jane for company. Eventually, Miles' Father came to him, "Be patient with her son. It will take time."

"How is Edward? She left orders at the hospital that we were not to be admitted to his room or given any information."

"He's alive. Archer and Grimes still aren't sure if he will make it." He pursed his lips and added, "Jefferson said he would look in on him but that we could trust Archer."

I kissed my Father-in-law on the cheek. "Does she know that he's receiving Magda's serum?"

"Yes, she doesn't like it, but Jane stepped in and told her that Edward would surely die without it." I stepped back and took Miles' arm when I saw Fiona glaring at us from the Earl's carriage.

Lord Melbourne came to our sides, so we turned our attention to him. "Sir Thomas will be greatly missed. I must say that Lady Jefferson and Sir Matthew seem to be handling his death well, a solid English family."

Jibben, Judith and Magda came to stand with us. "You should all be commended, but I heard that Sir Edward is still in serious condition. One can hope that we won't be back here anytime soon." I felt the muscles tighten in Miles' arm as he clenched a fist.

"Lord Blackburn tells me that you are off to Wales, which I think under the circumstances is for the best. The police seem to have everything well in hand here." Lord Shellard smiled at him, putting a hand on his shoulder and casually turning him around, and walked away with the excuse he needed to speak to him about some government business.

Jibben looked at Miles. "Calm down, my friend, now come along. We are expected back at the Jefferson's, then off to the docks."

Miles was still watching Melbourne, so I pulled on his hand. "Miles?"

He peered down at me and snapped, "What!" I arched a brow at him, sighed, letting go of his hand, and started walking toward our carriage.

I heard Jibben say, "You need to calm down, Miles."

"Mind your own business, Locke." I heard the crunch of gravel behind me and was poised to have my arm grabbed, but he didn't. Instead, he walked past me and up to the Shellard carriage.

I heard Fiona screech, "Get out!" as Miles climbed in and Lady Jane climbed out.

I stood with her and asked, "Do you think it was wise to leave them alone."

She shrugged. "Possibly not, but Fiona is one of the most contrary people I have ever met. One minute she's yelling about Miles not trying hard enough to see Edward. Then she's screaming that he had the nerve to show up and request to be admitted to see him." I moved towards the carriage, "No, Lissa, leave them alone. Edward would hate whatever it is between them right now."

There was muffled shouting in the carriage, and more than once, the door opened only to be forcefully shut by my husband. Suddenly everything went quiet. I glanced at Lady Jane, watching the carriage intently as everyone else was intent on speaking to Isabel and Matthew.

The door finally opened, and Miles hopped out, letting down the stairs and extending his hand to aid a tearful Fiona. He walked her over to Isabel and Matthew first to offer her condolences. Lord Shellard, I could see, was pleased with what he had observed. Lady Jane walked to Fiona's side and returned to me with her walking arm in arm.

Fiona glanced at me, and instead of anger, I saw embarrassment as she spoke in a choked voice, "I owe you an apology, Lissa. Edward is probably even more headstrong than Miles. I know it was his decision to leave your home and return to me. It could have been much worse if Miles had not been there to bring him back into the house for immediate medical attention."

She shuddered with a sob, and I took her into my arms, trying to comfort her. She pulled back, "Edward was trying to return to me—because I had made such an uproar about removing all signs of Anderson from our home. Because of my guilt, I lashed out at both of you when he was wounded. I contributed to all of this."

She licked her lips. "You have been through so much yourselves. Yet you and Miles always look ahead for what needs to be done. You don't look for who to blame. You take care of the issue and each other." Then she tried to smile. "Can you ever forgive me? I am lonely and afraid right now. I need all of you to help me get through whatever happens."

I hugged her once again. "We will always be here for you, Fiona. So you don't need to apologise. You forget I have been there too, looking for someone to blame to make myself feel better."

Then we both sobbed and hugged until Miles came up to us. "I have spoken to Isabel and Matthew. They understand that we won't be able to go back to Sir Thomas's home. I have to see Edward before we leave for Wales." I smiled at him, Fiona took his arm, and we walked to our landau. Once seated, we were off to the hospital to see Edward.

Edward was being cared for in the private wing with a room to himself. He was ghostly pale, lying on his back, unshaven and hair tousled. A sheen of perspiration was pronounced on his brow, and he was covered by only the lightest of linen sheets. Dr Archer was at his side and seemed to have just finished giving him an injection of serum. He quickly hid the syringe from view. Fiona smiled and sighed with resignation. "You needn't bother trying to hide it any longer. I know that you have been giving Edward Magda's serum."

Dr Archer grinned. "His fever has broken, and he's resting. I believe he is more comfortable than ever."

She went to his side and took Edward's hand as she sat down, asking Dr Archer. "Has he awakened?"

"Not really, he calls out, but it's nothing decipherable."

Miles and I stood back by the doorway until Fiona called us forward. Miles stood in shock, staring at Edward as if he didn't recognise the man in the bed. Finally, I whispered, "Miles say something. Magda tells me that people can always hear you even if they can't respond."

Miles clenched his fist and knelt by Edward's bed, his head lowered and his lips moving in prayer. Then he stared at Edward and said, "My house is a mess. I need you to come set it to rights."

Edward took a deep breath, setting Miles back as he glanced up at Dr Archer. Archer smiled, "It's still too early to tell Lord Tinley, but it's hopeful."

I came and took Miles' hand, then prayed. I didn't know what to say to Edward and blurted out brusquely. "If you don't get better soon, I will paint the breakfast room purple."

I could have sworn that I saw a slight tic of his lips that no one noticed. We let Fiona sit and tell him about the children, then Sir Thomas' funeral and finally, Miles explained we were going to move the fight to Wales. Then silence descended on us, and Miles pulled on my arm, whispering, "We need to go." He bent and kissed Fiona on the cheek. She squeezed his hand and stood to hug me. I leaned over, kissed Edward's forehead, and whispered,

"Remember, it will be plum."

As we made our way to the door, a barely audible raspy voice croaked out, "Not purple." We stopped dead in our tracks and turned to stare at Edward. Then he took a deep breath, followed by a barely audible "Green and cream."

Fiona gasped and laid her head near Edward's hand, and he moved his fingers to touch her hair and said, "Love you too." Then he swallowed and groaned.

Dr Archer was quick to shoo Miles and me out with the promise he would keep us apprised. Miles was grinning from ear to ear and musing, "Purple? A threat about paint colours is what rouses him." He shook his head. "That's my brother." Then he chuckled. I glanced up at him as a tear slid down his cheek.

Lady Jane and Lord Shellard were entering the private wing as we left. My Father-in-law saw Miles' tears and raced to him, grabbing him. "My God, what's happened."

Miles began to laugh. "Green and cream, not purple."

Lord Shellard's anxiety was crushing him when he glanced at me and back at Miles as his panic turned to bewilderment, and he said, "What are you talking about?"

Miles grabbed his Father's shoulders in return. "Those were his first words."

Lord Shellard beamed, "He's awake?"

Miles shrugged. "He's at least aware and attempting to wake up."

Lord Shellard let go of Miles, leaned over, and kissed my cheek. Then he and Jane moved briskly down the hallway calling back over his shoulder, "Have a safe journey!"

We proceeded to our carriage, headed home to gather our children, the Burley sisters, and then to the docks. We found the schooner Morgana bobbing in the London Pool, waiting for its passengers.

Andropov was there, and shortly after were joined by the Lockes, Hamiltons, and finally, my parents. Longboats came to the dock to transport us and our baggage out to the ship. Once on board, Captain Bruce welcomed us and took my Father and Miles aside to speak to them. When they finally joined us below, we were all anxious to know what the Captain had to say to them.

My Father glanced at a nervous Miles, biting his thumb, then said, "Our plan worked. The Russian crew of a nearby ship has been keeping an eye on Bruce and his crew. He says they are ready to sail and are waiting for us to leave."

Miles cleared his throat. "They are more heavily armed than we are. This will be a race, so we may not be putting into Pembroke. But, if need be, the Captain has arranged for land transportation to pick us up from Cardiff. Bruce hopes to be able to hug the coastline and tuck in behind the Isle of Wight, and if we're lucky, we will lose them in some summer fog in the straits there. So, pray for inclement weather."

I sat with my hands wrapped around a cup of tea, biting my lip. Then I asked, "Should we have gone overland?"

Miles shook his head. "No, we can see them coming at sea and hopefully outrun them. On land, we could easily be ambushed. Captain Bruce knows these waters better than any Russian captain."

We all sat lost in our thoughts, waiting for the schooner to move out for the English Channel. Nell enquired about Edward, and Miles' response brought smiles all the way around. Even Arabella and Marianne joined in our happiness.

On the other hand, Magda sat solemnly chewing on a biscuit, her eyes narrowed, staring at the door behind me. I reached out to touch her hand, and she jumped and then focused on me. "Edward is still very ill, Little One. Only time will tell us if he will recover." She sounded preoccupied, without any confidence or emotion behind her answer. She sighed, then smiled. "Come with me. We can go above now."

The door opened, and the first mate stuck his head in, saying, "Cap'n says you can come up on deck now." Then he ducked back out.

Marianne was giddy at the thought of going out to sea, yet Arabella looked positively green. I pointed this out to Magda, who nodded, pulling some herbs out of her ever-present satchel, which she added to a cup of hot tea and pushed over to Arabella. "Drink this slowly. It will help your stomach." Arabella smelled it, wrinkling her nose. Magda smiled and said, "Hold your nose or don't breathe when you drink it."

Then she rose, saying to Marianne, "Come with Lady Tinley and me—we will talk." She reached into the satchel and pulled out a smaller bag.

After climbing onto the deck, Marianne raced about like a child. She hung far over the railing to watch the ship's wake; finally, Magda caught her hand. "Come with us, child." Marianne looked down at their clasped hands and frowned. I waited for her to shake it off, but she looked up at Magda and seemed to drift off, almost as if she had been hypnotised. She calmly walked where Magda led, and I followed them to the boat's stern, where we sat down on crates in the sunshine. Magda shook the little bag she had and dumped her old knuckle bones out on the deck. Marianne was mesmerised as Magda scrutinised her casting. Finally, she glanced up at me and smiled. "A boy will be healthy and look just like his Father."

Marianne giggled. "Me next!"

Magda frowned and shook her head. "I cannot see you, Lady Marianne. Your mind remains —muddled. You have not chosen your path yet."

Marianne frowned. "Then why bring me with you."

"To help you clear your mind."

She glanced at me. "Why did Lady Tinley need to know the gender of her baby?"

Magda laughed. "She already knew in her heart. I brought her along to help you. She is well-grounded and sees things no one else does. I am hoping she can help you —un-muddle."

Marianne laughed. "People have tried to do that all my life. Only my Mother ever understood me. She told me that I thought on multiple plans simultaneously and that no one would ever find any pattern in my thoughts. She feared that I would be labelled mad one day. Unfortunately, it seems that her prediction has come true. I don't even understand myself. Sometimes I don't sleep for days because of conflicting thoughts. My drawing helps me organise them."

Magda nodded. "Men like you are called a genius at best and at worst eccentric, while women are called witch or mad." Marianne stood and left us to go back to the railing, this time staring back the way we had come.

The crew became more alert as we proceeded down the Thames and out into the North Sea and rounded the headland just past Margate. Once we were in the Straits of Dover, the Captain posted a lookout aloft and on the stern and bow, keeping an eye out for other ships and any change in the weather. When we passed Folkestone, Captain Bruce came below to tell us. "We have picked up a shadow. It's not a schooner nor frigate."

Jibben laughed. "That will be my yacht with Thornton and de Bearne."

The Captain was gobsmacked. "De Bearne, the wine merchant!" he chuckled. "He's a master seaman, but the rat catcher?"

Jibben grinned. "Thornton is a man of many skills, Captain."

"I hope so. My voyages with you tend to be challenging at times."

Miles chuckled, "As if you didn't enjoy those challenges."

The Captain chuckled, then sat down. "Aye, my boy. Now,

where's the food? I am starving." He yelled out to his cook, "Bring on the food!"

His cook yelled, "It will be there when it's ready and not a minute before. The cook's galley assistant brought in a plate of hard biscuit and placed it before the Captain. The Captain stared at it, saying, "I would replace the damn man if he weren't so good at what he does." Then, he chuckled and picked up a biscuit biting into it with relish.

The rest of the day and night proceeded without issue. The following day another ship appeared, coming up fast on our port side. Jibben's yacht appeared out of nowhere, causing the other ship to manoeuvre away to avoid ramming them. However, it was a near miss and sent the unknown ship further into the Channel. The yacht stayed nearby for most of the day, and then as evening came upon us, it veered off, heading towards St. Ives in Cornwall. I watched them leave as Miles came up with the children to stand by me. "Alex is demanding another story."

I peered down at Charlotte, then at Alex, who was almost asleep on his Father's shoulder. "Alex, is it?"

In a very muzzy voice, Alex just managed to say, "Story." Before closing his eyes, sighing, and drifting off to sleep.

Charlotte pulled on my sleeve. "I will listen to a story for him, Mama."

I smiled at her, then looked at Miles, who cocked a brow. "I think I was manipulated."

I chuckled. "No doubt." Marianne stared at me blankly until

410

Charlotte approached her and sat in her lap, catching her full attention. "I like happy stories, but you look sad, so I don't think you know any."

Marianne raised her chin and thought, "My brother Justin used to tell me a tale about a brother and sister who ran away from an uncaring Father." I was concerned that this would turn into a terrible story, but it included the vestiges of an old tale called *The Brother and Sister* as she started. This must have been Marianne's dream of her brother rescuing her from a cruel Father. She finished the tale in the tradition of the original story. "Her brother took her deep into the woods where they lived together until a prince and princess found them, and they fell in love and married the lonely brother and sister." Marianne finished just as Charlotte's eyes were getting heavy, but she reached up and kissed her on the cheek. "Thank you—that was beautiful." Then she leaned her head on her shoulder and closed her eyes.

Marianne was at a loss about what to do, so she hesitantly put her arms around my daughter and pulled her close. Then, she smiled up at me. "Your children are truly remarkable, Lady Tinley."

"I think so, but then I am their Mother." A tear trickled down her cheek as she stared at the setting sun. Miles stood with Alex drooling over his shoulder as I said, "Miles, Robert is not going to be impressed about having to get those milk stains out of your jacket yet again."

He snorted and moved Alex to the other shoulder, then looked down and frowned. "I don't suppose he will. I best take this young fellow down and put him to bed."

I rose. "Here, give him to me. You can carry Charlotte." He handed me our son and picked up Charlotte. Marianne was startled and gasped, reaching out for my child. Then she pulled back and wrapped her arms around herself. I felt like I should stay, but it was getting cool, so instead, I asked if she would join us, surprisingly. She agreed and followed us down below.

She stood in the doorway with Anne, watching us change and put our children to bed. Then, I heard her whisper, "Do they always put their children to bed."

Anne responded, "Not always. It depends on what they have going on. But they are devoted parents." It made me smile, and I saw Miles smile as well.

Once we were done, Miles excused himself and went back up on deck with my Father and Jibben, who had been waiting for him to follow. Marianne and I joined Mother, Judith, and Magda in the Mess. Judith poured coffee for us and then tipped a measure of whisky into each cup. Magda smiled at Marianne. "Your sister is finally asleep. She is strong-minded to fight my herbs so hard."

Marianne nodded. "Rupert used to drug her."

I stared at her. "Drug her?"

She nodded. "It horrified her when Brewster told her what was being done." I still had to wonder about Brewster and Arabella's stories, I had discussed it with Miles, but he felt it was just the confusion from the trauma. I suppose he could be right, but I still felt uncomfortable about it.

I abandoned that thought when Judith said, "Some men are

412

just pigs."

We all nodded, and then my Mother added, "Some are a blessing." To which we all nodded except Marianne.

So I decided to change the subject. "About your drawings. I have part of the one you gave Milly. It's impressive in its intricacy. Where did you learn to do that?"

She smiled. "From a truly mad man in Scotland named Gavin. He was very handsome and so lonely, but he rarely spoke. So I would sit beside him and watch him draw. Some of the words he used in his drawings were so small that it's almost impossible to read even with a magnifying glass."

"What was he writing about?"

"His life, madness—he was deeply disturbed and had terrible hallucinations that ended with debilitating headaches. He would sometimes lie on his bed and moan for days. Because of him, I decided I didn't want to be mad anymore. It was exhausting, though, trying to recapture the real world. It was so much easier to be mad. No one has any expectations of you when you are insane, while sanity has many demands. But, strangely enough, Gavin encouraged me to reach out for normal. It made me sad that he couldn't come with me, so I did it for him, but in doing so, I lost him."

"What happened to him?"

"He died." She grabbed all of our attention as she added, "We were on an excursion one day on the beach with several other patients. He waited until the staff were distracted, kissed me passionately, turned and walked into the sea—he never returned. After he died, I started to draw.

Oddly, I couldn't draw when I was younger, but using letters and numbers to construct a composition seemed to come naturally to me, as if Gavin had transferred his skill to me with that kiss." All of us were mesmerised by her story. It was beautiful and tragic at the same time.

Then she chuckled. "But it's only when I let myself float into the realm of madness that I can draw. So, Madam Magda, my mind will be forever muddled as long as I need to draw."

Judith had been watching her intently. "Then what drives you to draw?"

Marianne sighed and covered her face with her hands. "You will think it sounds silly, but I used to get terrible headaches like Gavin. He told me it was because I kept too much information in my brain, and it would run out of room. So he suggested that I empty it every now and then. I laughed at him, but it came to me after he died that perhaps he was right. I wanted to honour Gavin's memory, so I started to perfect his method of drawing, and my headaches disappeared."

Judith was captivated by Marianne's tale and reached out to pat her hand. "That is such a beautiful and tragic tale."

Marianne giggled. "Gavin is my daily inspiration to keep up my drawing."

Magda closed her eyes, and a tear ran down her cheek. Then, she opened her eyes and took Marianne's hand, examining it closely. "You will find another Gavin one day and never be muddled again."

Marianne leaned into Magda, wrinkling her nose and said cheekily, "I know, Grandmother. But, if not in this life, maybe in the next."

Magda cupped her cheek and stared into her eyes. "I believe you will."

My Mother had been silent the entire time, and when I glanced at her, I saw tears sliding down her cheeks. She rose. "If you will excuse me, I think I will get a breath of air before I retire."

I raised a hand to touch her arm. "Would you like me to come with you?"

"No, dear, I would like to be alone. I will be fine."

I turned back to see Marianne watching us. "You love your Mother very much, don't you."

"Yes, I do."

"I loved my Mother like that too." She didn't continue but turned her attention to her coffee which she gulped back and then rose. "I think I will retire for the night." She left Judith, Magda, and me staring at each other.

Judith was the one to give voice to a question paramount in my mind, "I feel like Lady Marianne just predicted her death?"

Magda waved a hand, dismissing the question, "We all die, my Judith, but no one knows when or where."

Judith shook her head. "I am not so sure about that. I felt a chill from her words."

Magda sighed and tried to explain what she meant. "She is tired and damaged. I want to help her heal—but I don't know if I can. Perhaps Wales and the ocean will calm her spirit."

I looked over my shoulder and saw Marianne standing with her forehead leaning against the door to the berth she shared with her sister. "And what of Arabella?"

Magda closed her eyes. "I see her walking along cliffs, the wind in her hair and looking out to sea. Someone is at her side, but I don't know if it's her sister."

I rose. "I think I will find Miles and see if we can't talk about something more cheerful. This conversation has been heart-wrenching."

I left and made my way on deck. I found Miles standing by himself at the rail. I linked my arm with his "What were you, Jibben, and my Father discussing?"

He smirked, still staring out to sea as he laid his hand on mine. "Options."

"That doesn't sound too dire."

He turned to look at me. "It's a matter of how we can discourage the Russians from their mission without killing them."

"And that's not something you would support?"

He snorted, "I admit I am a hothead, but I don't support outright murder either. I will not take a life except to defend those who require my protection. Still, I don't want to break my promise to Father and Edward. I will make those people pay." I leaned into him, and he removed my arm from his and pulled me into a hug. I relished his warmth and revelled in his scent and the sea air.

I glanced towards the stern and saw my Mother standing similarly with my Father. "Did my Mother interrupt your talk?"

"She did, but regardless there was little else to say." He glanced their way. "Tell me what upset her so much."

I pursed my lips, not sure how to phrase it. "I think Marianne fell in love with another patient in Scotland, but he died tragically. How she spoke of him was so heart-rending, it affected us all."

"Hence I have the pleasure of your company?"

"Indeed, sir, perhaps we should retire, and you can comfort me?"

He chuckled. "It would be my pleasure."

Captain Bruce strolled by to say, "We have picked up our Russian shadow again. But they are keeping their distance this time. I don't think they will try anything at sea now since we will reach Pembroke in the early morning, and from there, I can only wish you well. I promise to do what I can to delay anyone from disembarking from that ship until after you are on the road." He patted Miles on the back. "Stand firm, Miles. Sometimes revenge is necessary."

I should have been shocked by his words; before he moved on, he glanced down at me and winked, "It's the Viking in me—most

Scots have one in the family tree somewhere." Then he tipped his hat and walked on.

I glanced at Miles' stern expression as he stared out to sea and wondered if he was mulling over the Captain's warning about the ship or his advice.

I let him think for a bit. Then I pulled away from him. "Come, you promised to comfort me."

He smirked, "Yes, milady, how could I forget."

Chapter 17

Decisions, Diversions and Deceptions

In Pembroke, the plan was revised. Nell and Hamilton would wait for the arrival of the Irregulars on Jibben's yacht, which was expected at any time. To my surprise, Andropov agreed to stay with them. He wanted to keep an eye out for the Russians if they came that way.

Once they were settled in a comfortable Inn, we hired carriages and horses to take us to Blackburn Manor, where Sir Derwyn and Lady Stanhope welcomed us. I stood back and took in the vastness of Blackburn manor, realising I had forgotten how large the house was and how foreboding it could be. It was, in part, a medieval fortress that had stood there for centuries, repelling Viking invaders from the sea and the English from the east. But, eventually, it fell into English hands, and the enemy became the Welsh themselves, a proud, hardy, and intelligent foe that were a continuous thorn in the side of the English for years to come.

After we had changed out of our travelling clothes, we came down to the drawing room, which had been redecorated. I could see my Mother's and Lady Stanhope's influence. The dark half-panelling had been painted white. The formerly deep blue walls were painted pale mint green, making the room light and airy. The furniture was an eclectic mix of old and new, covered in burnished gold and shades of cream. Pale yellow velvet curtains hung to the sides of the windows, bringing the eye soaring up to the intricate mouldings on the ceiling. They included frolicking cherubs and the symbols of Wales, daffodils, and tiny Welsh dragons. While two prominent crystal chandeliers now hung from gilded rosettes equally spaced down the centre of the room.

Lady Lewis looked younger than when I had last seen her. The strain of her life as Lady Stanhope had been lifted from her shoulders. I ventured to ask her about her son Bennett the new Lord Stanhope. I remembered the troubled young man from earlier in the year when he had fled with Lady Adele north to Northumberland and asked for our protection from her malicious ex-husband, Johnathan Campeau. "Is Lord Stanhope well Lady Lewis?"

"As well as can be expected. He is still convinced that Lady Adele was the love of his life and that he will never marry. I feel for his loss. Yet if anything good came of it, it's helped him focus on his estates and his people here in Wales. He and Jean Campeau have become close, but we have kept an eye on that relationship.

Mr Campeau seems amenable, but he was his brother's man for most of his adult life. However, he's been invaluable to Derwyn. Jean has taken charge of the estate business and freed Derwyn to tend to the Brotherhood's day-to-day business."

I smiled, wondering if it was wise that Stanhope and Campeau had renewed their friendship, bonding over their admiration of Lady Adele, no doubt. However, I didn't voice my concerns and only said, "I look forward to seeing your son and Mr Campeau again."

She smiled. "They are out fishing right now. Bennett has made a retreat out of the old castle on the headland. He calls it his thinking place."

"I hope we will see him later."

Sir Derwyn stared at his wife as she frowned and said, "It is doubtful, Lady Tinley. He knows you are coming and told us seeing you again would bring back too many painful memories. So I imagine he will stay at the castle.

I glanced at Miles and then at the couple in front of me. "Hiding from the past isn't healthy."

Lady Lewis looked relieved. "I don't know what else to do. He needs to let go of Lady Adele and let her rest in peace."

As tea arrived, so did a slightly dishevelled Jean Campeau and Lord Stanhope.

Campeau was smiling as he said, "I was able to convince Bennett to come, after all, Lady Lewis."

They both bowed, apologised for their appearance, and then made as if to leave again. Lady Lewis quickly made the introductions forestalling their retreat, and my Mother insisted they sit down and not bother running off to tidy themselves.

Lady Arabella was noticeably uncomfortable under their scrutiny, and Lord Stanhope, ever one to put his foot in it, asked, "Lady Arabella, may I ask what happened to your eye?"

Arabella and his Mother were horrified. A Beau Monde custom was that you didn't ask such questions in public and never when the person with the disfigurement was present. The person was only ever talked about behind their backs, so in that regard, I applauded Stanhope for putting his foot in it. His Mother, though, was shocked and hissed, "Bennett!"

Marianne took her sister's hand and answered, "Her husband had his valet beat her almost to death, taking out her eye in the process. But both of them are dead now. I helped kill the valet. And since you're asking the most impertinent questions, I will tell you that I was in a madhouse in Scotland after witnessing several brutal murders and being repeatedly abused by my cousin and his friends, all with my husband's blessing."

Both Campeau and Stanhope sat there with their mouths open in horror. Campeau shook his head in disgust *"Ils devraient être tirés et coupés en quatre."*

Marianne smiled at him. "That's very thoughtful of you, Mr Campeau. Drawing and quartering them would have been a most fitting punishment— but they are all dead now regardless."

Campeau stared in astonishment at her, then smiled. "I am glad to hear it, Lady Marianne."

Stanhope had not taken his eyes off Arabella. I realised she resembled Lady Adele superficially, while Campeau seemed enchanted by Marianne's forthrightness. Judith and my Mother seemed to have noticed it from their expressions of concern as they looked from one couple to the next. I only hoped this wouldn't lead to trouble since all four people in question were not above suspicion, yet they all carried the scars of betrayal.

Lord Stanhope finally came back to himself and asked in his off-handed way, "So what mischief have you gotten into that has you people fleeing to Wales this time?"

My Father sat back and said smugly, "Russians." running a finger down a crease in his trousers.

Stanhope looked at Miles. "What is that supposed to mean?"

Miles smiled. "Exactly what he said the Russians are coming."

Stanhope shook his head in disbelief. "Why?"

Jibben chuckled. "What else would it be but the same old motivations, greed, the desire for secret information that they have no right to and murdering their opponents."

Stanhope rubbed his forehead. "You people never do things by halves, do you? But why here?"

My Father answered him with a deeply pained expression, "Sir Thomas Wiseman was murdered, along with several others that were merely in their way. We will see and hear them coming in Wales before they reach us, and here they have no allies and no embassy to hide within."

Campeau nodded. "There will also be no eyes passing judgement on your actions."

My Father abruptly turned on him. "We are not murderers, Mr Campeau. If we were, you would have been dead earlier this year and not working with Sir Derwyn to manage my estate."

Campeau's face flushed as he responded, "You are right. I beg your forgiveness, Lord Blackburn."

"No need to beg anything, Mr Campeau. I am sure you were

used to different methods of dealing with such inconveniences." Then he sighed and said more lightly, "We on the other hand, prefer to handle things differently."

Campeau glanced at Marianne, who was watching him intently, then looked back at my Father. "I am prepared to defend you and your family."

"Thank you, Mr Campeau. We may indeed need your assistance." Then he turned at Bennett. "Stanhope, can we count on you to protect our children at the very least?"

Stanhope looked gobsmacked that he would have to ask. "Of course—you needn't ask."

"Thank you. Now can we have some of that tea Lady Lewis? I am parched."

She nodded, and as she rose to send for it, she said, "I hope you don't mind, but when I heard you were coming, I invited Dr Stockton to join us for dinner this evening."

I smiled, thinking of the former Dials Crow. "How is Stockon managing?"

Sir Derwyn laughed. "He speaks Welsh like a native and has won the people's hearts, including that of the local beauty Miss Emma Cowin. You will meet her at dinner."

My Mother chuckled, "I suppose it's wise to alert him that we might require his services."

Lady Lewis frowned with concern. "Truthfully, I hadn't considered it, but I suppose you are right."

Father cleared his throat. "We had best inform you what is coming here and why."

He glanced at Stanhope and Campeau. "But first, I should warn you two gentlemen that if either of you tries to undercut us believe me when I say you will pay dearly for it." Both men accepted the admonishment without comment.

Then he switched his attention to the sisters "Ladies. I hope you understand that we do not tolerate betrayal from anyone." Arabella looked affronted, but Marianne nodded in agreement without hesitation.

My Father explained the details of what had transpired in London, everyone appearing to hang on his every word. Miles and Jibben occasionally interposed a comment, but no one asked any questions. I was watching Arabella while my Father spoke. Since coming off the ship, she seemed withdrawn, and I was sure it had nothing to do with seasickness. I felt like she hadn't told us her whole story. Something was missing. I wondered if Arabella had been working with Brewster and the Count all this time. Only time will tell.

I suddenly felt a weariness come over me. The peaceful surroundings were lulling me into a doze, so I whispered to Miles, "I am going to go lie down until luncheon."

He kissed my hand, saying, "I will come with you. A nap would be just the thing right now." We both rose and made our excuses. Miles pulled me aside once in the entry hall. "I saw you were watching Lady Arabella. What bothers you about her?"

"I don't know, Miles, but there seems to be something missing from her story." I turned to the sound of shuffling feet behind us as the sisters exited the drawing room.

Marianne came towards us, pulling her sister along. "Tell them now, or I will. They will never trust us until you do, and frankly, I am tired of being considered unreliable."

Arabella was in no mood to speak, so Marianne continued. "Fine, then I will tell them. In case you weren't aware, Arabella was the toast of her first season, a fact that angered a certain Russian Countess who had been sent to England to obtain some polish. It was also an excuse to remove her from the influence of a certain Count, you know." She glanced up at Arabella. "Well, say something!"

Arabella huffed and shook her sister's hand loose "It became a game for Irina and me. How many of the Beau Monde could we entice with our charms? While the Englishmen take such things for granted, the Russians expect something in return for their attention, at least Count Vasiliev did. I found myself in a compromising situation with him when Countess Irina came along at a fortuitous time, and he fled. Irina promised to keep what happened a secret."

She wrapped her arms around her waist and seemed lost for words. "I was a fool to think she meant to keep her word. She began spreading vicious rumours about me though nothing ruinous had happened to me. The scent of scandal would cause embarrassment for my family, and I would lose my chance for a good match. It was shortly after that when Rupert asked my Father for my hand."

Marianne nudged her. "Go on."

"I agreed to the marriage because my Father said it was the only way to stop the gossip. Even though I detested Rupert, he wanted me. He was well-heeled and an Earl, so I wasn't trading down or moving up in the social hierarchy, so everyone assumed it must be a love match."

She shuddered and chuckled unhappily. "It turns out he had worked out this scheme with the Russians to entrap me, but it backfired. He had offered for the wrong sister. He didn't realise Marianne was the one he should have asked for, it was she who knew about my Father's business dealings, but he didn't find that out until it was too late. The Russians compromising me made it possible for him to marry me. In return for the favour, he was to provide the Russians with information from the Home office and about my Father's business. He was furious when I pled ignorance about my Father's dealings. He had to adapt to the mistake, and I was supposed to ask my Father specific questions about his business and provide Rupert with the answers or endure a beating. My Father, however, wouldn't tell me a thing."

A tear rolled down her cheek when she added, "When I complained to him about my husband's threats of beatings, he said that it was my fault that I had let myself be trapped. Shortly after, he gave Marianne to Braithwaite, the Beau Monde's worst degenerate. It was a calculated move since Rupert, and he loathed each other and because Braithwaite was a confidante of my Father's."

Marianne, during this time, had been scrutinising the far corner of the large entry hall and smiling. I am not sure what she saw, but this manor was incredibly old, and anything or anyone was likely to be there. After being in Scotland for All Hallows Eve, I

427

couldn't pretend that sometimes the veil between life and death wasn't thin. Still, she noticed that Arabella had stopped talking and nudged her again without looking at her. "Go on, tell them the rest."

Arabella glared at her inattentive sister and continued, "Count Vasiliev accosted Brewster one day when we were shopping. He tried to get to me through her. I believed her lies that she had refused to help him, but she must have been working for them all along. Finally, she pressured me to agree with my husband to move Marianne to London and Blane House. He forced me to sign Justin's name to the papers making Rupert her exclusive guardian."

Miles had been patiently listening but finally seemed to have lost his patience. "Is there a point to you finally baring your soul to us?"

Arabella scowled at him. "Of course, there is! They are going to find us and kill us all."

"Are you going to assist them?"

"No! Of course not!

I saw my Father and Jibben enter the hallway and scrutinise Lady Arabella. My Father said, "Brewster talked quite a bit on the way to Newgate. You are both particularly good at telling us just enough truth to be believed."

Jibben smirked. "In other words, he's still not sure which of you is lying. But Brewster made a convincing case that you are working with Count Vasiliev. According to her, you two have been lovers for years. I believe the words she used were that *'you shared him with the Countess,'* unbeknownst to you."

He smirked and crossed his arms. "I, on the other hand, believe that you have been used all this time, Lady Arabella. You were right about one thing, your husband and the Russians thought you were the one who knew your Father's secrets. It seems that you were your Father's prized decoy. It was the bluestocking, Marianne, who they had wanted. Your Father must have found it amusing that he had deceived them into believing it was you."

Arabella started to cry, and the rest of the assembly in the drawing room came out to see what the commotion was. Lord Stanhope was flustered as he spoke. "I am sorry, milady, I told them that I met Lord Harris in London at the opera earlier this year. He was a friend of my Father's and introduced me to Count Vasiliev, who offered to introduce me to you. He thought you might be able to help me forget a recent loss. I realised then I needed to leave for Wales to avoid their corrupting influence and any association with my Father's old friends. They are all degenerates."

Marianne reached out to take her sister's hand, but Lady Arabella pulled back and slapped her hard across the face. "You bitch! All you had to do was give Brewster the damn drawings. We could have been free of them!"

Marianne shook her head. "No! We would have been dead, Arabella." She snapped her fingers and said dismissively, "Fish food—that's all we would have been. When will you realise that nothing good ever came from papa's business dealings?" Arabella sank to her knees, covering her face with her hands. Marianne knelt beside her, pulling her hands back and ran her hand over her hair. "Oh, Arabella—you've always made poor choices." Then she stood up, walked away from her distraught sister, and went back into the drawing room.

Lady Arabella climbed to her feet and screamed at her, "Father loved me more!"

And from the drawing room, Marianne yelled, "Yes, but he needed me more and used us both abominably."

Arabella looked up at Miles, then my Father. "What are you going to do with me?"

Jibben glanced at my Father, and Miles then pulled on his ear and asked, "What do you want us to do?"

She stared at him in disbelief. "I have worked with the Russians!"

He scratched his cheek. "No, you didn't. You were used. I am sorry, but you can't do anything to hurt us—unless, of course, you have a knife or gun, which I don't think we would allow." Jibben was always a pragmatist with a sense of humour.

She lost all her bravado as my Mother came to her side. "Come, Arabella, a good cry often brings things into perspective." She walked off with my Mother to the morning room across the hall.

Lady Lewis looked concerned. "What will happen to her?"

My Father nodded. "Nothing. She has no skills or information and is no threat to us."

She shook her head. "You can't be sure, Colin. The Russians can't be far behind. She may try to reach them."

Campeau interjected, shaking his head, "She is a liability to them now—they would kill her."

I turned to my Father. "Sometimes, I don't think I will ever understand you. Why bring her with us if you thought she was lying."

His eyes were full of concern as he answered, "I wasn't positive, and besides, would you have believed me? She was beaten at her husband's direction. You can't help but have sympathy for her despite any doubts we may have harboured."

I nodded, knowing that I did have doubts about both sisters, so I asked, "Do you trust Marianne?"

He shrugged. "I don't trust her because she is unpredictable."

Marianne called out from the drawing room, "You know I can hear you, and I am not unpredictable. I am insane."

I smiled at this exchange, then sighed, "I am going to see the children and then take a nap."

Miles nodded. "I will go with you."

We spent an hour with the children before their luncheon arrived. My brothers Daniel and Allan were full of questions about why James was allowed to stay home to study for Eton's entrance exams. Miles pointed out that our Father would likely take them fishing in the cove at some point if they behaved. Their mood immediately changed, and they began plotting with Jibben's son

John about when and how to ask our Father.

Our children, however, were a different story. They had picked up on our tense emotions. Charlotte was cranky, and Alex was being contrary. We tried to calm them both without much success. Finally, Anne seemed to have had enough and took them in hand with a stamp of her foot. "Miss Charlotte, Master Alex that will be enough of that. You both need a nap."

Charlotte was shocked. "Without luncheon."

"Yes, unless you can behave." Both children ran to Anne, pleading with her and promising to be good. To avoid interfering, we quickly and quietly snuck out.

Miles quirked a brow back towards the nursery. "Anne has turned into a fine nanny."

I smiled. "That she has."

We entered our room to find Meg and Robert still unpacking, but they were happy to leave and have a cup of tea. Meg was much healthier than before her holiday, and Miles and I agreed it was good to have the pair back. At some time, I would have to sit with Renee when this was all over and discuss her ambitions, for if she wanted to be a lady's maid, she would have to change some of her behaviours.

Miles and I undressed and lay down. We were both exhausted and fell asleep in each other's arms. I woke alone in bed to Meg bustling about as she approached. "It's time to dress, milady. Luncheon will be served shortly."

I groaned and stretched. "I take it Lord Tinley is already up and downstairs?"

She smiled. "Yes, milady."

I washed in the warm water that Meg had brought to refresh myself and let Meg help me dress and fix my hair. Then I hurried downstairs so as not to be late. As it was, I was on the tail end of those filing in the dining room. Lady Arabella sat beside my Mother, and I sat next to Miles.

Once the first course was served, the conversation began to flow. Magda, I noted, was picking apart a piece of bread and eating a tiny bit at a time. Finally, I leaned over and asked, "Magda, are you feeling well."

She glanced up. "Yes, Little One, I am lost in thought." Then, she turned to Lady Arabella and said, "You are not worthless, Arabella. On the contrary, you ultimately saved your sister when you could have betrayed her and us at any time."

Arabella stared at Magda with her one red-rimmed eye. "I hadn't thought of it that way. I have always felt marginalised by my brothers and my baby sister. Yet my Father didn't value any of us, not even Justin and Alexander, but they were the only ones he protected."

Marianne looked up from her soup "Mother loved us, Arabella."

Arabella sighed. "But she left us."

Marianne shook her head. "No, Lord Shellard's second wife poisoned her. Mother didn't drown. Father dumped her in the weir after discovering what Carolyn had done."

433

She took another mouthful of soup. "Poor Alexander, the only family he has left is a bankrupt brother and two damaged sisters. It's a wonder that Justin can afford to keep him at Cambridge though he's the true academic in the family." She chuckled. "Perhaps we will have a Cambridge don in the family."

Jibben had been watching her closely from across the table. "As you could have been if you had been born a boy."

She snorted, "I have an excellent memory and am good at Mathematics. However, I am not sure I would have an aptitude for creative thinking or philosophy."

Jibben smirked. "I beg to differ; you have played at being the haughty vapid lady and the insane waif. You can keep secrets, important secrets that people would kill to obtain. Why have you never given in to the temptation to use those secrets for your own gain."

Marianne put down her spoon and folded her hands in her lap. "Because such knowledge is poison Sir Stephen. It killed two of my brothers, my Father and, indirectly, my Mother. Greed and immorality have been my family's hallmarks for two generations and possibly more. I want that to stop even if it means I must give up my life."

Judith sucked in a gasp. "I knew you were thinking of killing yourself—so that you could join Gavin."

Marianne smiled sweetly. "Gavin was a good friend, that was all. I loved him like a brother. He wouldn't want me to kill myself. I want to live, Lady Locke. That is more important to me than anything. To be free and to live."

Jean Campeau was listening to her intently and smiling. "It is a wish that many of us have, Lady Marianne. If anyone can help you realise it, these people can." He blushed when she smiled at him, and he returned his attention to his soup.

Lady Arabella seemed withdrawn and sceptical, "How can either of you be positive about the future? You both have nothing!"

Jean Campeau scrutinised Arabella "I have made friends here, I have a roof over my head, useful work for which I am compensated, and I am free to come and go as I wish." He glanced at My Father. "I am free to come and go, am I correct?"

My Father chuckled. "You are correct, Mr Campeau."

Lady Arabella asked my Father, "How can you possibly know that he's trustworthy? I understand that his brother was one of your worst enemies."

Without hesitation, he said, "He has earned my trust."

She chuckled. "I have never heard of such nonsense. It will be interesting to see if my sister and I can meet your expectations well enough that we might also earn your trust."

He swallowed a spoonful of soup and then stared at her, unblinking, "Only time will tell, Lady Arabella."

Marianne chuckled. "Arabella, trust is not negotiable. It is either given or not."

Mother patted Arabella's hand. "We will help you adjust, my dear." I watched Arabella look at her with disbelief. I still wasn't sure that I would trust her.

Marianne was a different case; she had been exposed to another life without her family's influence for some years, even though it was in a hospital. Nevertheless, she would still bear watching, and I would keep an eye on Arabella as events dictated.

Campeau and Marianne carried on a conversation about Mathematics in which Jibben seemed engrossed and was chuckling over some mathematical equation. I wondered how they could find such a dry subject amusing, but it was beyond my understanding.

After luncheon, Miles and I went for a walk along the cliffs gazing out over the cove far below. I stepped as close to the edge as I could and saw to my right the steep path we had taken down to the beach the last time we were here, but six feet directly below me was a wide recessed ledge nestled into the cliffside where some seabirds had nested. Suddenly the earth under my feet started to crumble, and Miles pulled me back. "That is too close, my love."

I rolled my eyes. "It was only a bit of loose earth, Miles. I wasn't about to go over the cliff; that ledge is wide enough to catch me."

Marianne and Jean Campeau, with Arabella and Lord Stanhope, came up behind us. Jean leaned over, smiling. "The ledge belongs to a pair of Peregrines. Their young have reached maturity, so the nest is not in use now. Otherwise, they would be diving at us and screeching."

Arabella looked aghast as Marianne stood on the edge with

Jean, looking down and discussing falcon habits. Again, they seemed like a strange pairing but obviously enjoyed each other's company.

Lord Stanhope appeared to find Arabella's response to her sister's daring amusing. Still, he hid it well as we continued to walk along the cliff, talking about how he was working to restore his dilapidated estate. Surprisingly, she offered to consult with him on restoring his gardens. It was something in which she was singularly interested. So they walked off talking about how a kitchen garden could make a household self-sufficient. Then they turned to the possibility of recruiting a tenant farmer to put his home farm to rights. She made several suggestions of likely candidates, including usurping the farmer who was currently on her husband's country estate and hated it there. They walked off hatching plans, leaving Miles and me at a loss for words.

Marianne and Campeau came up beside us, and she said, "You should close your mouth before a bug flies in Lady Tinley. If you are surprised about Arabella's knowledge of gardening and crops, you should recall that she took over my Mother's place when she died. She had already learned a considerable amount about gardening before our Mother died. As my Father became wrapped up in his other business affairs, the estate's running was left to her. Randall and Julian were useless sods. Justin had been trained but was still at school, and Alexander was too young. Anything I tried to grow generally turned brown and died." She giggled and walked on with Campeau, talking mathematics once again.

I peered up at Miles shielding my eyes from the sun. "I have never seen two more unlikely couples."

Miles glared at me. "Lissa, we are not here to play matchmaker."

"I wasn't considering that, Miles. It's just the contrast I find interesting. I would never have thought that any of those four would be attracted to each other."

"Lissa!"

" All right—I said I only found it interesting."

He shook his head, took my arm, and assisted me to waddle down the footpath to the beach. We stood on the sand and looked out over the cove. "It is beautiful here." Then his focus shifted to the headland, and he frowned. "Even that derelict castle is not such an eyesore in the full light of day."

I followed his eye and noticed some movement on the headland. "Did you see that?"

Lord Stanhope came running towards us, shaking his fist, "Damn squatters!"

Miles arched a brow. "Have you had problems with squatters before?"

Stanhope nodded. "Occasionally, it's most often just fishermen who use the docks on the other side."

Miles pursed his lips. "You should pull them down."

"I know, but they are damn convenient. It saves me the effort of stomping up the giant's stairs."

Miles was intrigued. "You use the place that frequently?"

Stanhope frowned. "After I lost Adele, I retreated there. I considered being a hermit for a time. Then Jean kept coming out and bothering me about refurbishing my estate. He helped me get my finances straightened out. I took a loan from my Mother, and things are coming together now. I spend less time at the castle, so I am making progress. I am no farmer and have no eye for fruits, vegetables, and flowers, but Lady Arabella has offered me some valuable advice."

I nodded. "Yes, we heard."

He blushed, staring at his feet. Then he asked, "Care to row out with me and see if we can scare them off."

"That's been successful?"

Stanhope chuckled. "We will have to go up the giant's stairs and through the back of the castle, but I find that making enough noise while making my way to the western side usually works. I have never had to confront anyone with pistols drawn."

I looked over at the headland again but didn't see anything. "Do you think that's wise, considering who has been following us?"

Jibben and Judith came to join us, with Jibben pointing out, "Looks like you have company, Stanhope. We saw a man with a spyglass looking this way from up on the cliff. I waved but didn't get a response. I would say that they are decidedly not friendly. Shall we go have a look?"

Judith slapped his arm. "You would just row out there when you're not sure what or who you are dealing with?"

Lord Stanhope said, "It's probably just a fisherman that has put in for a rest."

Judith shook her head. "So they landed on the west side and decided to take a stroll and spy on the local Lord?"

Stanhope frowned. "She has a point. Do you think it is your Russians?"

Judith stared at him like he was simple. "Of course, I think it's the Russians!"

Miles shrugged. "We should arm up before we row out."

I turned on him. "Have you not heard Jibben or Judith?"

"Lissa, we can't just sit here and wait for them to come to us."

Stanhope agreed, "We can do some reconnaissance."

Miles glared at him. "You are going nowhere."

Stanhope scowled. "I beg your pardon, but that is my castle. I think the constable and I should pay a visit."

Jibben laughed. "It will get you both knocked on the head and dumped in the sea."

Stanhope pouted, "What are you going to do to stop me? Call the Truncheon lads to drop me in the *oubliette*?"

I shook my head. "Blackburn Manor doesn't have an *oubliette*."

He glanced at me and frowned. "What difference does that make? Your husband and Father have locked me up before."

Arabella had caught up with us and sounded shocked, "Would they drop you into an *oubliette*?"

Stanhope looked at her, then burst out laughing. "No, but I am already familiar with the dungeons of Blackburn Manor."

Jibben chuckled, and Miles scowled, saying, "I suggest we return to the Manor. We need to tell Lord Blackburn what we have seen and decide our next course of action."

Arabella looked horrified. "You aren't going out there without knowing how many men or armaments they have."

Miles pinched the bridge of his nose. "There is no other way to find out, Lady Arabella."

She snorted, "I am sure the footmen are very accomplished; let them go. Or are you relying on the locals with pitchforks and scythes to come to your rescue?"

Miles laughed. "Our friends that chased the Russians out at sea have been gathering others along the way. They should be arriving before too long."

Arabella gave him a quizzical look. "I heard nothing about this."

"There was no reason for you to know about it."

Stanhope chuckled, saying to Arabella, "They make plans and discard them as quickly as the events dictate."

Miles shrugged and moved ahead to walk with Jibben until we reached the footpath. Then our husbands turned to help Judith and me back to the top of the cliff, where we found my Father looking through a spyglass, then handing it to Jean. Campeau

441

shook his head. "I don't know them."

Marianne had taken it from him, "The blonde man, I have seen before—he is your Count Vasiliev."

My Father stared at her. "How do you know that?

"He came with a man named Sergi Popov to see my Father a few times."

"Were they friends?"

"If you mean they were business partners, no, they weren't. They were competitors."

I could tell that my Father's interest was piqued. "Competitors at what?"

Marianne leaned in as if meaning to whisper, then straightened up. "Information gathering. Most of it was about an organisation called the Brotherhood."

"And that's all you know?"

"They didn't need my services. Information is not a ledger item. However, my Father did make copious notes about these visits in his journals. I can tell you that he was more inclined to trust Sir Thomas Wiseman than those two Russians."

My Father frowned. "Wiseman, you say?"

Marianne nodded. "Yes, before he died, he had two meetings with Sir Thomas. I never knew what they were about, and he didn't include them in the journals I had access to. You might want to ask Justin, though, since Father left his diaries to him and some of the less nefarious ledgers that didn't go up in smoke in the townhouse fire."

Miles arched a brow looking at my Father, "I suspect you will want to speak to Lord Burley when we return to London."

My Father pursed his lips. "If not before. I told de Bearne to collect him and bring him along. They should have landed in Pembroke by now."

Marianne's face lit up. "Justin is coming here! That's wonderful."

Lady Arabella did not look so sanguine as she addressed her sister. "It will require a great deal of explaining from me about how and why you are here and not in Scotland."

Marianne took a step closer to Campeau. "I am not going back, Arabella, so don't even consider suggesting it."

Arabella reached out and took her hand. "No one is going to send you there or anywhere else. You are free now, Marianne, and you shall remain that way. I will handle Justin."

Marianne shook her head. "But I need to prove to Justin that I am not a lunatic, just eccentric."

Jibben chuckled. "Well, I can testify to that. No one with a mind that can handle complex computations as you can should be locked up anywhere. If you were a man, you would be teaching at Oxford."

Marianne shook her head, "Cambridge."

Jibben argued back, "Oxford."

He waved a hand in defeat as she answered back. "Cambridge."

Magda joined us and invited Marianne and Campeau to walk with her. They strolled away from us along the cliffside, but Magda's demeanour was such that we all knew no one else was invited to go with them. Stanhope and Arabella drifted off in the opposite direction

Judith came to my side while staring at Magda. "What is that all about?"

"I honestly don't know, but Magda has been noticeably quiet on this trip. I think the sisters are an enigma for her. She tried to read the bones over Marianne and failed miserably."

Jibben arched a brow. "Really? That's not like Grandmama."

Judith answered him, "She told me once that some people are so strong-willed that they can block you from reading them. But I have never known her to be confounded by anyone. But after all those two sisters have been through and survived, I imagine they are both extraordinarily strong-willed."

"I hope that doesn't bode ill for us."

Judith was still watching their retreating forms. "I don't think so. Grandmama said you could smell evil intent on people, and they apparently don't smell evil."

Jibben placed a hand on her shoulder that she reached up to clasp it. "I agree, my love. They are not evil."

I sighed. "But can they be trusted?"

Jibben snorted, "Now that I don't know. I wonder if Burley will be any easier to read?"

I shook my head. "I doubt it. He's more muddled than Marianne."

Judith leaned back against Jibben. "I would like to know what Grandmama is plotting."

Jibben wrapped his arms around her and leaned his chin on her head. "You think she's hiding something from us?"

"Grandmama always has a plan that doesn't include us. I would feel more comfortable if we knew what it was this time."

Chapter 18

Dinner, Daylight, Death

That evening Dr Terrance Stockton the former Crow or healer from Seven Dials, and his fiancé Emma Cowin arrived for dinner. So we had dressed to impress Miss Cowin for Stockton's sake. She was a charming young woman and extremely forthright. "Terrance has told me about his past and informed me that you are a kind of secret police working for the King. Is that true?" Stockton blanched and stared down at his clasped hands.

On the other hand, Miss Cowin looked directly at my Father, who was glaring at Stockton. She saw the exchange and smirked. "Come now, some of your adventures have been in the newspapers. Several of your number were even knighted. It was in the court circular, but the reason for the knighting seemed to be rather vague. It only said services to the Crown. And one of you was made Rat Catcher to the Crown. I thought that was a joke until Terrance assured me it was not."

My Father sighed in resignation. "It's all true, Miss Cowin."

"Is it true then that Terrance has been essential to some of your more nefarious missions?"

My Father smirked at Stockton's discomfort. "Yes, he has. Then he was kind enough to give up the cutthroat life and agreed to become this county's physician."

She smiled at an appropriately embarrassed Stockton as she said, "For which I am ever so grateful, Lord Blackburn."

Once dinner was over, and the usual entertainments of singing and playing the piano were exhausted, Stockton excused himself and Miss Cowin. He had promised her Father to have her home by decent country hours. We said our goodbyes, and he promised before leaving to return in the morning.

The evening wore on from there, with conversation at a minimum. Then, after the sisters had retired, Judith was at Magda to tell us what she had talked about to the young couple. But she refused, only saying that it needed to remain a secret. Then she said goodnight and retired, so we couldn't press her any further.

The following day we were at breakfast when a commotion arose in the entry hall, and the doors to the dining room were thrown open. In walked de Bearne, Thornton, Jilly, Rabby, Montgomery, McMaster and Janet, Captain Bruce, Derek Bruce, Dr Jefferson, and Lord Shellard. De Bearne was grinning from ear to ear and called out, "Locke, that yacht of yours is perfect, but you need to change the name to something more elegant than Pelican. I will think about it and tell you what it should be."

Lord Shellard took a seat by Miles as the rest sat down around the table, and the footmen scurried to provide place settings, and additional food was brought up from the kitchens. I noticed Jilly, Rabby and Thornton hanging back, as did my Mother. "Come along, you three, take a seat; you are guests here. Jilly arched a brow and hesitated while Thornton and Rabby dashed to take a seat. Mother took in Jilly's stiff posture and decided to ask, "Why are you here, Jilly?"

She rocked back on her heels, not expecting the question, "Sir Edward and Lady Johnson sent Rabby and me to take care of Lord Shellard." My Father-in-law shot her a withering scowl from which she recoiled slightly. "Well, maybe not, but that's what they told me to say. It wasn't my idea. We're actually supposed to keep Lord Tinley from doing anything stupid. I have no idea how we can do that—he can be a headstrong devil sometimes."

Miles perked up and chuckled. "Edward's awake?"

Jefferson nodded. "Off and on, Grimes told me that his first words after you left were to tell Fiona to send their best staff to look out for you since he couldn't."

Lord Shellard laughed outright, as did everyone at the table; while Jilly stood in the doorway frowning, Miles pointed to the chair beside him. "Will you sit, Jilly? I think I will need your counsel."

She snorted but came and sat down. "Did Lady Tinley never tell you that you are a terrible liar when you try to be charming?"

Miles looked at me. "More than once, I am sure, but when do I ever listen? After all, I am a headstrong idiot most of the time."

She leaned in, "I said headstrong devil, milord."

I shook my head, "Don't argue with him, Jilly. The idiot is correct." She covered her mouth, trying to stifle a chuckle.

Miles finally asked Matthew, "So why are you here?"

"That was the new Lord Gromley's doing with Isabel's approval. He has returned from the north and assumed command

448

of the Agency in Sir Thomas's place." He glanced at Miles, who looked relieved and added, "Archer and Grimes have our medical practice in hand, and for a change, we have a Johnson as a patient that is cooperating. If a touch dictatorial."

Rabby nodded and, in between mouthfuls of shirred eggs, said, "Ordering us about like we were his own army."

I stared across the table at McMaster and Janet. "What are you two doing here?"

Janet sighed. "I have had enough of wedding planning. Owen's Mother has things under control, and I prefer that she argue with Prince Talleyrand—he would make this a royal wedding if he could. So, when Montgomery sent Owen word of your dilemma, we decided to come and offer our assistance."

McMaster called out to my Father at the head of the table. "The Irregulars you called for are being organised by Hamilton and are ready to come at your call. Burley is too exhausted to continue the journey here, so Lady Hamilton and his valet are caring for him. Also, Lady Hamilton has set the locals to keep an eye out for the Russians. She is a wonder at earning people's respect and trust without much effort."

I nodded. "Nell has never forgotten what it was like to be raised as one of them."

He chuckled. "Their companion Misha Andropov is another story. He is a very annoyed fellow and feels you changed the plan to leave him out of any confrontation. So he's none too happy with you."

My Father grinned. "Indeed, I wonder what gave him that impression? But it is difficult to know who to trust these days."

McMaster arched a brow. "You don't trust him or Hamilton?"

My Father frowned. "Andropov, I don't know well enough to say, and Hamilton has divided loyalties."

"You mean that Hamilton is still Lord Russell's man."

My Father sat back with his coffee cup in hand. "Also, Palmerston's to a lesser degree. Hamilton enjoys the politics of these missions. At the same time, I would prefer to keep the Agency free of politics and adhere to Sir Thomas and the Brotherhood's original vision. Hamilton will undoubtedly be a great political ally someday, much like Lord Shellard. But I can't be sure if what he tells me right now is the complete truth. I believe his tenure as a seconded member of the Agency might end after this mission."

I frowned, knowing that such words would hurt Nell, but I knew she would understand since Hamilton did have serious political ambitions.

McMaster grinned. "Is he aiming for the Prime Minister's seat?"

Father chuckled. "I think he's aiming for the Foreign Secretary's position."

Lord Shellard joined in, "Should we warn Palmerston?"

Miles shook his head. "I am sure Palmerston is already aware of Hamilton and his ambitions. And he's willing to use that ambition to his own benefit."

I frowned. "Do you think Hamilton is that gullible?"

Miles paused to consider his response, "No, but I think he's willing to be used for what he considers the right reasons, which may not always be aligned with ours." Then, he saw my face fall and added, "I still like the man and consider him a friend, but I think our professional paths are on divergent courses."

I could picture Nell as a political hostess and said, "Nell should speak to Lady Cowper."

Miles was perplexed. "Why is that."

"The demands of a political hostess differ considerably from just being a society hostess. From what Lady Cowper has said, it can be exasperating." I looked down at Magda. "She may need your counsel as well, Magda."

She looked up at me. "Why should our Nell need my help?"

"She told me you taught her how to overcome her anxiety when she married and hosted her first dinner parties."

She waved a hand at me. "Mrs Spencer helped her with that."

"That's not what she told me."

She smiled. "Our Nell did not have the advantage of being raised in the fashion she should have been. As the wife of an ambitious husband, I told her of the skills she would need to help him separate the good from the bad. He will need her ability to suss out those that would use him and those that would support him for the right reasons."

Jibben snorted, "He is lucky, then. Politics is a cutthroat business, is it not Shellard?"

My Father-in-law took his time in responding. "A successful career in politics requires patience and the will to make compromises. Otherwise, you are correct. Ambition can be your downfall. If he asks me, I will advise him to take it in measured steps and prove his worth rather than selling his soul for patronage."

Thornton and Montgomery, up until now, had been concentrating on their meal. Thornton suddenly nudged him. Montgomery scowled and sighed, wiping his mouth; he sat back. "The Russians are practically on your doorstep if you don't already know it. One of the local men, Davie Riggs, was coming in with his catch and said he saw a big ship making for the headland."

I couldn't place the man and asked, "Who is Davie Riggs?"

Montgomery smiled. "An ingenious smuggler and fisherman. He was the one who brought your attention to that French frigate when you were here working on the Counterfeit case."

My Father chuckled. "How much did Davie charge you for that little tidbit."

Montgomery said, "Nothing, surprisingly."

Sir Derwyn beamed and patted Jean Campeau on the back. "You were right. Providing them with a small monthly stipend for information would be beneficial."

My Father arched a brow. "A stipend?"

Sir Derwyn pursed his lips, "It's a trial project. We pay a monthly stipend to people who are in the way of being able to collect information through the course of their everyday activities without risk to themselves. It's been most valuable up to this point for some of our endeavours, milord."

My Father nodded. "Perhaps we should look into expanding that." He noticed they had Thornton's attention and sighed, "Jacob, you are already on the payroll."

"Aye, milord, I know, but Jilly here and Rabby aren't. Are they eligible for such a thing?" He looked at Sir Derwyn. "A stipend yee called it?"

Sir Derwyn cautiously nodded, glancing at my Father, who said, "You are right, Jacob. Jilly and Rabby have often put their lives on the line for us. I will look into supplementing their income when they are involved, or we call on their services."

Jacob chewed his lower lip and stroked his chin. "That makes it complicated for yur bookkeepers. Maybe a monthly but smaller stipend than the Irregulars make, which can be subject to change based on the risk they take."

My Father quirked a brow. "Are you negotiating for them?"

Jilly had her arms crossed. "No, it just be his crazy way. He thinks we need to have a sum put aside if we get sick or injured or lose our positions."

Miles was stunned. "Jacob, do you think we wouldn't take care of them if they needed us?"

Jacob pursed his lips. "I see a lot of money going out of the

453

Agency and none coming in, does the Crown pay handsomely?"

My Father answered, "We have a budget from the Crown."

"Aye, and when the King dies, what if yur got the Duchess of Kent and her toady John Conroy to deal with then? I see her kicking yee to the curb. She hates the old King and his people."

Dr Jefferson offered, "Unless the Princess takes control away from them."

Jacob waved a hand, "Bah, they keep her locked up like some hothouse flower that will wilt under the influence of anyone but them."

My Mother spoke up, "Aunt Mary says she is a very opinionated young woman and fully capable of managing affairs of state. If the King lives until she sees her majority, we may find things are different." Up to this point, the Bruce men hadn't said a word. It was Derek who spoke up with encouragement from his Uncle. "I have had the honour of meeting the Princess, and I am inclined to agree with Lady Blackburn she may surprise us."

Captain Bruce chuckled. "She will be no Queen Bess. She's just a wee thing not even as tall as Bess, and she was no giant, am I right, Derek."

Derek looked at his Uncle shaking his head. "Since I've never had the pleasure of meeting the great Queen Elizabeth, I will take your word on her height. But yes, I would be surprised if the Princess was five feet."

My Father pinched his nose. "Rest assured, Jacob, the Agency and Brotherhood have extensive investments managed by a sound financial team of advisors, and we are solvent. The Brotherhood will continue even if the next ruler disbands Sir Thomas' organisation."

Jacob nodded. "Sound planning there, Lord Blackburn. I am duly impressed."

My Father turned to Derek. "I assume that Samuel sent you as well?"

Derek nodded between bites and said. "Aye, when he set out for London to take control of things there."

De Bearne had worked through an impressive plate of food before asking. "That castle out there, who does it belong to?"

Lady Lewis responded, "My son owns it. It is part of his estate. May I ask why you wish to know?"

Gabriel swallowed and took a sip of coffee. "Just that I would rather not be found trespassing by some surly local." Then he turned to Miles, "We need to row out there and see what these Russians are up to."

Jibben grinned. "Exactly, my friend."

Miles turned to my Father. "Colin?

My Father shook his head, "De Bearne, Montgomery, and McMaster can go. They are unknown to the Russians who may take them for townsfolk out fishing."

Jean Campeau waved his hand at my Father. "I speak Russian fluently, Lord Blackburn. Perhaps I should go with them."

Jibben stared at him in disbelief, "You are a bookkeeper, not an agent."

Campeau sighed. "And you, Sir Stephen, can be an idiot sometimes, but I don't hold that against you."

Jibben chuckled, smacking Campeau a little too hard on the back, rocking him forward while saying, "You have heart, Campeau. I will give you that." Then, he turned to my Father, "Isn't he more valuable behind these walls."

My Father was watching Mr Campeau. "I think he deserves the chance to prove himself in ways other than with a pen and a ledger—but not this time."

Campeau glowered at Jibben, who said, "You would have had to stay behind us at all times anyway."

My Father arched a brow. "What makes you think you are going, Locke?"

Judith snorted, "They know you, Jibben. So what are you thinking!"

My Father shook his head. "Neither you nor Mr Campeau are going this time. The fewer, the better."

Jibben slumped back in his chair and grumbled under his breath when Magda spoke up, "I will go with them."

McMaster glared at her, and she scowled back. "You may need me, Sir Owen. I have talents that could protect you and heal you if necessary." McMaster faced my Father to argue, but he shook his head at my Father's expression. "Fine, but you will stay behind us."

Jibben was sitting with his arms crossed and pouting as he said, "Good luck. Grandmama does what she wants—when she wants."

Once the meal was finished, Judith and Janet went off with my Mother. I was more interested in watching Arabella and Marianne since they had contributed nothing to the breakfast conversation. Marianne went straight to Campeau's side afterwards. They whispered together for a time, then approached Jacob, who was playing a game of draughts with Rabby. Marianne reached out as if to touch Jacob, then pulled back, and Campeau cleared his throat. "Mr Thornton, you raise ferrets, true?"

"Aye, that be true."

He smiled. "Lady Marianne was wondering what kind of pets they make?"

He took his pipe out of his pocket and chewed on it for a minute. "They not be much different from cats or dogs. They like people if they treat them well and be sociable creatures. I find them to be great company. Mind yee, a pair is better than just one. They can get lonely otherwise."

Marianne smiled and clapped her hands. "Are they easy to train?"

Jacob seemed to warm to the conversation, "Depends on what you want to train em for." He went on to explain his training methods. I discovered things I didn't know previously about ferrets. Then Marianne went on to negotiate the purchase of a pair.

I turned my attention to Arabella, who sat by the empty hearth with an open book in her lap as she chewed on her thumb. She jumped when I sat down across from her. I pointed at the book, having recognised it. "Mary Wollstonecraft? I would never have considered you an advocate of women's equality."

She glanced down at the book and frowned, then looked up. "I am not—I mean, I would like to be, but old habits die hard."

I nodded. "Are you concerned about your brother's arrival?"

"I have a great deal to explain to him. Other than Alexander, he is the only family Marianne and I have, and she seems ready to survive without us, perhaps because she has had to survive without anyone for most of her life. I fooled myself into accepting that my marriage wasn't that different from other women of the Beau Monde. But now that I have seen your family and friends, it's opened a whole different world that makes no sense to me. I am not sure that I can find my way alone."

"What makes you think you will be alone."

She reached up and touched her eyepatch. "I have no illusions about finding a husband again. Justin and Alexander will marry one day, and neither of them will want to have a widowed sister living off them and in their homes."

"May I offer you a suggestion?" she arched a brow. "Embrace your independence. I promise we will not desert you. It's not the way we do things."

She looked at our friends, the dark and mysterious Gabriel de Bearne, then McMaster, a man known as a bastard to Beau

Monde and his fiancé, a former maid. Then at Montgomery, he was an enigma to almost everyone. Thornton, Jilly and Rabby were from a different world than hers. Magda and Jibben were culturally rich but alien to her. Then there were the rest of us. I knew then that she didn't understand how we coalesced into a group of friends and family."

I watched her as she scanned the room, weighing and judging us all, "Miles was blind when he asked me to marry him, and there was no guarantee he would ever see again. He still gets terrible headaches, and the bright sun can be like a knife in his eyes. But more than that, he was still considered a bastard then. I accepted him for the man he is, not his pedigree. I was willing to trust his love, and he was brave enough to reach out to me and believe in my love."

She chuckled. "Give life a chance, Lady Tinley? I am sorry, but life is not a fairy tale." She then picked up her book and ignored me.

McMaster kissed Janet goodbye as Montgomery and de Bearne gathered at the doorway and saluted us as they walked out, with Magda scooting out behind them. Jibben and Miles rose to follow, but my Father called them back. "They don't need you two standing on the cliff watching, especially if the Russians have a guard posted. They will see you and know that we are up to something."

"They will know that anyway with them rowing out from your cove."

My Father shook his head. "They are going through the caves."

Thornton coughed. "Does Montgomery know that? He doesn't like enclosed spaces."

My Father pinched his nose. "It's a large cavern. He will be fine. The Truncheons will be their guides."

Thornton shrugged his shoulders. "Perhaps Magda can do some magic on him." then he turned back to his games of draughts.

Jilly and Marianne came over to me. "Would you care to show us the garden, Lady Tinley?"

I looked at my Mother, who was concentrating on Judith and Janet. Miles and Jibben were deep in thought over chess, and my Father was murmuring to Lord Shellard and Dr Jefferson. But two people were missing, the Bruce men, yet I couldn't recall them leaving. I stood up, answering, "I would love to."

We casually walked onto the terrace and strolled across the lawns to the concealing yew hedge. Once we were out of sight, we scurried around the side and out of sight, "What are you two plotting."

Marianne answered, "I am going to the castle; Jean is worried that the Russians might steal something important, and Jilly said you had been out there before."

"I didn't go through the caverns. We went in a boat then and climbed the giant's stairs."

Marianne waved a hand. "But you know where the caverns are."

"Yes, and they are dangerous."

Jilly grasped my hand. "Then tell us where the boat in the cove is. You needn't come with us in your condition."

Just then, Captain Bruce and Derek step out from behind the hedge. "You will need someone to row the boat, lassie."

I jumped, and Jilly cupped her hands over her mouth to suppress her squeal. Marianne didn't seem the least surprised. But I snapped at the men, "Are you two stalking us"?

Derek scoffed. "Of course not. We were waiting for you to do something. You are not someone to sit and wait for others. We should go through the back of the castle since you have been that way before. There is a great deal to be said for the element of surprise when facing a foe."

Captain Bruce nodded. "Come then, and we had better go before someone notices we're missing."

Derek looked over his shoulder. "Too late."

Miles and Jibben were standing there with arms crossed over their chests. Miles glared at me and snarled, "We had better hurry if we are going." Then he added a kinder tone to me, "I don't suppose you would consider staying behind."

I matched his posture with my feet apart and my arms crossed. "No."

He shook his head in resignation. "Then let's go."

We reached the beach without being called out, though knowing my Father as I did, I would be surprised if our absence

461

had gone unremarked. Miles and Derek dragged out the boat on the beach that Lord Stanhope kept there for his fishing excursions. However, there were no oars. Until Campeau came down the path, "You will need these."

Jibben reached for them, but Campeau pulled back. "Oh no—I am going with you."

Jilly looked out at the choppy water and then at the towering cliff. "It all looks smaller from up above."

Captain Bruce chuckled. "We will need a lookout on the beach, and it seems we have found a volunteer."

Jibben looked at the boat and back at our group. "There's not enough room for all of us." He glanced at Captain Bruce, then back at a fearful Jilly.

The Captain sighed, rolling his eyes. "Fine, I'll stay here with the wee lassie and keep an eye out for trouble. Besides, I am not as nimble at climbing cliffsides as I used to be."

Miles smiled and clapped him on the back, whispering. "You are a liar—but thank you, Douglas."

The Captain looked at me. "She's the one that should be staying behind." I glared at him. "Don't give me that look, lassie. You know I am right. But I also know you would find a way to go anyway."

He opened his jacket and on display was an impressive array of weapons. He grinned, saying, "Before you go, take one." Jibben reached for the largest pistol and got his hand slapped. "No one takes my Bonny." Then he passed out the weapons, Marianne was

462

given a knife, and I was handed a pistol. His last admonishment was, "Don't get yourselves caught. I have no desire to sail to St. Petersburg to rescue you. It's not the friendliest of ports. Now get on with it before I change my mind and hold you all hostage until Blackburn comes after yee."

Derek laughed. "As if you could." Captain Bruce arched a brow in disdain, and Derek abruptly stopped laughing.

"Off with you now, and no more of your cheek, nephew."

Once in the boat, Marianne became quiet and hugged herself close. Her usual quirky animation didn't return until we set foot on the shale beach. Then she looked up at the cliffside with curiosity. "Can you imagine what it must have taken to carve that staircase out of the side of the cliff?"

I shuddered, thinking of my last climb up it. "Plus the temerity of those that used it."

She giggled. "Such as us?" She didn't wait for instruction or guidance and bounced up the first few steps until hitting a patch of moss when one foot slid out from under her, and she canted to the open side of the stairway. Campeau pushed past the rest of our party and shot up the stairs to grab Marianne around the waist, pulling her back against the cliff face. She smiled at him and said, "Oops—I suppose I should exercise greater caution."

"Indeed, milady."

"Stop calling me that—it's Marianne."

He grinned. "Yes, milady—ah, Marianne."

Derek stood behind me and said, "Either kiss her mate or move it along, but I recommend waiting for a better time and a less public place for the kiss."

Marianne laughed and started up the stairs with a blushing Campeau close behind her. Derek chuckled with an impish grin on his face. I smacked his arm. "That was mean, cousin."

He arched a brow at me. "I beg your pardon, milady?"

I shook a finger at him. "This is not a time for teasing. Wait for the moment when your humour might be helpful."

He nodded and started up the stairs, followed by me, then Miles, with Jibben bringing up the rear. I could feel Miles almost reach out for me every other step as if he expected me to fall but would drawback when he saw that my footing was sure. When we reached the top and looked around, it was still just as barren as I remembered.

In the distance, I could make out the causeway that started halfway down and led to the back gates of the castle. The windows on this side of the edifice were still blank apertures, no glass and no coverings, and I imagined I could hear a mournful groan coming from them as the wind swept over the open plain before us.

Jibben stood with his hands on his hips and growled, "It's still a hellish place, nothing but scrub and rock."

Miles looked about him. "There's no cover at all. We are completely exposed."

I nodded. "It's not changed much. I keep expecting to see

464

Griffin and his wolfhounds come bounding out of the castle after us."

Jibben clapped his hands, jerking everyone's attention back from the wasteland before us. "Let's move, children."

Miles glared at him, and Derek chuckled nervously. Marianne was the first to move off in the castle's direction, skipping over the rock-strewn plain. Campeau quickly scampered after her. Derek looked at me and asked, "Does she have a death wish?"

I smirked. "You are not the first to ask that. But, honestly, I think she doesn't fear death like the rest of us."

Derek nodded, then frowned and said more to himself than the rest of us, "She has looked into that abyss and come back."

He moved off with his back to me. I glanced at Miles as he nodded towards Derek, "He's been there as well." And I thought to myself, you have to, my husband.

Jibben slapped Miles on the back. "Many of us have, my friend. Come, let's go."

Miles took my hand, and Jibben loped ahead, constantly looking about, checking for hazards. We moved forward quickly since moving cautiously was impossible, being out in the open like we were. As we walked onto the causeway, Jibben looked back at me. "Stanhope and your Father had that midden cleaned up, didn't they?"

I smiled. "Yes, Jibben, I can assure you they did." He smiled and heaved a huge sigh. "I still have nightmares about that."

Miles glanced at me with alarm, Jibben and I had never shared that part of our experience. I grimaced as I said, "You don't want to know." Miles only nodded as we continued.

Jibben was the one that guided our group to the hidden door that led us into Griffin's prior home. The remains of his habitation were still scattered about the room.

Jibben approached the door to the midden with some trepidation. He pulled it open, holding his breath, waiting to be assailed by noisome scents, but none came.

Marianne ran before him, looked through the door, and then up at Jibben. "This place made your gut turn?" She inhaled deeply. "That's understandable. It smells of death."

She rushed into the space ignoring the ledge, and spun around, looking upwards, making a face. "You said that they cleaned this up, Lady Tinley." She pointed upwards. "Then they missed someone." Miles and I stepped in and looked up to where she pointed at Sergi Popov, hanging out a hole in the wall at the height of the main floor. Marianne gave words to my thoughts, "I wonder who he annoyed?"

Then she dismissed him and passed over to the doorway that opened into the medieval kitchens. Nothing here had changed either. Stanhope had not repaired nor restored the lower floors. We walked up the ramp and paused in the main room where we had once found trestle tables of abandoned food and lit braziers.

The only signs of habitation now were one table, with a gathering of chairs around the enormous central hearth and a writing desk. No one was in the room, nor were there any signs of recent occupancy. Then a door slammed somewhere near the western side of the castle. Miles, Jibben and Derek rushed off in that direction.

Leaving Campeau, Marianne, and me alone in this cavernous banquet hall. Marianne turned around, taking in everything. "This is a beautiful place—but so sad. She looked over at a corner that was darkened by shadows and waved her hand. "Begone. You have no place here; you do not scare me."

I was stunned at her words, which must have shown on my face as she said with a lopsided grin, "It is just an ugly shade trying to make himself seen. But he has no power here." I merely nodded and stared at the corner but saw nothing. She grinned. "See, I told you, he has no power."

Then I heard someone laughing and snatches of a conversation above us, such as "I told you he would betray us." Then it was followed by whispers and a loud "Shut up! I don't care!" I motioned for Campeau and Marianne to follow me as I ducked into the room that had once held a printing press and now appeared to be a library. I pushed the door partially closed, thankful the hinges had been recently oiled and watched Count Vasiliev and Countess Irina come into view. He held her tightly by the upper arm as she watched him in horror.

The Countess cried out, "Urie, you killed the master! You can't go home. They will execute you."

"Bah—he was going to Wiseman. He would have told him everything."

"But you killed him too. Now what?"

"Now we kill Blackburn and Tinley. We need to cut off the heads of the beast and watch it die." They walked across the hall towards the western door. But he stopped suddenly and looked around. I pulled back as he said, "Did you hear something?"

The Countess shook her head, "Nothing."

He nodded, then continued walking in the direction our men had gone. Suddenly, the sounds of shots came from below and from the western door. He spun around, dragging Irina across the floor. Then abandoning her, he bolted. Racing out the way we had come.

The Countess screamed after him, "Urie!" Then she fell silent and froze as she focused on the dungeon doorway.

I moved to step out, but Campeau grabbed my arm and hissed, "Listen and wait."

Yelling and shouting were coming from the dungeon stairwell, accompanied by the sounds of a pitched battle. Then men spilt out into the hall and continued the fight. McMaster and de Bearne burst through, pursuing what appeared to be several professional soldiers. Pistols had been dropped, and now it was sword to sword. Coming from the western side was another raging battle with Jibben, Miles and Derek against a similar group.

Our men were outnumbered but seemed to be holding their own. They spread out into the more open space of the great hall. The Countess tried to edge herself around the battling groups and make for the western exit, and she was almost past our door when Campeau reached out and grabbed her clapping his hand across her mouth. She attempted to kick him, stomp on his toes

468

and head butt him, but she was unsuccessful as he managed to dance out of her reach each time.

"Stop it," he called out. "If you don't stop, I will be forced to hit you, madam." She continued to resist, and abruptly Marianne stepped up and, with a clenched fist, punched her in the throat, stopping her dead as she pitched forward onto her knees, gasping for breath.

Then Campeau jerked the Countess to her feet and walked into the Hall with a cocked pistol to her head. I assumed he yelled out in Russian to stop, but no one paid him any attention. Then Magda came through the dungeon door. A nonexistent breeze was blowing her clothes and hair before her, and then I saw her eyes glowing, and I knew it was Aneski, her ancient ancestor, who had taken possession of Magda.

She stepped into the hall and raised both her arms. Marianne was standing beside Campeau, watching it all, and a stunned Countess was on her knees again. So the battles still raged until an unearthly voice called out loud and clear, overcoming the sounds of clashing metal, "Stop!"

The men did as commanded and stared at Magda as she took from her pocket a pouch, and I recognised the sparkling sand she poured into her hand and raised it to let the summoned breeze send it flying about the room in a whirlwind. I yelled at Marianne and Campeau, "Close your eyes!" I felt the grit of the sand hit my face and waited for it to subside.

There was no sound of movement in the room. Yet the breeze had strengthened and still whistled through the space. When it ceased, Magda said, "Open your eyes, people."

All around us, the men who had been fighting, including our own, were unconscious on the floor. I looked over to where Magda was standing, she was once again Magda, and out of her satchel, she pulled out equal lengths of rope enough to restrain our adversaries. She came forward and divided the bundle of rope between us. When the Countess protested, Magda snapped her fingers, and the Countess fell unconscious onto the floor.

Marianne clapped her hands. "That was amazing!" Then casually and with skill, she began tying up the unknown assailants. We all joined in, and once we were done, Magda reached into her satchel and pulled out a bag of apples, a loaf of bread and four bottles of small beer, passing them around. We ate while waiting for our men to awaken—Jibben and de Bearne were the first, and their language was atrocious as they held their heads. Gabriel continued to curse, "Christ woman, what in the hell did you do to us? My head feels like it is about to split open.

Magda admonished them both for swearing, "You will watch your mouths. There are ladies present."

Then she pulled out two flasks of whisky and passed them out. "You will have a headache for the rest of the day, but I will give you medicine to help later. Now we must find our way back."

De Bearne rose. "I will check on the caverns."

Marianne stood, saying, "I will check on the boat."

Campeau shook his head and reached for her hand. "No, *Cheri*, Count Vasiliev went that way, and we have no idea where he might be lurking.

Jibben pushed past them and snapped, "I will go." He sprinted across the floor, calling out, "Vasiliev! Don't run away. Come out and play."

Countess Irina was cowering on the floor as Miles, Derek, and McMaster began to stir. The Countess said nothing. She only glared at us. Miles, Derek, and McMaster repeated de Bearne and Jibben's colourful expletives as I handed them the flasks the others had left behind and informed them where and why the other two had gone.

Miles leaned against the table with one leg bent, resting an arm on his knee, staring at the Countess. He offered her the flask he held, but she ignored it. "Well, Countess, it seems that you have been deserted. One of your allies is dead, and one has run like a coward."

I peered at Magda, who was observing the Countess with curiosity. She reached into her satchel, pulled out another pouch, and poured a blue powder into her hand. She was mumbling under her breath and focusing all her attention on the Countess. I looked away, then back again and noticed that something was wrong. The Countess looked different to me. Her nose was blunter, and her hair was less vibrant than I remembered. Magda stood up, walked behind her, and blew the powder all over her. The Countess growled and tried to break free of her bonds unsuccessfully. The powder engulfed her, and then as it dissipated, the woman before us was not the Countess but the Countess's companion. She stared straight ahead and said not a word. Magda walked around her, then sat down, asking, "Where is your mistress?" The woman refused to answer.

Miles and Derek were unruffled about the transformation, Marianne was fascinated, and Campeau was agog. The woman seemed to feel my scrutiny and turned to hiss at me in Russian. It meant nothing to me, but it upset Magda enough that she backhanded the woman and then spat at her; turning to me, she asked with a degree of anxiety, "Do you have your talisman?"

I nodded, "Of course, you have told us countless times that we should keep them with us. I pulled it out of my pocket, and though it was rather worn, it was still intact. She beamed and turned to sneer at the woman at her feet. "You have no power over her. Your witch has wasted her one chance."

The old woman's shoulders slumped. She frowned, looking down at her secured hands, totally defeated. Then, she did a strange thing and tipped her head to the side, baring her neck. One of the other men lined up against the wall, with hands and feet tied, snorted in disgust before saying in a heavy Russian accent, "She thinks you will kill her and is baring her neck for you to open the vein. If you don't do it, the Countess will— eventually." Then he chuckled.

Magda shook her head and addressed the woman. "They—" she motioned to Miles and Derek, "will not let me." The woman glared at Miles and spat at him. He watched it fall short of his boots and shrugged, indifferent to her contempt.

Chapter 19

Always Waiting

De Bearne returned with the Truncheon brothers to tell us, "The tide is coming in—we won't be getting out through the cavern for some time. He sat and glared at those around us and scrutinised the old woman. "Where did she come from?"

Derek nodded towards Magda. "She removed some magic that made us think she was the Countess."

Gabriel growled, "Hmmph—I hate that—." he grumbled an expletive. "Spells should be outlawed."

Derek snorted, "It is my friend; witchcraft is still illegal."

"Good." Magda glared at him but said nothing; he grimaced, saying, "Your magic isn't witchcraft." which brought a smile to her face.

Jibben returned not long after, "Excuse me, ladies, but that bastard stole the boat we came in."

Miles nodded. "He's probably already made it to that ship standing off the headland. But I should check to be sure."

He got up and walked out the western door. I rose and followed him. The ocean breeze buffeted us as we stood on the dock, staring out at the ship that floated there with its sails furled. A skiff was slowly making its way to its side, where a rope ladder had been lowered. I could make out two people standing on the captain's deck. One was a woman with her hair streaming out behind her. The man in our boat eventually reached the ship, scampered up its side, and ascended to the deck with the watchers. He went down on one knee, kissed the woman's hand, and rose to stand beside her. Then he had the cheek to salute us before they turned their backs.

Miles pulled me close, saying, "They don't appear to be in a hurry to leave. No doubt we haven't seen the last of them."

I leaned against Miles. "How many men do you think they have."

"Enough to overwhelm us if they choose. Our only advantage is having the high ground."

We returned to the hall, where Jibben scrutinised our prisoners; he looked up at our approach, saying. "What are we going to do with these fellows?" Miles shrugged.

Then he ran a hand through his hair. "If Jilly and Captain Bruce stayed on the beach, they would have seen Vasiliev leave in our skiff. He understands tides and should be able to figure out that the caverns will have flooded by now. Hopefully, reinforcements are on the way."

Derek prowled around the perimeter. He appeared to be looking for something. "Does anyone else wonder why they came here?"

Jibben shrugged. "To rid themselves of Popov and blame us?"

Miles nodded. "But he has no official position in their

government. He's a private citizen and only considered a Trade Attaché. So I doubt his loss would engender an international incident."

Derek ignored them and headed for the stairway leading up. "I am going to check the rooms above. Anyone care to join me?" De Bearne heaved himself up along with McMaster and followed Derek up the stairs to search the rooms. Derek called down, "Nothing up here." McMaster agreed with him.

Gabriel came out of the last room on the mezzanine. "This room has been utterly destroyed. Stanhope will need to find himself some new furnishings."

Campeau ran up the stairs. "That's not Stanhope's room. It's my private office."

Miles arched a brow. "Private office?"

Campeau ignored him and raced into the room. Miles, Marianne, and I followed him up and into the room. It was set up or had been set up as an office. He was tossing papers aside, apparently not finding what he was looking for—he stopped in the middle of the room, pulling his hair while turning around and muttering, "No, no, no!"

Derek came into the room, taking in what was transpiring and stood by Miles. "What's wrong with Campeau?"

"I have no idea except that this is his office, and something appears to be missing."

Derek walked over to Campeau and grabbed him by the shoulders. "Don't make me slap you like you are some hysterical

475

woman. What's wrong with you, man?"

He stopped and stared at Marianne. "Your drawing and my notes are gone!"

Marianne stared at him, lost as to what he was referring to, "What drawing, what notes?"

I touched her arm. "The one you gave Milly, I gave him a part of it."

She chuckled and waved a hand at Campeau. "It's nothing to worry about."

Campeau rushed to her side. "In and of itself, you are right. But it's like—like the Rosetta stone. It just needs to be deciphered properly. You use three languages in that drawing. One is referring to a location in the picture. The second is using words that appeared to be jumbled but must be a code, and the last is the language of mathematics."

She was stunned. "You think that will give them a blueprint to interpret my Father's ledgers and accounts?"

Campeau's shoulders slumped. "Yes."

She turned away from Campeau to my husband. "They will soon realise that picture is worthless. You must kill me, Lord Tinley." She threw her arms wide open. "I am the repository of all my Father's business dealings."

Miles just stared at her with arched brows. "We don't kill people on request, Lady Marianne, and I caution you that it won't be tolerated if you entertain the idea of taking your own life."

She sighed. "You are quite right, Lord Tinley. I owe it to my country to provide you with a record of all I know, and you will need it if the historical information is meaningful." But, again, I was somewhat confused unless she meant that things from the past would continue to come back to haunt us and make life difficult.

Derek appeared perplexed as he asked Miles, "Do you understand what she's talking about?"

Miles nodded, but I answered, "It's apparent when you consider it from her point of view."

Marianne grinned at me, and Derek merely shook his head in confusion. "Well, I am glad that someone comprehends what she's saying. Perhaps you could explain it to me in greater detail when we have time."

I smirked, "It would be my pleasure."

Marianne had returned to Campeau's side and cupped his cheek smiling. "Without me, they have nothing. I am just as important, if not more important, to Lord Blackburn and the Crown than to the Russians."

Campeau grasped her hand with his, "We have the same problem; someone will always want what we know."

She smiled. "So we will beat them and live. I trust these people to help us—they understand that being different is not wrong or threatening."

Derek looked from them to Miles, who was chewing on his lip, then said, " All right, there is nothing else that can be done here."

Then, addressing Campeau, he asked, "Is there anything we should take back to Blackburn Manor?"

Campeau looked around, then picked up a few items but nothing that seemed terribly important, only personal items. I recognised a rock from Northumberland, probably from Lady Adele's cairn, a seashell that must have come for the cove here, and a Napoleonic coin. He smiled at me, watching him with the small pile of items cradled in one arm. "Some are mementoes of things I love, and some are reminders of things that I hate."

I smiled. "I have a similar cache of my own, Mr Campeau. I find it comforting, like a talisman for the future and against the past."

He nodded, pulling out a worn talisman that looked very much like mine. He smiled at me. "My Grandmama made this for me when I was a boy."

Magda shuffled into the room and took it from it, "It is very powerful young Jean; rest assured, she watches over you." Then she handed it back and poked at the debris on the floor, leaning forward and rubbing her hands together. "Ha! Now I have you."

In her hand was a ribbon that appeared to have been torn. She smiled, clasped it in her hands, and then shoved it into her pocket. She smiled up at Miles. We can win—I will make them come to us when, where and how we want."

Then she walked straight and proud out of the room. Usually, after manifesting Aneski, she was drained, but finding this bit of the ribbon energised her. Derek leaned in and asked, "Do you know what that's about?"

"I have no idea whatsoever."

"Good, I hate being alone in these things." He turned to the others. "Do any of you have an idea?"

Campeau frowned. "Not really, but if she intends what I think she does, it's powerful magic."

Marianne was staring at him in surprise. "You look afraid, Jean."

He nodded as he watched the door that Magda had left through. "We should all be afraid."

Below I heard Jibben bellow, "Grandmama, you can't do that!" Derek and Miles rushed out the door while Marianne, Campeau and I stepped out to look over the railing down at the Hall below. Magda had her Templar knife out, cutting a lock of hair from each of our prisoners and placing them into her satchel. Jibben stood by, muttering, "You cannot do this thing."

Miles had reached Jibben's side, as he said. "We must try and stop Grandmama—this is bad, very bad."

I had no idea who he was talking to, but I felt the serious import of his words. Jibben was afraid, which made me more nervous. Magda finished collecting her tokens by taking a piece from the old woman's dress. Then she walked towards the back of the castle and the way we had come in. I rushed down the stairs and grabbed Miles by the arm. "You have to go after her." He looked at me, then Jibben and they both set off at a run.

Marianne sat in a chair, staring at the old woman, who seemed to have aged even more since we had been upstairs. She tipped her head from side to side, but the woman ignored her, and then Marianne sat on the floor before her. She closed their eyes and sucked in a deep breath. They stayed like that until the older woman fell over, and Marianne opened her eyes, screaming. I knelt by the Countess' companion while Jean went to comfort Marianne.

Marianne pushed Jean's arm aside and asked me, "Is she dead?"

I nodded. "What happened, Marianne?"

She shivered. "I don't know; I think I fell asleep. Then I saw something dark hidden below in the caverns, and it was alive."

I looked back at Derek. "We need to leave."

He nodded and headed out the western door. In a few minutes, he returned with a troubled Captain Bruce and my scowling Father, who growled. "Anyone care to tell me what the hell all of you are doing here!"

I sucked in a breath and stammered, "Well—we felt that—"

He glared at me. "No—none of that, we felt anything! You deliberately ignored my orders. All but the ones I sent here are on probation until I decide what the repercussions of your actions might be."

I swallowed. "There's more, papa."

He stared at me, showing his disappointment. "What else could there possibly be?"

I sucked in a breath and squeaked out, "Mr Popov is dead.

Count Vasiliev killed him."

He pinched his nose and closed his eyes. "Do you have irrefutable proof of that?"

I shook my head. "No, only he was dead when we arrived, and the Count was here, and the old woman said he killed him, but she's dead now."

My Father was incensed, "I am sure the Russian Embassy will be impressed that you have no evidence to corroborate his guilt or your innocence."

I nodded and whispered, "Point taken."

Jibben and Miles came back into the Hall. Jibben pulled up short and hissed, "Tinley, we are in for it now." He was right.

My Father tore into them in a fashion I had rarely seen or heard. "What in God's name did you two hope to achieve? Melbourne is going to want your hides nailed to a door! Have you any idea how difficult you have made this situation? I suppose you have all been seen by Vasiliev with your running around here! He will use that against us! And I have no idea how I will keep you out of the Tower! You imbeciles!"

Jibben ventured to add, "But they were trespassing."

My Father exploded, "SO WERE YOU!" He continued in a similar vein for a bit, then he looked about him and pointed to the old lady once he was done. "Who is that?"

I meekly offered, "I believe that it's Countess Irina's companion."

He tipped his head to look at the ceiling. "Wonderful. How did she die?"

"I shrugged. I don't know."

Marianne bit her lip. "I think the beast in the cavern ate her spirit."

My Father moved to look at her directly. "I beg your pardon?"

Her eyes were wide and full of innocence "The dragon in the cavern that's guarding the treasure."

He closed his eyes and pinched the bridge of his nose. "Not that nonsense again."

Her brow furrowed. "It's not nonsense Lord Blackburn. But, you will see, Madam Magda intends to awaken him."

Jibben groaned. "This is not going to go well."

Miles sounded perplexed. "You believe her?"

Jibben shook his head, "Awakening a dragon—no. Causing some major incident that Grandmama loses control of—yes."

The idea that she would lose control of anything piqued my curiosity to ask, "Jibben, how old is Magda?"

He opened his mouth to answer, then shut it and furrowed his brow. "I have no idea; she's just always been there." I nodded, trying to reflect on the first time I met her. She never seemed to age. I recalled times when she appeared younger or older than usual. It gave me something uncomfortable to ponder. But I was concerned that whatever she had planned might destroy Magda, and it appeared that Jibben was too.

My Father organised getting our prisoners back to the mainland and, I believe, purposely made us stay behind until the last one was removed. Once they were gone, he looked at the old lady's body. Then asked, "Where is Popov?"

Jibben pointed up, "The jakes."

My Father threw his head back and sighed, "Bring him down here."

Jibben glanced at Derek, then Miles. They were all looking at each other while McMaster and de Bearne stood there with their arms crossed, smiling. Miles finally said, "Come with me, Locke." and headed for the stairs.

Jibben shook his head. "No, thank you, I think I will stay here."

He scowled at Jibben, then headed for the stairs as Derek called out, "I'll come." and hit Jibben on the back of the head as he passed.

Jibben gritted his teeth and growled, "Fine—I am coming."

While they were gone, My Father came to me, glaring. "I have come to expect this kind of recklessness from Miles, but I expected better judgment from you."

I felt he was unfair to Miles and me, but all I could respond with was, "You know that's not true. You have called me reckless, foolish and selfish."

He rubbed his forehead and pulled me into his arms. "I worry about you. I know that Miles tries to discourage your more dangerous impulses, but you are just like —"

I interrupted and said, "Just like you?"

He cleared his throat. "I was going to say your Mother."

He kissed my forehead as we heard the men wrestling with Popov, only to drop him as his stiff leg caught hold of the handrail and pitched forward, literally rolling down the stairs. Derek threw up his hands, palms out. "Sorry, his foot caught." Father ran a hand across his forehead.

Jibben glanced down at me and called out, "Lissa, will Jefferson be able to prove that any bruises from the fall happened after death?"

I shrugged. "I have no idea, but I would assume so."

My Father yelled, "Just pick him up and take him out to the boats."

Then My Father turned back to look at Campeau, Marianne and me. "I want a full report back at the manor. By the way, where is Magda?"

Marianne perked up. "She has descended into the caverns to battle with the Dragon Sorris."

My Father shook his head in disbelief. "That woman is beyond comprehension."

I tried to deflect his attention. "Do you know where Montgomery is?"

He glanced at me. "Montgomery fell in the caverns." I gasped, and then my Father added, "He's fine. He hit his head, and the Truncheons carried him out." Then he chuckled, "However, he will be nursing a headache, a goose egg and a massive amount of embarrassment that the Truncheons aren't about to let him forget."

The men had stormed down the stairs, and collected Popov, then marched out to the docks while we followed.

Marianne and I climbed into the boat with the old woman and Popov's bodies while Campeau, Miles, Jibben, and Derek rowed us back to shore. My Father jumped from his boat, and after taking my arm, he ordered Campeau and Marianne to move up the path ahead of us, leaving my husband, Jibben and Derek on the beach with the bodies. McMaster stood at the top of the cliff with de Bearne smiling, so as I passed them, I hissed, "You can wipe those smiles off your faces. Both of you have made a mess of things before."

My Father laughed and said, "She's right." their faces fell as we moved on.

As we entered the hall, Arabella came flying down the stairs. "My God, Marianne, where have you been? I have been worried sick! Justin is here, and he's been frantic since you couldn't be found. Come with me now and change. He will want to see you." She reached out and grabbed her hand, pulling her towards the stairs.

Marianne shook her off. "I will come after I have finished my report to Lord Blackburn. This is serious, Arabella. People died out there."

Arabella drew back from her and snapped, "You are talking nonsense!"

Campeau stepped forward. "She is not talking nonsense. It is true two people died, both Russians. This is profoundly serious, Lady Arabella."

Arabella glared at Campeau and pouted, "Fine." Then she wheeled and stormed back upstairs.

Marianne paid no attention to her. Instead, she glanced at my Father and, with due seriousness, said, "I am ready to provide my report, Lord Blackburn.."

He smiled but waved a hand towards his study, and in they went. Each of us went in one at a time. Miles and I were last, and I refused to go in without him. I noticed several pages of hastily scratched notes before my Father when we entered. He put his pen down and pushed his papers aside. "I think I have all I need, including that neither of you instigated this venture but rather went along; I suppose that was out of a sense of duty to protect the others."

Miles sighed and opened his mouth to respond just as my Father added, "Please don't say a word; just let me believe that to be the case."

My husband nodded, then said, "That sounds reasonable, but I think you can add that we hate being left out. Might I remind you that the outcome could have been much worse if we hadn't been there, sir? We could have lost McMaster and de Bearne."

"I am fully cognisant of that, Miles. That's why I am about to apologise for my tirade at the castle. However, Sir Thomas and I have discussed plans for you, and I think it's time for you to know what your new role in the Agency will be. We need someone willing to question our methods, especially now that Samuel will be taking on Sir Thomas' role."

Miles quirked a brow. "Milord, I don't want to be a bureaucrat. The idea of sitting behind a desk and meeting with representatives of the Crown or parliament turns my stomach. I haven't the patience nor the diplomatic skills."

My Father chuckled. "I am aware of that, Miles; it would be a disservice to pull you out of fieldwork. Instead, you would act as a consultant when we need more creative thinking on our difficult cases, even those you aren't involved in."

Miles nodded. "I understand, milord."

"There is one problem." Miles looked intrigued but said nothing, Father sighed and pursed his lips tightly before quickly saying, "You will have a partner in that role."

Miles sighed with resignation and pinched his nose. "Who? McMaster or Locke."

My Father steepled his fingers once again and shook his head. "McMaster will be my continental operative and liaison. Locke is our investment and financial advisor. Your partner in this new role would be Lissa."

No one was more surprised than I, but when I stole a peek at Miles, he sat forward and asked in a very calm voice that belied his look. "May I ask how you came to this decision?"

"Yes, it was on the unsolicited recommendation of Mr Thornton. He said that the shadow council of Seven Dials respects you both. However, you will not supplant Sir Edward unless he gives up his council position. It seems the members find you both amusing and highly creative in getting out of trouble, qualities Thornton assures me are needed in the Agency. His exact words were, *'There be a need for fresher and younger ideas in the Agency.'* I will concede that you both approach problems with unconventional flair, if not wisdom."

I felt the flame of anger race up my spine as I said, "I suppose that's where you and Uncle Samuel come in."

My Father looked taken aback by my tone. "I beg your pardon?"

Miles chuckled. "I believe she means you and Samuel will provide the wisdom to curtail our more outrageous suggestions?"

"Yes, well, Lord Shellard has thoroughly acquainted me with some of your lesser-known exploits, Miles, so I think it is advisable that Samuel and I have the final say for the time being, at least until we understand each other's methods."

Miles sat back, crossing his arms. "That rather defeats the purpose. If you and Hughes are so inured in your way of doing things, then having us consult with you is superfluous, and the Agency will run the risk of becoming predictable to our enemies."

My Father scowled at him. "Point taken. The fact is, I know that you two will go off and bloody well do what you want anyway. But, at least this way, I will have some idea what you and Lissa might be getting into."

Miles looked affronted. "I would never take Lissa knowingly into danger."

My Father smirked, "I know that, though danger still seems to find her often enough."

I hated being talked over and slammed my hand down on the arm of my chair. "Will you two please stop talking like I am not here!" They both gave me a quizzical look and smiled. "Miles and I accept your proposition, Father. It will save us a great deal of time by not having to go behind your back." Both men burst out laughing and acknowledged I was right.

Miles sobered and asked, "Where is my Father?"

"He and Jefferson went for a ride to Pembroke. I want the Hamiltons here, along with the Irregulars. After today I would prefer not to have my resources scattered. Captain Bruce is taking his ship to sea and will monitor the Russian vessel from a discreet distance."

I sat up at the mention of the Hamiltons. "Then how did Burley get here without the Hamiltons?"

Father snorted, "The idiot snuck out and stole a horse. I have no idea how he rode all that way, but Jefferson says he should be confined to bed even if we must tie him down. The leg is badly inflamed again. Luckily he didn't rip out the stitches."

He didn't seem to have anything more to say, so we made to stand, but my Father waved us back into our chairs. "I am not done with you. Now, what is this nonsense about Magda? Jibben is terrified that his Grandmother will unleash hell and that we will all die. Lady Marianne says she's gone to battle with a dragon named Sorris or something like that. Can either of you tell me what's going on?"

We both shook our heads no, but I offered, "Aneski made an appearance today."

He looked astonished. "That clever glamour Magda conjures at times."

I didn't have the heart to tell him that it wasn't a glamour, but people have a tendency when they can't explain things by the rules of this world to reduce it to something simplistic or call it a parlour trick. So I merely agreed, "Yes, that Aneski."

He waved it off. "Well, we will leave Magda to whatever she's up to—but a woman her age should be at home caring for her grandchildren."

I chuckled at the thought of Magda staying home. "In a way, she is caring for her grandchildren, Judith, Jibben and their family."

He scratched behind his ear. "True." Then he asked the question plaguing me, "Do you have any idea how old Magda is? I've never been able to figure out if she's fifty or a hundred and fifty."

I thought she might be even older but answered truthfully, "I have no idea. Even Jibben isn't sure. He says that she has always been there."

Father smiled. "Spoken like a true grandchild. Now then, perhaps we should join the others for luncheon."

Everyone was already gathered in the dining room, including Lord Burley. I was surprised to see him, "Lord Burley, I understand that Dr Jefferson threatened to tie you to your bed."

Burley glanced at me with open hostility as Ewen poured him a glass of wine. "He could try."

I decided to take the chance and address his hostile tone, "What has you in such a surly mood."

He set down the glass before taking a sip. "If you must know, it is you, Lady Tinley. You took my sister into a dangerous situation without considering her safety."

Marianne bit into a roll, glared at her brother, then threw it down and swallowed. "That is unfair, Justin, and you know it. I am not a child to be coddled, and nothing happened to me. I was the one who was intent on going out to the castle. Lady Tinley only came along to keep me out of trouble."

Lord Burley sucked in a breath. "Marianne, stay out of this."

She glowered at him and snapped, "Do not speak to me like that. I will not stand for it."

He scowled at her. "We will speak of this later; you have been ill."

"NO! We will speak of it now. I intend to stay here for as long as Lord Blackburn will have me. I have information and skills that he will find invaluable. Moreover, he has offered me his protection." I glanced at my Father, who seemed to be enjoying the confrontation, but I wondered if he expected either one to give away any secrets in this confrontation.

Burley looked at my Father. "Is this true? Have you offered her your protection?"

My Father sighed, "Your sister is a widow and therefore independent and has sought employment and protection from me. Which I will gladly extend to her."

Burley then turned to his other sister. "What are your thoughts on this."

Arabella had been spreading butter on her roll, which she had set aside. She took a deep breath. "Marianne doesn't need doctors or us anymore. She has always been different and always will be, Justin. You know that better than anyone. So if you want her in your life, I suggest you let her go."

Marianne appeared gobsmacked. "I am surprised to hear that coming from you, Arabella."

Arabella looked down at her lap. "I don't intend on continuing as I have either. I hope that whatever I can beg from Rupert's brother it will be enough to allow me an independent life. Perhaps we could share a cottage, Marianne."

Justin shook his head. "You will be able to afford more than a cottage Arabella. Do you honestly think that Father was that poor of a negotiator?"

Arabella responded, "Father didn't care one wit for me."

"He cared enough to ensure that should Harris die before you, you would have a comfortable living. As a result, you will have a small but profitable estate in Gloucestershire."

She was puzzled. "Rupert didn't own such a thing."

He smiled. "No, but our Mother did, and she willed it to you. Father hid that from Harris for just such a day. And you will have the equal of your marriage portion from Rupert's estate. Arabella, twenty thousand pounds, a handsome sum for a widow."

My Father cleared his throat. "May I suggest that this family business be left for another time? We have more pressing problems to deal with currently."

Burley glowered at him and said, "My family and I are leaving for Pembroke until suitable transportation can be arranged to leave Wales."

Just then, a decidedly harassed and dishevelled looking Lord Shellard entered the room with a distraught Nell and Dr Jefferson. My Father stood and looked over Lord Shellard's shoulder. "Where's Hamilton."

Jefferson plunked down in a chair. "He's coming. He is just dispersing the Irregulars around the perimeter."

"What happened?"

My Father-in-law guzzled back a drink from his flask "Russians. They surrounded the village and planned to take the Hamiltons hostage." He looked at Burley and said, "Someone in Pembroke told them where they were staying."

Burley was gobsmacked, then covered his face with a hand, saying, "A nun stopped and asked me where she could find your party. I told her that the Hamiltons were the only ones still in town and exactly where they were."

Nell walked up to him and slapped him hard. "You risked the lives of my husband and sons so you could escape by giving away our whereabouts to the enemy!"

Burley glared at her, then put up his hands as if to ward off another blow. "How was I supposed to know that a damn Nun was the enemy! She seemed credible enough."

Nell took a deep breath, hands on her hips. "I swear if you ever try anything like that again with me or mine, I will cut off your balls with a dull knife and feed them to you."

Jibben started to laugh. "She could do it too." Nell snapped her head to the side and glared at Jibben, and he meekly added, "Or not—"

Hamilton stood in the doorway with their oldest son in hand and a baby tucked under his other arm. He relinquished the children to Nell and yanked Burley out of his chair, hissing, "You ever even think about doing something like that again, and I will kill you." Then he let go, and Burley painfully dropped into his seat, gasping and grimacing, blood seeping through his trousers. No one bothered to commiserate with him.

Even Jefferson said, "I should let you sit here and fester, you blithering idiot. Ewen, will you call Lord Burley's valet and help carry his Lordship back to his room? Once I am done here, I will tend to his wound—again."

"Yes, milord."

Once a contrite Lord Burley was removed, my Father-in-law and the doctor explained how they almost rode into a trap.

"Hamilton signalled us from the upper story of the Inn with a mirror that they were surrounded. Jefferson pretended to have been summoned for a medical emergency and declared it was the plague."

I looked at him and said in disbelief, "The plague? And they believed you!"

He tipped his head towards Jefferson, who grinned, saying, "Moscow 1771, there was a terrible plague which decimated the citizenry. Fortunately, the memories of such an event stay in the collective memory for an exceedingly long time, so the Russians ran."

My Father nodded. "Excellent work Matthew, but that won't hold them off for long." Then he turned to Hamilton. "Where are the men?"

Hamilton smiled. "Positioned around the property in the outbuildings and empty cottages."

"Good. Now we sit back and wait for the Russians to make their move."

Chapter 20

What have Dragons got to Do with It?

The previous evening had been dedicated to checking weapons and assessing defensive positions and protection for the children. Gregory, the cook, worked hard to ensure enough food to last a few days for the Irregulars dispersed about the estate. Finally, there was a review of all viable escape routes. Lord Stanhope surprised us by arriving with the men from his estate.

Magda was still nowhere to be found, but she had left her medicine satchel in Dr Jefferson's room at some point. Then Terrance Stockton arrived with Mercy Cousins and Afon Thomas, bringing additional medical supplies. Stockton saw my Father and told him, "Jenkins down at the pub said the villagers are at your service if you need them."

My Father smiled. "That's generous of them."

Stockton just laughed. "He's just pleased that there isn't any plague, and he wasn't obliged to serve the Russians any longer. The villagers love playing up the plague story."

So, we waited, yet nothing happened as the day wore on and evening descended on us. Some of us sat beside each other, speaking quietly. Others paced from room to room, checking and rechecking windows. Mothers checked on their children and reassured them that all was well. There was no changing for dinner or formal dining. Instead, an extensive buffet was set up in an inner room without windows that had once been a medieval armoury. There were still spears and swords from a bygone era hanging on the wall and resting in the corners. Those that could eat filled their plates and ate where they could find a seat.

As we waited for the sun to set, my Father invited Derek, Miles, and myself up to the battlements on the oldest part of the manor's once-grand medieval keep. The sky was a deep glistening blue, without a cloud to be seen anywhere, and as the sun started to set, the first evening stars began to appear and still there was nothing to see in the cove until the Russian ship appeared at its mouth.

Its draft was too deep to sail in, and their longboats would have a long and exposed pull to reach the shoreline under the cliffside nearest Blackburn Manor. None of us could determine what advantage they would have by anchoring there. Derek even said, "Any guns they have wouldn't be an advantage at this distance."

Behind them, on the horizon, the clouds were building into mountainous billows of an ugly, bruised colour in the west, and the wind started to pick up, blowing strong. The air was suddenly heavy with the sweet, pungent odour I associated with lightning, portending a horrific storm.

My Father studied the horizon. "Odd for such a storm this time of year. I suggest we descend below; it's quickly moving our way."

As we turned to the stairway, thunder reverberated across the sky, followed by the first heavy drops of rain that began pounding on the parapet."

Jibben was waiting for us below. He was pacing back and forth. "This is Grandmama's doing."

Miles looked puzzled. "What?"

Jibben threw out his arms. "This! This storm is her doing."

My Father snorted, "Magda can do many things, but she can't control the weather."

Jibben waved a hand in dismissal. "Have you forgotten Egypt and the sandstorm!"

My Father was equally dismissive. "Mere coincidence."

Jibben took a step closer to my Father. He was livid as he pointed at him, growling, "We shall see—this is not natural, mark my words." Then he stormed off down the hallway. I glanced at Derek and Miles to see what they might think, but both stared blankly at Jibben's retreating figure.

Miles looked at my Father. "Has anyone seen Magda?"

I shook my head and said, "Not since she left us at the castle."

Sir Derwyn came around the corner, "Lord Blackburn. We have a bit of a problem. Mr Thornton, Miss Jilly and Mr Rabby are missing."

Father was perplexed and testy. "What do you mean missing? Surely someone saw them leave."

Sir Derwyn exhaled, "Lady Marianne says they have gone to Madam Magda in the caverns."

Father exploded, "The caverns! They will be underwater in this storm!"

He nodded at my Father. "Yes, milord."

Father snapped back, "I want to see Lady Marianne and Mr Campeau in my study, now."

Burley yelled down from the wing to the family rooms as he marched across the hall. "Blackburn! I need to speak to you about this nonsense of my sister having any knowledge of my Father's business dealings."

He glanced up at him. "If you can hobble down here, I will hear what you have to say. But I warn you, don't try my patience."

We followed my Father into his study and took the seats furthest away from his desk. Campeau, Marianne, and Burley came in, as did Derwyn, Jibben, my Father-in-law Lord Shellard and Andropov for some unknown reason.

My Father sat, and everyone started talking to him simultaneously. He pinched the bridge of his nose and just let them shout over each other. Finally, Derek let loose an ear-splitting whistle and ordered, "Sit down!" None of them complied, but they did stop talking, "Fine, have it your way; don't sit."

Then he nodded to my Father, "Now you can speak one at a time on Lord Blackburn's command." Miles seemed to find the spectacle humourous and could barely contain his delight, which Derek succumbed to after issuing his edict.

My Father gave them a withering glance, then scanned the room and said, "Will you all please sit down!"

Everyone scrambled for a seat except Marianne, who plopped down on the floor. Like a child and leaned up against Campeau's chair. He received a contemptuous glare from Burley, who sat in the chair opposite him. Campeau ignored the slight. Instead, he concentrated on my Father while laying a hand on Marianne's shoulder. Father cleared his throat " All right then, Burley, since you don't need to be here, let's get your business out of the way first."

Burley didn't appreciate the thought of his family business being spoken of in front of relative strangers, but my Father had not offered him any other option. "I am not—" Then he seemed to rethink his words and instead said, "In my Father's will, he stressed that the documents he had left in my charge were the only true accounting of his business activities."

Marianne laughed. "God, he even lied in his will."

Burley ignored her. "While Marianne was deeply involved acting more or less as his secretary even after her marriage, she should be aware of that fact."

Marianne chuckled again, and then her expression hardened. "The other books Justin, about his most profitable dealings, can be found in only two places. One was in the room that went up in flames when our Father set fire to his study to escape Brocklehurst. He died in that room because he destroyed what they thought was the only record. Jean can confirm that."

All eyes turned to Campeau, but he only nodded. "The second place they can be found is burned into my memory." Then her expression softened. "For heaven's sake, Justin, do you think Father wanted you tainted by what he had done? He left you with his personal diaries, estate ledgers and those from his few legitimate business concerns."

She sighed and closed her eyes. When she opened them, she stared at her brother with steely-eyed purpose. "His illicit activities started as a small concern. He thought it was a harmless smuggling operation, and everyone was profiting from the war in one way or another. But it turned into a multi-headed serpent, and he lost control of it and ended up selling his soul to the devil to protect you."

She chuckled, then added, "The last great hope of saving the honour of the Browne family were you and Alexander—the heir and the spare. You two were the only ones he protected. He knew Randall and Julian were just as twisted inside as he was, and he wasn't surprised or remorseful at their deaths." She smiled at him. "The information everyone wants is up here, brother dear." She tapped her head.

Lord Shellard and Mr Andropov leaned forward and, at the same time, said, "About that information—"

Lord Shellard waved a hand for Andropov to continue, "Lady Marianne cannot be allowed to give that information to anyone else."

My Father glared at him. "And how do you propose we stop her if she so desires?"

Andropov didn't hesitate. "We kill her."

Burley reared back, "Now, wait just a minute there! No one is killing my sister."

Campeau's eyes were full of loathing as he glared at Andropov and said, "You think your people in Moscow should have that information?"

Andropov chewed on his lip before answering, "That is irrelevant. We can at least protect her, hide her somewhere from others who want it."

Campeau sneered, "Like Siberia, where all political prisoners go to die of cold and starvation! No, I will not allow it!"

Burley glared at Campeau but added his voice, "Neither will I."

Then Andropov shrugged. "Fine, then she dies." He quickly withdrew a cocked pistol and pointed it at Marianne. But before he could pull the trigger, Miles grabbed his arm, jerking it upwards and firing into the ceiling to rain down a dusting of plaster on Miles and Andropov.

Surprisingly, no one reacted with panic or outrage. Miles casually brushed off the dust from his shoulder and arms, then shook his head like our dog Bard, flinging plaster and dust everywhere. He took the pistol out of Andropov's hand and said, "I knew there was a reason I didn't like you."

Just then, a gust of wind rattled the windows, followed by a crack of lightning and then thunder. It was so loud that the windows and floor seemed to shake. Once the noise had subsided, my Father scowled at Andropov. "That is not the way we do things here, Mr Andropov. You will cease to threaten Lady Marianne and anyone else in the household, or I will throw you out into the storm."

He rubbed one eye as if exhausted by the topic already. Then he turned to my Father-in-law. "You have something to say, Lord Shellard?"

He glared at Andropov. "I just wanted to emphasise that no one should die. The Russians are diplomatic visitors to this country. Whitehall, Moscow and Windsor would take a very dim view of any of them being killed by any of you."

My Father stared at him for a few seconds before saying, "So, would you have me turn Lady Marianne over to them in a diplomatic pouch."

Lord Shellard snorted with derision. "Of course not, Colin, and you know it."

"Then what do you propose I do?"

No one said anything and stared at the floor until Sir Derwyn ventured, "We could send her out through the old escape tunnels."

It was Miles who responded, "Then where?"

He shrugged. "At least Lady Marianne wouldn't be under threat here."

"She will still be hunted. There has to be a better solution."

Jibben had been glaring at everyone like we were simple. The driving rain was coming down in sheets, and the harder it came, the harder the wind blew and the more frequent the lightning and thunder. It became so intense it was as if it was responding to the moods in the room. Our nerves were stretched taut and darker

503

emotions crackled in the air. Then Jibben said "Grandmama."

My Father looked up and said, "Look, Jibben. Magda has always done whatever she wants when she wants." He gestured towards the window. "She can hardly be responsible for the weather."

Jibben arched a brow. "You think not?"

Derek chuckled. "It would be a blessing if that damn Russian ship was wrecked on the rocks and all hands lost."

I stare at him in disbelief. "Derek! That's a terrible thing to wish on anyone!"

"I heard the stories about what she did in Egypt, cousin dear. That didn't seem to bother you too much."

He had no idea how I had wrestled with what I had seen there, and it still haunted my darkest dreams. "I had no hand in condoning what was done, cousin. It was a sandstorm that took them, nothing else." And that was what I had to believe—the alternative that it was conjured somehow was just too impossible for my mind to comprehend.

A still wrathful Jibben yelled. "Enough! What was done cannot be undone, and what will be; will be. We cannot change Grandmama's course. We shall have to wait and see." He spun on his heel and made for the door. Then he stopped to point at the window where darkness had descended. "Mark my words. Death awaits us in that storm." Then he opened the door, where I saw Judith standing in the hallway biting her fist before he closed it behind him.

Father ran a hand down his face. "This is becoming beyond ridiculous. There is nothing that can be done until this storm abates." He turned and smiled at Marianne. "Let me think about what I can do for Lady Marianne. Until I come up with something, I would prefer that you weren't alone, and didn't venture outside, milady."

She took Campeau's hand. "That shouldn't be a problem, Lord Blackburn. Between Jean and my brother, I doubt they will let me out of their sight." She smiled warmly at her brother and giggled at the look on Campeau's face. She stood, pulling Jean to his feet, then, looking down at Burley, said, "I will call Sorely to come to aid you, brother." Then she glided out the door with Campeau in tow.

Her brother growled as they disappeared, "I will not let her wed that French trash."

I arched a brow at him. "I don't think you have anything to say about that, Lord Burley. She is of age and no longer dependent on your support since she has a position here."

Burley leaned his head back and groaned, "I have a sister who will be a secretary to a man not of her own family and appears to have aligned herself with a Frenchmen who has questionable forebears."

My Father-in-law chuckled. "You will get over it and survive any accompanying scandal. Lord knows you have weathered your Father's exploits well enough. When I left London, I heard Lord Tomlinson is considering your offer for Lady Edith's hand. It has been brought to his attention that you were at Palmerston's estate and were injured foiling an assassination attempt against

Lord Blackburn, a close confidant to the King.

Burley looked confused. "Who put that claptrap about."

Lord Shellard chuckled and pointed to my Father. "He did—he's taken a liking to you, or he wouldn't have bothered. But for the life of me, I can't imagine why."

Burley glared at my Father. "Why did you do that?"

My Father stared off into space for a time. Then said, "Consider it reparations for the trouble we caused you indirectly with the deaths of your brothers."

Burley quirked a brow. "And my Father?"

"We had nothing to do with his death."

He nodded. "Tell me then, is my bother's education at Cambridge being paid for by an anonymous donor, or are you also doing that?"

My Father sat back before answering, "Alexander has a fine mind—he could prove valuable one day."

"He will not work for your Agency! Over my dead body."

My Father chuckled. "I didn't say he would. But a man like him working for the good of the people in Parliament would be invaluable. You should encourage him to give up a life of academia and apply his considerable intellect to improving this country."

"You think he could?"

"It never hurts to try, especially with a brother in the house of Lords, to help guide him."

Burley snorted, "And if you ever need a favour?"

My Father smiled. "I will know where to find you—both."

Marianne and Campeau returned with Sorely, and he assisted Burley out of the room.

Then my Father turned to Sir Derwyn. "What is this about Thornton, Rabby and Jilly disappearing?"

Sir Derwyn glanced at Campeau and Marianne, seated primly on the settee. I wondered if sometimes her outrageous behaviour was for her brother's benefit, just to set his teeth on edge. It was also a way to assert her independence from anyone, including Campeau. Sir Derwyn took a deep breath. "The three of them have been as thick as thieves since they arrived, and considering their backgrounds, I have been keeping an eye on them."

I was insulted on their behalf and growled, "They are trusted friends, as well as employees, Sir Derwyn."

He didn't back down as he added, "That might be who they are in London, Lady Tinley, but here in Blackburn Manor, they are unknown. Their very butchering of the language sets them apart."

I could feel my brow wrinkle. "Butchering of the language. All three of them speak respectable English."

He arched a brow in disbelief. "That might be your experience with them, but since coming here, they speak in nothing but a low cant from the slums of London, according to Mr Murphy, your

Lordship's secretary."

"Did you ask Mr Murphy what they were talking about?"

"I did, and he said it was none of my business."

I almost burst out laughing as my Father scratched at his ear and mumbled, "Yes—well, that sounds like something he might do. Would you do me a favour and locate Mr Murphy and come back here with him."

Sir Derwyn bowed and then walked out. Lady Marianne watched him go and said, "He feels threatened by all the new people here, Lord Blackburn."

My Father nodded. "I daresay he does. I will have to see what I can do to rectify that. Now tell me what you know about where Madam Magda has gone."

Campeau nodded for Marianne to go ahead. "She's gone to wake the dragon. That's what this storm is all about. She told me to expect it and not to be afraid. That she would help Jean and I disappear from the world."

My Father looked intrigued. "And how does she plan on doing that?"

Campeau shrugged. "She said something about obliterating us, then bringing us back." I shivered, thinking of what Magda could be doing.

My Father looked at the rest of us, and everyone shrugged. He rubbed his forehead. "Derek, please find Jibben and bring him back here."

Derek left and returned with Jibben and Judith in tow. Jibben came reluctantly and stood with his arms crossed in the doorway. My Father glared at him. "Would you care to sit down, Locke?"

"No."

Derek and Judith came in, and as they sat down, she said, "My husband wants to look for Magda. But no one could see past the end of their nose out there. It's very dark, and the rain is torrential. It would be suicide."

My Father resigned himself to Jibben being difficult. "I agree with you, Lady Locke." He stared at her husband. Very well, have it your way, Jibben. Feel free to look for her. But may I ask if you know where she has gone."

Jibben's eyes flashed, his brow furrowed, and his shoulders slumped. "No."

"Then where were you planning to look?" Lord Stanhope was standing behind him, chuckling. "He asked how he could get out to the castle through the caverns. I told him, in this weather, you don't. But he is determined. Would you like me to have the Truncheons put him in the dungeon?"

"I don't think that will be necessary, Stanhope. Now, will you two please sit down?" He sat back and tapped his fingers on his desk as they took their seats. "What is your Grandmother up to."

Jibben was still disgruntled and answered petulantly, "How should I know; I can't find her!"

Miles shook his head. "Then just tell us what you think she might be doing."

Jibben pinched his nose while looking up at the ceiling. "God, I wish I knew Tinley. If it's what I think, it could kill her. This magic is incredibly old. It is so ancient that I have only ever heard it whispered about by Old Dora—the one who died at the picnic. She saw it done when she was a girl, and it killed the caster."

Miles sighed. "What is it, Jibben?"

He pulled on his ear. "It's a legend, history if you like—it's called Dragon's Breath."

Derek chuckled, and Jibben glowered at him. "I don't laugh at your legends."

Derek arched a brow. "Oh, really."

Jibben smirked. "Well, maybe I do a little." Derek snorted.

My Father watched this exchange smiling, and then he asked, "What is this Dragon's Breath?"

Jibben swallowed. "I need a drink."

Derek pulled out his ever-present flask and handed it to him. I thought Jibben would drain it, and when he passed it back to Derek, he looked at it. "Jesus, did you leave me a dram?"

Jibben had clasped his hands between his legs and leaned forward. Judith's hand was on his back. "Once, long ago, the clan had to disappear or be eradicated. So their most powerful Mother took it upon herself to hide the clan. She could not cast her magic from outside where she would hide them, but they never saw her again. The elders said that she was consumed by the spell she cast."

My Father looked incredulous. "What does this spell look like."

Jibben pointed out the window, "It starts like that."

"Jibben, it's just a freak storm."

"No, that is the beginning of the spell—exactly like that!"

Before he could go on, Sir Derwyn returned, "Mr Murphy, Mr de Bearne and Sir Owen all seem missing; I have set the Truncheons to searching for them."

Father's brow furrowed in concern, but he dismissed it quickly, seemingly because they were all experienced agents and could take care of themselves. Instead, my Father asked, "Derwyn, you were born and have lived most of your life here. I am sure storms like this happen with a certain degree of regularity at this time of year?"

He shook his head. "No, milord, I don't recall anything like this in August. In November possibly, but not this time of year."

My Father sighed and ran a hand through his hair. " All right then, if we accept that Magda has done something to change the weather, what can we expect next."

Jibben fidgeted. He looked back at Judith. "In a day, the rain should stop, the sun will be blotted out, and a fog thicker than anything you have ever seen will descend on us."

"How far will this fog extend."

"As far as she needs it."

My Father nodded. "Then why did she need Thornton, Jilly and

Rabby?"

Jibben cleared his throat. "She needs Thornton's thoughts as a wise man. Jilly will give her a hair of the virgin, and Rabby—" he glanced around "will provide the seed of a stallion."

Derek and Miles coughed and looked anywhere but at Jibben. I smacked Miles' arm and glared at him, whispering, "Stop it, both of you." Derek tried to look contrite but was having difficulty holding back his laughter.

Jibben glared at them. "Laugh if you like Bruce, but that's what I know of the spell."

My Father ignored my husband and Derek. "So this Dragon's Breath is the fog?"

Sir Derwyn scratched his ear. "Pardon me, Lord Blackburn, but that sounds very much like some of the legends of Merlin."

Now Derek was shaking with laughter. "What's next? King Arthur and his knights come out of the fog to rescue us?"

Jibben rolled his eyes. "You weren't in Egypt! There were forces within the sand that came to fight our enemies."

Derek tried to control himself, but Miles looked concerned when he asked, "Can Magda control this Jibben? In Egypt, she had Amir, and he seemed to be fairly powerful."

Jibben shrugged. "That's why I am worried that she is doing this alone and has no one to back her up if she loses control. I have no idea what it will do to those caught in it. The time Dora recounted to me was used to protect the clan from being

512

discovered. Who's to say it is not like the sand in Egypt, and whatever it touches dies? That's why I must find her. I have to stop her."

Sir Derwyn seemed ready to accept this. The Welsh had a long history of magic in their folklore. "If she's in the caverns, Sir Stephen, there is no way to get to her now. The storm surge will have flooded this side of them, and it would be suicide to try or take a boat out there. Even if we could reach the cliffside stairway, it would be like climbing glass. We are more likely to run aground on the submerged rocks and sink. You can't swim in that and survive. It's a boiling cauldron on the best of days."

My Father sat forward and slapped his desk. "Then, I guess we wait. I suggest you spend some time with your loved ones while you can, pray if you like and hope that one crazy Gypsy can make a miracle happen."

Judith chuckled. "What a recipe for disaster. We can't kill the Russians, we need two people to appear to have died so the Russians will leave, and we need a miracle from Grandmama to make it all happen."

Andropov snorted. "What a bunch of superstitious nonsense! It is ridiculous that you people believe in magic of all things. If you don't kill Lady Marianne, then the Russians on that ship will bombard you from the cove if they can. Then they will take Lady Marianne, and what will you do then? They will torture her for her knowledge and rain chaos down on us."

Lord Shellard arched a brow, then his expression hardened, and he snarled, "That's a bit melodramatic, don't you think, Misha? I am not opposed to the Russians dying and having it look

513

like self-defence or even an accident at sea. But one thing you can be sure of is that if you don't stop threatening my family and friends, you will be counted among the dead and missing. I will make sure of it."

Andropov threw up his hands. "Fine, I was only sent to observe and find out what the Russians were up to and inform Lord Blackburn that he had trouble on his shores. My work is done. I am just a casual observer now. But if you let me, I can get Lady Marianne and Mr Campeau out of here."

Miles chuckled. "I hardly think we could trust you to save their lives now."

My Father folded his hands in front of him. "No, Mr Andropov, you are welcome to leave anytime. But you will be leaving alone, with my thanks to our brothers in Russia."

Andropov crossed his arms in resignation. "No, I will stay and help protect you. After all, it is my duty to protect even the foolhardy."

Father smiled, but there was no warmth in it. "That is entirely up to you." He rose. "I don't know what the rest of you plan for the day, but I will spend time with my wife and children."

He stopped next to me, took my hands, and pulled me to my feet. "You have made me extremely proud, poppet." He glanced quickly at Miles. "Even your unconventional choices have proved you to be a young woman of superior intellect and impeccable taste." He leaned in, kissed me on both cheeks, and hugged me tightly.

Miles, who was now standing, shook his hand and then suddenly pulled him into a hug, whispering something that made Miles chuckle before saying, "You have my word, sir."

He walked out of the room, leaving us. Andropov rose. "I have some letters to write if we don't survive." he left, shaking his head and muttering in Russian, then Romani.

Derek watched him leave and asked, "What was that about."

Jibben jerked his chin up. "He thinks we're doomed. He has heard the stories of Dragon's Breath though he would rather not admit it." He turned to Judith. "Come, my love, Rosalyn will want her mama, and I promised the boys I would play soldier with them."

I perused the room for those that were left. Sir Derwyn was contemplating the raging storm outside, he looked worried and abruptly stood, and as he did, he looked at Stanhope. "Shall we go find your Mother?"

Stanhope started to grin but suddenly stopped after scrutinising him closely. "You actually believe this nonsense about Dragon's Breath?"

Sir Derwyn glanced back at the window. "Believe it or not, that storm is not natural, Bennett. You have lived here long enough to realise that."

Bennett's expression sobered immediately. "Yes—." He, too, stared out the window before following his natural Father out the door.

Lady Marianne and Mr Campeau scooted out behind them,

whispering to each other, but nothing I could hear.

That left my Father-in-law, Derek, Miles, and me. It was Lord Shellard who spoke first. "Well, that was a fraught conversation. I don't know about the three of you, but I could use some laughter, and there is nothing like children to supply that." He glanced at Derek. "Care to join me, nephew?

"Aye, Uncle William, I will. It's much better than drinking alone." They left but not before suggesting that we join them.

I rose and started for the door, but Miles beat me to it and closed the door, locking it. He came to me and unloosed my hair from its pins, then began on the row of buttons on my bodice. I pushed at his hands. "Miles not here?"

He smirked. "Why not—everyone has gone their own way. Besides, the next time I am summoned to this room, I won't feel like a child sitting in front of the headmaster."

I rolled my eyes. "Miles, we hardly ever come here."

He shrugged, then began kissing away any objection I might have. I only managed to get out one last protest. "You will have to restore my hair."

Miles chuckled and nuzzled my neck. "Done."

Chapter 21

Do Dragons Breath Fire?

The storm continued unabated, lashing at the manor with a terrible fury. It was impossible to see further than a few feet at any given time. As a result, we were often confronted with a sheet of water pounding against the doors and windows. It rattled them so hard in some cases that they had weakened the panes and seals to the point where water was entering some of the rooms—requiring the constant diligence of the staff.

One of the Morning Room windows facing the cove cracked then shattered, allowing the rain to pour into the room. The furnishings and artefacts were rescued. Then four men risked life and limb to put storm shutters in place. The room was then locked and abandoned to its fate. The sounds emanating from the room were like a wild animal roaring and throwing its weight against the door, rattling the frame to the point that it was eventually barricaded to prevent it from bursting open.

Murphy, de Bearne, and Sir Owen returned soaked to the skin. They explained that they had been testing the perimeter of the storm but had consistently been pushed back. Janet was relieved beyond belief, and Lettie gave Murphy an ear full. All three scoffed at the idea of Dragon's Breath, but their bravado did not reverberate in the timber of their voices.

The children were brought down to the old keep's central

room. It was devoid of windows other than arrow slits in what had once been the medieval banqueting hall. It was part museum and library but considered safer than the far-removed nursery. Bedding and cots had been moved here for the children and were piled at one end near one of the three massive hearths. It was also the place where one of the four escape tunnels could be found. Andropov and Derek had spent considerable time investigating them all. Only two still had a viable exit. One led down to the beach was partially filled with water, and another opened into a small woodland well east of the manor.

The space in the keep was ample, and the children were making the most of it. Their adventure was charged with unbridled excitement accentuated by the palpable tension of the adults. Alex was asleep on my lap while Charlotte and her Father listened to Lord Shellard tell a story that had been one of Miles' and Edward's favourites about King Arthur.

My Mother decided that we would not eat here in hiding. Instead, we would enter the formal dining room with the children and our servants for dinner. The meal was laid out in a buffet, and while the Welsh staff were initially unsure about this break with convention, the London staff soon helped them relax, and we found ourselves a mixed and amenable group. Even Lord Burley and Lady Arabella spoke to Lettie and Murphy as equals after their initial shock at our table companions.

It was during this meal that there was hammering at the main entrance. Whether it was the storm or not, everyone stopped to listen. The hammering was not repeated, but the conversation was muted from there on out. Hamilton turned in his chair, looking towards the hallway, "What do you suppose that was?"

Jibben narrowed his eyes and said without inflexion, "That was the Dragon's tail—the battle has begun."

Everyone looked at him with mouths open, but no one asked for an explanation. Afterwards, he rose from his seat and walked out; Judith looked around the table. "Please excuse him—he's very distressed about Magda." Then she stood, saying, "Come, Alma, boys, let us see if we can stop him from doing something stupid." She picked up Rosalyn, then their Nanny Alma, and the boys followed.

The other nannies rose and took the children back to the Keep as we finished the meal. The servants who sat companionably with us reverted to their typical roles and left to go about their duties. The rest of us remained seated until Derek suddenly said, "Listen."

I strained to hear any noise. "There's nothing, Derek."

"Exactly—nothing, the storm has passed."

De Bearne squeezed his eyes together, listening intently. "It hasn't passed, Derek; we are in the eye of the storm. I have been in hurricanes in the West Indies; it's just like this."

Derek bit his lip, looking towards the window, the sight outside was still impenetrable, but instead of sheets of rain, it was fog so thick that it appeared to push against the window. There was absolute silence, not even a hint of the moaning wind that had haunted us since this had started.

Nell whispered. "It's worse than the yellow fog of London—do you think it's as deadly as Jibben believes?"

Hamilton took her hand. "I don't think so, Nell. It's only thick sea fog." No one dissuaded him of the idea, and we were all hopeful that he was right.

Then night fell on us, and nothing changed. Jibben paced the drawing room. Some tried to read and play cards or chess, but most of us whispered our fears and hopes to each other. Judith finally lost patience with Jibben. "Stephen, if you don't stop pacing, I will pay Derek to knock you down."

Derek's eyes lit up. "With pleasure, and I will do it for nothing."

McMaster added glibly, "I will help—Locke is a big man, and Bruce might not be able to handle him."

Gabriel was grinning from ear to ear. "I forgot how much fun you people could be under stressful circumstances. You are like the Vikings celebrating the possibility of your death in battle." Everyone in the room stopped and turned to look at him. He scanned the room, considering the glowering expressions, adding, "Perhaps I am reading more into it than exists. I think I shall retire. There's no telling when the Dragon will bring the fight to us."

People nodded and slowly followed his lead, checking on children before retiring. I walked around the ground floor with Miles and Derek checking windows and doors. When we came to the morning room, it was eerily quiet until we made to turn away. I swore I could hear a whimper and hissed at Miles and Derek talking as they walked away, "Shush, listen!"

Once again, the whimper emanated from the other side of the door. Then I tried to remove some of the barricade but found it almost impossible "Miles move these things, please! Someone is in that room."

He and Derek stopped and appeared annoyed as Miles snapped, "That's impossible."

I stomped my foot. "I tell you, someone is trapped in that room!"

They both sighed and came to my side, leaning towards the door. Then we all heard a very human moan followed by a whimper that galvanised them into action. They hurriedly pushed aside the items blocking the door, garnering the interest of my Father, Mother, and Dr Jefferson, who were coming out of the study. I explained what I had heard, and they added their efforts to clear the barricade. My Mother rifled through a key ring in her pocket and found the one to open the Morning Room door. A thick and cloying fog rolled into the hall knee-high and crept higher. Miles and Derek covered their noses and dove into the room, calling out, "Who's in here? Call out so we can find you!"

Three distinct voices called out. Derek stepped through the door with a dishevelled and barely conscious Jilly in his arms. Then he ducked back in as Miles dragged an unconscious Rabby out next, and finally, Derek came out with Thornton barely on his feet, holding him up with an arm around his waist and one of Thornton's arms thrown over Derek's shoulder. Father quickly reached in and pulled the door closed, and my Mother locked it just as something bumped up against it.

He looked at my Mother as she nodded her head. He was about to turn the key in the lock when the door shook again, and an inhuman cry echoed from the other side. Jilly's eyes snapped open, and she yelled at my Father, "No! Don't open it."

"But it could be Magda."

She shook her head. "That is not Magda." There was the sound of something slithering on the other side of the door. It was unmistakable that whatever was in that room wasn't human.

Jilly then relaxed back into my Mother's arms as she asked, "Jilly, where is Magda?

The young girl tried to open her eyes but shook her head. "I don't know, the storm came on us, and the caverns started to fill; she told us to run." Jilly's eyes welled up with tears, and she was shaking.

Mother cradled her in a tight hug, "It's okay, Jilly, you are safe now."

Jibben came racing down the stairs. "Where is Grandmama?"

Jilly answered. "I don't know, Sir Stephen. She told us to go, so we ran. The last I saw her, she was—" Her brow furrowed as if trying to think of the right words. "Her eyes were glowing, and she was limned in a blue light."

My heart dropped, and I breathed, "Aneski." the manifestation of a glamour that she could wrap around herself always unsettled me, mainly because I couldn't believe in Aneski's existence in our world. After all, this was the 19th century!

Miles was staring at me. "You mean her ancestor, Aneski?" I nodded.

Jilly was asleep now, and Jibben was on his knees beside her. "Aneski—was the first of us. She was a powerful conjurer in ancient Egypt and Pharoh's lover. But the priests feared her and convinced the King that her powers were evil and that he should kill her. But, despite being afraid of Aneski, he couldn't bring himself to kill her, so the Pharoah abandoned her in the desert to the will of the gods."

Dr Jefferson was examining Rabby, interrupted, drawing us back to the present to ask, "Where will we put the causalities from our coming conflict." Mother chose the drawing room for its size and proximity to the Keep and the kitchen. They then started organising the space and calling for supplies to be brought in. After examining the three in the hallway, Dr Jefferson moved them to the drawing room. "Nothing seems wrong with them other than exhaustion and dehydration."

My Mother sighed. "Well, that's a relief. I would hate to explain to Mave Manners that an unknown assailant attacked her daughter."

Jibben shook his head. "Not unknown—a dragon."

Mother went to him and cupped his face "Jibben, there is no such thing. Whatever Magda is doing out there, she will be fine. She is a survivor."

He smiled at her. "Yes, Irene, my brain agrees. But, unfortunately, my soul is not so sure."

Judith had come down the stairs to join us, and she looked at Jilly, Rabby and Thornton, each so pale with dark circles under their eyes. Then she went to Jefferson, "You should get some rest. Jibben and I will watch over them. I doubt he will be able to sleep, and if he can't, then I won't."

Jefferson nodded and gave her instructions to encourage them to drink and be prepared for nightmares and hysterical outbursts, considering what they may have endured stumbling about in that storm.

Miles and I consulted with my parents and then checked the rest of the ground floor to see that it was locked up tight and secure. Then we made our way to our room. I sat at my dressing table as Meg came in. She was pale and had lost her glow after returning from her holiday. "Meg, sit down. I plan on dressing in my boy's clothes and plaiting my hair. I can manage that without you. Go to bed."

"I am worn out, milady, but it is not physical. Whatever is happening outside is unnatural and terrifying."

"That it is." She assisted me in pulling off my dress. I released my stays and breathed a sigh of relief. "One day, there will be no stays, and women will be as comfortable as men."

Meg chuckled. "I don't think I'd like to wear those skin-tight trousers and jackets, milady. Could you imagine wearing those high collars and cravats that make some men purple in the face?"

I laughed. "You have a point, Meg."

Miles joined us. He had changed into more comfortable clothing and wore only a simple neckerchief. "Glad to hear that someone realises how we suffer too."

"I will finish helping my wife Meg; you and Robert are free for the evening. Stay away from the windows. We have no idea who's out there." She nodded and picked up my dress and underthings, leaving the room through our shared dressing room.

Miles undid my hair. I chuckled. "You didn't want her to know that you had already taken my hair down once today."

He smirked, "Oh, I believe she knows—she knows her work when she sees it."

I suppressed a giggle and stopped his hand as he ran it through my hair. "What do you think is happening outside."

"I think it's a freak storm that rarely happens that no one is alive to remember the last one. There's no magic. Magda is simply good at reading the signs of change and uses them to her advantage."

"The glowing eyes and limning that Jilly saw?"

He shrugged. "Electricity in the air."

"So, another case of the right circumstances coming together?"

I saw him nod in the mirror I was facing as he plaited my hair, "Or the vivid imagination of a terrified young woman in unfamiliar surroundings. Some plants and insects glow in caverns in the right conditions—I wouldn't worry about it, my love."

I spun around to rest my hand on his chest. "You are so practical."

"I prefer to think I am rational. Now come and lay down. We should try and get what sleep we can."

"I will need to dress in my boy clothes."

"No, you don't, at least not yet anyway." He swept me up in his arms and carried me to the bed.

We awoke as Meg pulled back the curtains to show that it had lightened outside, and the fog seemed to have dissipated somewhat. It was more like smoke that would stalk you in your dreams, hiding things at the most inopportune times and showing disturbing shadows in the blink of an eye.

I turned to shake Miles awake, "Look."

He opened one bleary eye and stared toward where I was pointing, saying. "Yes, it's still foggy."

"But it is not as bad."

He opened the other eye and groaned. "But it is still foggy."

I slapped his arm and lifted the sheet taking note of our nakedness just as I had been about to rise. Meg laid our wrappers at the end of the bed, then walked into the dressing room, giving us privacy to clothe ourselves at least partially. She returned with a day dress for me, and I sighed in disappointment at the sight. "Lord Blackburn orders. Everyone is to appear for breakfast appropriately dressed. When the fog blew off for a bit, Mr de Bearne caught sight of the Russians lowering a longboat."

I nodded. "So it's clearing?"

She wrinkled her brow and frowned. "Just when you think it is, it closes over everything again like someone is pulling a curtain over the world."

Miles and I dressed quickly and met the others in the breakfast room. The buffet was set up as usual. Near the head of the table with my Father and Mother sat Count Vasiliev, Countess Irina and a rather regal-looking gentleman introduced as the Countess's Uncle, Prince Andre Gregor. No one seemed to have much of an appetite. But a few went through the motions of making their selections from the buffet. The rest of us waited for coffee or tea to be poured. None of the staff withdrew, and I saw that they were strategically positioned around the room. I suspected that weapons were hidden within easy reach.

Once everyone was assembled, the Prince grinned, looking down the table's length, scrutinising each of us before saying. "So, you are the members of the famous Agency. I expected more, but perhaps not everyone will come to Lord Blackburn's call. After all the events around the death of Sir Thomas Wisemen, you and your people are suspects. Are they not Dr Jefferson?"

Jefferson glowered at him, but Father tapped on the table to ignore his provocation. Finally, my Father turned his attention to the Prince. "I find it interesting that you should be so well informed regarding an internal matter."

"Oh, we know a great deal about you, Lord Blackburn and your organisation."

My Father smiled. "I rather doubt that Your Highness, considering the murder of Sir Thomas was most certainly committed by someone in your diplomatic entourage."

The Prince stopped smiling. "And you have proof of this?"

My Father smirked. "Witnesses including the murderer's own words just before killing another British citizen."

The Count huffed, "This is make-believe! They are trying to provoke a diplomatic incident."

My Father leaned forward, smiling at the Count. "On the contrary, we were ordered here to prevent such an occurrence. Lord Shellard is our government's representative to observe that we do nothing more than defend ourselves and believe me that I will not hesitate to do so."

The Prince ran his tongue over his teeth as he seemed to consider his options. Then, he looked at Hamilton and smiled. "Lord Hamilton, are you here as the representative of my friend Lord Russell the Home Secretary?"

Hamilton flicked at nonexistent lint on his jacket, then said in a snobbish fashion that I rarely heard him use, "In part, Your Highness."

The Prince was not satisfied with the answer and tried again by excluding my Father. "Then until new leadership for the Agency is selected, if it continues to exist, I will address my requests to you and Lord Shellard."

My Father chuckled and sat back. My Father-in-law didn't seem surprised, and I wondered if this had been worked out ahead of time. Lord Shellard tipped his head towards Hamilton, who was more relaxed than I had ever seen him. He nodded to Lord Shellard, then asked, "What is it you want, Your Highness? I seriously doubt that you came to Wales for your health, considering the most recent change in the weather."

At this point, the Countess hissed, "The witch."

The Prince reached out and patted her hand. "Yes, my dear, it is not your fault that she is more powerful than you initially surmised." His tone indicated anything, but. "I suggest we dispense with the usual pleasantries and get down to business. You have something we want. The truth is you have two people that we want. Your attempt to discourage us was impressive, but even the most powerful have their limits."

He gloated while pulling at his goatee before continuing, "As you can see, the fog is dissipating, and you have directives not to attack us. On the other hand, we have no such directives to keep us from killing all of you. I suggest you give us Lady Marianne Braithwaite and Mr Jean Campeau, then we will leave peacefully, and you and your children will be safe.

Mother sucked in a breath and lashed out, "You would kill innocent children!"

He grinned maliciously at her. "Innocent children tend to grow up to be angry and vengeful adults. I cannot have my people constantly looking over their shoulders in the coming years." He chuckled and spread his hands out, palms up. I am sure that you understand, Lady Blackburn."

She glared right back at him. "No, I do not understand, Your Highness."

He puckered his lips and shrugged. "Then we see things differently."

Stanhope sat sneering at Count Vasiliev, who was almost laughing at us. The Countess's head would swivel at every noise, making me wonder if she was waiting for Magda to appear. Lady

529

Marianne stared at Irina from the other end of the table and grinned as she said, "How does your God look down on you now, Countess? You have failed him, haven't you? The glamour you conjured for the old woman was so poor that she died."

The Countess pretended not to hear her, but it did affect her, she frowned, and there was a tick present at the corner of her right eye. Marianne continued, "Did your lover tell you that he ran like a coward and left her? Your companion willed herself to death—she protected you to the end? She didn't answer a single question. Her body is in the cold house here. Do you want to see her? Of course, we will bury her here unless you want to take her back to her family."

The Countess glanced at her Uncle. He was irritated that he had lost control of the conversation and said as much for the Countess' benefit as much as ours, "I don't care what you do with her. She was just a servant." I was disgusted he didn't even consider that she might mean something to his niece, whose lip was now trembling.

The Prince sliced the air with his hand. "Enough! You, Lady Marianne and Mr Campeau will come with us, or I will have my men crush this estate, and we will take what is ours. All of these people, their servants and children will die."

Marianne tipped her head sideways like a bird, "I doubt that, Your Highness." Then, suddenly, outside, there was a crack of lightning, followed by rolling thunder that shook the dishes on the table. The Prince glanced over his shoulder and glowered, "We will leave for now, but this cannot last, and when we return, I want what we came for."

My Father chuckled. "You think we will let you walk out the door?"

The Prince sneered at my Father, "You have no right to hold me."

"You are correct, but I doubt you would make it back to your ship without being swamped. The people who own the nearby estates are sitting here as my allies. "Your men are on a ship, not here other than those in our dungeon that were arrested for trespassing. You should know that your title means nothing to me. We all know that the Russians hand out titles like Christmas candy. So we are not impressed, Your Highness."

Jibben glared at them, McMaster leaned back in his chair annoyingly tapping the table, and de Bearne sat smiling at Count Vasiliev, squirming under the attention. The Countess seemed to be assessing the people at the table. I suspected she was looking for a way out of this through seduction or appealing to the ladies. I am afraid she would lose on both counts, and by the slump of her shoulders, I believe she had reached the same conclusion.

McMaster stood. "I will get the Truncheons and the key to the dungeon."

My Father glowered at him. "That will be enough, Sir Owen. They stay as my guests if they remain while this storm rages."

Jibben stood up, knocking his chair back. "I will not sit at the same table with murderers!" Then, he thundered, "How can you even consider allowing them to stay? Throw them out. Let them weather the Dragon's rage." He took Judith by the hand, pulled her to her feet and walked out of the room.

Count Vasiliev started to chuckle until my Father gave him a contemptuous glare. He then turned his attention back to the Prince. "I think I should correct you regarding my relationship with the Agency. I work with them, not for them, and those that work for me are independent of the government and Crown. Therefore, I am not constrained by any edicts issued by either side, especially if they wish to retain my goodwill."

The Prince was caught off guard for a split second but recovered quickly with an outward show of indifference. Then, just at the point when he seemed to be prepared to refute my Father's claim, Misha Andropov walked into the room. Andropov was as stunned as the Prince. But Andropov recovered first; clicking his heels together, he bowed, "Prince Andre, what a surprise."

The Prince glowered. "Misha, I had no idea you were still in England." He glared surreptitiously at the Count.

Andropov said, "I am not in England, Your Highness; technically, I am in Wales and at the invitation of Lord Blackburn."

The Prince raised his chin and sneered. "On what business?"

Andropov moved to the buffet, helped himself to the dishes, and sat. "I beg your pardon, Your Highness, but I do not answer to you as I am sure you are aware."

"Bah—ancient orders have no place in today's world. So you play at being knights—what do you accomplish by meddling in affairs you have no business interfering with?"

Andropov finished chewing on a mouthful of shirred eggs, took a sip of his coffee, then wiped his mouth. "That is its beauty of it. No one knows how we affect things. But if our participation upsets you, we seem to be doing the right thing."

He grinned at the Prince's discomfort and returned to his meal. "I see the Dragon is awake once again. You must have roused his ire coming here."

The Prince dismissed his comment, but the Countess hissed, "I told you it was Dragon's Breath. You have no idea how dangerous it can be."

The Prince waved her off. "Enough of your superstitious nonsense." When she went to open her mouth again, he sliced the air with his hand. "No! Not another word."

As if in answer to his command, the manor was shaken by a crack of lightning that limned the windows in an eerie purple-blue light and was followed immediately by a deafening *'BOOM'* of thunder. The crackle of the lightning continued around the windows, then suddenly it stopped, and everything was unearthly quiet. The rain continued as the fog started to roll in once again. It moved as if it was a living sinuous being looking into the manor for weaknesses and a means of entry.

Andropov looked up from his plate and grinned. "Yes, the Dragon seems most upset by your presence." Then, he turned to my Father, "If I might suggest milord, I would throw them out as an offering to the Dragon."

Derek and Stanhope started to snicker as they concentrated on their plates. McMaster and de Bearne joined in, and then Lord Shellard and, surprisingly, Lord Hamilton laughed outright. Soon everyone was chuckling until another crack of lightning and thunder shook the house. It was accompanied by the sound of something scraping against the building. Then a hollow roar sounded as if the ocean was crashing on top of us. Andropov was the only one who continued eating. Nell rose, saying with a certain bravado, "I think I will eat now. Tea is hardly sustaining when whatever is outside seems intent on getting in."

The rest of us that hadn't eaten followed her lead. Much to the chagrin of the Prince, he had lost his audience. We all made our selections, then sat and continued what would normally be a typical breakfast conversation. My Mother even asked Lady Lewis about the harvest festival plans this year. The Prince was furious. He had little choice but to accept the snub. He snapped his fingers at one of the footmen who looked at my Mother. She shook her head and smiled, delightfully saying, "When we are informal here, Your Highness, we serve ourselves. May I pour you some more tea or coffee?"

He grumbled as he glanced out the window at the cloying fog. Then he slipped out of his chair to serve himself from the buffet. The Count and Countess followed his example. Our table conversation continued and excluded our unwanted guests. When my Mother was done, she rose, saying, "I will see that rooms are prepared for our guests. In the meantime, Colin, I can count on you to keep them entertained—and disarm them if you please."

My Father took her hand and kissed it. "Of course, my dear." He nodded at McMaster, de Bearne and Derek. They rose and surrounded our guests. "I would suggest you voluntarily hand over your weapons, and I mean all of your weapons or be subjected to a search."

Father rose then, as did the rest of us. Miles and Hamilton stayed behind, and I waited in the hallway with Nell listening to the English, Russian, and French curses. While waiting there, Lady Marianne came to my side. "Lady Tinley, I was told to speak to you about disguises."

"What do you want a disguise for?"

"Oh, they aren't just for me but for Jean and the sheep."

I was stunned. "Sheep?"

"Yes, I need two male and two female costumes of a similar type."

Nell could barely hide her amusement. "Do the sheep have a say?"

Lady Marianne looked confused. "No, they're dead. Jean and I need to look like the sheep."

I was lost. I had no idea what her intent was. "Why don't we go to my Mother's writing room, and you can explain what this is all about."

Nell came with us, and once the door was closed, Lady Marianne sat down, giving us a beseeching look. "I need you to listen to me first. I am not crazy when I tell you that Madam Magda came to me last night. She wishes to shield Jean and me and needs two costumes to match what Jean and I will wear."

I took her at her word. It seemed that I had no choice, and she appeared sincere. After all, Magda had made stranger requests. "Do they have to be identical, or will similar do?"

535

Marianne shrugged. "Madam Magda said you would know what would work best."

I rubbed my forehead. "Leave it to Lady Hamilton and me. We will find something. But why dead sheep?"

Marianne shrugged. "I have no idea. One other thing, you are to leave one of each costume in the locked morning room." She grinned and then slipped out of the room.

Nell glanced at me with an arched brow. "And she said she's not crazy?"

I sighed. "This is Magda we are discussing. No matter how mad it may sound, I can't ignore the request."

Nell exhaled and stared out the window. "Then I suggest neutral colours, nothing too distinctive. But who does she hope to fool with dead sheep?"

"All of us, except Marianne, Jean, you and I."

Nell shook her head. "To what end?"

I shrugged. "To protect Marianne and Jean?"

"I suppose we will find out. Let's go see what we can find." It took us most of the morning to settle on the earth-tone costumes. Finally, we took one set to Marianne's room. She was delighted with our selection. "When can we expect this transformation to take place?"

She tipped her head to the side as if listening to something none of us could hear. Then she came back to us and smiled. "I don't know." The windows rattled, and she looked wide-eyed at us, "I don't think we should speak of this again." Then she turned her back on us to examine the costumes. It was clear that we had been dismissed.

As we stepped out into the hallway, I asked Nell, "Would you care to come with me and visit Jilly? She might have more answers for us."

Nell smiled. "Lead the way. I would love to know what Magda has planned. What about the second set of clothing we were to leave in the morning room?"

"I will have to try and sneak the key out of the butler's pantry."

We went to Jilly's room and found the dark-eyed, hollowed cheek young woman staring out the window with a fright clearly noticeable in her clenched fists. "Jilly?"

She jerked around to look at us. "Lady Tinley, Lady Hamilton!" She took one last look at the window and then took a seat, inviting us to join her. The windows rattled just then, and the fog swirled as if writhing in pain. She glanced over her shoulder and, strangely enough, smiled. She looked back at us. "Madam Magda is still alive. I was concerned when the lightning started up again. But as you can see and hear, she has tamed the Dragon again."

Nell's expression was fraught with concern as she asked, "Jilly, what happened out there?"

She looked back at us with haunted eyes. "To be honest, milady, I have no idea. The last thing I remember was her plucking a hair from my head. When I woke up, I stood beside Uncle Jacob and Rabby, and she shouted at us to run." She clasped her hands in her lap. "I have no memory of even finding our way back here other than the feeling of being thrown into that room where you found us."

"Have Jacob and Rabby told you what they experienced?"

She sighed. "Uncle Jacob said it felt like someone had their hand in his head, and it hurt mightily. Rabby won't speak of it, saying it's too personal."

I nodded. "Do you have any idea what Magda is doing?"

She shuddered. "If you'd asked me before I came to Sir Edward's house, I would have said magic and made the sign to ward off the evil eye. Now that I am better read, I would say it's science. She knows how to read the signs and—aug—augment what is naturally occurring."

I raised a brow. "Then why all the showmanship."

She stared at us and said, "Where's the fun without it?"

I smiled. "You have a point, so Magda augments the effects and heightens the fear. But it would be nice if she informed us first."

Jilly turned serious, then said, "Madam Magda means no harm, but she needs our enemies to believe, and for that, she needs you to doubt that there is a rational explanation."

Nell chuckled. "That does sound like Magda."

I nodded. "I am afraid the children will have nightmares about this for years."

Nell cocked her head to the side. "I don't believe so. Have you ever heard anything but the sounds of a normal storm where they are in the Keep?"

I thought about it; she was right. The six-foot-thick walls kept the noise of the storm's full force at bay. "You're right. But I doubt I will forget it."

"Nor will I," Nell answered

Jilly sighed. "I am not used to sitting and doing nothing, milady. I would like to see what I can do to help here. Perhaps I could assist in caring for the children."

I nodded, knowing the thought of being sheltered from the storm attracted her to that notion and being with her sister Anne. "I think that's an exceptional idea."

She smiled. "I'll get Rabby then. He's a good one to have for games."

"And what of your Uncle Jacob?"

She laughed. "I think he's stomping around with Libby Truncheon assessing the vermin threat here. Uncle Jacob is always looking out for another business opportunity."

I rose first and offered to take her to the makeshift nursery, but she begged off, saying she'd find Rabby first, and they would go together. So Nell and I made our way back along the hall.

We encountered the Countess coming out of the room assigned to her. She stopped and stared at us, so attempting to be hospitable, I stepped forward and asked, "I hope your room is satisfactory, Countess?"

She glared at me before her expression melted into an insincere smile. "Without clothing or a maid, yes, it is satisfactory."

Nell shrugged her shoulders. "Then next time, you will know not to sacrifice your maid to the vanity of a coward."

She snarled out something in Russian, and Nell responded in kind, astounding me. The Countess was shocked and turned around, entering her room and slamming the door. I glanced at Nell. "When did you learn Russian?"

"Brian taught me while we waited for Henry to be born. Having a hovering husband can be most annoying, so I badgered him into teaching one of the several languages he knows. I wanted to pick the most complicated. My only choices were Ancient Greek or Russian. I chose the one I could put to practical use, never dreaming I would be using it so soon." She stared at the closed door, saying, "I do hope I got the verb tense correct. I would hate to think I complimented her unintentionally." She grinned, then giggled.

We wandered downstairs and found Miles and the Count in a heated discussion. Jibben and Derek were at his back, calling the Count a liar. I waited with bated breath until the Count noted our presence, and then he laughed and walked away. I went to Miles and took his hand in mine. "What was that about?"

"Nothing important, my love."

Jibben sighed, "The louse was found in the children's room

with an exposed knife in his hand and Alex on his lap. I thought Tinley was going to kill him."

Nell and I were both astounded. "How did he get in?"

Hamilton came into the hall just then. "That was my fault. I sent the guards to check all the entry points. I didn't think he would have the audacity to threaten the children."

Jibben growled, "Where did he get the weapon."

Gabriel, who had just joined us, laughed at the question, "In case you haven't noticed, this manor is part fortress and museum. There are weapons on display everywhere!"

I looked at a livid Miles. "What exactly were you going to do to the Count?"

"Other than rip his head off his shoulders—nothing."

"I take it that Alex is all right ?"

He arched a brow at me. "You are very sanguine about this."

"One of us has to be—since you seem bent on murder."

He wrapped an arm around my shoulder and smiled. "What have you been up to?"

I considered telling him about the sheep and the costumes. Instead, I decided against it, especially with Jibben standing nearby. Derek and de Bearne wandered off to find where the knife had come from, leaving Nell and me with my husband, Hamilton and Jibben staring at us with arched brows.

I smiled at them feeling my gut roll, knowing that I was holding back information. "Nell and I went to see Jilly."

"How is she?"

I looked at Nell, and she offered, "Rattled—not afraid exactly, but tense."

Jibben interjected, "Did she say anything about Grandmama and what happened?"

I sighed. "She has little memory of what transpired other than Magda plucking a hair from her head, and the last time she saw her, she was hale and hearty."

Jibben was desperate for more, "Where were they?"

"As best I can tell, they were in the caverns, Jacob suffered an ear-splitting headache, and Rabby isn't talking about his experience." Jibben opened his mouth to continue, but I put up a hand. "That's all I know, Jibben, and Jilly couldn't remember anything else, so don't pester the girl. She and Rabby have gone to organise a play session with the children.

He nodded and headed for the stairs, "Judith will feel better knowing Grandmama is safe." I hadn't exactly said that, but I wasn't about to call him back as he raced up the stairs.

Miles looked at me. "Now would you care to tell us the rest, what you didn't tell Locke?"

Nell looked at me as I glanced at her. "I have no idea what you are referring to."

He arched a brow. "I know when you're withholding

542

information—what is it."

I sighed, and Nell shook her head. "You might as well tell them. Brian will get it out of me before dinner, and you know it."

Hamilton chuckled. "She's right there."

"Fine, but I am not standing out here and discussing it."

We adjourned to my Mother's writing room to find it a disaster. The window was wide open, and the fog was pouring in. The papers on my Mother's desk were windswept and strewn about the room. On the wall was a message *'four o'clock.'* Written in what appeared to be blood."

Miles closed the window as Hamilton set a few chairs back to rights. Then we stood and stared at the message. Hamilton was the first to say, "Magda's getting rather melodramatic, isn't she?"

Behind us, I heard an intake of breath and peering over my shoulder, I saw the Countess. The blood had drained from her face, and her hand was at her throat. She whispered a few words in Russian, swirled around and rushed out of sight. I glanced at Nell. "What was that about?"

Nell shrugged, looking at her husband to answer, "Something about a curse."

Miles examined the message, "Well, it is not blood—it's paint. How impressive that teatime was selected as the unveiling of her plan." He cocked his head. "At least, I assume it's an unveiling. Perhaps we will get to see the Dragon." I gave him a nervous side-eye recalling the shades we had seen in Egypt.

Hamilton stared at him in disbelief. "You are joking, of course." His voice trembled, so I was sure he recalled the same memory.

Miles sighed. "Come now, people. It's all theatre. Magda is a master of the spectacle. Now ladies, can you tell us what you didn't want to say in front of Jibben."

I peaked at Nell, and she nodded, so I told them, "It's Aneski—I think she was channelling her ancestor from what Jilly described."

Miles scrutinised us both. "Aneski is a glamour, a trick Lissa. I thought we had agreed on that."

"I know. But Jilly believes that what Magda is doing is based on science and not the supernatural. That Magda only augments natural occurrences and uses them to her advantage."

He nodded. "Jilly is an intelligent young woman."

Nell sighed. "It takes the romance out of it, though. Unfortunately, no Dragons or King Arthur are coming to our rescue."

Hamilton stared at his wife. "How did King Arthur enter the mix?"

"You know the old legend that he's waiting to be recalled by his country in its time of greatest need."

Hamilton rolled his eyes. "I hardly think this qualifies, and besides, what does that make Magda—Merlin?"

Nell smiled. "I am not going to debate that possibility with you, Brian."

Miles started to laugh. "Will you listen to us? We live in an enlightened century, not the middle ages."

My Mother entered just then, looking about her. At first, she was shocked, but then she went to the message and said, "I have wanted to redecorate this room for a while. But I think red is too dark." Then, speaking to the ether, "Thank you, Magda, for making that choice clear."

She began picking up the papers that were strewn about the room. "I will have to get the maids in here before the water ruins the floorboards and carpets." She moved about the room taking account of all the damage, then called out to Mr Collin, the butler. He came to her side, and they decided what needed to be done, and then he left, assuring her that all would be taken care of as required.

After watching Mr Collin leave, she turned around to look at us. "I am bound to be looking for a new butler before long. Did you see the look in his eyes?" She sighed and looked up at the clock on the mantle. "The message says four o'clock. Perhaps I should order tea earlier. What do you think?"

Nell smirked. "These things rarely go as planned. I wouldn't change a thing. It might alert our adversaries that something is about to happen."

She smiled at Nell. "I think it's a little late for that. The Countess is already shrieking at her Uncle that they need to leave. So far, he is unconvinced that there is anything to be concerned about, but then he's never seen Magda at work."

She left the room, saying, "Tea will be at the usual time."

545

Miles sighed, looking at Hamilton. "What should we do next, collect weapons, lock up our guests or go to the billiard room?"

Hamilton seemed to consider it "Billiards."

Nell and I shrugged. "We will join you shortly, Nell, and I have something to take care of first." We gathered the duplicate clothing we had hidden and made for the Morning Room. Surprisingly my mother's key was still in the lock. I opened the door, and Nell threw the clothing in. Then I slammed it shut and locked it again, slipping the key into my pocket.

We joined our husbands and sat removed from them to converse quietly. I quizzed her about Hamilton's political aspirations. She was very circumspect about what she shared, but I could tell she was nervous. Finally, I reached out and took her hand. "Nell, you will be a brilliant political hostess. Don't second guess your abilities."

She chuckled. "I think I can handle the parties and dinners; controlling my mouth will be an issue. Brian is far more conservative than I am. He believes change comes slowly by gradually winning over your opponents. But, on the other hand, I believe in fighting for it." She looked over at her husband, smiling at her, and she smiled back, sighing, "I am afraid that he may ask me to give up my charity work."

"Oh, Nell, he would never do that."

"He doesn't like me going into the rookeries, and he will like it even less if he gets a position in government. He will support my contributing money to my causes but not being actively involved. So I will have to change my whole way of thinking."

I watched my husband make his shot and thought about the day Miles would take his Father's place in the House of Lords, wondering how much our lives might change."You will find a way, Nell, but don't change who you are."

Her husband seemed to have been paying attention to our conversation. As he finished his shot, he knelt in front of her. "I have given this considerable thought, Nell. I don't want you to change. You do not need to hold grand political dinners to advance my career. You and our family will always come first. I am happy to remain as a voice for change in the House. I do not need a grand appointment. Shellard has managed to be influential without sacrificing his family time and core beliefs. At heart, my love, I am still the Brian Murray you met in the Dials. Besides, it's good to know that I can always fall back on being an apothecary if my political career fails and I lose my fortune."

She laughed at him. "You were an awful apothecary, and you know it."

Miles coughed, "Your wife is right. You were terrible at trade."

We all laughed, and then Nell said, "Hush! Do you hear that?"

We all paused to listen. It was eerily quiet once again. We stepped out into the hall and waited. Through the double windows on either side of the main door, we could see that the vista had started to clear. Even though the fog was still pervasive, the sun was trying to break through. The Countess stood near one of the windows, her back rigid. Count Vasiliev came from the library to join her asking. "What do you see?"

She leaned back against the Count. Unaware of our presence,

he put his arms around her. "It's the end."

He pulled her around to face him. "The end of what?"

"Just the end."

"Bah, your seeing is a waste of time if that is all you can say." He abruptly let her go. "I am leaving. Are you coming or not?"

She shook her head. "Urie, don't go out there. It's not safe yet."

He looked over his shoulder at her. "I am not afraid of fairy stories. You can join me or not. I am going back to the ship."

Prince Andre Gregor was coming down the stairs and, ignoring us, growled, "You are not going anywhere, Vasiliev!"

The Count had reached for the door and looked over his shoulder, sneering, "We need to have the ship blow this place off the face of the earth and teach these people a lesson."

The Prince had come even with them. Still, none of them seemed to have noticed our presence. "You will do no such thing. I am not leaving here without what we came for."

The Count dismissed him. "Bah—it's just stories that the woman couldn't possibly know her Father's business dealings so intimately that she can recreate all his accounts and journals from memory. Besides, what is in those journals that worries you so much? It is not just about gaining control over some English Lords."

The Prince clenched his fists and snapped back, "Do not try my patience, Urie. Have no illusions that your family would seek to

548

avenge your death because they wouldn't."

The Count clicked his heels together and stormed off into the library, slamming the door behind him. The Countess had turned back to the window, and the Prince asked her, "What do you see."

She turned, and this time she saw us and paused, then looked at the Prince "Death." And she walked away and up the stairs.

The Prince stood looking out the window. "I know you are there, Lord Tinley, Lord Hamilton. What she said means nothing. Irina tends to be theatrical."

Miles scoffed, "It seems to be contagious today." He took my hand, and then we, with the Hamiltons, made for the drawing room, where I could hear Miles' Father and mine arguing over a chess move.

Chapter 22

Tricks and Consequences

Time progressed, with luncheon being an uneventful affair since our Russian guests had decided to take their meal in their rooms. The clock seemed to move slower after the meal, and everyone went their separate ways. We all knew that four o'clock held special meaning, but what that would be, no one knew.

We spent time after luncheon with the children. Then we gathered in the drawing room, watching the clock tick down. And as time moved on, it began to lighten outside. With each hour, the fog lessened, and for the first time since this had started, we could see the outlines of the landscaped gardens and the hint of glistening water every now and then in the distance.

Lady Marianne and Jean Campeau joined us, wearing the clothes Nell and I had chosen. The young couple sat side-by-side, whispering and holding hands while rebuffing Lord Burley's attempts to come between them or interject himself into their conversation.

There was a hollow pounding on the front door at precisely four o'clock. We all moved into the entry hall and watched Mr Collin move sedately to answer the door. Above us in the gallery stood the Russians. The door opened, and Magda was standing there. It was not Aneski—it was just Magda. I hadn't realised until that moment that I held my breath. She smiled and walked in, addressing my Mother, "I hope tea will be ready soon."

Mother smiled. "I believe you are just in time, Magda."

Magda smiled as Jibben walked up to her "Grandmama—you and I need to speak."

She reached up and patted his cheek. "We will, Jibben, but not now. I am very hungry."

He took her arm and was greeted by smiling faces as she passed us. We followed her back into the drawing room to join Lady Marianne and Jean Campeau, who had not followed us into the entry hall. They stood as she came in and went to her, kissing her cheek. Jean was the one to speak, "Thank you, Magda, for making it clear what we must do."

She smiled sweetly at them. "Death, in your case, will not be so painful."

With that, they clasped hands and ran out of the drawing room, followed by everyone but Magda. The front door was still open. Outside, the sun shone brightly, showing the line of the cliffsides and the cove below. The sunlight glistened so brilliantly on the water that it hurt the eyes. Still holding hands, the couple ran out into the sunshine and straight for the cliff. Miles and Derek started to run out after them, with all of us yelling at them, "No!" and "Stop!" but they ran straight for the cliff.

The Count pushed past us hard on my husband's heels when the young couple jumped and fell out of sight. The rest of us ran to the cliff edge. Looking down on the rocks below were the crumpled bodies of the couple.

Swimming around them was a pack of sharks. As the incoming

waves crashed on the rocks moving the bodies closer to their jaws, the sharks became more frenzied until one had successfully dragged Marianne's body into the deep water and swam off. Many of his fellows followed. While another group waited patiently for Jean Campeau's body to slide off into the water on a wave. Everyone stood there in disbelief except for Nell and me wondering where the real Jean and Marriane had gone.

Lord Burley had hobbled out behind us, and Arabella ran back to him. "Don't look. It's too horrible!"

The sharks were thrashing about in the water in competition for their prey. Sir Derwyn was at the greatest loss, "I have never seen sharks in this cove."

Miles answered quickly, "Perhaps the storm drove them in."

He nodded. "Perhaps. If the Orcas who come here have their young nearby, they will run them off."

The last vestiges of the shark's meal disappeared, and as if on cue, the Orcas returned and drove off the sharks. Lord Burley stood by my side, holding onto Arabella. "Tell me—that it wasn't real. Did my sister fling herself off a cliff?" He turned to me with tears in his eyes. "Why?"

I bit my lip and told him what I could with the Russians standing nearby. "To keep what she knows out of the hands of the people that would abuse it."

He looked at Count Vasiliev, standing on the brink of the cliff, and yelled in rage, "NO!" and charged the man pushing him over the edge. Prince Andre Gregor held his niece back as she screamed.

Burley turned on them. "Be thankful that you are a female, or you would join him. I am not without influence. He looked about him and said with conviction, I am not without friends. I suggest that you leave now." The rest of our men lined up behind Burley, giving veracity to his words.

Lord Shellard and Andropov stepped forward in tandem. My Father-in-law looked the Prince over with disgust. "I suggest you leave. I intend to report to the Prime Minister and the King about your part in what happened here."

Andropov sneered, "The Tsar will also hear of this, and you know that we have his ear." He meant his country's version of the Brotherhood when he referred to *'we'*. An organisation that worked in the shadows and was not above seeking revenge. I felt the Prince's death sentence had just been declared before us.

The Prince wasted no time dragging a distraught Countess with him as she yelled at us in Russian. Andropov made a dismissive gesture and called back, "I doubt it, milady. You will not live that long." She went white and stumbled down the path to the beach, where a boat was making its way towards them.

Then my Father turned on us. "Now, would someone tell me what in hell I just witnessed?"

I wet my lips to speak just as Magda came walking out. "The tea is ready. If you want answers, Colin Blackburn, then come inside."

Burley was beside himself with grief. "I should have killed them all, flung them off the cliffside."

I took one last look to see that the Prince had sailors retrieve the Count's body, despite the threat of a shark attack. At the same time, the whales seemed to concentrate on corralling and pushing the sharks back to sea. So I didn't wait to see if the Prince and Countess reached the ship.

De Bearne and McMaster assisted Burley as everyone moved inside, harassing Magda to tell us her story, but she refused until Thornton, Jilly, and Rabby had been fetched to join in the telling. When asked why she grinned at me, "So they can tell you the scientific reasons for what happened."

Jibben's lips curled as he said, "Grandmama, what have you done?"

She lifted her chin and said, "Stephen, this is an enlightened age. The time for magic is long past."

Judith shook her head. "There is always a time for magic Grandmama. It is just that so few believe today."

I added, "Or are afraid to believe." She grinned at me and tapped the side of her head.

The others she had requested came in and sat down. Mother passed the tea around, along with plates of cakes and sandwiches. Magda took her time but finally looked at Lord Burley and smiled at him.

Then she began her story. "I spoke to Afon Thomas about the fishing here. He told me the weather was strange this summer, and the water was so warm that they had to go further and further out to get a catch worth taking to market. The conditions were so odd that he couldn't remember a similar time. But old Pol, the village fishmonger, remembered hearing stories when she was a child about a hundred-year storm that had covered the land in sheets of rain and fog, both so dense that no one dared venture forth. So I read the signs and saw that the conditions were ripe for such a storm."

Stanhope asked, "Then why disappear and be so mysterious?"

She grinned. "I had to convince the Russian witch that I was conjuring. So, I chose people I could trust and who would not be immediately missed. Then, I asked them each for something personal so that when they returned and told their story, it would rattle the Russian Countess."

Miles put up a finger. "Then why do Thornton, Jilly and Rabby remember so little about what happened?"

She shrugged her shoulders. "Lightning struck nearby in the caverns, and they ran at my command. They were terrified enough that they must have forgotten our little deception."

Thornton scoffed at the assertion that he had forgotten anything because of fear. "I've never been afraid enough to take leave of my wits, woman! Yee wiped our memories clean of any recollection. Don't know how yee did it—probably happened when yee was glowing all blue like."

Magda just smiled as she continued. "When they ran back to the manor, I made my way to the castle on the headland and settled in to wait. I banished a few malevolent ghosts while there, but mostly I just waited and watched."

Jilly looked doubtful, but she responded affirmatively, "I told you, Lady Tinley, that it was all scientific-like and nothing supernatural." Thornton and Rabby did not join in her declaration, nor did they naysay her. On the contrary, Jilly appeared more confident now that she had expressed it aloud. But her hands were tightly clasped in her lap, and her eyes showed she was not as convinced as she would like us to believe.

Burley, who had listened and was still highly emotional, stared at Magda. "So, it was necessary to kill my sister to achieve what? Tell me!"

Magda stared at him with compassion. "I only needed to convince those that required to be convinced that she and her companion were dead. The eye sees what it expects to see. They are not dead but will now be known as Helen and Paul. Now come with me, all of you."

We rose on her command and followed her to the cliffside looking over the cove. The Russian ship was gone. The sun was muted, winking in and out behind clouds. Magda whistled shrilly, and a set of hands popped up over the cliff's ledge. Campeau and Marianne called out, "We could use a hand up."

Burley was in shock and the last to come to the edge as the man now known as Paul hoisted Helen onto his shoulders. Burley reached for his sister pulling her up and into a hug, crying, "I thought I lost you forever."

Marianne cupped her brother's cheeks. "Oh, Justin, you lost me a long, long time ago. I am Helen now. Maybe I can be a friend who reminds you of your dearly departed sister Marianne." Miles and Derek had pulled Jean up from the ledge.

556

Burley stepped back from her. "What farce is this that you think I will deny you."

She smiled as Campeau came up and took her hand as he said, "If you want her to remain safe and alive, then you must. Our lives will depend on it. So we will live here, learn Welsh and become Helen and Paul."

Justin grimaced. "Are Arabella and I to go through a sham funeral?"

Marianne now Helen shook her head. "Nothing public, my dear brother. Arabella will be in mourning for her husband, and I was only your mad sister who died tragically in the hospital."

Arabella came to Justin's side. "It's a good plan, brother. I will return with you to London for the funerals. Then I shall retire to Hampshire, and with whatever Rupert left me, I will repair our grandparent's estate to a state fit to sell, along with the home you say I have in Gloucestershire. The profits from their sale should recoup some of what was once yours."

"They are yours, Arabella. You must keep them."

She smiled and looked about, dismissing his assertion for the time being, "We can discuss it later."

Their family unit now seemed to include Jean Campeau, known now as Paul Michaud, a distant, long-lost cousin of Emilie Hughes, my Uncle Samuel's wife. We moved back to the manor and out into the garden. Judith and my Mother had their heads together, with Lady Stanhope saying, "I think an Autumn wedding would be perfect for them." I smiled at them, then glanced at Nell, who

557

watched our newly minted Helen Turner and Paul Michaud walk off hand in hand beside the slower-moving brother who leaned on his other sister.

Magda came to my Father, "I owe you two sheep."

My Father arched a brow. "I beg your pardon?"

"The bodies that the sharks devoured were two of your sheep."

My Father was perplexed. "How did you get them down there and dressed?"

She gave him a cheeky grin and said, "Magic."

Epilogue

We returned to London to clear up the mess left there. My Father and Uncle Samuel met with the King and the Prime Minister to explain the death of Antoni Gzowski. He had been seeking a secret meeting with Melbourne through his old friend Sir Thomas Wiseman. But, unfortunately, what he had wanted to discuss was lost with both men's death.

Publicly their deaths were attributed to Foreign assassins. However, the occurrence raised the ire of Parliament and the Crown to such a degree that Lord Hamilton proposed a new funding bill for the Agency. It was taken up and would permanently fund the Agency to work for the people's benefit against all enemies.

Rupert Harris' death was attributed to footpads as yet unidentified. Sergi Popov, the old crone and the Count's deaths were never mentioned. The Russians had not lodged a complaint or even mentioned their loss. Popov and the old woman's bodies were consigned to the sea by Captain Bruce, who swore it was the last time that one of his ships would be used as a means of funeral transport. "It's not good for business and makes the crew tetchy." Magda had gone with them to dispel any residual spirits that might cling to the ship.

Prince Andre Gregor and his entourage had set sail for St. Petersburg after collecting the men we had taken prisoner from Pembroke, where we had sent them. The Prince's excuse for leaving so abruptly without returning to London was that the Tsar had recalled them.

The King himself alluded to having sent a sharply worded dispatch to the Tsar about his interfering with British subjects.

A communication from Andropov was delivered several months after his departure, and all it said was *'Paid in full.'*

The Jeffersons took possession of Sir Thomas's home and made it their own, making our neighbourhood a collection of close family and friends. My Uncle Samuel, now Lord Gromley, opted to remain in his current London home next to my parents. It made it so much easier for those late-night surreptitious meetings of the minds that were given the care and safety of Britain's subjects.

McMaster and Janet were married early in September in a ceremony that would have rivalled a royal wedding, except the couple had managed to contain the guest list. Instead, Prince Talleyrand got his own back by having a magnificent firework display and a Paris symphony play for the wedding and the reception, a party that went on for three days before the couple left for a month-long tour of Italy.

Back in London, the year's social event that eclipsed all else was the Tower picnic for Lord Shellard's birthday. It was a terrible crush, but the Beefeater guards were outstanding at dealing with the visitor's requests to be thrown into the cells once inhabited by some of England's most notorious scoundrels and the most famous members of the royals and aristocracy who had been housed there.

John was back from the sea and was sure he would be better off in the Army. He spent most of the day attached to Derek and, of all people Jibben who pledged to put a good word in with his old commander in the 1st Dragoons.

Edward had recovered sufficiently to be wheeled about in a bath chair basking in the attention of all our friends and relations. All three of his doctors agreed that he would suffer no ill effects, but he would have an impressive scar.

Meg gave birth in late September to a daughter Lilly Alice just before we returned to Wales for the Harvest Ball and the wedding of Paul Michaud and his bride Helen Turner. It was a brilliant and joyous affair.

With Jibben's help, Lord Burley had successfully sold a massive cache of French wine and brandy that Helen had discovered under their Father's warehouse, significantly improving his finances.

Fortunately, he and his Arabella happened to be in the neighbourhood with his fiancé Lady Edith Tomlinson and were invited to attend the nuptials and the gala Harvest Ball. Nothing was said about Helen being family. Burley's fiancé attributed his emotional response to the young bride reminding him of his dead sister.

While Arabella didn't dance, she did enjoy the festivities and Lord Stanhope's attention. They had struck up a friendly correspondence when he offered her advice for setting her grandparent's estate to rights.

Helen never told us if she had hidden anything in Edward's home and refused to discuss it, saying she wasn't that person anymore. And despite what Miles, Fiona and I considered a thorough search, nothing turned up.

Then on the 15th of October, Richard William was born to us at the Rambles, surrounded by family and friends. Dr Archer, Dr Jefferson, and Dr Grimes were all in attendance at the birth, taking Magda's direction.

Charlotte was highly disappointed that we had not named her baby brother Crispin Corwin as she had suggested. But she adored him after she swore he had laughed at one of her stories.

Alex was indifferent, except I heard him say one day, "I am first." I knew then that he would bear watching if he was jealous, and I alerted Miles so that he could be more attentive to *the first,* as Alex now insisted on being called.

It was sometime later, when I was having tea with Magda that I finally had the nerve to ask her, "I haven't been able to figure out how Thornton, Jilly and Rabby were able to find their way back to the manor from the caverns in their condition and that fog?"

She paused for a minute as if choosing her words. "Sorris carried them there."

I was confused. "Who?"

She grinned, and I thought I saw her eyes flash for a moment before she said in a hushed voice. "The Dragon."

About the Author

Hello, my name is Wendy Bayne. I am a Canadian author who has always been fascinated with the 19th century since finding myself lost in the works of well-known authors such as Jane Austen, Charlotte Bronte, Charles Dickens, and Thomas Hardy.

I was an ICU nurse for over forty years, and I have seen a great deal of man's inhumanity to man, how disease and age ravage a body, and how people deal with loss and triumph. Personal experience and tragedy have influenced my writing.

So, why did I choose the post-Napoleonic period for my book? It was an exciting time, a world aswirl in silks, seduction, and the intrigue of the post-war period, full of political and economic duplicity.

Radical new ideas and innovations were clashing with the past's conventional thinking. Moreover, society was changing; people challenged class norms and their society's fundamental values. As a result, there was a renewed interest in the novel during the late Georgian and Victorian eras. A key theme of these novels was social commentary, satirising the nobility's lifestyle and offering keen observations regarding the class and gender distinctions of the time.

It was a period marked by change and one in which I can find relevance to today's struggles and conflicts. Therefore, I endeavoured to infuse my cast of characters with values significantly opposed to the era, thus making them curiosities to the others in their class. Add some intrigue and suspense, a few outrageous personalities, a murder, and more than one harrowing rescue, and the book is complete.

Thank you for reading THE DRAGON'S BREATH Book 7 in the Crimes Against the Crown Series. The Adventure is not over. Watch out for CHASING SHADOWS, book 8 in the Crimes Against the Crown Series.